P9-ELX-862

Tempest Unleashed

ALSO BY TRACY DEEBS
Tempest Rising

Writing as Ivy Adams
The International Kissing Club

Tempest Unleashed

Tracy Deebs

WALKER & COMPANY ✳ NEW YORK

Copyright © 2012 by Tracy Deebs

First published in the United States of America in June 2012
by Walker Publishing Company, Inc., a division of Bloomsbury Publishing, Inc.
www.bloomsburyteens.com

For information about permission to reproduce selections from this book, write to
Permissions, Walker BFYR, 175 Fifth Avenue, New York, New York 10010

Library of Congress Cataloging-in-Publication Data
Deebs, Tracy.
Tempest unleashed / Tracy Deebs.
p.   cm.
Sequel to: Tempest rising.
Summary: Half-human, half-mermaid Tempest must again choose between
land and sea as two boys vie for her affection and the evil sea witch returns.
ISBN 978-0-8027-2830-2
[1. Mermaids—Fiction.   2. War—Fiction.   3. Identity—Fiction.]   I. Title.
PZ7.D358695Tg 2012   [Fic]—dc23   2011037220

Book design by Donna Mark
Typeset by Westchester Book Composition
Printed in the U.S.A. by Quad/Graphics, Fairfield, Pennsylvania
2 4 6 8 10 9 7 5 3 1

For Omar

Tempest Unleashed

PART ONE
Initiation

"The land is dearer for the sea, the ocean for the shore."
—LUCY LARCOM

Chapter 1

I didn't know what I was doing there.

Didn't know what I hoped to accomplish.

Didn't know, even, how I'd found myself in these cold, dark waters when I was supposed to be thousands of miles away, in the heart of the Pacific Ocean.

But the fact that I shouldn't have been there didn't mean I didn't want to be. Because I did.

I wanted to know.

To see.

To *feel* what I once had—even temporarily.

The need to reassure myself—of their safety and happiness—was a throbbing wound inside of me, one that grew larger with every day that passed. I'd left here eight months ago because I had to. Because I couldn't *not* leave.

Choosing the sea had been as necessary to me then as the beating of my heart. It still was. But in doing so, I had left a lot behind.

Too much, maybe, including huge chunks of that still-beating heart.

I couldn't resist the urge one second longer. With a few swift kicks of my tail, I lifted my arms above my head and began to swim straight up. Within moments, I'd broken through to the surface. And was completely disappointed by what I found.

The sky above me was dark and endless, with stars dotting the landscape like an overabundance of fireflies. When I'd been human, this had been my favorite kind of sky—and my favorite time to walk along the sand.

But now it meant the beach was completely deserted, the only movement that of the waves crashing against the shore under the tall, yellow lights lining the adjacent street. I looked as far as I could in both directions, but it was so dark that I had to struggle to see, even with my enhanced vision. I was hoping for a glimpse of something familiar—*someone* familiar—but there was nothing. Just the endless cycle of the ocean.

I had come all this way for nothing. The thought seethed inside me like an open wound, even as I told myself I needed to return to Coral Straits, the mercity where I now lived. The longer I floated here, the more I risked being discovered—by some lonely soul wandering the beach, by a passing boat, by another creature of the sea. For a second, Tiamat's face flashed in front of my eyes, and I whirled around, half expecting to find the evil sea witch or one of her crazy henchmen behind me. God knew they'd been plaguing me for months.

But there was no one, nothing save the cold lap of water against my shoulders. Just like always.

Knowing it was the wrong thing to do, but needing even this most superficial of contacts so badly that should-nots didn't matter, I swam a little closer to land. It had been so long since

I'd seen them—months and months—two-thirds of a year in human time—and my soul cried out for them like they held its very salvation in their too-fragile human hands.

As I moved ever closer, my gaze fell unerringly on the large glassed-in house at the end of the block. My father's house. *My* house—or, at least, it used to be. It was as beautiful as I remembered, though as different from the underwater castle where I now lived as I was from the girl who had dived into the ocean all those months ago.

The house was dark, the windows sheets of glass that reflected the omnipresent ocean, as everyone inside was still asleep. The lamp my father had left burning the first time I went under was now extinguished. The lack of that light told me louder than words ever could that he had given up on my ever returning.

The thought was an all-encompassing blow, and I reeled under it like a boxer at the mercy of a too-strong opponent. Even after all this time, after all the choices I had made, my feelings for my family were too strong to be ignored.

My father.

My pain-in-the-butt brother Rio.

And Moku, sweet Moku, the brother I had all but raised in my mother's absence. I still saw the blinding sweetness of his smile every time I closed my eyes.

But I needed to see him—see *them*—for real.

Needed to reassure myself that they were all right.

Needed to prove to myself that I had made the right decision choosing Kona and embracing my mother's clan—and purpose—so completely. No matter that being mermaid was almost nothing like I had expected it to be.

That reassurance wouldn't come as long as I was out here and they were in there.

So again, I flirted with danger. Again, I swam just a little nearer. A few yards, then ten, twenty, thirty. And willed Moku to wake up with each inch that I covered.

I didn't want him out here on the beach—it was dangerous, a lesson I had learned all too well last winter. But it would be nice if he turned the light on in his room, wandered to the window. Let me get just a peek at his skinny shoulders and crazy hair.

I smiled as I wondered if the nanny my father had hired had managed to tame the crazy curls. God knew I'd given up on doing anything with them long before I'd ever gone under.

For long minutes I floated there, in the choppy waters off the shore of La Jolla, but Moku didn't stir. No lights came on in my house, no slight figure looked out to sea. I really had come all this way for nothing.

Which is how it should be, I reminded myself viciously as I dived beneath the ocean, trying to open myself up to the salt water, to the pain of that first, fiery gulp. It hadn't gotten easier, even after all these months. The water filled my lungs, and the fear that I was drowning swamped me before my lungs stopped working and the small gills behind my ears finally kicked in.

When was I going to get used to this mermaid thing?

When was my body going to give up its painful fight to be human and embrace what it had become? Kona kept telling me to relax, that it would get easier, but instead, everything kept getting harder and more complicated, until the simple act of breathing underwater burned like hell itself.

I needed to let go. Hailana, the merQueen, had pointed that

out to me the other day, had told me that my body was fighting the change so much harder now because of the ties with the land I refused to completely relinquish.

And on this point, I knew she was right. I could feel it in every part of me as I stretched out on the ocean floor that was nowhere near as far down as it should have been. In my desire to see my family I had wandered into much too shallow water.

But how was I supposed to just let go of everything I had been for so many years? When I'd grabbed on to Kona all those months ago—grabbed on to my feelings for him and the images he painted of the life we could lead—I'd been certain that, despite all the protests that had come before, what I found below would more than make up for the loss of my friends and family.

And it did, I told myself sternly. It really did. I had Kona and the freedom of the entire ocean. I had friends and responsibilities and more magic than I had ever dreamed possible. I had my mother's clan. Wanting anything else was silly, selfish. Not to mention dangerous, when my mother's people needed me so much.

I was supposed to save them, supposed to protect them from the most evil sea witch who had ever lived. Even supposed to one day become their queen in my mother's stead. Getting cold feet now wasn't an option.

So what if things were different, harder, than I had anticipated? So what if being mermaid was not everything that I'd expected it to be? My doubts didn't matter. I was exactly where I had to be.

My mother had done it for years. Had relinquished her life

in the sea to be human. If she could do it, surely I could do the reverse.

And if it hurt to be this close to what had once been my life, I could fix that pain easily enough—by not coming back. When I was deep under, my previous life felt like a dream, nothing more. A bittersweet dream, absolutely, but a nebulous, unsubstantial one that was easy to ignore. It was only being here that made it all tangible again.

The thought had me arrowing through the water like a bullet from a gun. I needed to get away. The pain of no longer belonging was crushing in on me from every side.

And yet, even with the need for escape foremost in my mind, I couldn't force myself to dive deep without one more look. One more memory to hold tight inside of me when I was miles and myths away from here.

I shot to the surface again, and as I did, I realized my mistake. My sense of direction had failed me again and I had swum toward the shore instead of away from it.

Damn.

The pull was so much harder to resist when I was this close. It was so much easier to forget what I now was and remember what I could be.

I closed my eyes, determined to tamp down on the longing. Kept them closed for as long as I could stand it, and when I opened them again, I realized more time had passed than I originally suspected. The first rumblings of dawn were beginning to streak their way across the Southern California sky, painting it in shades of violet and pink and yellow.

I could see the sand now, see the rocks and

washed-up seaweed that lined the beach. I wanted to feel the rough graininess of the sand between my fingers, wanted to burrow in like I had when I was a child and my father buried me up to my neck in the warm, powerful weight of the stuff.

I was almost there now, was so close that my toes brushed against the ocean's floor even with my head above water. The cold squickiness of the sand squished between my toes as the waves crashed against my shoulders, and it was all I could do to keep my balance against the raging of the early-morning ocean. In that moment, as I dug my feet into the ground in an attempt to keep my balance, I figured out what I had done.

For the first time ever, I had changed without conscious thought. For the first time ever, my tail had effortlessly become legs again. Despite all of the powers my mother had handed down to me, shifting had never come easy. Moving between human and mermaid form usually took long, agonizing minutes.

Kona told me it was normal, as did my queen and many, many others. They assured me that, with time and practice, it would get easier—and faster. *What would they say now?* I wondered as I stumbled through the last bit of the shallows toward shore. Would they be proud of my instantaneous change, or alarmed by it?

I didn't know, and as voices rang through the still-cold morning air, I didn't care.

Because they had come.

Yanking my bikini bottoms out of the small, waterproof backpack I carried, I shimmied into them even as I strained to get a good look down the beach.

At first I couldn't see anyone, could only hear them. A laugh, a shout, the excited murmur of people about to do what they loved. But I knew those voices, those laughs. They belonged to—

Scooter strolled across the sand, his beloved surfboard under his arm and his long, disheveled hair blowing in the soft wind.

Tony came next, his dark skin shimmering in the first rays of dawn.

Then Bach and Logan, my best buds from my former life. God, they looked good. It took every ounce of concentration I had not to run to them, to hug them. Logan was grinning hugely, and I felt my own lips curve in answer, though I didn't know the punch line.

Something strange happened then. A low-grade energy whipped through me, one I normally felt only when I was underwater. I began to glow, heat pulsing through me with each breath I took. My legs trembled, my heart raced, and panic shot through me. Had Tiamat followed me after all? Had I somehow endangered my friends by coming here? But I'd been so careful . . .

I glanced around wildly, freaking out at my own stupidity. There was no sign of the sea witch, but she *was* sneaky. She had tricked me before. Maybe she—

And that's when I saw him. A little late, a little rumpled, he was bringing up the rear and closing fast the gap between him and the others.

Mark.

The mild hum inside of me became a maelstrom in an instant, my power rising, ripping through me until it was all I could do not to rend the sky with lightning. As it was, the wind picked up, and I watched the guys glance at the sky to see if they'd somehow missed an early-morning storm watch.

If only they knew.

I shuddered as I fought to rein in the energy, to hold on to my emotions. *How could this be happening?* I wondered frantically. How could one look at him stir me up this much? I'd put Mark out of my mind for all these long months, had refused to dwell on what we'd had. Or, more precisely, what I'd thrown away. But now he was here, right in front of me, and I could barely catch my breath. All my training, all my efforts at control these last, long months, dropped away like they were nothing. I strained for a better look, even knowing just how dangerous the game I was playing could become.

It didn't matter. In those moments, nothing did but seeing him.

The board in his hands was new—and sweet—but everything else about Mark was exactly as I remembered.

Same wild blond hair.

Same warm brown eyes.

Same strong jaw and broad, well-muscled chest beneath his favorite electric-green wet suit.

Same wicked grin.

I melted at the sight of it, was more than a little surprised I didn't turn into a puddle and mix right into the ocean that had taken so much from me. *And given me so much,* I reminded myself. The sea had given me everything these last months—as had Kona. But never had it been so hard to remember all this as it was in these moments, when my vision and my heart and my very soul were filled with Mark.

Just Mark.

I took a deep breath and could almost smell the sweet,

musky scent of him. I longed for it, as I longed for the feel of his arms around me.

Will it ever go away? I asked myself bitterly. *Will these feelings I have for him ever disappear completely? Or am I stuck with them forever?* Mark had been such a big factor in my life for so long that there was a part of me—even after all this time—that felt empty without him. Incomplete. Like a surfer without a board, an ocean without a shore.

Though I didn't make a conscious decision to do it, I found myself moving farther up the beach. Not so close that I could hear what they were saying but close enough that I could get a good look at Mark's gorgeous face.

Like the rest of him, it was exactly as I remembered.

God, I've missed him. The thought I had held at bay, that I had refused to acknowledge for far too long, came crashing down on me like a tsunami. I missed him so much that I ached with it, glowed with it.

Missed him so much that I had embarked on this crazy, reckless trip just to see him.

Oh, I had told myself it was to visit my family. To feel the land. To remember who I used to be. But here, now, looking at Mark, I knew that I had lied to myself. I had come to see him too.

How stupid could I get? How ridiculous? How wrong?

I turned, ran back into the water, no longer able to look at the boy I'd once loved. I'd made my choice, after all. Long before Mark and I officially broke up, long before I returned to the ocean to carry on my mother's duty, I had chosen Kona. Beautiful, wonderful Kona, whose eyes were so deep and silvery that I could drown in them. Whose smile wasn't wicked but sweet, whose scent wasn't dark and musky but clean and fresh like a summer sea.

And Mark had made his choice as well—Chelsea, a cheerleader, for God's sake—as different from me as he could have possibly gotten. No matter what I had told him, no matter what I had told myself, it had been a slap in the face.

As I swam backward away from shore, I held on to that thought and to the emotions it brought back. I didn't belong here, didn't belong with Mark any more than he belonged out at sea with me. I couldn't let myself forget that.

But as I scanned the beach, memorizing the tableau they all made standing there, Mark turned . . . and looked straight at me.

Our eyes locked—across the wide swath of sand, across the endless yards of ocean—and I saw his beloved chocolate-brown ones widen in shock. For long seconds, he didn't move and neither did I. And then he was tossing his surfboard on the ground and running straight into the water.

Straight to me.

Chapter 2

I froze for one long moment, then dived deep as panic swamped me. *Swim,* my brain screamed. *Get away from here! Get away from him. It's too dangerous! Swim, swim, swim!*

I started to put as much distance between me and the beach as I could as quickly as possible. But I hadn't gone very far before I realized, with utter certainty, that self-preservation wasn't what I wanted.

Maintaining the status quo *wasn't* what I wanted.

Instead, I wanted to talk to Mark, to hear his surf-and-sand-roughened voice as he demanded to know where the hell I had been for all these months.

Of course, that could just be wishful thinking. Maybe he'd forgotten what we'd been to each other, the same as I had so desperately tried to forget him.

Suddenly, I knew I couldn't go any farther until I was certain. I stopped swimming, turned around. I didn't go back—I wasn't that stupid—but I wanted to know what Mark would do. Would he write off his sighting of me to his imagination? Or would he stand in the ocean and call my name, sure that his eyes hadn't been deceiving him?

I hoped it was the latter, even as I told myself I was being selfish, petty. I should be happy that he'd moved on with his life, with Chelsea. I had moved on with Kona. But nothing I told myself just then mattered—in those few minutes, all I cared about was whether Mark missed me anywhere near as much as I missed him.

"Tempest!" The wind whipped my name straight to me in Mark's snarly voice. "Tempest Maguire, damn it, I know you're out here!"

I didn't answer. I couldn't. My heart had nearly stopped at the first sound of his voice. Instead, I stayed where I was, immersed in the ocean up to my chin, and watched as Mark's powerful body waded through the water. He was thigh deep, waist deep, chest deep, and still he yelled my name.

It made me feel awful, made me feel wonderful, confused me as nothing had since I'd made the decision to be mermaid. I yearned to go to him, everything in my body straining to answer his call. My skin ached for just one touch of his fingers.

As I was watching him, memorizing him, Mark dived deep into the water. He was looking for me, as determined today as he had been eight months ago when I'd nearly drowned during a routine early-morning surf. Back when this whole alternate life of mine was just beginning.

I watched the surface anxiously, waiting for him to come back up. One minute passed as I counted numbers in my head, then two as I struggled to reassure myself he was okay. Mark was a terrific swimmer, could hold his breath for a long time underwater. Not as long as I used to be able to, but then he was human and I never had been. Not really. Not completely.

My internal count had reached one hundred and fifty-seven before I saw Mark bob back to the surface. I was too far away to see him clearly, but the verdant green of his wet suit stood out against the opalescent azure of the waves. I knew he was sucking in air, gulp after gulp, and my lungs ached in sympathy.

I waited for him to catch his breath and head back to shore and the board he had so carelessly tossed aside. Instead, he disappeared beneath the water yet again.

And again, I began to count and wait and worry.

Every second dragged. *One hundred one, one hundred two, one hundred three.* There he was, his head and shoulders popping powerfully above the surface. He was closer to me now, so close that I imagined I could see his chest rising and falling.

I started to back up. To submerge myself, to flee. But I watched as he went under again and accepted that I wasn't going anywhere. I had caused this mess and I had to see it through.

Mark was the most stubborn person I had ever met. Since it was obvious he hadn't forgotten me, I knew if I just disappeared, he would keep looking until he was completely exhausted. Already, he had swum a good distance from shore. Who knew how much farther he would swim before he finally figured out it was hopeless? And who knew if he'd have enough energy to make it back to land?

I ducked under the water, started to swim toward where I had last seen him. *Ninety-four, ninety-five, ninety-six, ninety-seven.* He should be heading up for air soon. When I got to one hundred nine, I propelled myself to the surface with a few powerful kicks of my legs.

He wasn't up yet. I dived back under, swam a little more. Came up again. Still no Mark.

I started to panic. Was he in trouble? Was he caught in the undertow? Was he *drowning* because of me? I looked back at shore, saw that the guys had all jumped in after Mark. They were still pretty far back, but I knew they were good swimmers. I didn't have much time.

Going deep again, I searched the water around me for the green of Mark's wet suit. I didn't see it, didn't see him. Oh my God, he was drowning. He was—

"Tempest!" The word was low and growly and so close to my ear that I couldn't mistake it for anything but what it was.

I whirled around. "Mark!"

"What are you—"

I threw myself at him, nearly took him under as I wrapped my arms around his neck and squeezed as tightly as I could. And then he was hugging me back, his firm, hard body pressed against me from shoulder to hip, while our legs kicked again and again to keep us from going under.

He pulled away. "Where have you been? I've been looking for you for months—"

My voice froze in my throat. What was I supposed to say? What *could* I say after all this time?

"Damn it, Tempest!" he snarled. "Answer me."

I opened my mouth, my mind racing for a response. An excuse. Anything. But before I could do more than take a breath, his lips were on mine and any hope I had of thinking dissolved like so much sea foam.

He tasted just the same, only wilder. Better. Like lemons and peppermints and my Saturday-morning mocha.

He tasted like home—with an edge.

I knew I should stop him. I even started to push away, but in the end all I did was wrap my arms around his neck and kiss him back with all the emotion this crazy, mixed-up roller-coaster ride of a day had awakened inside of me.

I couldn't do anything else, not while one of his hands cupped my jaw and the other pressed against my lower back in a hold so possessive I forgot for a minute that we no longer belonged to each other.

Kissing Mark, being held by him, reminded me too much of everything I'd given up by becoming mermaid, and for those few, brief seconds I wanted it all back.

Wanted *him* back.

But if there was one thing my mother's life—and death—had taught me, it was that it wasn't possible to go back. Whatever we've done, whichever path we've chosen, we have to walk down it. Or in my case, swim down it. Either way, going back to the way things had once been was impossible.

I knew this, understood it—or at least told myself I did. And still I didn't pull back from Mark right away. Instead, I pressed myself more tightly against him and gave us, gave myself, this one perfect kiss. I felt certain it was the last we would ever share, and I was determined to hold on to the first boy I'd ever loved as long as I could.

But the ocean had other plans for us. A huge wave came along, sweeping us up in its wake until our only choice was to let go or drown. I pulled away immediately, but it took Mark longer. Almost as if he didn't mind being dragged under if it meant we would be together again.

But that was fanciful thinking, I reminded myself as the

splash of cold water against my face brought me back to my senses. He had Chelsea and I had Kona. Kissing him had been just one more mistake. It seemed like I was making a lot of them these days.

Knowledge flashed through me at the thought, an understanding that I was coming precariously close to where I'd been eight months before. At the precipice of a cliff I had no chance of backing away from. And like eight months before, I wouldn't be the only one who got hurt.

The thought had me propelling myself backward, away from Mark and the wary, wanting look on his face.

"This isn't over, Tempest." His voice was dark, dangerous, sexy. "You don't get to just show up here, kiss me in the middle of the frickin' ocean, and then disappear again."

"You kissed me." It was an inane answer, especially considering the way I'd twined myself around him like a piece of seaweed. But I didn't know what else to say. What excuse to level for my imminent disappearance. All I knew was that I had to go. The air was closing in on me, the shore far too near for comfort—especially with Scooter and the others paddling straight toward us on their boards.

Mark cocked an eyebrow, gave a sardonic little grin that got to me even as I forced myself to keep retreating. "Is that the excuse you're giving yourself?"

"It's the truth," I insisted. "Besides, I have to go."

"Let's go then. I'll take you back to shore and we can talk—"

"I'm not going back, Mark. I think you know that."

"Where are you going then, Tempest?" His eyes narrowed and he started to swim toward me. "Where *can* you go?"

His advance galvanized me to action like few other things

could have. If he came near me again, if he touched me, I knew without a doubt that I'd end up right back in his arms. And I couldn't do that—not to myself, not to Kona, and not to Mark.

I needed to tell him the truth, needed to let him know why things would never work between us. But I didn't know how to say it in a way that would make him believe.

So, in the end, I did the only thing I could do. I swam forward, reached out my hand. Stroked it down his cheek. Then I turned and dived deep, knowing a word from him could melt my already shaky resolve.

At the last second, I shifted—again so easily that it surprised me—and turned my legs back into a tail. I might not be able to find the words to tell Mark why we couldn't be together, but that didn't mean I couldn't show him. Which was why I very slowly, very deliberately, extended the bottom half of my tail just above the surface, slapping the water with it and no doubt spraying droplets of sea water all over Mark's face.

Then I took off without bothering to try to find my bikini bottoms, too cowardly to stick around and wait for his reaction.

Chapter 3

My head was on the verge of exploding as I swam away from Mark as quickly as I could. *Did I really just do that?* I wondered. *Did I really just show him my tail?*

Now I had to live with the consequences, whatever those might be. I could only hope that they would only affect just me, and not the entire mermaid population who worked so hard to maintain secrecy.

What was Mark thinking right now?

Did he understand why I'd run away, why we couldn't be together?

Or was he completely freaked out by what I'd become?

I really hoped he wasn't. But because just the idea of it hurt, I swam faster in an effort to escape my thoughts and the invisible lure that seemed to stretch between us.

Why did I still feel this messed-up connection to Mark? This inexplicable feeling of rightness even after all the things that had passed between us?

It was stupid. Absolutely ridiculous, considering the fact

that I couldn't even be sure Mark still wanted me now that he knew the truth. He had kissed me, yes, and it had been as wonderful, as powerful, as ever. But I was smart enough to know one kiss didn't mean anything, especially when he was human and I was . . . not.

Which was why I needed to stop thinking about him. It had been just a kiss, nothing more. It wasn't like he'd pledged his undying love for me—or even his like for me. I would do well to remember that.

Just as I would do well to remember that humans and mermaids didn't mix. My parents had proven that. And though my mother had said she'd left to protect her people—not because she didn't care about my father, the boys, and me—it didn't really matter because the outcome was the same. Rio, Moku, and I had grown up without a mother, and my father had lived the past seven years of his life without the wife he loved more than anything.

Knowing that, how could I even be worrying about what Mark was feeling? The two of us had been completely doomed from the very beginning; I had just been too stupid to figure it out. Back then, I'd been so sure I could stay human. Little had I known how limited my choices would really be in the end.

No, I told myself firmly, using my tail to propel my body through the water like a torpedo. Freaking out about Mark and one silly kiss wasn't going to do me any good. It was over between us. He had Chelsea and I had Kona—which was more than enough for me.

I loved Kona, adored him, wanted to spend every waking moment with him. He was perfect for me. Perfect for the

Tempest who was adviser/whipping girl to the merQueen and second in command of her mother's clan. Perfect for the Tempest who had chosen water over land.

But if all that was true, why were my lips still tingling? And why did I still hunger for the feel of dry sand between my toes?

Wrapped up in berating myself, I was focused so completely inward that I forgot the first rule of the ocean. The first rule that Kona had taught me when he brought me down here—never, *never* lose your concentration.

The ocean was filled with dangerous predators, and though I was slowly learning not to be afraid of sharks or be squicked out by octopuses, there were other, more dangerous creatures down here. I knew better than to leave myself open to them.

And yet that was exactly what I'd done. I had been so busy thinking of all the reasons I couldn't go back to land, I hadn't noticed the shadows creeping up behind me until it was too late.

One minute I was swimming as fast as I could toward my mother's clan—*my* clan—and the next I was surrounded by five of the ugliest-looking creatures I had ever seen. Half human, half shark, each of the shark-men had a great white's tail with a human torso and head, while their faces were a weird amalgamation of shark and human. Small, black eyes, long, rounded nose, with rows and rows of sharp teeth behind their humanlike lips.

They circled me and I jerked to a stop, though every instinct I had screamed for me to flee. These were Tiamat's henchmen, predators of the first order, and as usual, her instructions seemed to have something to do with tormenting me. I could only hope they didn't also include ripping me limb from limb.

But as the five of them got closer, their beady eyes terrifyingly flat and their mouths stretched in crooked, macabre grins, I knew they hadn't hunted me down just to hassle me. Tiamat was making her move, trying to force me to join her while I was confused and vulnerable and isolated.

I had to get out of there, had to maneuver so they weren't surrounding me. Adrenaline coursed through my body, made me shaky. Or at least that's what I was blaming for the fine trembling of my hands—adrenaline, not total and complete terror.

I knew better than to let the nerves show. I had learned at an early age that the best defense really was a good offense, and though I wasn't going to be the one to attack first, that didn't mean I couldn't play a little. Try to distract them.

Hi, guys, I projected telepathically. *Long time no see.*

Not long enough, answered the biggest one. *You're in Tiamat's territory.*

I froze for a minute, wondering if I had somehow managed to wander that far off course—I was still learning my way around down here and sometimes I made mistakes. But Tiamat's territory was far north from my own clan's waters, and from Kona's as well. Had I been traveling in that direction all this time when I had thought I was traveling west?

I glanced around, but it wasn't like there were street signs down here to help me get my bearings. There was, however, a huge trench to the left of me, and I recognized its odd zigzagging pattern. I was nowhere near Tiamat's territory.

These are selkie waters, I told him defiantly. *You have no business here.*

You mean they were *selkie waters,* answered the big one. *Now they belong to Tiamat. She has claimed them for her own.*

A new spurt of alarm coursed through me. They were bluffing. They had to be. These were Kona's family's waters, and I knew Ari would never give up his territory, and his people, without a fight. He would have called for reinforcements and put up a battle of epic proportions. There was no way all of that had happened in the time I swam to my old stomping ground and back.

Now didn't seem the time to call shark-guy a liar, though. Not when he and the others were circling me, moving nearer and nearer. Closing in for the kill, as Kona called it. Months before, he'd told me I had nothing to fear from the ocean's sharks unless they were in attack formation. These guys were only half sharks, but I knew from bitter experience that this just made them more dangerous. They had a shark's predatory instincts combined with human intelligence and Tiamat's amorality. *Not* a good combination . . .

And especially not a good combination for me. If I didn't do something quickly, I wouldn't have to worry about Mark or Kona or what I liked and didn't like about being mermaid. I would be too dead to care.

I didn't realize things had come under new management, I said. *I apologize. I'll chart a course around this area from now on.*

It's too late for that, little Tempest, and I think you know it.

One reached out to grab on to my wrist, but I jerked back. There was no way I wanted these monsters to touch me. But that quick movement brought me within arm's reach of the one directly behind me and he latched on—one arm around my waist from behind and the other around my neck. The flat of his hand rested against the gills behind my right ear, making it difficult to breathe.

It hurt, especially as he started pressing his forearm into my throat. I struggled against him, but he was a lot stronger than I was. Everything my mertrainer, Jared, had taught me required distance—something I just didn't have right now—so I searched my mind for the rusty self-defense maneuvers I'd learned a couple years before in PE. Nothing came to mind—at least nothing that I didn't need legs for. And since I'd lost my bikini bottoms in that last shift, I really didn't think it was a good idea. Not to mention that if it took me as long as it normally did to shift, I would be vulnerable for at least five minutes. I couldn't afford that.

The more I jerked and pulled, the harder the guy pressed against my gills, until the ocean around me went even grayer than usual. My head started to hurt, and soon everything was spinning. I was on the verge of passing out, I realized with horror. And if I did, it would be game over.

If they'd wanted to kill me, they could have done that already—one teenage girl against five grown men who knew the ocean, and how to fight in it, a lot better than she did hardly stood a chance. But my death wasn't what they were after. If I passed out, if I stopped fighting even for a second, they would take me to Tiamat. And I had a feeling what awaited me at her hands was far worse than death could ever be.

As things started to go dark, I knew I had only one shot to get away. Desperate, frightened, I drew every ounce of power I could from deep inside me. Then I wrapped my tail around shark-guy's tail and yanked as hard as I could. At the same time, I drove my elbow straight back into his belly. The combined attack had him stumbling, his grip loosening, and that was all I needed.

Whirling away from him, I threw my hands straight in front

of me and blasted out with the power I had amassed. It wasn't as much as I would have liked—something about being strangled to near-unconsciousness made it difficult to gather energy. Who knew? But at least it was strong enough to shove the four men looming over me a good fifteen feet back.

I didn't wait around for them to recover. Instead, I took off toward Kona's place at top speed. As I swam, I heard them behind me, felt the vibrations of the water as they tried to catch up. I wanted to know how close they were, how much of a head start I had, but if I slowed down even a little to look over my shoulder, they would have me.

I felt fingers brush against my fins, and I lashed out with my tail, knocked the hand away as I dived straight down. The tactic didn't work, though, because a minute later fingers had fastened on to the tip of my tail. They dug in with superhuman strength, and I screamed before I could stop myself.

And then we were spinning, somersaulting, spiraling through the water over and over again as I tried to shake him off. He held on like a limpet and I felt a sharp slice across my tail. It hurt like hell, but I didn't have time to pay much attention to it, not when I was sure that his buddies were just waiting for their own chances to make a run at me.

And not when his fist was coming at my face at an alarming rate.

I ducked and twisted, managed to dislodge his grip on me a second time. But that didn't matter, because his friends were right there to grab on when he lost me. A huge hand seized a chunk of my hair, fisted around it, and yanked.

I saw stars, but that second jolt of pain was just what I

needed. Anger blossomed inside me, leaving no room for fear or worry or confusion. Instead, there was this overwhelming heat skating along my nerves, taking me over. Fiery, electric, full of rage at Tiamat for wanting me to turn to her side so badly that she was willing to resort to kidnapping to make it happen.

The heat was getting worse, the strange feeling growing until I was literally vibrating with it. I didn't know what this feeling was, knew only that it was as different from the energy blasts I usually wielded as good was from evil.

It scared me a little, but not nearly as much as the men who were presently pinning my hands behind my back and trying to tie them with seaweed. The only thing stopping them was that I was trembling so badly they could barely get the strands around my wrists.

Furious, uncertain, determined not to be captured, I closed my eyes and prepared to let loose with everything I felt building inside. Some instinctive part of me realized that it was the only thing that could save me. I just hoped I could survive whatever happened—God knew, water and electricity were far from a perfect mixture.

Flexing my hands, I relaxed, letting go of my natural barriers. Then nearly screamed as something bright and powerful shot out of almost every pore in my body—and straight at the five men who surrounded me.

They yelled, pushed back, but it was too late. The one holding my hand gasped and then his grasp loosened. I watched in dismay as his eyes went blank, and he slowly, so slowly, started to float away from me—carried by the ocean's currents rather than his own power.

I stared at him for one long second, horrified by the idea that he was dead. He wasn't the first person I'd killed since being in the Pacific—in self-defense, I'd been forced to kill one of Kona's friends who had turned traitor, not long after I'd discovered the underwater world. This time it wasn't any easier, despite the fact that shark-guy had been trying to kill me, just as Malu had.

Even as the thought was forming, even as I was grieving at what I had become, I was turning, prepared to meet any other threat head-on. But there was no more threat—the other two men who had been touching me were also dead, their eyes wide and vacant as the ocean slowly carried them away. The last two hadn't been hurt by my strange new power—or at least they didn't look hurt as they swam away from me as quickly as they could.

I watched them go, but then my instinct for self-preservation kicked in. Who said they really were running away? Maybe they were just going for reinforcements. And if that was the case, I certainly didn't want to be caught floating here, waiting around for them like an imbecile.

I started to swim, glancing around for something familiar to prove that I was going in the right direction. There was nothing—no trench, no oyster bed, nothing but the feeling that I was heading where I needed to be.

More than once I was certain I caught glimpses of Tiamat lurking in the darkness, watching me, her long, red hair floating on the current and her black tail curled up like a sea horse's. But every time I turned to where I thought I saw her, she was gone. Was it my imagination or was she really there, waiting for me to falter?

Just the idea that she might be lurking pushed me to swim faster.

My throat hurt, my stomach hurt, my head hurt—but I wasn't sure if that was because I had actually been injured in the struggle or simply because I was doing my best not to cry. The tears were right behind my eyes, but I wouldn't give in to them. Not this time.

Yes, I had killed three people, and no matter how sick that fact made me, I had to live with it. If I hadn't lashed out at them, if my power hadn't done that weird electric thing, I wouldn't have stood a chance. And I could be sure that they would *not* have experienced the same attack of conscience at my demise that I was suffering at theirs.

And speaking of my powers, what had happened back there? I knew that I could call down lightning and cause storms, knew that I could blast out at people with bursts of energy. But this latest power—this electric thing taking over my entire body and consuming whatever was in its path—was new. Not to mention creepy in the extreme.

I shivered, and for the first time realized I was still trembling. And not just trembling but shaking violently. *Adrenaline?* I wondered again, because I certainly had enough of the stuff coursing through my body to power a small city.

But this didn't feel like the crash after an adrenaline rush. This just felt . . . awful. Like I was slogging through mud with every swish of my hands and flip of my tail.

My eyes started to close against my will, and that's when I realized how tired I was, my whole body assailed by a bone-deep weariness. What was wrong with me? Was it the fight? The electric thing? The fact that I had killed three people?

Or was it something else entirely?

For the first time since I'd gotten away, I realized that my tail was hurting. Glancing back at it, I froze as I saw blood in the water all around me. A lot of blood. And it was pouring out of a long, deep cut down the center of my tail.

One of Tiamat's henchmen had stabbed me.

Chapter 4

I stared at the jagged cut for several seconds, trying to wrap my head around the reality of it—and the consequences. I was bleeding out, obviously, which meant I didn't have much time before I fainted. And once that happened, I'd be a sitting duck— not just for Tiamat, but for all the other ocean life that was drawn by the scent of blood. I might as well be wearing a sign that read ALL-YOU-CAN-EAT MERMAID BUFFET.

I glanced around. I had to get moving, fast. But I was still about seven hundred miles from mer territory, and judging from how dizzy and confused I felt, I didn't think I could make it that far, even if the copious amounts of blood leaking from my tail weren't announcing my weakness to the world.

There was only one place to go—Kona's. If my underwater GPS/homing-beacon instinct was working properly, I was about ninety miles from the outskirts of his territory. At the rate I swam, it would take me about fifty minutes to get there. Surely, if I concentrated, I could make it that far.

Speeding up, I used every ounce of strength my arms had to

propel myself through the water as I tried to give my tail a rest. It took only a few minutes for my arm muscles to get tired, though, and I worried about how long I could keep this up. I could feel myself growing weaker with every second that passed.

Long enough, I told myself grimly. I could keep this up long enough to get myself to safety. The alternative was dying out here alone, and I wasn't about to give Tiamat that satisfaction.

Or Kona and my family that heartbreak. Then I would be just like my mom—my father and Moku and Rio would never know what had happened to me. They'd think I just drifted away, drawn by the call of the ocean, and forgotten all about them.

I couldn't let that happen. I *wouldn't* let that happen.

A great white shark swam past, its black, beady eyes completely focused on the blood trail behind me. I stifled a mental scream, reminded myself of all the times Kona had told me I had nothing to fear from sharks—even big ones like this. But when the thing made a U-turn and came back, swimming so close that its tail brushed against me, I knew I was in serious trouble. Sharks might not bother mermaids in everyday life, but my open wound was obviously too much for the predator to resist. It was only a matter of time before it tried to eat me.

The thought terrified me—and made me angry. I would be damned if I had just fought off a whole coven of Tiamat's sharkmen only to be done in by a normal shark.

Gathering my power was a lot harder this time around. I was weaker, close to physical collapse, and scared out of my mind. Trying to focus my gifts, to use them to defend myself, was difficult at the best of times. Now I was afraid it would be downright impossible. Especially since that new electricity thing seemed to be MIA.

Then again, when the alternative was becoming some shark's afternoon snack, I had a lot of motivation to get things right.

The fire started in my stomach, the way it always did, as I gathered more and more energy to me. It was smaller than usual, didn't burn as hot, but I forced myself to tap into the last of my reserves. They were incredibly low, and I instinctively started seeking power outside of myself.

Even as I tried, I wasn't sure I could do it. I'd never tried this before, had never even known it was possible. But some latent instinct was demanding that I tap into the energy of the current—of the ocean itself—before it was too late.

Closing my eyes, I focused everything I had into channeling strength from the water. I could almost see its energy—a glowing, cerulean light that wove through the whole world around me. Kind of like a net, it permeated all parts of the ocean as far as I could see. I reached out to touch it, felt a jolt rip through my body that was unlike anything I'd ever felt before—a million times more powerful than what it would feel like to get hit by one of my lightning bolts. Or at least, what I *imagined* it would feel like.

Ignoring the pain of touching a million live wires, I focused instead on drawing the energy inside of me. On capitalizing on the strength, the potency, that the ocean was offering me.

I continued moving, and each foot of the bright blue electric net zapped me, burned me, but also somehow gave me the strength to go on even as it shocked me. I could feel the intensity of the jolts coursing through my body, feel them making my journey easier. Already, I was moving faster, the swish of my tail no longer an excruciating exercise but more like slogging through Jell-O than swimming.

The shark came at me again, this time trying to brush against me with its long, sleek body. It was testing me, I knew, and I braced myself for the feel of it—cold and a little bit prickly against my sensitive mermaid skin—but I felt nothing. Except an odd jolt that added more heat to the flame burning inside of me.

The shark must have felt something else, however, because that one lengthy touch had him swimming in the opposite direction as fast as he could. Part of me wondered if he was just trying to build up speed—if he was going to come at me with the full-power attack from the side that great whites were known for. I really didn't want to be shaken to death in the grip of some shark's rows upon rows of teeth.

Just the thought of it had me speeding up again, processing more and more energy as I moved faster and faster through this strange new power interlace with the ocean. I reached the edges of Kona's territory a few minutes later, a fact that shocked me as I would have sworn I was nearly an hour away. Maybe I was even worse at this underwater-navigation thing than I'd thought I was.

Either way, I'd never been so relieved to see any place in my entire life.

Guards met me at the border. They took one look at my injuries and called for help. Within minutes, I was carried through a long, dark passage that led back to the surface to a small land clinic not far from Ari's dwelling. They'd taken me to Kona's brother's territory because the clinic was much closer than anything in Kona's waters.

Nothing like being the girlfriend of the selkie crown prince to have everyone jumping to keep you alive.

It's not like I was in any position to argue, though. The influx of energy I'd gotten from the ocean had faded as I swam those last miles, until I was now so exhausted and woozy that I could barely keep my eyes open as the healer examined me. I think the only thing keeping me awake was the shivers racking my body. I was freezing.

Whatever the healer found must have alarmed him, because the next thing I knew I was getting a blood transfusion—directly from his arm to mine. Which, I admit, would have totally grossed out my human side if I was coherent enough to fully understand what was going on. As it was, I was hanging on to consciousness by a thread and didn't have the energy to argue about something that was pretty common practice down here.

In the ocean, there is strength in blood, and in bloodlines. The purer your blood, the stronger it is—and the more talents you have. That's why I have such power—because my mother, Cecily, had even more and passed much of it on to me. Most healers have a lot of talent and the strongest blood around—it's where their healing talent comes from. By sharing his blood with me, my healer was giving me an infusion of pure, unadulterated strength. Kind of what I imagined a speed cocktail would be like, only a lot healthier.

As soon as the blood hit my veins, I started to feel better. Less dizzy, more focused, though my tail still burned like hell itself. Of course, that could be because he was prodding at it and muttering a bunch of things I would have been better off not hearing. Things like *near amputation of caudal fin, breach of membranes, lucky to be alive* . . . Needless to say, his bedside manner left a lot to be desired.

Once the transfusion was over, the healer pulled out a couple of very big, very long needles, and that's when I nearly lost it. There are only two things in the world I'm truly afraid of without just cause—needles and sharks (although after having almost being eaten by one, I was going to start considering my fear of sharks justified).

"What are you planning to do with those?" I demanded, and this time I was shaking for a whole different reason than blood loss.

"One's a painkiller. It will stop you from feeling me clean out your wound and stitch you up. The other is an antibiotic shot, to stop infection."

"Can't I just take pills?" I babbled. "I swear, if it keeps you from jabbing me with that thing, I will *never* miss a dose. *Ever.*"

He gave me a droll look. "You're going to be in the ocean. It's kind of hard to keep pills dry down there."

"Oh, right." *Crap, crap, crap. I so don't want to do this.*

"Come on, Tempest. Any maid who can take on Tiamat can surely handle a little shot." Relief rushed through me as I heard Kona's voice.

I turned to face him and was shocked at how haggard he looked. He was trying to put on a smile for my sake, I could tell, but his eyes wore the pinched look he got only when he was really upset. Plus, when he reached out to grab my hand, he was trembling worse than I was.

"You got here fast."

"Yeah. That tends to happen when I hear my girlfriend got

herself injured." He dropped a kiss on my forehead before settling in beside me, his arm wrapped around my waist. "I can't believe you have such a hard time staying out of trouble, Tempest."

That got my back up a little. "I wasn't exactly looking for it, Kona."

"I know, baby. I know." He skimmed his lips over my hair. "How is she doing, Zarek?" he asked the healer.

Again, that little niggle of annoyance. "I'm sitting right here, you know."

"Yes, well, you've been so busy complaining about those shots, I wasn't sure you were aware that you'd been *cut*."

"I'm the one who had to swim hundreds of miles that way—I think I know better than you what's wrong with me," I snapped at him. As I did, I was a little amazed. Were Kona and I *fighting*? We never fought. Not like this, obnoxious little volleys fired at each other through clenched teeth.

I turned around and looked at Kona, really looked at him, and realized that behind the worry was an anger I'd never seen from him before. Kona was furious, and if the gleam in his dark eyes was anything to go by, he was furious with me.

My mind immediately went back to those minutes with Mark. Did Kona know? I wasn't sure how he could. But then again, I was reminded often that Kona's reach was farther than I ever suspected.

God, that's why I didn't do this kind of thing. I didn't date one guy and kiss another—or at least I never had before I met Kona eight months ago. Of course, then everything had been the other way around: I'd been dating Mark and sneaking out with Kona. Something I had felt equally guilty about.

So, what was wrong with me? When had I become completely incapable of being faithful? My inability to properly commit wasn't in the mermaid genes—I knew this because I'd seen hundreds of loyal, happily bound couples while I'd lived down here, couples who had been together for decades and even centuries.

So if it wasn't a mermaid thing, then what was it?

What was I turning into?

Wasn't it bad enough that I'd grown gills and a tail and now swam around the ocean all day? Was I also on my way to becoming a siren, those maids who couldn't be faithful to any male? Who spent their nights seducing men and then lured them to their deaths?

Just the idea made me shudder.

Which was stupid, because any idiot could tell I didn't have what it took to be a siren. I mean, I'd never met a siren, but I'd overheard Kona's brothers talking about them numerous times. They always said the same thing—they're dark and dangerous and have irresistible voices. Which ruled me out. While I can hold my own in a fight, no one's ever described me as dangerous before. And my voice . . . let's just say it's far from irresistible.

Then what was wrong with me? I loved Kona. I really did. So why did I suddenly feel so drawn to Mark again? Why, in those moments with him, had I wanted him more than I'd wanted anything, ever?

It just didn't make sense. And it was dangerous—to me, to my people. Look what had already occurred, and I had let my guard slip for only a second. What would happen if I actually let myself pine after him?

No, I couldn't do it. I had to stop this, had to stay away from Mark forever. He was part of my old life, a life I couldn't go back to. Not when the clan needed me so desperately.

"Ouch!" A sharp pain in my tail yanked me forcibly out of my head and back to the present, where the healer had just stuck one of the very long, very thick needles mere centimeters from the stab wound.

"It's almost done," he said soothingly. "A couple more seconds and you won't feel anything."

He was right, thank God. The lidocaine, or whatever it was he was injecting into me, took effect, and suddenly I felt a whole lot better—at least about him and the shots. As for the Kona/Mark situation, it was going to take a lot more than a shot of anesthetic to make that pain go away.

On the bright side, one look at Zarek holding the needle and special thread they used to keep the saltwater from dissolving the stitches and I was instantly distracted from my other problems.

"You know," I told Kona as I turned my face into his chest, unable to look, "I think it really sucks that selkies have magic healing powers while mermaids get stuck with regular medicine."

He stroked a finger over the back of my hand. "I'm sorry, Tempest. If I could, I'd give you my ability to heal. I hate seeing you like this."

"I know." I snuggled deeper into his arms, relishing the feel of his hard chest and warm skin. Before he'd arrived, I'd been freezing. But with his arms wrapped around me, the chill didn't seem so bad. "I'm glad you're here," I whispered, running my lips over the only parts of him I could reach—his right shoulder and bicep.

He shuddered a little as he buried his face in my hair. "I was so worried," he told me. "When I got the message and realized how far away you were, I nearly lost my mind. A wound like that could have easily killed you."

"I was more concerned about the sharks, to tell you the truth," I said, trying to make him smile. "I know you say they won't hurt me, but I ran into one on the way here who looked like he thought I'd make a good lunch."

"With all the blood you were losing, I'm not surprised." Kona shook his head. "What were you doing all the way out there, anyway? I thought you were home, training?"

And here was the tricky part, the question I had been dreading. How was I supposed to explain to him that on one of my rare days off, I chose to go to the place I still considered my real home instead of hanging out with him? It barely made sense to me.

I couldn't stand the idea of lying, though, so finally, I just told him. "I was on my way back from La Jolla."

He stiffened, his arms growing rigid and unyielding around me. He didn't pull away, which I might have taken as an encouraging sign except for the fact that he kept glancing at my tail, as if gauging how much longer he was stuck sitting with me, so that he didn't jostle me and mess up Zarek's stitches when he got up.

"Please don't be mad," I told him. "I just wanted to check on my family. I wanted to see Moku, to make sure he was okay."

Kona's jaw was rigid. "And is he?"

"I don't know. I miscalculated the time, so it was late when I got there. Everyone was asleep."

I was suddenly aware of how deathly quiet the room had gotten. At my confession, the guards had made themselves scarce, while the medical personnel were all trying to look as busy as possible. Which was nowhere near busy enough, considering they were hanging on my every word. But then, that was no surprise. These were selkies, and Kona would someday be their king. Everything about him was news.

It was that realization that made me decide to omit any mention of Mark. The last thing Kona needed was for the entire kingdom to know his girlfriend wasn't completely over her ex.

"It was a total bust."

"Why didn't you tell me you were going?"

I shot him an incredulous look. Wasn't that obvious? "I thought you'd try to stop me."

He looked away, his jaw working furiously. "Tempest, when have I ever tried to stop you from doing anything?"

I didn't have an answer. Kona had always been incredibly supportive—and tolerant—of me. No matter how whacked out I got.

"I don't care that you went home. Frankly, I expected you to want to check on your family a lot sooner than this."

Shock jolted through me and my whole body twitched, which earned me a hiss from Zarek. "Sorry," I told him.

"It's your tail. If you don't mind scarring, neither do I."

His threat had the desired effect as I froze, resolving not to move my body another inch until he was done. Turning my head back to Kona, I murmured, "I thought I wasn't supposed to see them."

"I knew you were going to say something like that," he told me, his frustration palpable. "But why? You're not in prison, Tempest. Hailana and I want you to be happy. Whatever you need to do to make this transition work is okay with us. If you want to go home and see your brothers, why would we stop you?"

It sounded so reasonable when he said it like that. But it didn't feel reasonable, this need I had for the land. For my family. For Mark. It felt illicit, dangerous, like I was skating too close to a line I wasn't supposed to cross.

But why did I feel it was wrong to wonder about my family? If the vibes I was getting weren't coming from Kona, where were they coming from? Sure, Hailana was making my life difficult in a lot of different ways, but even she had never hinted that my half-human status was a problem.

A picture of Cecily flashed through my mind. My beautiful, powerful, doomed mother, who had chosen the water over her family many years ago. And who had never looked back.

I'd spent years angry at her, resenting her, convinced she was one small step up from a monster. Now that I'd seen her die—because of a mistake I'd made—I felt guilty about those feelings and the fact that there was a part of me that was still bitter.

Was that what was motivating me? Despite all the mixed-up feelings between us, despite all my anger and resentment, was I drawing my ideas about land versus sea from my mother?

Was I seeing things in black and white because that was how she'd seen them?

I hated to admit it, but it made a twisted kind of sense. My mother had left us when I was ten years old, when my brothers were much younger than that. My father had thrown away seven years waiting for her to come back; only she never had. Even with all my anger, all my assertions that there was no excuse for what she'd done, had I tried to absolve her of guilt? To make things easier on her, and on me, had I chosen to believe that it was an all-or-nothing situation, when it truly didn't have to be?

If that was the truth, then Kona's anger really didn't make sense. I told him as much and he looked at me like I was dense. "I'm angry because you went alone. You know Tiamat is gunning for you, and yet you went anyway. What if you hadn't made it back? What if you'd died? This isn't pretend, Tempest. This is real."

"I can take care of myself! I'm not a child playing make-believe."

"Then stop acting like one, running off in secret instead of owning up to what you want. If you need to see your family, let's go see them. But there are precautions that have to be taken. What if you'd run into Tiamat or one of her crew? What would you have done?"

"Exactly what I did do. I fought them and then swam to the nearest ally and asked for help. I'm not a moron."

"What are you saying?" Kona demanded. "That. You. Fought. Tiamat. *Alone?*"

Chapter 5

I only *thought* people were staring at us before.

As Kona's words thundered through the clinic, I realized every eye in the place was on me. Even Zarek had stopped stitching to stare with his mouth agape.

Obviously, telling Kona how I'd gotten hurt had been a supremely stupid move.

"Not Tiamat," I was quick to reassure him, my heart pounding in my chest. "Just a few of her henchmen. Shark-shifters."

The eyes Kona turned to me were a dark, endless black—no silver in sight and with none of the light I'd come to associate with him. "How many is a *few*?"

"Umm . . ." Suddenly telling him I'd gone up against five of Tiamat's crew didn't seem like such a solid idea. Especially considering what I'd had to do to get away from them.

"Tempest." In that moment, in that one word, I saw a side of Kona I had never seen before. Royal, entitled, unwilling to be denied. I could tell he was using his power to influence me, but

I was not without power of my own, and it annoyed me that he thought he could force compliance.

Heir to the selkie throne or not.

I tried to shove back, to show him I wouldn't be coerced, but I was still too weak. The second my defenses lowered, he reached through the path we used to communicate—one that was exclusive to us—and snatched the answer right out of my head.

"Five!" It was as close to a yell as I'd ever heard from him. "You fought off *five* of Tiamat's goons alone?"

Fury bloomed deep inside me. How dare he use our bond like that? I elbowed him, struggled to push him off the bed. I was rewarded by a raised eyebrow from Kona, who didn't so much as budge, though I'd put all the strength I had left behind it, and a hiss from Zarek, who was still, unbelievably, working on the last part of the cut.

"How many stitches do I need, anyway?" I demanded, completely frustrated that, though I was beyond angry with him, I was forced to stay cuddled up to Kona like some good little girl.

"So far?" Zarek answered with a downward twist of his lips. "One hundred and fifty-seven. Before I'm done, more than two hundred."

His answer only enraged Kona more, though he never moved an inch. "What the hell happened out there? And don't even think about lying to me."

"What is *wrong* with you?" I asked, annoyed. "You're acting insane. I've never lied to you, and I don't appreciate being treated like some damsel in distress who can't take care of herself. Back the hell off!"

One of the nurses dropped a tray of instruments, and for long seconds, the only sound in the room was the clatter of steel hitting tile. Obviously, no one was used to hearing the crown prince addressed so bluntly. But I wasn't one of Kona's subjects. I was his girlfriend. If he thought he was going to get away with beating his chest and acting like a total caveman around me, he was going to be sorely disappointed.

Kona glared at me as he tried to accept the fact that I wasn't going to bow and scrape for him. I glared right back, refusing to give an inch. Finally, with a sigh, he closed his eyes and buried his face against my neck.

"I'm sorry, Tempest. The idea of you in danger makes me crazy."

"Obviously." I stayed stiff against him, not willing to relax just yet. "Don't ever do that again—you know how I feel about you reading my mind."

"I didn't—"

"You know what I mean."

He sighed. "Yes. And I'm sorry. It won't happen again."

His obvious sincerity, coupled with the torment I'd seen in his eyes, was enough to make me relent. "I was about halfway back to Hailana's waters when they ambushed me. We fought, I killed three of them, and the last two ran away."

My synopsis of the events didn't exactly explain everything that had happened, but unlike Kona—who had grown up with servants everywhere—I wasn't used to airing my private business in public. Some sixth sense kept urging me to be quiet about the electric thing, to not let anyone but Kona know about it.

I finally spoke to him using our private line of communication. *Kona, can you please trust me on this? I swear I'll tell you everything later.*

You'd better. He didn't look happy, but he gave in, asking only a couple of benign questions for show. Of course, that just meant he was going to be in my face about this as soon as I got out of here.

"That should do it for the stitches," Zarek finally said.

"Thank God." I glanced down at my tail, saw he'd done such a good job that already the cut was barely visible. "Thank you," I told him sincerely. "I'm sorry I was such a pain."

Zarek grinned. "I've had much worse patients." He looked meaningfully at Kona, who was suddenly very interested in the striped pattern of the wallpaper. Which totally piqued my curiosity . . .

But before I could ask what Zarek meant, he continued. "Besides, I got my entertainment for the week. It does my old heart good to see Kona being led on such a merry chase."

Kona groaned. "Don't encourage her. If she leads me on any more of a chase, I'll end up lost somewhere in the darkest depths of the ocean."

I ignored him. "Can I leave now?"

"After I go over the rules with you." Zarek gave me a stern look.

"What rules?"

He went over to a cabinet and pulled out two pills. "You take these now, for pain."

"I feel fine—"

"Because the numbing agent is still blocking the ache. These will take the edge off for the next twelve to fifteen hours, and by then you should be well on your way to healing. I did everything I could to speed the process along."

Which meant not only had he given me his blood, he'd also drained his reservoir of power trying to heal as much of the damage as he could. "Thank you," I said again. "I really appreciate it."

"Well, show your gratitude by staying out of trouble, will you? I don't want to have to stitch you up again anytime soon. Got it?"

"Believe me, I've got it."

"Good. Now, no shifting for at least twenty-four hours and you should be good to go."

"No shifting?" I stared down at my tail. "How am I supposed to get back to the water?"

Zarek actually winked at me. "Kona's got a strong back. Use it. Somehow, I don't think he'll mind."

⚭

Fifteen minutes later, I was, indeed, back in the ocean, along with Kona and the largest contingent of guards I'd ever seen. To keep me from exhausting myself, he had me wrapped snugly in his arms and was using his legs to propel us quickly through the water.

Not taking any chances, hmm? I asked him along our private telepathic link.

Not with you, he answered grimly.

I'm fine.

I'm still not sure how that's possible, by the way. And just so you know, I expect my ignorance to be remedied very soon.

I didn't argue with him. Not when I wanted answers as badly as he did. *It was strange. I had been in the middle of the shark-men, thinking I didn't stand a chance—*

His arms tightened around me, and I stroked his bicep in an effort to calm him down. *I'm fine,* I reminded him. Then I went on to explain everything that had happened, including the weird electric current I'd managed to pull from the water.

You really did that? Kona demanded. *Pulled electric energy from the ocean?*

I think so. That's what it felt like, at least. Is that a bad thing?

It's a rare thing. I mean, through the years I've heard of some mer being able to do that, but I've never actually met one who could.

Yeah, well, I'm not sure I ever want to do it again. Throughout the whole thing I was convinced I was going to electrocute myself.

I bet. He paused. *So nothing like that's ever happened to you before?*

Never. I shook my head. *I would have told you if it had.*

He relaxed imperceptibly. *We need to tell Hailana. See what she says.*

I paused. *Are you sure that's a good idea?*

Of course. Why?

When I didn't immediately answer, I sensed his attention getting sharper, narrowing in on me exclusively. *What's wrong, Tempest?*

Nothing. I tried to shrug off the whole topic. Now wasn't the time to tell him that things between Hailana and me weren't quite like he assumed. *I guess the painkillers are kicking in. My thinking's going a little nuts.*

He didn't say anything for so long that I thought he'd

dropped it—at least until he replied softly, *I thought you knew that you don't have to do that with me.*

Do what?

Front. You always deflect, like you don't want to burden anyone with what's bothering you. When are you going to figure out that you're never a bother to me, Tempest?

I think I was a pretty big bother today, I said with a quick grin.

He sighed. *There you go again.*

I don't deflect, I told him. But even as I protested, I sensed the truth in his words. From the time my mother left, I'd hidden most of my concerns or worries. Partly because I didn't want to stress out my dad—he'd had enough to deal with—and partly because I was embarrassed to be such a mess.

And then, when I got older and the whole half-mermaid thing came up, I felt like I couldn't talk about it. Not to Mark, who knew something was wrong but who I didn't think could ever understand if I told him the truth. Not to my friends, because they would have thought I was a candidate for the mental institution. And, except there at the end, not to my dad, because I was so worried about hurting him, of reminding him of my mom, that I would rather bumble through things alone than ask his advice.

Kona didn't bother to contradict me, but then I figured that was because he had a pretty good idea of what I was thinking.

Can we talk about this later? I asked. *The pain medication really is starting to kick in.*

Of course. Close your eyes and relax. Let me do all the work.

His words startled a laugh out of me. *You know what that sounds like, don't you?*

His lips twisted in reluctant amusement. *Only to dirty girls like you.* But his arms tightened around me even more, until we were molded together like we had been in the clinic—my back to his chest. Out here, in the water, it felt so much better. Sexier. Even with all the guards around us.

Besides, he continued, *when we get to that situation, I am* not *planning on doing all the work.* His teeth nipped at my earlobe. *Lively participation is pretty much a requirement, after all.*

His words sent crazy shivers through my body. My heart sped up and I could feel a flush spreading through me that had nothing to do with embarrassment. *I love you, you know.* The words—and feelings—were there, unable to be denied despite what I'd done in La Jolla.

That whole thing had been an aberration, I told myself sternly. A mistake. I'd confused my feelings for home with my emotions about Mark. That was all it could have been, all it would ever be.

I love you, too, Kona said, his voice soft and sweet and sensuous as it brushed against the corners of my mind. *Now sleep, baby. I've got you.*

Giving in to temptation, I relaxed, let myself drift. I knew he would take care of me. I didn't sleep, though, despite the narcotic effect of the painkillers. There was something so nice about being held securely by Kona as we zipped through the sea that I didn't want to miss any part of it. With both of our lists of responsibilities, we didn't get to see each other enough as it was.

Ocean life teemed around us, bold and bright and beautiful, and the deeper Kona took us, the more vibrant the colors became, until it seemed like the whole world was one huge psychedelic kaleidoscope of color. Reds and yellows, pinks and greens, whirling by at an amazing rate.

Fish, octopuses, selkies, mermaids, and even sharks seemed

to surround us—to be watching us from every angle. At first, I thought it was the medication, making me see double or triple. But the faster Kona swam, the more of them there were, until they lined the water on all sides of us.

I glanced up at a particularly beautiful school of fish—purple masked angelfish, I think, in shades of canary yellow and violet. I was spellbound by them, the way they darted around one another, spinning and diving, until they all blended together into what looked like one long, glowing rope.

Look, I told Kona, pointing up. *You can almost see their halos.*

He laughed.

What? I asked. *You don't see it?*

I think you're the only one who sees it, Tempest. You're hammered out of your mind on painkillers.

No. I reached a hand up to touch the long, glowing line—to show him that I was right—but there was nothing there. *You really don't see them?* I whispered, sad for him. Those angelfish were some of the most gorgeous things I'd ever seen, even down here where the waters were filled with one beautiful mystery after another.

Oh, I see them, just not like you do, he teased.

Why are they all here? I glanced between the different types of sea life that surrounded us. *Shouldn't they be trying to get away from the sharks and viperfish?* I looked all around. There was even a giant squid following us—I'd never seen one this close before—and yet none of the fish or other creatures seemed the least bit concerned.

He kissed my back, his lips soft and sweet against my shoulder blade. *They're here for you, Tempest.*

What do you mean? It was hard to concentrate when he was

doing that, especially knowing that there were thousands of eyes watching us. I shrugged, tried to get him to stop, but he wasn't quite ready to let go. Instead, he trailed his lips up my spine until I all but melted into a puddle of goo.

Only then did he lift his head.

And that's when I knew. He was claiming me in front of the whole ocean—letting every creature out there, including those loyal to Tiamat, know that I was under his protection. It was a warning, pure and simple, to anyone who tried to mess with me.

I wasn't sure how I felt about that, wasn't sure if I should argue or appreciate it.

In the end, I decided to just let it go. Obviously, Kona was taking Tiamat's attack even worse than I'd imagined.

Are you doing this? I asked, struggling to think clearly through the medication. *Are you calling all these fish to us?*

No, baby. They're here to protect you.

To protect me? I was baffled.

By now, news that Tiamat attacked you again has to have spread through most of the Pacific, as has word of your injury. They're here to make sure you get home safely.

Why?

No one's forgotten what you did eight months ago, Tempest. The sacrifices you made to keep us all safe. This is their way of giving back.

And you know this how? I asked, suspicious.

Because they told me, of course.

Right. I'd forgotten that another one of the talents selkies had was being able to talk to almost all the other species in the ocean. It made my electric show seem kind of pathetic in comparison.

I looked back up at the rows upon rows of sea life surrounding us, hammerhead sharks swimming next to sea turtles, squids drifting along next to clownfish. Predators and prey organized into a gauntlet of sorts—not one meant to harm, but to show the selkie prince support. It was an awe-inspiring, if intimidating, sight.

They stayed with us the whole way—all six hundred miles through Kona's territory to Hailana's. Some of the smaller fish grew tired, dropped out, but they were quickly replaced with others of their kind.

Less than four hours later—even in human form, Kona was a faster swimmer than I—we reached mermaid territory. Coral Straits was about twice the size of the waters ruled by Kona's father, stretching thousands of miles and covering some of the Pacific's most prosperous areas.

It was ruled by the merQueen Hailana. She'd been my mother's queen, and her best friend, if everything I'd heard about the two of them was to be believed. Now she was my queen, and we were still working out the kinks in that system. To say we had a volatile relationship would be something of an understatement.

I think when she took me under her wing, she'd expected me to be a carbon copy of my mother. To behave exactly as Cecily had.

Unfortunately for her—and for me, I sometimes thought—I wasn't any better at conforming than I was at taking orders. Which meant Hailana and I butted heads. A lot. So much so lately that she would probably be disappointed to hear I hadn't perished in the deep-sea attack. It would certainly have made her life easier if I had.

As we cruised the last hundred miles to Hailana's castle, we slowly lost our escorts. The selkies were the first to go, followed by most of the large predators, so that by the time we reached the deep, narrow trench we needed to take to get into the city, we were alone except for Kona's guards.

Kona dived into the trench, his natural silver phosphorescence guiding the way through the long, winding tunnel. In places, it narrowed so much that I thought he would crush me between his arms, but somehow we made it through. The closer we got to the city, the more uncertain I became about returning here.

Part of me wanted to head to Kona's place instead—there I would be coddled and taken care of. Here, with Hailana, it was a different story. She would have heard about the attack by now, and I was sure she would find some new and unique way to make me pay for my mistakes. Of course, now would probably be a great time to get my punishment over with, considering I felt so drowsy and floaty that I could barely focus. It might very well be the most painless encounter I'd ever had with Hailana, besides the time we first met.

We took the final, twisty upturn into the center of Coral Straits at dazzling speeds, bursting like a minicyclone into the place I'd called home these last eight months. I clung to Kona, more than a little dizzy after that last wild ride.

What was that for? I asked, trying to make sense of the crazily spinning world around me.

I don't know what you're talking about. He sounded so innocent that I almost bought it, probably *would* have bought it if the first thing I saw when I was finally able to focus hadn't been Hailana.

She was floating a few feet away from the trench's opening, arms crossed over her chest and blue eyes completely disapproving. So much for being summoned to her chambers—she'd been so pissed off she'd actually come to me.

You did that on purpose, I accused Kona. *You knew she was going to be here and you wanted to make her mad.*

I guessed she was going to be here and I wanted to send her a message.

What message? Kill Tempest now instead of later?

More like: you mess with Tempest, you mess with me.

I didn't know whether to be charmed or annoyed, so I settled on a little bit of both. *I can fight my own battles, you know.*

I never doubted it—especially after today. But since I'm amazed you're still reasonably coherent after the pills you took, I figure you could use a little break before she starts in on you.

I can deal with Hailana.

He shrugged. *Okay, have at it, tiger.* He dropped his arms from around me and pulled back, leaving me dazed and disoriented and at Hailana's mercy.

I see you've been busy, Tempest. She thrust the words into my head, her voice reeking of disapproval. For a woman who looked every one of her centuries of life, her words slammed across our personal connection with incredible force.

You know me, I returned with a guileless smile.

I do, indeed. Her eyes, faded with age but still sharp, shifted to Kona. *What's wrong with her?*

She's had a rough day. She needs to go lie down.

I noticed he didn't refer to my injuries at all, and briefly I wondered if perhaps Kona knew more about what was going on between Hailana and me than he let on. But trying to think

about it made my head hurt, so I resolved to figure things out
later when I was back to normal.

Playing nursemaid, Kona? The queen opened up our conversation as she watched him with careful eyes.

Better than playing sea witch, Hailana.

I'mstillhereyouknow, I interrupted. *StoptalkingaboutmelikeIdon't
haveabrain.* I wanted to say more, to tell both of them to stop
posturing, but it was obvious I had garbled the words so badly
that neither of them had understood a word I'd just said. I tried
to start over, but now that I was finally home, I was crashing
quickly, and it was all I could do to keep my eyes open.

I can see this is a waste of time, Hailana said. Then she glided
over to me, stroked a soft hand down my cheek. *Poor child. Your
life isn't easy down here, is it?*

I blinked, positive I'd misheard her. She hadn't shown me
that much compassion—or any compassion at all, really—since
the day of my mother's funeral. I must be more doped up than
I thought.

Before I could say anything, she turned to Kona. *Take Tempest to her room and get her settled. I expect to see her in my chambers
the moment she is feeling more like herself.*

And there she was—every inch the merQueen again. Kona
and I watched as she made her way through the small crowd
that had gathered, all members of her court. When she was
gone, he turned to me with a grin. *Right. Bed for you. Now.*

You sound entirely too excited by that prospect, I told him as he
swept me back into his arms.

What's not to be excited about? He started swimming. *So, do you
want surface or water?*

I closed my eyes, rested my head against his arm. *Pick one.* I was fading fast.

Water's closer. We followed the queen back to her underwater palace, then swam through the halls quickly and quietly. My suite was on the fourth floor of the palace, which—except for me—was reserved for royalty. But when I'd chosen to be mermaid, Hailana had given me my mother's old chamber, which basically meant I had my own wing of the building. Cecily, it seemed, had needed a lot of room to stretch out. I just found it lonely.

Kona carried me into my suite, locking the door behind us. I raised an eyebrow at him, but he only shrugged. *Even with the queen's guards—and my own—I'm not sure how secure it is for you here. Better to be safe than sorry.* He laid me on the bed, then stood behind me, hands shoved into the back pockets of his black-and-gray-patterned board shorts. *Do you need anything?*

It was the first time in months that I'd seen him look so nonplussed. He was always so confident, always seemed to know what he wanted, that this sudden discomfort in my bedroom was kind of charming. Okay, really charming, if I was honest.

I just want to sleep, I told him as I reached for his hand. *I'm exhausted.*

Okay.

Stay with me?

Yeah?

Of course. Though it hurt, I scooted over on the bed. He settled down next to me, sliding his arm under my head so I could use his bicep as a pillow. *Thanks for coming for me,* I told him as I traced the intricate tattoo that softly glowed where it wound around his arm from shoulder to wrist.

Don't be stupid, he said, dropping a kiss on my cheek. *I'll always come for you. And thanks for staying alive. I don't know what I'd do if I lost you.*

For one brief second, Mark's face flashed before my eyes. Then I banished it as I had banished my feelings for him so many months before. *I guess it's a good thing you don't have to find out.*

A very good thing. His other arm wrapped around my waist, pulled me even closer. It felt so good, so deliciously warm, to be held by him that I drifted to sleep without another word.

Chapter 6

I woke up slowly, feeling like I was swimming through cotton as I reached for consciousness. My tail hurt, but it was more of an ache than the sharp pain I'd felt when I was first injured.

Stretching slowly, I checked out all my muscles. Was relieved when nothing else so much as twinged. I seemed to have escaped my latest encounter with Tiamat's evil goons relatively unscathed. Thank God. And as long as I didn't think about the shark-shifters and what they looked like after I'd—

I cut myself off, refusing to go there. Not now, and maybe not ever. I did what I had to do, I reminded myself. That didn't mean I had to like it, but I wasn't going to make myself sick over it either. Not this time. Not when I'd come so close to death myself.

Rolling over, I bumped against Kona's warm, hard body and nearly jumped out of my skin. My eyes flew open, met his silver ones. He smiled lazily and, flushing a little, I smiled back. He was propped up on an elbow, watching me. Totally relaxed, with the attitude of someone who had been doing the same thing for quite a while.

How long have you been awake? I asked softly.

I don't know. A couple of hours, maybe?

Oh. Sorry. You should have woken me—

Why? I like watching you sleep. When you're awake, you're usually running in so many different directions that sometimes it's hard to keep up.

I snorted, then choked on a mouthful of water. When was I going to stop doing that?

Kona's laughter echoed tauntingly in my head. *Good one.*

Yeah, I can see why you have such a hard time keeping up, I told him sarcastically. *Nothing like trying to anticipate what your idiot girlfriend is going to do next.*

He ignored that. *How are you feeling?*

Almost as good as new. I stretched again.

The medication all worn off?

I think so. I mean, I can actually focus now, so that's a plus. Why?

Because I want to make sure you're completely lucid when I do this.

He leaned over and his too-long black hair fell around his face, brushing against my cheeks. I reached out, rubbed a few strands between my thumb and fingers. It felt so good, soft and silky despite being immersed in salt water most of the time.

You really scared me, he whispered, his lips brushing over my forehead and down my cheeks.

I'm sorry. My breath hitched, as if my gills had suddenly stopped working. *If it makes you feel better, I kind of scared myself too.*

That doesn't make me feel better at all, actually. He skimmed his mouth along my jaw, paused to nibble at my right ear.

I jumped a little, tangling my fingers in his hair and pulling him closer as delicious shivers worked their way down my spine. *Kiss me,* I told him.

I am kissing you. To prove his point, he pressed a firm, open-mouthed kiss against my collarbone.

My head fell back and I clutched at him, pulling him even closer. *You know what I mean.*

Do I? He nibbled his way up my neck to my other ear.

Kona!

Yes, Tempest?

Please. Kiss me.

But instead of waiting for him, I closed the distance between us and captured his mouth with my own.

It was exactly as I remembered it, exactly as it always was between us. All brilliant colors and sparkling fireworks and loud, raucous music. Amazing, intense, like catching the perfect wave and riding it all the way into shore.

His arms tightened around me until our chests were pressed snugly against each other. *I love you*, he told me in between kisses so sweet and salty that they took my breath away. *I love you so much that it scares me sometimes.*

I love you too, I answered, running my hands over his back. Because I did. Despite what had happened with Mark earlier, I knew that I loved Kona. Knew that he was the right choice for me. The only choice.

He felt so good, so strong, so *perfect*, that I wanted this moment to last forever. I could do anything, could face down a great white shark, could deal with a selfish, over-the-top merQueen. Could even take on Tiamat herself if I could also have this.

Could also have Kona.

I don't know how long we lay there, kissing and touching and reveling in the feel of each other.

Long enough that the dull ache in my tail disappeared completely.

Long enough that I forgot everything but what it felt like to be held by Kona.

More than long enough for the events of the previous day to become distant memories, like a bad dream that fades, grows less scary, with time and distance and a light in the middle of the darkness.

We might have stayed like that forever—or at least for the rest of the day—but a knock on the door finally reminded us that we both had things we should be doing. We both had responsibilities.

Slipping out from under the waterproof violet comforter I had picked out months before, I ran a self-conscious hand over my hair as I opened the door. My friend Mahina stood there, looking embarrassed about interrupting Kona and me, but also gleeful as she took in my flushed cheeks and kiss-swollen lips.

Tempest! She threw herself at me, wrapping her arms around my neck in a giant hug. *I'm so glad you're okay.*

I'm fine, Mahina, I answered, gently extricating myself from her grip. *Sorry to worry you.*

I wasn't that worried—I know you can take care of yourself. She winked. *Queen Hailana, on the other hand, nearly wore a new trench in the ocean floor as she waited to see you with her own eyes.*

Yeah, right.

I'm serious. She was more frantic than I've ever seen her—she'd be screwed if she lost her star mergirl. Which is why I'm here interrupting your little lovefest, by the way. She glanced mischievously at Kona, who was now standing next to the bed and looking a little like he wanted to run.

Not that I blamed him. The way Mahina was looking at us—like she was imagining exactly what we'd been doing before she knocked on the door—made even me uncomfortable, and I'd had eight months to get used to her teasing bluntness.

Mahina! Stop. I sent the request along our private communication path. *Can't you see you're embarrassing him?*

She eyed Kona without apology. *He needs to lighten up. For such a hottie, he takes himself way too seriously.*

Selkies are different than mermen. They don't have quite the same sense of humor.

That's too bad, she sniffed, somehow managing to do it without snorting a noseful of water. The fact that I loved her despite her teasing spoke more to what a fabulous person she was than to any generosity of my own.

I was planning on getting myself a selkie for my next birthday—preferably one of those F.I.N.E. specimens Kona brought with him—but you know I like a guy who can make me laugh.

Kona makes me laugh, I defended.

I bet. She waggled her eyebrows lasciviously.

Mahina!

Fine, fine. I swear, you're getting to be as bad as he is. Anyway, she went on, talking on the general communication pathway so Kona could hear us again, *the queen requests your presence in her chamber at your earliest convenience.*

I sighed. *Which pretty much means now, right?*

Actually, I think it meant five minutes ago, but who's counting?

She is. I glanced over at Kona. *I should probably go see her.*

I know. I need to head back anyway. I'm sure my dad's ready to kill me by now.

Why? I asked, concerned.

When I got the news about you, I walked out in the middle of one of his you-need-to-take-more-responsibility-for-the-kingdom speeches. He saves up his complaints for months before one of those things, so he's probably apoplectic at being denied the chance to list everything that's wrong with me.

There's nothing wrong with you! You do ten times more than any of your brothers or sisters.

Yeah, but they're not next in line to be king. Unfortunately. He bent his head, pressed a long, lingering kiss on my lips that practically had me swooning all over again.

I'll see you in a few days? he asked. *For the Bringue?*

Yeah, of course. You know I'd never miss that party, not after everything I've heard about it.

Don't go getting yourself into any more trouble, okay? I don't think my nerves could take it.

Kona . . . You're beginning to sound like an old man.

He grinned before dropping another quick kiss on my lips. *Love you.*

I love you too.

Bye, Mahina, he said with a wink before slipping out the door.

We both watched him go, admiring the way his tattoos shifted with every flex of his muscular shoulders and back.

When he rounded the corner, I turned back in time to see Mahina pretending to fan herself. *I don't care if he doesn't have a sense of humor. That boy is freakin' gorgeous.*

He really is, I agreed with a sigh.

I forcibly pulled my mind back to the matter at hand. *Did Hailana say what she wants?* I asked as I crossed to my closet and pulled out a bikini top that wasn't ripped or stained with blood, along with one of the long, ceremonial pareos we were supposed to wear during command appearances with the merQueen.

Probably to yell at you. What does she ever want? Mahina pawed through my closet along with me. *Hey, can I borrow this?* She held up a bright turquoise bikini. *I have a date tomorrow night.*

I thought you said you were checking out the selkies?

I was. She rubbed her knuckles against her chest and then blew on them. *What can I say? I'm a fast worker.*

With that genius IQ of yours, I'm not exactly surprised. And in honor of your fast work, you can have the bikini. I eyed her dark bronze skin and black hair. *It'll look better on you anyway.*

Thanks, Tempe! She gave me a quick hug, then spun to face the closet as I changed tops. When she turned back, I was struggling to get the pareo to lie correctly and she rolled her eyes. *You've been here eight months. When are you going to get this thing right?*

About the same time I finally understand Hailana?

I guess I better plan on sticking around for a long time then, huh? Here, give me that. She grabbed the pareo, folded it in an intricate pattern I couldn't seem to get no matter how many times she explained it, then draped the floral fabric softly around my tail.

Good? I asked as she tied a knot over my left hip.

You look great for someone who just survived a violent attack.

Somehow, that doesn't seem like much of a compliment.

She shoved me out the door. *I'm not going to lie. You'd look better without that massive hickey on the back of your neck.*

What? I slapped my hand over the body part in question.

Kidding, just kidding. Kona's way too much of a gentleman for that. More's the pity . . .

I refused to dignify that remark with a response. Instead, I concentrated on what I was going to tell Hailana. Should I ask her about the weird electric thing? Kona had told me I should, but I didn't have the same trust in Hailana. He seemed to think that she was only out for my best interests, but I knew it was a lot more complicated than that.

Did Hailana want to see me survive this whole death spiral with Tiamat that I was locked into? Absolutely.

Would she go so far as to interfere to keep me alive? Only if it benefited her.

Eight months of living under Hailana's rule, trying to please her *and* follow in my mother's footsteps without actually making her mistakes, had taught me a lot. Namely that being a mermaid—at least at court—was much more political than it was fantastical.

I might be in the middle of a war with an evil sea witch, but *The Little Mermaid* really was just a Disney cartoon. Real life in mermaid territory was much more treacherous than Ariel could ever have imagined.

I'm not sure what I would have done if I hadn't become friends with Mahina and her pod soon after I came here. Probably died of a knife in my ribs from one of the mermaids who had been less than impressed by my presence here. As it was, much of my life in the ocean was a tightrope walk between pleasing Hailana and remaining true to myself.

So far, the score definitely seemed to be in Hailana's favor.

Kona didn't understand because he was selkie—and selkies, in general, were honorable and compassionate. Sure, there were exceptions to that rule—like Malu, the selkie I'd been forced to kill eight months ago to defend myself—but for the most part, the ones I'd met really did seem to care about each other and the world around them. I'm not sure I could say the same about mermaids—at least not most of the mermaids I'd had the misfortune of getting to know.

But Hailana's court didn't represent all the mermaids in the world, I told myself. It was just a small portion. Which meant that if I could stick it out here long enough to finish this death match with Tiamat, then—if I somehow managed to survive—I could find my own place, far from here. Cecily's legacy, and all that comes with it, be damned.

I often wondered why my mother had chosen to return here. Could she really have been best friends with Hailana, like everyone said? I liked to imagine that the stories were mistaken, that they couldn't be true, but honestly, I wasn't so sure. My mother had abandoned her husband and three children without a backward glance. A woman who could do that, who years later could still plot to use her only daughter for her own means, was pretty much capable of anything.

Shoving the disquieting thoughts out of my head, I concentrated on clearing my mind. Doing some deep-water breathing. I needed to be as close to Zen as I could get when I went in to see Hailana, or she would dig until she found my weakness and exploited it.

Not this time, I assured myself as I stopped in front of her chambers. Today I was not going to let her rattle me. At all. As for the electric thing? I'd play it by ear, see how it went. If it was beneficial to me, and not just to her, maybe I would ask for help in understanding my new power. And if not, then there were other ways to get the information I needed.

After knocking on the door, I waited patiently to be admitted by one of her servants. But when it finally swung open, the merman standing there was definitely not like any servant I had ever seen.

Dark and gorgeous and full of life, with piercing blue eyes that looked right through me, he exuded power from every pore. He was as tall as Kona—which meant he was huge, as my boyfriend was close to six and a half feet tall in his human form—and heavily muscled. Even more disarming than that, though, was the series of dark blue tattoos covering nearly every inch of skin between his neck and his waist. They weren't the kind you got in a tattoo parlor.

No, I thought as I tried to press forward into the room. These tattoos, with their slight phosphorescent glow, were like mine. Like Kona's. Like Hailana's and my mother's. They were gifts from the sea, markings of true oceanic power.

I couldn't help staring in astonishment. Not because he was the first merman I'd ever seen with such marks—he wasn't, of course. But never before had I seen so many on one person. Not even my mother or Hailana, or even Kona's incredibly powerful father, had close to this number.

Who is he? I wondered as I shifted uncomfortably under his scrutiny. And why was he looking at me like I was a present he couldn't wait to open?

Chapter 7

Come in, Tempest, Hailana called from within the chamber. Tearing my eyes from her mystery guest was more difficult than it should have been, but I managed as I stepped into the large, opulent room that served as Hailana's meeting place while she was below the surface.

I expected the merman to move aside as I entered, but he didn't. Instead, he stood right in the middle of the doorway so that I was forced to brush against him as I passed. Jolts of electricity shot through me, sizzled along my nerve endings, and if we hadn't been underwater I would have sworn that I'd been burned. A quick, startled look at him confirmed he had experienced the same thing. Only he didn't look at all surprised.

Who is he? I wondered again. He didn't look much older than I was, but I'd learned that, down here, looks could be deceiving. After all, Kona—despite just having reached the end of selkies' teenage years—was actually over two hundred years old.

Even more important than who the guy was, however, was the question of how Hailana was planning to use him against me. Kona would think it was crazy of me to be so suspicious, but I'd been around the merQueen long enough now to know that she never did anything without a purpose. And that purpose was always self-serving.

Come over here, Hailana told me impatiently. *I don't have all day, especially considering I've wasted most of the morning waiting around for you to wake up.*

I'm sorry. My experiences yesterday left me quite . . . drained.

She studied me through narrowed eyes, this frail, old mermaid who looked like she might shatter at any moment. But eight months of exposure to her had taught me that the frailty was only on the outside. Inside she was as tough, as unyielding, as a rock. And as she looked me over, I knew she was being meticulous in her search for a weakness. She found it in my almost completely healed tail. *Did one of Tiamat's soldiers do that to you?* she asked.

Yes. I straightened my shoulders, tried to look as healthy as possible. If she sensed I still wasn't 100 percent, she'd poke at me until I was too weak to continue. *But it's fine now.*

Well, I guess we'll see about that, won't we?

Shit. I obviously hadn't done as good a job of faking it as I thought. *What do you want, Hailana?*

Queen Hailana or Your Majesty! she snapped back at me.

I stared at her with a look that was deliberately insolent. *Of course. Your Majesty.*

She looked ready to take offense at my provocation—which I knew was juvenile but so satisfying—when the merman cleared his throat.

Hailana looked at him and some of the fire died out of her

eyes. *Tempest, I called you here to introduce you to my grandnephew, Sabyn. Sabyn, this is Cecily's daughter, Tempest.*

Nice to meet you, Tempest. He stuck his hand out to shake mine, a friendly look on his face that did nothing to put me at ease. I'd learned from bitter experience with Hailana that sometimes smiles were sweetest right before you got stabbed in the back.

Even worse, the second our hands touched, electricity once again rocketed through me.

Sorry, he told me, so softly that I knew he didn't want his aunt to hear.

No problem, I answered, though half my body ached from our contact.

Sabyn is going to take over your training, the queen said.

This startled me enough that I spoke without thinking. *But why? Jared and I are doing great together.*

Yes, well, Sabyn has much more experience with mermaids of your . . . ilk. As for Jared, he's been transferred up to the Alaskan borders. I think he'll do well there, don't you?

I fought to keep my face free of the turmoil churning inside of me. Besides Mahina, Jared was my closest friend here—which was probably why the old hag had banished him. She was working overtime trying to bend me to her will, and the more I struggled to remain my own person, the worse it became for me.

Hailana could use whatever excuse she wanted, but I knew the truth. Jared was gone because he was one of my staunchest allies, and as such, was not to be trusted. *What about his family?* I asked, because I had to know. Jared adored his wife and infant daughter. *Did they go with him?*

The queen looked amused—and very satisfied—meaning I

hadn't sounded as nonchalant as I had hoped. But sometimes it was hard to keep my mouth shut. She was so heinous, so determined to get me to fall into line behind her, that she never missed a chance to exert her authority.

They'll be joining him within a few months, if things go according to plan.

I started to say something else, but she cut me off. *Enough, Tempest. We need to talk about this next phase of your training.*

What if I don't want to do the next phase? Jared said—

Jared was wrong, which is why Sabyn is your trainer now. Her voice dropped, lost its saccharine quality. Became as harsh and vicious as she was. *You are here at my behest, Tempest. I think you're forgetting that.*

I don't have to be here, you know.

Oh, really? Are you planning to run back to Daddy, let him take care of you against the big, bad sea witch? Tiamat would rip him apart before he even figured out he should run. And Kona? She laughed. *You don't actually think the selkies will accept a mermaid for a queen, do you? Oh, they all come down to play with the maids, but in the end, they marry their own kind. Always. Kona will never marry a non-selkie, and there's no way his father would ever allow him to put a half-breed mermaid on the selkie throne—no matter how well they put up with you now.*

It took every ounce of control I had to keep my jaw muscles loose, relaxed. But I managed it. I would *never* give her the satisfaction of knowing she'd gotten to me. *I don't need anyone to take care of me.*

No offense, darling, but you don't know what you need. You may have power, you may be as special as everyone says you are, you may even be the one who will kill Tiamat as the prophecy states, but you are noth-ing if you don't understand how to manipulate that power. Sabyn can show you much more than Jared ever could.

I eyed her suspiciously. I had trouble accepting that she would do anything to help me. *What happens when I'm stronger than you?*

As if I would ever let that happen. She got up from her jeweled throne, swam slowly toward me. *You're a weapon, Tempest*, she told me on our private line of communication. *A top-of-the-line, first-class weapon. If you aren't careful, if you don't do exactly what I say, that's all you'll ever be. One I wield and then discard once it's fin-ished being useful.*

I will never let you break me.

She held up one elegant, beringed hand and slowly began to make a fist, her fingers closing one after the other. Inside me, my heart stuttered as a crushing weight pressed in on it from every side. Tighter and tighter until the pain was so excruciat-ing I couldn't breathe, couldn't think. I tried not to react, tried to ignore what she was doing. But my heart was stuttering, skip-ping beats, and I knew, absolutely, that if she didn't stop soon, I would be dead.

Please. It was all I said, all I could get out, but it was enough. She opened her fist and the pressure and pain dissipated. Imme-diately, I tightened every inch of my tail to rigidity—it was the only way I could have stayed upright in the aftermath of her attack.

My whole body burned with mortification and hatred as I looked at her, this woman my mother had blindly served. I wanted to walk away, wanted to tell her to go to hell. The only thing that kept me standing there was the knowledge that I had a long way to go before I could take her down.

I glanced at Sabyn, saw him leaning against the back wall, a look of amusement on his face as he watched my humiliation. The bastard.

I turned back to Hailana. *When do you want me to start?*

PART TWO

The Split

"For whatever we lose (like a you or a me),
It's always ourselves we find in the sea."
—e.e. cummings

Chapter 8

So, how are you really feeling?

I stiffened at Sabyn's question as we floated into the elite training circles Hailana had set up for me months ago. Located behind the palace grounds, they were three interlocking circles that were meant to be private. Even so, it was not unusual to find a small group of mer watching as we practiced, trying to get a glimpse of me. *I'm fine, why?*

Oh, I don't know. Maybe because you went a few rounds with Tiamat's goons yesterday? There was laughter in his voice, and the same condescending smirk on his face that he'd been wearing earlier.

I'm fine, I told him again, which was almost true, as my tail no longer hurt. That didn't mean my chest wasn't throbbing from my encounter with Hailana or that my brain wasn't focused on finding a way to get as far from her as possible instead of on this sparring match. Which, considering the number of tattoos Sabyn had, was a truly stupid move on my part. Nothing like getting her ass handed to her twice in twenty-four hours to really make a girl feel good.

Glad to hear it. He turned, winked. And then shot a blast of energy at me so fast I barely had time to leap out of the way.

What the hell was that? I demanded when I could breathe again.

He didn't answer, just shot another energy blast—and another and another—straight at me. Soon, it was an unending stream that I was afraid would fry me at the first opportunity.

So much for training. This felt more like an assassination attempt.

At first I dodged, but then his careless disregard for my life started to tick me off—imagine that—and I fired back, using my own energy to block his. The first time our energy forces actually met, a shock wave blasted out from the middle of the ring that knocked us both back about twenty feet and then slammed past the boundaries of Hailana's grounds and into the city behind us.

The power of it shook buildings, flattened nearby merpeople and sea creatures alike. Had even more people ducking their heads out of doorways and windows to see what was happening. Some went back about their business, but others came down to the ring to watch us spar. Which was *so* not what I wanted.

As I pushed myself off the ground, I regretted that I still had my tail. I wished I had shifted back to human legs for this battle—even after months as a mermaid, I was still more confident in the response of my body in human form, not to mention more powerful. Eight months didn't trump nearly seventeen years of reactions and experiences, after all.

But since that wasn't to be—and it was too late to shift now even if I could—I put my wishes out of my head and prepared for Sabyn's next strike. He looked as shell-shocked by that last explosion as I was, but that didn't mean he wasn't going to try to strike while we were both off balance.

Sure enough, a huge blast of power came flying straight at me. But this one was different; I could sense it. Instead of the wide, sweeping blasts he'd been sending my way, this was focused, an arrow of pure power headed right at the center of my body.

I pulled up my own energy—more as a shield than a weapon— but it wasn't good enough. His power flew right through mine, and though I was able to slow it down quite a bit, it still hurt when it hit. Enough so that I stumbled backward, then fell.

There was a burning across my midsection, and when I put a hand to it, my fingers came away bloody. Damn it. I ducked my head, checked out the damage. It didn't seem too extensive, just a half-dollar-size circle in the center of my stomach where the blow had struck, along with thin, ribbonlike slices that crossed my torso on both sides of it.

Still, it completely pissed me off. I was getting sick of being used as a punching bag for the entire ocean.

Ignoring the blood and the pain, I sprang back up. And went at Sabyn with everything I had. I sent wave after wave of energy crashing into him until I was exhausted, but it wasn't enough. His shield was about a million times more effective. No matter what I threw at him, I couldn't get past it. Blast after blast, wave after wave, with nothing to show for it. Nothing, that is, except Sabyn standing there, laughing his ass off in front of everyone who cared to watch.

Frustrated, furious, I pulled back. Concentrated. Tried to focus my power the way Sabyn had, so that I could push it right through his shield. But no matter what I did, no matter how hard I tried to condense my energy into a powerful, unbendable weapon, I couldn't do it. The knowledge grated.

Around us, the water grew choppy with my agitation, until the whole area was literally pulsing. I could feel the storm brewing inside of me, feel the lightning begging to be unleashed. I held firm against it, knowing that the only people who would be hurt by my temper tantrum were those on the surface, or those down below who couldn't defend themselves. Sabyn, the jerk, probably wouldn't even be touched.

Come on, Tempest! he called mockingly. *Is this seriously the best you've got?*

I gritted my teeth, tried to ignore the taunts as I struggled for control.

I came down here because my aunt said you had real talent. Told me you were our best shot againt Tiamat. Now I'm not sure what she meant. Best shot at getting our butts kicked, maybe?

I clenched my jaw, tried to ignore his words. Either they were true, which was shocking since Hailana never missed a chance to insult me, or he was trying to feed my ego, which was just as dangerous as believing Hailana might actually think I wasn't a waste of space.

Either way, though, Sabyn needed to go down. The lightning was right there, but I remembered the first time I'd unwittingly let it go, how I'd struck Kona in the chest and nearly killed him. Since then, I'd been working on control, on channeling the lightning, but I couldn't take the chance, not right now. Not with all these merpeople around.

Instead, I pulled inward. Gathered up the last pulses of energy I had within me. And then focused as hard as I ever had in my life.

I pictured a spear, pulsing silver with power. With strength. Long. Unbendable. Wicked sharp. And then I went about creating it, one unbreakable inch at a time.

It wasn't perfect—not by a long shot. Even as I was forming it in my head, I could see the cracks, the fissures, the little mistakes I was making. If I had more time or more energy, if I wasn't so drained I could barely swim, I would have stopped and fixed all the weaknesses. But I didn't.

Sabyn had grown suspicious by my sudden cessation of activity, had once again begun lobbying energy strikes across the divide between us. I fractured my attention, left half free to dodge what he was sending my way and kept the other half on the weapon I was building.

When I was done, when it was as sharp and as strong as my flagging energy could make it, I reached out a mental hand and grabbed the spear. Then heaved it as hard as I could straight at Sabyn and his unbreakable shield.

He saw it coming, laughed. Waved a hand to deflect it, but he wasn't strong enough.

A look of alarm flitted across his face and he threw out both his arms to increase the energy of his shield. To strengthen his defenses.

But I was having none of it. I would lose this battle—I knew that. I was still weak from everything that had happened the day before, and I would have no energy left to follow up this attack. But I *would* strike him, *would* make him bleed as he'd done to me.

Closing my eyes, I focused on pushing the spear a little bit farther, a little bit faster. Imagined it spinning, burning, crashing through Sabyn's shield and straight into him.

Sensing that this was it—good or bad, succeed or fail—I opened my eyes and watched as the spear shot right through Sabyn's shield in a blaze of purples and reds and golds. The colors bounced off, slamming through the water like electric sparks. And the spear—the spear passed right by Sabyn, but not before it took a healthy chunk out of his right bicep.

It wasn't quite what I'd had in mind, as I was aiming to mess with more than his bicep, but it would do. Especially considering the look of abject shock on his face. Yes, it would do very, very nicely.

Around me, people cheered—I was definitely the hometown favorite between the two of us—and I took a bow. Then, calling a draw, I crossed the circle to see if Sabyn needed help. Not that I was in much better shape, but still—it seemed like the right thing to do, no matter how annoyed I was with his so-called training methods.

Nice shot, he called to me as I approached. He didn't look nearly as angry as I felt. Which, strangely, only made me warier. Most guys I knew didn't like it when a girl got the jump on them, especially publicly. And Sabyn definitely didn't strike me as a laugh-it-off kind of guy.

Not as nice as yours, I answered. I was still bleeding from the earlier blast to my midsection.

He shrugged modestly. *I do what I can.*

The crowd looked a little disappointed at our civility, but once they realized there wasn't going to be any more fighting between us, they took off, exchanging random bets regarding our next training session. Fantastic. Because I really wanted nothing more than to become the new entertainment down here. People already spent way too much time staring at me as it was. They didn't mean to be rude, I knew, but always being watched, always being whispered about as the mermaid who would finally vanquish Tiamat, got old really fast.

So, was that really necessary? I asked once the last stragglers finally moved on.

What? he answered with an innocence that was obviously feigned.

I thought you were supposed to be training me, not trying to kill me.

For one second there was a deadly serious look in his eyes, one that sent shivers—and not the good kind—up and down my spine. Then he grinned, and the tension dissipated. *Trust me. If I'd been trying to kill you, you'd already be dead.*

Why does that not reassure me? I asked, eyebrow raised.

I don't know. I certainly meant it as a reassurance.

And not a threat?

His face went blank. *I have no idea what you're talking about.*

Of course you don't. I glanced over my shoulder at the now-empty training circles. *So, can I expect this kind of thing every day that we're under the water?*

Not at all. He grinned wickedly. *That was just a warm-up.*

Fan-tas-tic. So not. *What happens if I can't keep up? Theoretically?*

He glanced down at my stomach wound. *Oh, you'll keep up.*

How do you know? Was he impressed with the spear? With my technique?

Because the alternative sucks. And you don't strike me as suicidal. With that parting shot, he took off for the castle, hand pressed firmly over his wound.

I watched him go, wondering if Hailana had brought him here to help me . . . or destroy me.

Chapter 9

Two hours later, I was still stewing over the whole encounter. Sabyn might be an incredible fighter, but he was also a world-class jerk. The idea that I was going to have to spend hours every day learning from him, training with him, made me insane. Particularly considering his last comments.

Keep up or die? What kind of teaching strategy was that? I mean, I'm all for real-life experience, but Sabyn was taking it to a new level.

I finally gave up any hope of concentrating on my other duties. I'd tried to focus on my homework for mer-school, but since I was new to the whole underwater-world thing, my teachers were treating me like an imbecile. And I could memorize only so many ocean species a day before tangling with a great white seemed like entertainment instead of certain death.

My other studies—watched over by Hailana—were even less interesting. She'd given me a new book last week—*An Unabridged History of Mer Society*. It was two thousand, three hundred and ninety-four pages long. And it was definitely *not* a page turner.

Hailana swore there was a lot of useful stuff in there, but then she thought there was useful stuff in the princess etiquette class she was making me take as well. And call me crazy, but learning to float with a book on my head or learning the entire lineage of the merCrown somehow didn't seem quite as important as finding a way to bring down Tiamat.

I'd said as much to Hailana a million times, but so far, she hadn't budged. And whenever I asked any questions about Tiamat, she found a way to change the subject. Which was crazy, but then it hadn't taken me very long to figure out that Hailana wasn't necessarily playing with a full deck. And the deck she *was* playing with was definitely a little . . . confused. I wasn't sure that senility hadn't driven her just a little bit around the bend.

The only good thing we agreed on was that she let me train, let me figure out how to use my powers these last few months. Besides my time with Kona, the hours I spent in the training circle with Jared were the only things that kept me sane.

Except now, it looked like even that sanctuary had been taken from me. I fumed as I swam away from Coral Straits and out into the ocean. I wasn't planning to go far, but I was going stir-crazy sitting in my room. Besides, I figured I should take advantage of my free time. Between school and training and learning to be an "adviser" to the merQueen, I didn't get nearly enough of the stuff.

Part of me wanted to hightail it over to Kona's, to pour out my latest problem in his lap and let him solve it, but just the idea seemed ridiculous. Kona had enough to worry about right now without my adding to the mix complaints about my psycho-Queen and new trainer. I had to deal with this on my own.

Which, for now, meant not dealing with it at all. Shoving
Sabyn and Hailana out of my mind, I concentrated on swimming. On pulling one arm after another through the water.

I dived deep, went through a forest of kelp and seaweed, and
relished the feel of the feathery stuff as it brushed against my
highly sensitized skin. Then I swam back up some and shot the
North Pacific current—it wasn't nearly as exciting as surfing,
but it was as close as I could get down here.

I let the current take me for about fifty miles, tumbling head
over tail part of the way before dropping out to just float. I tried to
clear my mind, tried not to think, but everything that had happened these last two days crowded in on me.

I didn't know what to do. I felt stuck, trapped, like every
way I turned was fraught with disasters and every decision I
made was wrong. I wanted to love it down here under the
ocean, wanted to be proud of the decision I had made to become
mermaid, but it was hard. Harder now, even, than it had been
eight months ago.

It just seemed like I didn't belong here, no matter how hard
I tried. I had Kona, who treated me really well and said he loved
me, but Hailana's words kept replaying in my head. That Kona's
parents would never let him end up with a mermaid, and most
definitely not one who was half human.

Was she right? Was I being naive to think that this thing we
had would last forever? And if it didn't, what would that mean
for Kona and me? What would happen to us when it was time
for him to settle down? What would happen to *me* if he had to
pick some nice selkie girl to be with?

Ugh. I was turning into one of those weepy, indecisive girls who couldn't do anything without her boyfriend to guide her. Just the thought made me break out in hives.

I don't need Kona, I assured myself. I loved him, wanted to be with him, but I didn't need him. I could do this, could be mermaid alone, if I had to.

But I wouldn't have to, I told myself. Kona loved me and wanted to be with me as much as I wanted to be with him. He didn't care about me not being selkie—he would have told me before now if he did.

Yet, even as I protested, I knew Hailana's words made sense, too. How could they not when I'd witnessed back on land how right they were? I'd been with Mark, had loved him completely, but even with that we hadn't been able to make it work. Not when I was only partially like him. Only half human.

Either way, I wasn't normal. Wasn't like everybody else. Which left me with the same question I'd had most of my life. Where did I fit in? Where did I truly belong?

An octopus swam close enough to brush against me with its long, dangling tentacles, and I yanked my attention back to the present. I was doing it again—swimming in the open ocean like it was no big deal. Like there wasn't a war brewing that could wipe me, and the other shifters who lived in the water, right out of existence.

Shoving my worries away for good—or at least until I had more time and energy to deal with them—I turned and started to head back to the city. Though Hailana's waters were relatively safe, it wouldn't pay for me to get too far from civilization.

I was about halfway to Coral Straits when I felt a tug deep inside myself, like a chord had been played that only I could hear. It vibrated through me, called to me in a way nothing but the ocean itself ever had before.

At first I tried to ignore it, but the vibrations quickly grew worse until I felt like I was going to shake apart. Slowing down, I glanced around to see if I had somehow managed to swim into a trap. If, even now, Tiamat was lying in wait for me.

I couldn't see anything though, couldn't sense the dark acid of her energy anywhere around me. Which meant that whatever I was feeling was not coming from her. I didn't know if that made me feel better or worse—or even if it mattered, when the noise and the vibrations were getting worse until I had to move. Had to dive.

At first, I thought I was getting away from the sound, from whatever it was that had burrowed inside of me, because the deeper I went, the lower the vibrations became. But as I got near the bottom of the ocean floor, I realized it wasn't getting harder to feel because I was getting away from it, but because I was getting closer. I was heeding its call and being rewarded by the lessening of pain.

The knowledge immediately threw me into retreat, and I swam straight up. Only to get to a point where I was shaking so badly that I could barely breathe, barely think. Barely swim. The water seemed to get thicker, until I felt like I was slogging through quicksand. No matter how hard I fought, I was getting nowhere. Just sinking down, down, down.

A little freaked out, I finally stopped fighting the pull. Figuring I could either wear myself out completely or meet this thing—whatever it was—while I still had some energy to fight back, I decided to dive deep again. I arrowed straight down until the weird feeling inside of me was all but gone and I was only a few feet from a series of caverns carved into the ocean floor.

I eyed them suspiciously. The last time I'd been in an ocean cave, I'd nearly died—and had ended up having to kill someone to escape. So to say that I really, really didn't want to go in there was a little bit of an understatement.

Still, I was smart enough to know that whatever this was wasn't going to leave me alone until I did. For a second, I longed for life before my seventeenth birthday, when my body actually did what it was supposed to, what I wanted it to. From the moment last fall when I'd been surfing and my legs had tried to become a tail, I'd been losing control—over myself, my life, my destiny.

This was just one more betrayal.

Sucking in a deep gulp of water, and what I hoped was a bunch of courage to go along with it, I swam right up to the mouth of the cave.

If the opening was anything to go by, this cave was a lot larger than the last one I'd been in. I didn't know if that was good or bad. More places for me to hide, but that went both ways. Whatever, whoever, was doing this to me could be somewhere inside, just waiting to spring the trap.

And yet I was going in anyway. If Kona ever found out, he would kill me. So would Mahina. She was constantly on me about doing stupid things that put me in jeopardy—part and parcel of having a certified genius as a best friend. This definitely counted as both foolish and dangerous, but it wasn't like I had a choice. I'd tried to leave, I really had.

Screw it. Annoyed with myself and just about everyone and everything else in my life, I put every ounce of strength I had left behind my kick-off, then plunged through the opening of the cave and straight into the middle of the first room.

It wasn't anything like what I was expecting. The last cave had been black, empty—filled with sharp rocks and barren rooms. This one was alive with color and life. Though it was dark, my natural phosphorescence partially lit up the world around me with a purple haze. Plus, there was an entire school of fish in this room, all glowing a beautiful orangey red.

Thanks to their light, I could see clusters of multicolored coral and sea anemones lining the floor, as well as gorgeous stalactites dripping down from the ceiling. They made a kind of maze for me, around long, sharp, rainbow-colored spears arranged with no rhyme or reason, that I had to navigate through and around to get to the back of this first cavity.

As I swam, the fish darted up to me. Some whirled back and forth in front of me, while others circled my arms or played peek-aboo in my hair. I couldn't help laughing, and tried to send them a sense of my amusement. If I'd had Kona's talent, we actually would have been able to talk to each other, but since I didn't, I settled for reaching out to pet them.

Most of the fish zipped away the second my hand came anywhere near them, but a few curious ones stuck around and let me stroke their sides or tails. They felt a little rough, scaly, but kind of silky too. I liked it.

Two huge stalactites loomed in front of me, the opening between them too narrow for me to squeeze through. I dived deep, got under them, but ended up brushing the tip of my tail against a fire coral.

Crap. It wasn't the first time I'd been stung—while mermaid

or human. But fire coral was obnoxious, its sting hurting more than a lot of the other kinds.

I swished my tail back and forth in an effort to shake off the last of the stinging cells, as Kona had taught me. The burn lessened a little, and I realized it was already healing. Huh. I'd been stung a lot in human form and it had never healed this quickly. Always nice to discover something else cool about being mermaid.

Feeling better already, I finished the obstacle course of the front room and ended up in a long, dark passageway. With the sting feeling better by the minute, I concentrated on exploring the cave, trying to figure out what it was about this place that called to me so completely. I had no sense of danger, no little niggle at the back of my neck telling me something was wrong.

In fact, I felt more right in this place than I had in a while. I certainly felt healthier and better than I had since getting attacked yesterday. It was like being here, in this cave, was feeding my energy, my power.

It sounds crazy, I know, but with every room I swam into, I seemed to get a little bit stronger.

Which was pretty much a guarantee that I wasn't going to stop until I'd explored the whole cave—or as much as I had time for today. As I swam through a room that branched off the main passageway, I found another, narrower route. I followed the path—I couldn't help it—and about halfway down found a hole in the floor that was barely big enough for me to swim through.

For long seconds, I contemplated it. Told myself it was a bad idea to go down there when I had no idea where it led and, unlike the rest of the cave, there seemed to be no other life forms in it.

And yet, somehow, I knew it was exactly where I was supposed to go. Sick and tired of the mysteriousness, of the unknown forces pushing at me when what I wanted most was to be normal—a normal human or a normal mermaid, at this point I didn't care—all of a sudden I wanted nothing more than to turn around and leave. No matter how beautiful the cave was, I didn't want to communicate with forces I didn't understand. Any more than I wanted to be the subject of that stupid prophecy that had everyone treating me like I was different. Special.

Better to just do it, I told myself. *Get down there, see what it is you're supposed to see, and then get back to the city.* Mahina was probably looking for me, and God only knew what Hailana would say about this latest disappearance of mine.

So that's what I did. I arrowed myself straight down into the small hole in the cavern floor. My arms were out in front of me, helping me swim, and the second they came into contact with the hole, an electric current jolted through me, paralyzing me even as it knocked my teeth together in the closest thing to a seizure I had ever experienced.

I tried to pull back, but I couldn't move. The electricity was zinging through my body, pulling me deeper and deeper into the hole without any effort on my part.

There was a whole section of my brain that was terrified, convinced I was going to die down here. But at the same time, it was kind of fascinating, this strange pull the current had on me. Even though it hurt, like getting zapped by a bunch of shocks at exactly the same time, another part of me understood that if I could just keep calm, just go with it, the pain would soon be over. Whatever oceanic force had grabbed on to me would relinquish its hold as soon as it brought me where I needed to go.

I floated down into the hole, through a passageway so narrow that I felt the rocks scrape at my shoulder blades and hips, then somehow moved into an even narrower tunnel. At one point, I had to hold my breath—just the in and out of my gills was too much for the tiny space. And then I was at the end, opening into a cavern so large that I couldn't see the top or bottom of it.

The second I slid into the room, the electric force released me. I plummeted a few yards, straight through water so icy I knew it had never seen sunlight, before realizing my body was once again under my control.

Slowing my descent with a flick of my tail and a few strokes of my limp arms, I took a second to assess my physical condition. I was weak, tired, my skin a million times more sensitive than it had ever been before. My breathing was harsh, my gills sucking water in like they were afraid it was about to run out. And my head—it hurt almost as much as it had yesterday, after I'd lost all that blood. I couldn't help wondering how many brain cells I'd killed in the last twenty-four hours, between the blood loss, Sabyn's attack, and now this. With my luck, enough to cause some serious damage. This whole underwater thing was working out so much better than I'd planned.

But self-pity wasn't going to get me anywhere. Of course, neither was sitting around in the dark. Though I was still glowing, it was nowhere near enough to actually help me out. This part of the cave was so huge that I didn't illuminate much of it. Closing my eyes, I concentrated as hard as I could, praying I had enough power left to do what I needed to.

My palms grew warm, tingled, and I wondered if there was a way to use what Sabyn unwittingly taught me to help me down here. In the training circles, I'd used my energy and light to create a spear. Down here I only wanted something to help me see.

Rubbing my hands together as I focused, I pulled them apart slightly when they started to burn. Opening my eyes, I could see the small spark of light resting in the center of my left palm, and I pulled my right one back a little, rolling them around so that I could mold the light into a ball. Then I used my mind to send the light straight out in front of me. It stopped about fifteen feet away and cast an eerie glow on the wall in front of it.

I grinned, startled but also pretty impressed by my first attempt at making light.

Focusing, I did the same thing again, but this time I sent the light straight down twenty feet or so, until it hovered a few inches above the rocky bottom of the cave.

Two more times I bent energy to make light, until I had a light source in all four directions, north, south, east, and west, with me directly in the center. Then, and only then, did I let my concentration falter.

Turning in circles, I got my first good look at the room around me. What I saw had my eyes widening and my heart nearly pounding out of my chest.

Chapter 10

Swimming toward one end of the chamber, I blinked several times, certain that I wasn't actually seeing what I thought I was. But the closer I got to the wall—which was elaborately carved with scene after scene of mermaids—the more certain I became that I was not imagining what was in front of me.

Someone had carved five shelves into the cave wall, whittling the sharp rocks into long, rounded platforms that ran the circumference of the room. And on four of the shelves, spaced equidistantly apart, were hundreds upon hundreds of pearls—in every shape, color, and size imaginable. The top shelf, which contained no pearls, held large pieces of sea glass instead, their ragged edges polished away by years under the surface.

Though the water in the cavern was ebbing and flowing with the cyclical, never-ending rhythm of the ocean, neither the pearls nor the glass moved so much as an inch. Instead, it was as if each one had been glued in place with something even endless exposure to salt water couldn't wear away.

I'd never seen anything like it, couldn't imagine who would

have the patience—or the time—to painstakingly create the shelves, let alone collect this variety and range of pearls. With the different shapes and colors, I knew they had to have come from all over the Pacific, and maybe the Atlantic as well.

So what were they doing here? I wondered dazedly. And why would someone want me to see this so badly that they'd all but electrocuted me to get me here?

Not sure what else to do, I reached out a hand and touched a pearl directly in front of me. It was one of the biggest I'd ever seen, maybe fifteen or sixteen millimeters across, and it was the lustrous, shiny black of the Tahitian pearls my father used to give to my mother on special occasions.

To my surprise, it came away from the shelf easily, as if it had just been waiting for someone to pick it up. The moment my hand closed around it, however, pain shot through my head, so all-consuming and terrible that for long seconds I was convinced my mind was literally being ripped apart. It was like someone had shoved giant, poison-tipped claws straight into my brain and started shredding.

I stumbled back from the shelf, tried to drop the pearl as I clutched my head, but now that I was holding it, the same magic that had kept the pearl on the shelf for God only knew how long was also keeping it attached to my palm.

It burned wherever it touched, and I opened my fingers, tried to shake it loose, but nothing I did worked. Even scraping my palm against the side of the cave wouldn't dislodge it—all it did was increase the blistering pain in my hand and the agony in my head, until the electric shocks of earlier seemed like mere tickles.

Uncontrollable tears poured down my face, blending with

the salt water all around me. I didn't know what to do, didn't know how to make it stop. All I knew was that if something didn't happen soon, I wasn't going to survive. Already, I could feel my heart pumping so fast that I was sure it would burst.

With each second that passed, I grew more terrified, less able to function, and slowly I sank down to the cavern floor. I continued to struggle, to try to pry the pearl away from me, but nothing worked. The water around me turned red and I realized, distractedly, that my nose was bleeding.

Then I started to convulse, my body jerking in twenty different directions. Darkness beckoned. Instead of trying to resist it as I normally did, I rushed toward the blessed numbness of unconsciousness, embraced it with what little will I had left.

The second I stopped fighting, the convulsions ceased. My body went limp and the agony that had raked me for what seemed like forever dissipated. In its place was light, bursting behind my eyes in a dazzling rainbow array that stunned me in a way even the pain couldn't. The colors spread out, widened, until they were all that I could see. And then it was like I was being sucked under, sucked through them as the cavern, the colors, the whole world, began to spin around me.

And then she was there. Cecily. My mother.

But not. She was younger than I remembered, younger than when I knew her. And about a million times more vulnerable. She was in human form, kneeling in the middle of Coral Straits in nothing but an emerald green bikini. Her body was covered in cuts and scratches and the water around her was bloody. So bloody that I couldn't imagine how she'd survived—until I realized that she was not the only one injured.

On the ground in front of her were five merpeople—a man, a woman, two teenage boys, and a little girl. Though everything was a little grainy, out of focus, they all looked familiar to me, and as I looked back and forth between them and my mother, horrified knowledge filled me. I felt like I knew these people, because looking at them—especially the kids—was like looking at my mother. Like looking at me. Like looking at the unknown woman on the ocean floor, a huge, gaping hole where her heart used to be.

This was my mother's family. *My* family. My grandparents and uncles and aunt. This scene, these deaths, were the reason I had no relatives down here, no one who cared about me besides Hailana, who had all the motherly instinct of a hammer-head shark. Of course, that was probably an insult to those sharks, even if they were known to eat their own young.

As I watched my mother stagger to her feet—bruised, bloody, broken—the pain came back. It wasn't quite as excruciating this time, tempered as it was with knowledge and distance, and I realized what it was I was feeling. My mother's pain and grief, so raw and acute that it had brought me to the brink of madness. Is that how she had felt, then, watching as her family lay murdered in front of her?

I thought of Moku, of Rio, of my father. Thought of what it had felt like to see Cecily ripped apart in front of me, and I knew that yes, that was exactly what I was feeling. What I *had* felt.

How had she borne all that anger and hatred and grief and pain without literally destroying herself? In those moments, when I'd been caught up in it, I had prayed for unconsciousness, prepared for death. Had thought either, both, would be better.

The pain was there again, a burning in my gills that made it nearly impossible to draw air. I wanted to put the pearl down, to throw it as far away from me as I could, but I didn't move, didn't even try to let go this time. I couldn't, not when I knew there was still more to see, more to understand. This glimpse into my mother's life was unprecedented and I wanted, *needed*, to know.

Cecily stumbled back from their bodies, turned, and limped across the ocean floor. It seemed strange to see her like that, so delicate, so human. Which didn't make sense. Except for brief moments of my childhood and that last, terrible encounter with Tiamat, I had only ever seen my mother in her human form. So why, then, did it seem anathema to me? So strange and awkward?

Because I had spent so long thinking of her as mermaid? Spent so long resenting the choice she had made that I had forgotten how many ways we were alike?

I didn't know the answer, wasn't sure I wanted to, as my mother lurched back toward the palace. Toward Hailana.

When was this? My mother looked so young and vulnerable, but something about the expression on her face and the set of her shoulders told me she was a lot older than I had originally judged her to be. Mermaids aged at a different rate than humans, so their adolescence and young adulthood could last centuries—as long as they stayed in the water. Once they hit land and lived as humans, they aged at the same rate people did.

Then Hailana was there, holding her arms open to my mother. She looked tired, worn out, and I could see that she was injured too, though not as severely as Cecily. I have to admit, it surprised me a little to see the blood on Hailana's temple and shoulder. For

as long as I'd known her she'd seemed so invulnerable, so indomitable, that it was hard to imagine she could actually bleed.

The knowledge that she was, indeed, mortal was nowhere
near as reassuring as it should have been.

What was even more unexpected, though, was that my
mother—Hailana's self-professed best friend—walked right by
her like she wasn't even there. For one brief moment, Hailana's
face registered shock and then she was rushing after Cecily,
grabbing on to her.

Cecily flinched away, and I could see clearly now the livid
bruises on her arm. I couldn't tell if Hailana had given them to
her or if she had received them in whatever battle had gone
down.

When Hailana reached for her again, tried to put herself in
Cecily's path, my mother shoved the merQueen as hard as she
could. Hailana hit the floor and then my mother was lurching
painfully across the sea bed. Moving as quickly as she could
away from the queen.

She paused once, and I knew it was because Hailana had said
something to her. I would have given anything to know what
it was—what the two of them were saying to each other—but
the sound effects of this memory (or whatever it was) couldn't
breach the walls of telepathic communication between them.

Then my mother started moving, and again I wondered why
she didn't shift—it would be so much easier for her to move with
a tail, especially if she wasn't used to human legs. Then I remembered what the healer had told me about shifting, about how
I had been stuck with my tail until I healed up a little more, no
matter how much I longed for the comfort of my legs.

The memory changed then, became less sharp, more confused. The pain was still there, but it was different. More bearable, less all-encompassing.

Cecily was being tossed from wave to wave, current to current, and as I watched, everything took on an even blurrier feel, as if the camera that had recorded these memories was just a little out of focus. She was numb, I realized, recognizing the feeling from some of what I'd been through. Completely disconnected from what happened to her family, from what was happening to her now. The pain I felt, like a hard punch blunted with cotton, was her physical reaction, her body's response to its injuries. The white-hot agony I'd felt before had been my glimpse into her emotional devastation.

My stomach clenched as I watched her, sometimes swimming, sometimes floating unconscious. Though I saw only small sections of time, I got the impression that her disoriented flight lasted a long while. And then things changed again, grew clear and crisp like the razor-sharp edge of a scalpel.

Cecily, in human form, was lying facedown on a beach. Hair matted, body bruised and scabbed over, bikini top missing. I narrowed my eyes, tried to look more closely, but couldn't figure out where she was. It was too tropical to be home, but we'd been to a lot of different beaches in my life—it could be anywhere from American Samoa to Tahiti.

Then I saw my father—or at least a much younger version of him—shooting a barrel, and I knew. She was in Hawaii. This is where they met. I'd heard the story a hundred times through the years, but neither of my parents had ever portrayed it as happening quite like this.

My father spotted her as he came into shore, ran to her. Checked for a pulse. Then carried her to his car.

My heart hurt a little, watching them, realizing that nothing was ever quite what I expected it to be. It was like the ocean changed everything, twisted it, until what was left was barely recognizable. Like my mother and, I was very afraid, like me as well.

The pearl grew dim, its fire weakening against my palm. There was one last scene, though. My mom in a hospital bed with my father beside her. He was spooning green Jell-O into her mouth and cracking jokes. Though I couldn't hear what he was saying, I recognized the look on his face and the smile on my mother's that said she was more amused than she wanted to admit.

I hoped to see more, to know more, but the pearl turned cold—one second before it floated from my hand like I'd never had trouble shaking it loose.

As I sat there on the jagged rocks that made up the bottom of the cave, I didn't know how to feel. For seven years now, I'd resented my mother and the choices she'd made. The choices I'd had to make because of who she was and what her genetics had made me.

And now, having watched all of that, I still resented her. This time, however, I felt guilty about those emotions. My mother's life, her choices, had not been as easy for her as I'd always imagined they were. And maybe in time, that knowledge—I looked around the cavern at the many, many pearls on the shelves—and all the knowledge that was to come, would somehow change my feelings.

For now, I just felt numb. Except, of course, for the pain all that seizing and crashing around earlier had inflicted on my already messed-up body.

I stood slowly. Carefully. Suddenly I felt a lot older than seventeen, though I didn't know if that was because of what I'd just seen or if it was a result of all the injuries I had sustained in the last twenty-four hours.

I should leave. I didn't know how much time had passed, but I figured I'd been gone long enough for it to have gotten late. Kona was probably trying to check on me, and God only knew what Hailana had planned in my absence.

Yet I was strangely reluctant go. Half an hour ago I would have done anything to get out of here, to run away from the horrors swamping me. But now, now that the pearl had done what it was supposed to, now that the enchantment that had brought me here had finally let up, I wasn't sure what to do.

Go or stay.

Get another pearl or get the hell away from them.

Learn more about my mother or keep my memories of her exactly as I was used to.

I shook my head, fought the urge to bury my face in my hands. I was sick of all these questions, all these dilemmas. In some ways, it was just like being back on land with my birthday looming. I'd been forced to make choices I wasn't ready for, and I felt like I was being forced to do it again now.

I was tired.

I hurt.

And nothing was turning out quite the way I had expected it to when I'd first decided on this life. Maybe it never would.

With that thought foremost in my head, I coasted closer to the wall. Examined pearl after pearl without actually touching any of them. Trying to decide which one I would drop into next.

On the second row there was a brilliant white blister pearl in the shape of a thumbprint. I liked it, felt it call to me even with the awkwardness of its contours. Despite the warnings in my head, despite all the reasons I had to back away and simply disappear, I found myself reaching out. Wanting to touch it. Wanting to know more about the woman I had spent so much of my life despising.

I was almost there, my fingers almost brushed against the cool, slick surface of the pearl, when I heard Hailana's voice in the back of my head. Low, cool, and oh so urgent, it sent chills through me—as did all the things she refused to say, even though no one would think about dropping in on Hailana's private lines of communication.

Get back to Coral Straits right now, she told me impatiently. *I need you!*

Chapter 11

What's wrong? I demanded, even as I shot straight up to the hole at the top of the cavern, pausing only to extinguish the lights I had created.

We have a situation. How far away are you?

I sucked in my breath, held it while I shot through both narrowed passages like a rocket. New scrapes bloomed on my shoulder and stomach, but I didn't let myself pay attention to them. I'd known Hailana for eight months now and never had I heard her sound so anxious.

I'm about two hours away, I told her, already wincing as I prepared for the ass-kicking I knew was coming.

Two hours away? she demanded. *While injured? And on duty?*

Technically, I'm not on duty. Because of my injuries—

I didn't remove you, she snapped. *Which means,* technically, *you're in direct violation of our training protocols.*

Direct violation? Training protocols? I nearly snorted up lungfuls of water as I struggled not to laugh. But seriously . . . *When did you start talking like we were in a James Bond movie?*

*Since we've been overrun by refugees and I need every pair of hands
I can find.*

Refugees? The word felt strange, foreign, here in the ocean
where life was so different, so much less politicized, than it was
on land. *From where?*

Get back here and I'll explain everything.

Hailana— I started to ask more, but she was gone, the connection between us severed so completely that it was like it had
never been.

I tried to reach for her, to speak to her, but no matter how
hard I'd been training, I still couldn't get the hang of initiat-
ing long-distance telepathy. I could answer when someone—
usually the merQueen or Kona—spoke to me, but I couldn't
figure out how to reach across miles of ocean and open the
conversation.

I sped home as fast as I could, ignoring the fish and other sea
creatures that wanted to play. Refugees? I mused. From where?
And why had they come to Hailana? I had trouble seeing her as
the altruistic type.

About ten miles out of Coral Straits I saw them, mermaids
carrying messenger bags, backpacks, and duffels as they inched
their way toward my city. Some were in groups, some were
straggling on their own, but they all had something in common—
they were moving slowly and looked so bruised and defeated
that it was like they had already given up.

What could have done this to them? What could have turned
such normally vibrant creatures into these hopeless people? An
underwater volcano eruption that buried their city? A massive
earthquake along one of the fault lines?

I could only imagine.

I wanted to stop, to help, but there were so many of them that I was afraid of being buried in their stories, in their grief, and never making it back to the city where I could do more good. I sped past them, determined to make it into Coral Straits where I could take up a position to help get the refugees settled. But as I rocketed along, it grew harder and harder to keep going.

So many people, so much suffering. I wished I had some food on me, some blankets for the little ones shivering despite the relatively warm water. Were they in shock? Injured? Because mermaids could regulate their own temperatures, despite being warm-blooded creatures, it was rare for us to be either too hot or too cold—at least in the water.

My concern for the little ones doubled. I swam faster—maybe I could gather up some supplies and bring them back here. These people didn't need to suffer any more than they already had.

My headlong flight stopped abruptly the second I saw him. Young, no more than five or six, he was curly-headed with bronze skin and huge brown eyes ringed with lashes. And he was injured, his little arm wrapped up in a bandage and a sling that was way too big for him.

I couldn't help it—I had to stop. He reminded me so much of Moku that it just ripped my heart wide open.

Swooping down, I squatted—or did the closest thing to a squat that I could with a tail—and asked, *Hey there, big guy. You doing okay?*

His lower lip trembled and those huge eyes filled with tears. *I want my mommy.*

Of course you do, sweetheart. I looked around. *Where is she?*

One of the women on the trail—who had three young children hanging off her—whispered to me, *She didn't make it.*

Didn't make . . . I froze in horror as I realized what she was saying. *And his father?*

The woman shook her head. *I've been watching out for him on the trip, but it's been hard.* She gestured to the kids in her own arms, none of whom looked older than four.

Let me see if I can find someone to take care of him. Okay?

She nodded gratefully as I picked him up in my arms. *What's your name, baby?*

Liam, he told me. His lower lip was trembling.

I'm Tempest. How about a piggyback ride?

His eyes grew wide. *A what?*

Hmm, maybe some things didn't translate from land to water. *How about a ride on my back?*

A sea-horse ride?

Sure. A sea-horse ride.

He nodded, and scooted so that his arms and legs were wrapped around me. Like all mer children, he wouldn't grow a tail until he'd proven himself, sometime after his adolescence hit.

How fast do you want to go? I asked him as I took off, careful to keep a secure grip on his legs.

Superfast! he cried, bouncing up and down a little.

Superfast it is, then. Hang on!

I sped up, staying low to the ground to cut down on the current for him. I also moved away a little from the refugee path. It was so depressing, so awful, that I wanted Liam to have a little break from it. He had a hard road in front of him—the least I could do was give him a few minutes of fun to try and take his mind off everything he'd lost.

When we arrived at Coral Straits, I whipped through the huge gates that were more decorative than protective. I'd planned on swimming right up to the castle, but one look at the city had me stopping dead, my head whirling with the difference a few hours made.

The training fields were filled with huge white tentlike structures. At the entrance to each one were two long tables, staffed with merpeople from my clan. They were checking in the long lines of people that snaked from the tent, handing out packets of food and the waterproof blankets we used down here. It looked so much like the scenes I used to see on TV after disasters on land that I almost couldn't process it.

I don't know why, but I guess I'd never thought anything like this could happen under the surface. It was strange to realize that it could. Even more so that it *had*. Looking at all those people who were wounded, hungry, who had lost their homes and their families, made me realize that, in some ways, the ocean wasn't as different as I'd thought.

Tightening my hold on Liam's legs, I swam as fast as I could toward the castle. Hailana often spent evenings out of the water, on her island, but I was guessing that with everything going on, she was in the ocean.

I didn't even make it to the castle before I spotted her. She was on the outskirts of the tent city that had sprung up from nowhere, deep in discussion with Sabyn, a couple of her advisers, and a number of mer that I didn't recognize. I wondered if they were from the incoming clan.

Liam and I zoomed up to them, and though I had planned to lurk at the back of the group, Hailana spotted me right away and waved me to the front. I'd never seen her look so grim, which was saying something as Hailana was not a big smiler. Now, however, she looked like the world really was crashing down around us.

What happened? I asked, suddenly not sure I wanted to know. Something told me that a natural disaster wouldn't put the slightly bemused, slightly horrified look on Hailana's face.

Tiamat attacked another mer clan. She wiped out about half their numbers, including the entire royal family.

The strangers winced at Hailana's blunt summation of the facts, but no one said anything. *Is this it?* I asked, instinctively shifting Liam around so that I could shelter him in my arms. *Is this the beginning?*

We'd known war was coming, but Hailana had said she'd hoped to put it off until I was better trained. I'd been hoping to put it off indefinitely. I might have power, but fighting would never be something I enjoyed.

Not yet, Hailana answered. *I believe she's just running amok, causing trouble. It's something she's infinitely good at.*

That's not— Sabyn started, but a swift look from the mer-Queen shut him down quickly. I looked back and forth between them, wondering what he'd been about to say. And what Hailana hadn't wanted to share.

Who is this? she asked, looking at Liam like he was a rare and exotic species she had no interest in getting too close to.

I found him on the path in, I told her on our private channel. *He's lost both of his parents.*

Oh, well, that's certainly a shame. The reply was brisk, without feeling. *You should probably get him settled at the tents. We have a lot to do in the next few hours.*

I glanced down at Liam. The tears were gone, for now anyway, but he still looked lost. He probably would for a while—his whole world had been yanked out from under him. And Hailana wanted me to just dump him in with all the others?

I knew it was stupid, knew that he probably wasn't the only child in this situation, but I wanted to help him. And not just in the abstract, but personally.

I didn't bother telling any of this to Hailana, however. She wouldn't understand. She was great at doing what had to be done to save the many, but she'd never paid much attention to the individual. And while I recognized that sometimes you needed to be like that, I also knew that sometimes you couldn't. Sometimes objectivity had to fly out the window.

What do you need me to do? I asked. *Do you want me to help out at the tents? I could—*

I want you to get the boy settled. And then you need to train. You have to master your talents. Quickly.

I started to protest, but her warning look cut me off. Apparently now wasn't the time to undermine Hailana. She would never forgive me if I made her look weak in front of another clan. I might not like her, but I understood how important respect was.

Go get the boy settled and get yourself something to eat, she told me. *There's a strategy session in my chambers aboveground in an hour. I expect you to be in on it. You can do a late-night training session after that.*

Yes, ma'am.

I reluctantly headed over to the refugee section, everything inside of me crying out at the injustice of leaving Liam. Even if there were people in these tents who knew him, even if I was sure that he would be taken care of, I still didn't want to let him go. It didn't seem fair, especially considering the way he clung to me. I don't think he wanted me to leave any more than I wanted to walk away.

There had to be a solution. Glancing back over my shoulder, I saw Hailana still staring at me, though she was technically engaged in conversation with someone else. I knew she wouldn't stop paying attention until she saw Liam ensconced in the refugee tents. Which meant I had to think fast if I was going to find a way around her. There had to be someone I could count on, someone who could help me . . .

I was searching the crowd when my eyes fell on Mahina. She was working the second refugee line and looked like she was going to cry at any second. Which she probably was—I'd never met anyone more tenderhearted than Mahina. And that's when the lightbulb went off. Mahina had seven younger brothers and sisters and, despite that, loved children. And they loved her. Liam would be safe with her while I was off following the merQueen's bidding.

Maybe I couldn't keep him with me forever, couldn't keep him safe from all the bad things waiting for him, but I could give him a little time, a little attention, while I tried to find a family member of his to take care of him.

Swooping down on Mahina, I didn't bother to waste time on niceties. *I need your help*, I told her.

She turned at the sound of my voice, threw her arms around

me and held on as tightly as she could. *Where were you?* she demanded. *I was so worried. I thought . . . I thought—* Her voice broke.

I'm okay, I assured her, pulling back slightly. *I was on my own the whole time—I didn't see anyone.*

Thank God. She sniffled a little, then glanced at Liam with wide eyes. *Who is this?*

Again, I explained his situation, and bless her, Mahina caught on right away. Holding her arms out to Liam, she said, *Come on, honey. Let's get you something to eat, okay?*

Liam's arms tightened around me and he shook his head, refusing to go. My heart melted just a little bit more, even as it ached for him. If he didn't go to Mahina, I was out of ideas. Hailana was simply being practical, as she always was, but I couldn't be. Not in this. Not when I imagined Moku every time I looked at Liam. Not when I prayed that my brothers would never be in such a precarious situation. I would care for Liam, because it was the right thing to do. And because I prayed that someone would do the same for my brothers if anything ever happened to my dad.

For a second I was blindsided by the knowledge that something could happen to one of them and I would never know. Rio could get hurt surfing, Moku—who was notoriously clumsy—could fall and hit his head. My dad, well, he was in great shape, but he wasn't getting any younger. What would I do if something terrible happened? What could I do when I had chosen a life far removed from them?

Tempest? Liam's little voice tentatively called my name, and I yanked my attention back to him. If I had any chance of maintaining my sanity, I had to let this new fear go. If I didn't, it would *paralyze* me.

Yes? I asked him.

I'm scared.

I know, baby. I hugged him tight, then pulled away a little so I could see his face. *This is my friend Mahina. She's really nice.*

He buried his face against my neck, but after a second shyly peeked out at her.

Mahina, this is Liam.

It's nice to meet you, Liam. She held her hand out, fingers curled into a fist.

At first I didn't think Liam was going to do anything, but at the last second he reached out his own little fist and softly bumped hers. Mahina melted, her expression going all gooey with sorrow and affection.

You want to know a secret? she asked him.

He nodded, his eyes widening.

I have a little brother who's six years old. And he has the biggest box of toys I've ever seen.

Really? Liam asked.

Cross my heart, she answered, drawing an *X* over her chest. *Would you like to see?*

He nodded vigorously.

Okay, then. Come on. She reached out her arms and after another quick glance at me, Liam opened his arms up and grabbed on to Mahina.

We both breathed out a sigh of relief. *I'll come get him later,* I promised her. *Hailana needs me in a meeting and then I have to train more with Sabyn.*

Lucky you, she said with a wink. *I wish I had some of your powers. Maybe then I'd get to train with him too.*

I thought of the session from hell and just rolled my eyes. *Believe me,* I told her, *it's not all it's cracked up to be.*

Yeah, well, I'd probably choke on my own drool anyway.

I laughed because that was what she wanted from me, but it was hard—especially when I looked into Liam's forlorn little face. *I'll see you later,* I told him, holding out my own hand for a fist bump.

He gave me a hug instead. I hugged him back, then turned away before I started crying all over him. That wasn't quite the tough, in-charge image I wanted to project.

Then again, nothing down here was living up to my expectations. Why should I be so concerned about living up to everyone else's?

Chapter 12

I grabbed dinner on the way to Hailana's chambers, throwing it down on the run. Tonight it was shrimp ceviche and kelp salad, which were both delicious, especially the way the merQueen's cook prepared them. Still, I found myself longing for a burger and fries, which was funny since I was never much of a meat eater when I lived on land. Lately though, I practically salivated at the thought of a steak. And don't even get me started on how much I missed Cherry Garcia ice cream . . .

Despite my rush, I was a few minutes late getting to the Council meeting. Shifting took a few minutes, as did examining the brand-new scar that ran the length of my calf. *Thank you, Zarek*, I said silently. The cut was bad enough that I wouldn't have wanted to walk on it if it wasn't fully healed. When I got to Hailana's chambers, everyone turned to stare at me. Which was a little intimidating, considering the fact that Hailana's entire Council was present. But I'd done the best I could—shifting back to my human form had been crazy difficult this time around and it had put me behind.

Hailana was sitting at the end of a long, polished table carved from the wood of a sunken Spanish galleon (I knew this because she was very proud of that table and took every chance to extol its heritage). On either side of her were Veracruz and Rafael, the two mermen she trusted almost as much as she'd trusted my mother. Both wore fierce frowns on their faces, which softened a little when they saw me but by no means disappeared completely.

Next to Rafael was Alastair, the newest addition to the Council (even newer than I was). He'd been a member of Hailana's staff forever, but it was only a few months ago that she'd seen fit to promote him to the Council. Mahina said it was because they'd been having an affair since forever and Hailana hadn't wanted to show favoritism, but I wasn't so sure. One, because she'd had no trouble showing favoritism toward me—at least in the beginning, before she realized what a pain in the butt I was going to be. And two, because Alastair, despite his very austere name, was one of the nicest men I'd ever met. I couldn't imagine him being caught in Hailana's web for long. At least not voluntarily.

Next to him was Faith, who had been one of my mother's closest friends. She'd spent the last eight months looking out for me and I liked her a lot, except I could never quite shake the feeling that she wasn't really seeing me. She was seeing who she wanted to see—namely, Cecily.

And finally, across from her sat Violet, who I absolutely adored. Hailana couldn't stand her, only put up with her because she was her sister, but I thought Violet was the coolest mermaid I had ever met. Though she was almost as old as Hailana, she still dressed like a teenager. Her bikinis were skimpy, her body jewelry plentiful, and I'd never seen her when she didn't have some kind of object woven through her hair. Today it was glittering abalone shells and ribbons in the same shade of hot pink as her tail.

I hurried across the room and sank into the chair next to hers, grateful that she was the one on this end, especially since the alternative was sitting next to Sabyn. Which so wasn't an option, considering my stomach still burned from the cut he'd given me that afternoon. The only thing that made my failure against him bearable was the large, bloodstained bandage around his bicep. At least he hadn't gotten away completely unscathed.

No one specifically acknowledged my presence and I relaxed a little as the conversation continued to ebb and flow around me.

"I'm telling you, Hailana, this is it!" Rafael's fist slammed down on the table. "Tiamat will be here any day now and we are completely unprepared."

"We are not unprepared," Alastair answered. "Our defenses are better than they've ever been. Halaina's powers are at their peak. And now we have Tempest and Sabyn to help us. If Tiamat comes, we'll be ready for her."

"I think you mean *when* she comes," Rafael corrected him.

"Whatever." He shrugged.

"That won't be now," Faith told them both, stretching lazily, as if she were sunning herself on the beach instead of locked in a meeting about the fate of her entire clan.

Our entire clan, I reminded myself.

"You don't know that, Faith," Veracruz told her. "Tiamat just attacked Stormy Point. It's shortsighted and suicidal not to assume that we're going to be next."

"It's shortsighted to assume that we are," Faith countered. "Yes, she just decimated Stormy Point. Yes, she's been gaining power consistently ever since she escaped Cecily's prison. And yes, we should be concerned. We should take every precaution, but I still assert that we have time. She isn't ready to come here yet."

"You sound awfully sure of yourself," Rafael told her.

"I am sure of myself."

"But what are you basing that on? This isn't the first city she's taken in the last few months and, if you plot coordinates on a map, we're the logical next choice." Alastair rubbed his eyes as if the whole discussion was giving him a headache. Of course, it could be the situation and not the discussion that was upsetting him so much. I knew it was upsetting me.

"She's afraid of us." Violet spoke up for the first time. "She won't come to Coral Straits yet because she's too afraid of Tempest to show up here. Not until she's garnered more resources, more power. More magic."

I started to protest, to tell them that the last thing Tiamat was afraid of was me, but then Sabyn laughed. The jerk actually laughed.

"Tiamat isn't afraid of anything or anyone," he told them. "If she isn't planning on coming here yet—and I'm not saying that I think she is or isn't—it's because her plan doesn't call for it. She's too cagey to let emotion get in her way."

"But she is letting emotion get in the way!" I told him, speaking up for the first time. "This whole thing is motivated by emotion, by her need for revenge."

"That's not the same thing—"

"Of course it is! I agree that she's powerful and scary and

definitely operating from a plan, but her biggest weakness is the fact that she will do anything to avenge the time she spent imprisoned."

"She's already done that," Veracruz told me. "When she killed Cecily."

I winced at the matter-of-fact way he said it, like my mother's death was barely a blip on the radar. At the same time, though, I appreciated his candor—everyone always tiptoed around my mother with me, even Hailana. It wasn't nice, but at least it was a relief to find someone who talked about it without lowering his voice and gazing at me with pity.

"Cecily's death wasn't enough," Hailana said, voicing the same thought that was currently in my head. "Tiamat's out for blood—my blood, Tempest's blood, Malakai's blood."

I started at the mention of Kona's father. "Why would she care about Malakai?"

"He worked with Cecily for years to imprison Tiamat," Violet told me quietly. "It was Cecily's magic, Cecily's plan, but if Malakai hadn't fed her as much of his power as he had . . . Well, a lot of people believe your mother would never have succeeded."

"Now isn't the time for that." Hailana's voice was sharp.

Violet regarded her calmly. "I disagree."

Hailana said something else, but to be honest, I wasn't listening. I was too busy reeling from Violet's big reveal. Cecily hadn't imprisoned Tiamat by herself. She'd had help. Selkie help. From Kona's father of all people.

I didn't know how I felt about that. One, because of the way everyone always treated me—like they truly believed I was going to single-handedly bring Tiamat to her knees. Part of that, I knew, came from the prophecy they believed was about me, but I'd always assumed the other part came from the fact that Cecily was my mother. One of the most powerful mermaids in existence, she had brought Tiamat down once. Was it such a stretch, then, that I could do it a second time? Even if I disagreed, even if I didn't feel powerful, I could at least understand where people were coming from.

Finding out she didn't do it alone . . . that just left me thinking that I didn't have a chance. Like everyone really was expecting the impossible from me, expecting something that had never been done before.

Even worse, I couldn't help wondering about Kona. I knew he was strong, knew he had a lot of power on his own. But was one of the reasons he was my boyfriend simply that he knew we had to combine our talents to have any chance of defeating Tiamat?

Kona loves me, I told myself fiercely. I was being ridiculous. Letting a bunch of stupid assumptions undermine my confidence in him. Kona had always been there for me, had never let me down. I owed him more than to suddenly start second-guessing him now.

At the same time, though, Hailana's conviction kept running through my head, that there was no way Kona would ever marry a nonselkie, no way his father would ever allow him to put a half-breed mermaid on the selkie throne.

Was there a kernel of truth to it? Or was I just allowing my fears, my own doubts about myself, to latch on to the most reasonable explanation I could find? I didn't know, and from the stricken look on Violet's face, I wasn't doing a very good job of hiding those anxieties.

So I did what I found myself doing more and more down here: I buried my worries deep inside myself and instead focused on presenting a brave face. On showing everyone in this world that I really was okay. And if most days I felt anything but, then that was no one's business but mine.

"Tempest." Violet's voice was tentative. "Just because your mother had help doesn't mean—"

"It's fine, Violet." I cut her off.

"Tempest, really—"

"I said, it's fine. We're not actually here to discuss my delicate emotional state, are we?" I injected as much sarcasm into the words as I could manage. Was it rude? Maybe. But I was struggling just to keep my head below water. I didn't need anyone else to know that, though.

I glanced down the table at Hailana—I couldn't help myself, though the last thing I wanted was for her to think I was seeking her approval. She gave it to me anyway, eyes gleaming and head nodding, as if I had passed yet another one of her incomprehensible tests.

"You're right, Tempest. That's not what we're here to discuss tonight," she said, her voice ringing with authority.

Although it might be interesting to explore those vulnerabilities. Sabyn again, this time on an intimate path into my thoughts that I'd never felt before. One I hadn't given him access to.

One he'd been powerful enough to forge anyway.

Of all the disturbing things that had happened to me in the last forty-eight hours, that freaked me out the most.

"Tiamat is playing with us," Hailana continued, her voice weak but still ringing with authority. "She has no particular grudge with Stormy Point—"

"Except that they're our allies," interrupted Veracruz.

"Yes, except for that," Hailana acknowledged. "She hit them because she wants us to be afraid. She wants us strung out, always looking over our shoulder waiting, so that we jump at the mere thought of her. It's classic psychological warfare."

"It's working," Violet told her. "I jumped at shadows all the way over here. And I know I'm not the only one."

"Exactly," Hailana said, leaning back as if her point had been proven.

And, in part, I suppose it had been. But there was more to this, I could sense it—a nebulous knowledge floating just out of reach.

"You really think that's all this is?" Sabyn questioned sharply. "Intimidation tactics?"

"No," I said, as things suddenly became clear. "This isn't intimidation—it's strategy. She knew Stormy Point would come to us when they were attacked—where else would they go?"

"Exactly," Hailana said. "She's using the attack to divert our attention, so she can strike when we least expect it."

"Or when we're tired." I leaned forward, more convinced of my argument with every second that passed. "Think about it. The refugees from Stormy Point come here, and what do they do? They weaken us. Drain our food resources, take our medical supplies, splinter our attention between defense and caretaking.

"Doing both will work our soldiers into exhaustion very quickly," I continued. "Even if we stagger shifts, try to rest them, there just won't be enough time. Enough manpower. Enough resources. There won't be enough of anything."

I looked around, saw that for the first time the Council was listening to me. Really listening. Only Sabyn looked like what I was saying was amusing.

From the end of the table, Hailana smiled at me. Then used our private path of communication to say, *It looks like you've got quite a bit of your mother in you after all, Tempest.*

I knew she meant it as a compliment. I just didn't know if I was going to take it that way.

⚬

"Hey, Tempest, wait up!" Sabyn called to me as I left the Council meeting.

I closed my eyes, resisted the urge to groan. Hadn't I been through enough tonight? All I wanted to do now was to see Liam and then fall, face-first, into bed.

"What?" I asked, not even trying to sound polite as I turned to him.

"Whoa!" He held up his hands. "What's got you so upset? I thought you'd be flying high after what happened in there." He jerked his head toward the room we'd just left. "By the end, you had the whole Council behind you one hundred percent."

"But not you." The words came out before I even knew they were there.

He looked uncomfortable, like he hadn't been expecting such honesty from me, either. "It's not that. I just think we need to be ready for an imminent attack from Tiamat."

"But we're not ready. I think that's the point all of us were making. We're not strong enough to fend off a sustained attack from her forces."

"You're ready," he said.

"Yeah, right. I couldn't sustain an attack from you this morning, let alone one from Tiamat."

"You held your own." He glanced outside. "In fact, I thought I'd see if you had time to go back down, do another few rounds. My aunt wants us practicing twice daily from now on."

I actually felt my shoulders slump. I knew Hailana had said she expected me to practice tonight, but I hadn't thought she was serious. Not after the council meeting from hell. It was already close to midnight.

"Come on," he said. "It'll be good for you. Tire you out so that you can sleep."

Not being able to fall asleep hadn't even entered my mind. I was so exhausted that the only worry I had was actually staying awake long enough to get to my room.

Still, he was looking at me like he expected I'd refuse. And that's when I knew—he hadn't chased after me because he'd actually wanted to spar. He'd come so that he could tell Hailana he had tried and I'd been the one to say no.

Anger spiked inside of me, chasing away the foggy tendrils of exhaustion. When I'd lived on land, I'd hated guys like him. Guys who thought they were so slick, that the rules didn't apply to them. Guys who thought they could be total jerks and then turn on a little charm and all would be forgiven.

My chin came up and I glared at him, even as we dived back into the water. *Where do you want to practice? The training circles are a little full right now.* I gestured to the huge white tents full of refugees.

How about the park? It should be pretty quiet at this hour.

Fine. I'll meet you there in ten minutes.

He raised an eyebrow. *You wouldn't be planning on standing me up, would you?*

Do you always think the worst of people? I mimicked his tone and his eyebrow.

That startled a laugh out of him. *I guess I do.*

Well, stop. It's not good for you. I glanced behind me, toward Mahina's house. *I'll be there in a few minutes. There's just something I have to do first.*

He nodded and I turned around, swimming straight for Mahina. And Liam. I hoped he was okay . . .

A couple minutes later, I was standing over his sleeping form, rubbing his back. *He was waiting up for you,* Lily, Mahina's mother, told me. *But the poor little thing ended up crashing. He's so tired.*

Guilt trickled through me. *I'm sorry. I didn't mean to just abandon him here.*

Don't be silly. The kids had a great time. Besides, he's got a bed, toys. I have extra clothes. Leave him until you find a family member.

I hugged her, and after assuring us both I'd be by first thing in the morning, I headed back outside. I knew Mahina's family would take great care of Liam, but I had started to think of him as my responsibility. I didn't like pawning that off on anyone else.

Besides, I'd rather be tucked up with Liam right now than facing down Sabyn for the second time today.

He was waiting for me as I approached the well-trimmed kelp forest—in the middle of a huge clearing surrounded by gardens of sea anemones and oyster beds, it was the closest thing to grass we had down here.

I stopped about fifteen feet from him, braced myself for an imminent attack. I'd let my guard down this morning. I wasn't about to do it again.

You look ready for battle, he called to me.

More like bed, I answered.

Oh yeah? A spark of interest lit up his face. *That could be fun.*

I rolled my eyes. *That's why you brought me out here? To make innuendos when I could be sleeping? Can we just do this thing?*

Sorry. The look he gave me was a little disgruntled, like he couldn't believe I didn't want to flirt with him. Which seemed ridiculous considering he'd tried to kill me less than twelve hours ago.

You have good form, he told me, covering the distance between us with a couple swishes of his tail. *But you leave yourself too open during battle.*

Intrigued despite myself, I asked, *What do you mean?*

You're very straightforward. You face every threat head-on. He came around behind me, placed his hands on my hips.

I stiffened. *What are you doing?*

Relax. You former humans are so uptight. He applied a little pressure, turning me so that I was at an angle. *You're left-handed, correct?*

Yes. I didn't like him touching me, wanted to knock him back a few steps. But again, I wasn't going to be the one to end this little practice session. I'd already pushed Hailana as far as I could this morning—if she thought I was blatantly disobeying her orders, there would be Hell. To. Pay.

So you should stand with your right arm forward. He turned me a little more, ran his hand over my waist and up my rib cage.

I elbowed him in the stomach.

He just laughed. *You have really soft skin for a mermaid.*

And you have a really soft brain for a merman superstar. Don't do that again.

Why not? What Kona doesn't know won't hurt him.

I yanked away. *You're disgusting.*

I'm joking, I'm joking. His fingers clamped down on my hips and he yanked me toward him again, so that we were pressed together—my back to his chest.

Sabyn, I said warningly.

Stop being such a prude and just listen, will you? He slid his hand down my right arm, then cupped my elbow and lifted away from our bodies. *This is your shielding arm. If you keep it to the front, it gives you an advantage, a little extra boost that can mean the difference between living and dying.*

Shields thrown up flat are more vulnerable, he continued, *easier for your enemy to find a weakness in. If you keep it off-kilter, the energy is harder to read. Not impossible, but harder.*

What do you mean? I turned back to look at him, realized our faces were only an inch or so apart, and jerked back.

He laughed.

When you're fighting, you can actually read the other person's energy? I asked him, intrigued. *You can see how they formed their shield?*

Of course. He looked surprised. *Has no one ever told you that before?*

No. I just thought you hit at it until you found the weakness.

Which is what you did to me earlier? he asked.

Pretty much, yeah.

Wow. I'm impressed.

Why? It was sheer luck that I got the spear through.

No. He shook his head. *It was sheer strength of will on your part.*

I warmed, unwittingly, at the compliment. *It wasn't as impressive as what you did,* I told him. *You sent that arrow straight into me.*

Because you were facing me head-on. If you'd been to the side, I never would have gotten that shot. He held his hand out about an inch in front of my chest and waved it up and down. *Always protect your midline.*

Right. I brought my right arm back up. *My midline.*

The next half hour passed in a blur as Sabyn patiently showed me technique after technique, none of which I'd ever seen before. As we worked, I couldn't help wondering why no one else had ever bothered doing this with me. Had Kona, Hailana, even Jared, relied on my power so completely that they failed to teach me even the most mundane blocking exercises? Considering how Sabyn had kicked my butt earlier, it seemed ridiculous.

Not to mention shortsighted.

Okay. Sabyn finally stepped back. *You want to try out your new form?*

I kind of did. Whereas training was usually something I suffered through, tonight I was excited. I wanted to see if Sabyn's tips would help.

Absolutely, I told him.

Good. He moved back to the other side of the park. *Hit me with your best shot.*

Seriously? I asked him.

Hey, Pat Benatar knew what she was talking about.

Hmm. Maybe I'd been a little too suspicious when he'd been touching me earlier . . . I didn't think most straight guys even knew who Pat Benatar was, let alone quoted her lyrics.

Shifting my body like he taught me, I threw up the strongest shield I could manage. Then I lifted my left arm and sent a blast of energy slamming right into him. It wasn't as sophisticated as the spear I'd done earlier, but it was a great calling card, an announcement of my intentions.

He let loose with his own energy blast, and this time I managed to stop it and volley it back at him. Sabyn just laughed and let loose with another pulse of energy that rocked me onto my heels.

We continued this way for a couple of minutes, and then Sabyn did it again. Snaked an arrow straight through my shield and nailed me in the right shoulder.

My shield dropped—I couldn't help it—and instead of waiting for me to raise it again, he pressed his advantage, coming after me full on now. Blast after blast hit me, knocked me back until he finally got one through my own energy bursts that landed me flat on my butt.

And still he didn't stop advancing. I wasn't scared this time, wasn't worried. Even though he'd hurt me when he broke through my shield, he'd been pulling his punches since then, keeping me from getting my groove back but not actually hurting me.

Now. He floated a little above me, a wicked gleam in his eyes as he stared down at me. *Ready to admit defeat?*

Not even close. I used every ounce of energy I had to construct a hasty shield, then braced myself for impact. This close it was going to hurt, even if he went easy on me.

Sabyn pulled back his arm and launched a blast straight at me, and it didn't look like he'd pulled his punches at all.

At the last second, I rolled away from him. And then several things happened at once.

I sprang back up.

Sabyn let loose a powerful blast of energy at the spot he expected me to be.

A new blast of energy met it—one that didn't come from me.

And then Sabyn was flying backward, tumbling through the water like a broken ragdoll.

I turned to see where this new threat had come from and saw an enraged Kona charging straight at me.

Chapter 13

Correction. Charging past me and straight at Sabyn.

Don't even think about touching her, he yelled at my sparring partner, his arm pulled back to deliver another energy blast. One look at his face and I knew he was out for blood.

I was up and racing toward him as soon as the thought registered. *Kona, don't!* I screamed at him along our private path.

It didn't even faze him. I grabbed on to his arm as he let loose and the blast went wide, striking a statue of Hailana that graced one of the park's walkways. The huge thing went tumbling backward, landing with a crash that sent fish scurrying and waves flashing out in all directions. I stared at it, shocked. If it had hit Sabyn while he was unshielded, the blow would have killed him.

Kona, it's okay, I told him, holding on to his arm as tightly as I could. This time I spoke on the general pathway so Sabyn could understand what I was saying too. The last thing I needed was for him to get up and fire back on Kona. World War III would probably erupt right here in the middle of the Pacific Ocean. *He's training me.*

Kona's silver eyes were wild when he turned to me. *Training you? It looked more like he was trying to kill you.*

Sabyn drifted slowly to his feet, an insolent look on his face. Even the blood coming from the corner of his mouth didn't soften the effect. *I would never hurt Tempest,* he said silkily—and a little untruthfully, but I didn't feel the need to point that out right then. *Hailana has asked me to get her ready for battle.*

Bullshit. Hailana would never be that stupid. Kona was practically foaming at the mouth and I stared at him, shocked. I'd never seen my boyfriend like this, not even the times he'd stood up to Tiamat. He looked like he wanted to tear Sabyn apart limb from limb.

It's true, Kona, I told him, trying to defuse the situation. *Hailana appointed Sabyn my trainer.*

Yeah, well, you're going to have to find a new one because that's not going to happen. He positioned himself in front of me so that I had to float up and peek over his shoulder even to get a glimpse of Sabyn's face. *Why don't you go crawl back under whatever rock you came from?* he snarled at Sabyn.

For a second I couldn't move—that's how shocked I was at this whole bizarre confrontation. Kona rarely lost his temper and even when he did, it was never in such a chest-pounding, testosterone-fueled way. He'd liked my last trainer a lot, had joked with Jared even as he'd nursed me through the various bruises and sprains our sparring had caused.

Have you completely lost your mind? I asked Kona, shoving against his shoulders.

Stay out of this, Tempest.

Stay out of it? It's my *training session you're interrupting.*

Not anymore. You're through. He turned back to Sabyn, and the look on his face was so powerful, so incensed, so *frightening*, that I probably would have fallen apart had it been directed at me. And I don't scare easily.

Sabyn merely snarled back.

If I ever catch you near her again, I'll kill you.

You can try, Sabyn told him.

Oh, I'll do more than try. Kona slammed him with another blast, one that went right through Sabyn's shield and hit him full-on. His nose and right ear started to bleed.

I shoved Kona out from in front of me. *Are you okay?* I demanded, rushing to check on Sabyn.

He's fine, Kona answered for him, throwing up a wall of energy between us so that I could do nothing but watch Sabyn weakly wipe the blood away. *Bottom-feeders like him always find a way to hold on to their tails.*

He's hurt!

He's fine, Kona snapped again.

Sabyn smiled at me even as he wiped blood from his face. *I am fine, Tempest. Let the little boy have his temper tantrum. It won't change anything.*

Kona stepped forward and hauled him up by the hair. *Stop it,* I cried, trying to use my own power to blast through the wall he'd created.

You don't know what's going on here, Tempest.

You're making a mistake, Kona.

Not about this guy, he told me. *He's been bad news from the day he was born—if Hailana doesn't remember that much, then she's obviously gone senile.*

Maybe I've turned over a new leaf, Sabyn said with a smile that didn't reach his eyes.

You wouldn't know how. Kona shoved him away with his free hand, hard enough that he ripped a chunk of hair out of Sabyn's head. *Get away from Tempest and stay away from her. If I ever catch you near her again—*

You'll what? Sabyn chose that moment to strike out, to blast Kona with every ounce of power he had inside of him.

I watched in horror as the energy struck Kona's shield and then powered straight through it, knocking him back about thirty feet.

Kona was up in fifteen seconds, but this time he was bleeding too. He and Sabyn started to circle each other.

Stop it! I yelled, but they both ignored me.

Desperate to put an end to this before one of them killed the other, I drew energy from the water around me, focused every ounce of power I had, and punched a hole right through the wall Kona had tried to lock me behind.

That's it! I shrieked, sounding like a crazy woman but not caring at all. *Don't we have enough problems without the two of you acting like imbeciles?*

He is a problem, Kona growled. *That's what I'm trying to tell you.*

You're the only one causing a problem right now, Sabyn told him, striking out with a blow that should have knocked Kona into next week.

Kona roared, the sound so low and mean that it sent shivers up my spine. I turned to look at him, to try to calm him down, and felt fear skitter through me at the sight. His eyes glowed, his fingers were curled into claws, and he fairly vibrated with the need to rip Sabyn in half, though they were still circling each other. It was the first time I'd ever seen him like this and it reminded me, forcibly, of the fact that he wasn't human.

He might be able to shift to human form, but Kona was selkie. As I watched him look for an opening to get at Sabyn, I finally realized just what that meant. In those moments, he was much more the animal defending what he considered his than he was the human.

Kona, please. Don't do this. I turned to Sabyn, who didn't look any more civilized. *Please, just walk away. I'm so sorry—*

Don't apologize to him! Kona reached for my arm, but I shook him off.

I was so furious with both of them that I could barely think, barely speak.

Don't tell me what to do! I yelled at him, the last of my patience eroded by his barbaric attitude. *Tiamat is on the verge of a major strike, we're in the middle of a humanitarian crisis, and you two want to pick a fight like a couple of children. What the hell is wrong with you?*

You don't understand—

And you're not trying to explain it to me, are you? I waited, but Kona didn't say anything and neither did Sabyn. *Fine, then, I'm done.* I turned and started swimming away.

Tempest! Kona called after me, but I was too angry to turn around. Too angry to do anything but flip them both off as I swam away.

Judging from the choked sounds echoing behind me, I wasn't sure which of the three of us was more shocked.

⚉

I was in my room half an hour later, sitting cross-legged on my bed while combing out my hair—and the snarls that two days of hell had caused—when Kona finally caught up to me.

He didn't bother knocking, just flung open the door and stormed in like he had the right to be there. Which only ratcheted up my anger another three hundred notches. Normally, I had no problem with him coming right in, but that courtesy definitely did not extend to him when he was acting like a crazy person.

Get out! I said.

Not until we settle this. He stalked toward me, eyes blazing with a crazy kaleidoscope of colors.

I didn't realize there was anything to settle. You acted like a maniac out there.

You don't know Sabyn like I do. You can't trust him.

First of all, isn't that up to me to decide?

He gritted his teeth. *Not in this case. I know more than you do—*

Excuse me? I swear I thought my head was going to explode.

I've lived down here my whole life. I know things about Sabyn that would completely freak you out.

Like what? If you're going to go around beating your chest, you need to at least tell me why.

I—He— For a second I thought he was going to lose it all over again. But he pulled back at the last minute. Gritted his teeth and curled his hands into fists.

Look, I'm already freaked out. I gestured to the window. *In case you haven't noticed, things are completely screwed up around here and the last thing I need is for you to lose your mind along with everyone else.*

I don't want you training with Sabyn.

You don't get to make that decision.

He snarled, *Don't push me on this, Tempest.*

No, Kona, don't you push me. I don't know who you think you are that you can barge in and nearly kill my trainer. I don't know who you think you are that you come up here and start issuing orders like I'm supposed to jump just because you said so.

You know, you could give me the benefit of the doubt, Tempest. I'm acting like this because I don't want that bastard anywhere near you. He's bad news.

Kona stalked straight up to me, until only an inch or two separated us, and glowered.

Don't try to intimidate me. I shoved him away, hard.

He moved back a little, but made it abundantly clear that it was his choice, not mine. *Jesus, Tempest, do you know me at all?*

I'm not sure. You've been growling and snarling like an animal since you showed up. And what are you doing here, anyway? I thought you were preparing for the Bringue.

It's canceled in light of what's happened. My family and I came to help. With Stormy Point, he clarified when I looked lost.

Oh, right. I felt awful for getting so wrapped up in my own angst that I'd forgotten the refugees.

He sighed, ran a hand over his face before asking, *Can you at least try to look at it from my perspective? I'm already worried about you—it was only yesterday that you were at death's door, remember—and the first thing I see is that jerk leaning over you, preparing to deliver a killing blow. Was I supposed to just stand there and watch it happen?*

You were supposed to trust me!

I do trust you. It's him I don't trust.

My mouth dropped open. *Did you really just say that? How old are you? Ninety?*

More like two hundred, but who's counting?

Ugh. You know what I meant. That sounds like something my father would say.

And he would be right.

I narrowed my eyes. *I really want to punch you right now.*

The last of his anger dissipated and he grinned. *Go ahead.* He leaned down to give me a free shot.

I didn't take it, not because he didn't deserve it but because in the space between one blink and the next, he went from a seething animal on the brink of losing control to the charming guy I'd grown used to. It was strange to witness the transformation, and though I wanted to relax, I couldn't forget the darkness I'd seen in him.

Where did all that power come from, anyway? I demanded. *I've never seen you like that.*

What do you mean? You've seen me wield energy before.

Yeah, but not to that extent. Sabyn kicked my ass earlier and you took him on like it was nothing.

You lost half your blood volume yesterday—that's the only reason Sabyn could take you.

That's not true. I hit him with everything I had earlier and he rolled right over me. He's got a lot of power.

Not as much as you do. Kona seemed convinced of it.

In that case, you should have had more faith in me. Do I really look stupid to you?

Of course not. The fact that I was still furious must have finally gotten through to him, because he reached for me placatingly. *Tempest—*

Don't Tempest me. Did it ever occur to you to ask me what was going on before losing your mind out there? Of course I don't trust Sabyn. I'm working with him because Hailana ordered me to, not because I want to.

Still, it's dangerous. He shook his head. *You don't know—*

You can't have it both ways. Either he's a poser without any power or he's dangerous.

The two aren't mutually exclusive, you know. He's sneaky and he doesn't care about anyone but himself. He'll do whatever it takes to get ahead.

But we're on the same side.

Are you? Really?

He was helping *me, Kona, showing me how to focus. How to shield better than I've ever been able to before.*

And what's in it for him?

Oh, I don't know. Maybe not being ripped into pieces by Tiamat? For a start?

You're being naive, Tempest.

And you're being insane. Find one more way to call me stupid and you can look for somewhere else to spend the night.

Seriously? You'd pick him over me?

Are you kidding? I rolled my eyes. *It's not a competition. You're my boyfriend—he's just some guy who's supposed to teach me how to use my powers.*

Then why are we fighting about him? If he's just *a guy?*

We're fighting because you seem to think you have the right to tell me what to do. We're dating, but you don't own me.

Dating? A minute ago I was your boyfriend. Did I just get downgraded?

Are we seriously having this conversation? I yelled. *I can't figure out if you're being deliberately obtuse or if you're just trying to make me insane!*

Jaw clenched, eyes darker than I had ever seen them, Kona said, *I'm trying to keep you safe. I don't understand what's wrong with that.*

Nothing, except that it's not your job.

I think it is.

Well, then, I'm not sure what to tell you. Except that we have a problem.

For long seconds he didn't say anything, just stared me down. His hands were curled into fists and his throat was working overtime, like it took every ounce of self-control he had to swallow back the words burning inside of him.

I waited for him to speak, to say something else, but he didn't. He just looked at me, completely implacable. Completely immovable. It scared me, because I felt exactly the same way.

Finally, he turned away. Walked over to stare out the window.

I watched him and wondered what he was looking at, considering it was after two in the morning and pitch black outside except for the bright balls of energy lighting up the temporary housing. Maybe he was looking at that, picturing the training circles that used to be there. Picturing his clan or mine dispossessed.

He didn't move for the longest time. Didn't so much as glance at me to indicate that he knew I was still in the room. It frightened me a little, this ability he seemed to have to completely tune me out. I'd never seen it before, but then, we'd never been in quite this situation.

Now that the actual yelling was over, it seemed worse somehow. I didn't know what to do, how to act, what to say to make him understand. I wondered if he felt the same way.

The thought galvanized me, had me moving toward him

before I'd even made the decision to do so. I put a hand on his shoulder, though I didn't have a clue what I was supposed to do next. On land, Mark had always made the first move.

Kona's hand came up to cover mine.

Do you love me, Tempest? he asked evenly, never turning away from the window. The only indication I had that the question mattered to him at all was the way his shoulders tensed beneath my hand and his fingers clutched at mine. His grip was tight enough that I would have winced had the pressure not felt so good, so reassuring.

Of course I love you. You know that.

I love you too.

I know. It's why I— I broke off, not willing to finish the sentence truthfully. Not willing to admit, even to myself, that he was the reason I'd given up everything. Not the only reason, but definitely the most important. Standing there, waiting for him to turn to me, I wondered for the first time if it was enough.

Kona didn't seem to notice my lapse. He was as locked in his head as I was in mine. *Do you trust me?*

Yes. Kona would never deliberately hurt me. I knew that.

He turned from the window then, caught my face in his hands. Looked deep into my eyes. *Do you really?*

Yes.

Then will you trust me on this? *Sabyn is bad for you, Tempest.*

How do you know?

Again with the jaw clenching. But at least this time, he unlocked it enough to speak. *He hurts girls just because he can. Because he likes it. He acts all smooth and charming, but there have been a lot of girls who end up injured around him. He always has an excuse, an explanation, but that only works so many times before it doesn't.*

He took a deep breath, blew it out slowly. *He's dangerous. I swear to you, he's dangerous, and if you're not careful, he* will *turn on you. He* will *hurt you. Please, please, please, watch yourself with him. Never lower your guard.*

I haven't, I said, still reeling from what he'd told me. *I won't.*

Don't let him get you on the ground again.

We were training.

It doesn't matter. He could have killed you.

It was my turn to move away from him. *Thanks for the vote of confidence.*

Not because he's better than you, but because he'll come at you when you least expect it. He'll hit you when you've lowered your guard and are at your most vulnerable.

Sabyn's mer. How do you know so much about him anyway?

Because he used to be my best friend.

Wow. I felt my eyes widen in shock. *I didn't see that coming.*

His laugh was ironic. *Yeah, no one ever does.*

What happened?

I trusted him.

And?

He killed my youngest sister.

Chapter 14

I awoke early the next morning with a headache and a stomach so unsettled that I was sure I was going to throw up. Of course, it was no more than I deserved after tossing and turning all night while Kona's words dogged my dreams.

I wanted to know specifically what had happened. But after telling me about his sister's death, Kona had shut down completely. Refused to say anything more. And I hadn't felt comfortable pushing. Not after our fight. And not about this.

Was it true? I wondered. Was Sabyn a murderer?

Oh, I had no doubt that in Kona's mind he was, no doubt that he had somehow been involved in Annalise's death. But down here, there were a lot of ways to die—I'd seen a bunch of them firsthand. Had Sabyn actually killed her or had he simply been a party to her death?

Then again, Kona had said that a number of girls had been hurt around Sabyn. I agreed that didn't sound like a coincidence.

Which only made my forced association with him worse. I

understood Kona's anger now. Understood his irrationality when it came to me training with Sabyn. I just didn't know if I could do anything about it.

I'd already pissed off Hailana enough with my defiance. If I refused to work with Sabyn, what would she do? And worse, what would I lose by not letting Sabyn train me? She had to have put us together for a reason. Plus, he'd already taught me more than any other trainer had.

It could have been because Sabyn was really what I needed to get ready for Tiamat, but it could just as easily be because Hailana wanted to hurt Kona, wanted to break us up. Knowing the merQueen's diabolical nature, a big part of me was rooting for the latter scenario.

Beside me, Kona stirred, stretched. He didn't awaken, though, and I was glad. He looked exhausted, like the weight of the entire Pacific was on his shoulders. I hated that, hated more the fact that I was adding to his stress.

Reaching out, I brushed a hand gently over his cheek, relishing the feel of the prickly stubble on his jaw. He was so beautiful, with his too-long hair and too-pretty face, that I could lie here looking at him forever.

But that wasn't going to work. I had things to do, responsibilities to take care of. My mind jumped to Liam and I wondered how he'd done on his first night without his parents. Poor baby. I hoped he'd been all right.

There was a soft knock on my door and I sprang out of bed, wanting to keep Kona from waking up. I figured it was Mahina, with news about Liam, and threw the door open without bothering to put on a robe. And then nearly freaked out when I saw

Sabyn standing there, looking like his night had been as restful as mine had been restless.

I guess you're not quite ready to train? he asked, his eyes traveling over the short, waterproof nightie I was wearing. I could be wrong, but it looked like he lingered extralong on my legs. The jerk. *Not that I would object if you wanted to wear that.*

Seriously? Could you be more disgusting?

His smile faded. *I thought we'd gotten past all that last night. But then, I guess Kona couldn't just let things rest?*

You didn't actually think he would, did you?

No. Sabyn shook his head, and for the first time since I met him, he looked sad. Weary. *Did he at least tell you it was an accident?*

I shook my head to let him know I wasn't going to talk about this. Not with him, no matter how much I wanted to know. *I think you need to leave.*

Okay. Why don't you come with me?

Not right now. He smiled sadly and I felt compelled to add, *I'm tired—it was a long night.*

Oh yeah? He looked over my head, to where Kona slept in my bed. *Tired yourself out, did you?*

The smirk was back, and with its advent, all my sympathy went right out the window. *Get lost,* I told him, trying to shut the door in his face. At the last second he slapped a palm on the door, and though I pushed as hard as I could, the door didn't budge.

What do you want? I asked with a sigh.

I know you want to trust your boyfriend, but there are two sides to every story.

Yeah, well, the only side I'm interested in is his, I lied.

I figured. His eyes gleamed wickedly. *You know selkies can't be trusted, don't you?*

Funny, he said the same thing about you.

I bet he did. But then, last night proved he's not exactly rational on the subject, is he?

I don't want to do this, Sabyn.

Why would you? Why rock your pretty little boat if you don't have to, right? He let go of the door, stepped back. *I'll be in the park in an hour, if you can tear yourself away from lover boy. There is a war to fight, after all.*

I know that, I snapped.

Of course you do. He winked. *I just thought it'd be a good idea to remind you.*

Well, thanks for that.

You're welcome. He glanced behind my shoulder again, and this time, when he looked at me, there was a wicked glint in his eye. *See you later, sweet Tempest.* Then, before I could figure out what he was going to do, he leaned down and brushed his lips over my cheek.

I was so startled that it took me a second to shove him away. And when I finally did, my hand caught only air because he was already gone. But Kona . . . Kona was there, of course, right at my elbow, a black scowl darkening his face.

The second Kona turned his back, I swam away from Coral Straits like my tail was on fire. He'd been in the mercity three days, and I swear this was the first time since our fight—and Sabyn showing up at my door—that he'd let me out of his sight. He'd even tagged along to my training sessions—some with Sabyn and some on my own—as well as to my visits with Liam. On Liam's second day in the refugee tents, I found his aunt, and he was settling in with her as well as could be expected. Still, I went by twice a day to check on him and make sure they had whatever they needed—and Kona insisted on coming with me.

He was seriously freaked out by just the thought of Sabyn being near me, convinced that the second he turned his back Sabyn would do something terrible. I knew he was only being so protective because he cared about me, but it was getting to the point where his motives didn't matter. He was driving me completely and totally around-the-bend insane.

As I swam into open water for the first time since the refugees flooded Coral Straits, I knew exactly where I wanted to go. It was far enough away that my absence would probably make Kona nuts, but to be honest, I couldn't bring myself to care. Not now, when he saw danger for me lurking around every corner.

Hopping on the current, I let it speed me to my mother's cave. I'd been wanting to go back ever since I'd left, but I hadn't been able to get there on my own. And, though I didn't know why, it felt wrong to bring anyone else with me. I sensed that it had been my mother's private place, and now it was mine.

I got through the cave more quickly this time, since I knew where I was going, and within a few minutes of entering the front room, I was in the cavern I thought of as belonging to Cecily. It looked exactly as I remembered, which surprised me. I don't know why, except that the three days that had passed felt more like three hundred.

After creating enough light to see by, I spent a few minutes swimming around the chamber, looking not at the pearls and sea glass, but at the beautiful carvings on the wall. I recognized my mother's subtle touch in the artwork, knew it well from the paintings she used to do when I was young. I had spent a great deal of my artistic life trying to imitate that style, but had never gotten it quite right. Seeing it here now touched me like few things ever had.

Floating all the way to the ceiling, I traced my fingers along one of the scenes that was carved up there. It was a picture of my mother with Hailana. I'd never seen the merQueen look better, and couldn't help wondering how long ago this picture had been done and if she had ever really looked that good or if my mother had taken creative license.

Either way, she and my mom looked really happy—exactly like two best friends should. Which, to be honest, disturbed me. I thought of the people I'd been close friends with in my life— Mark, Brianna, Mickey, Logan, Bach, Skeeter, Tony, and now Kona and Mahina. I was friends with them because they were nice and cool and because we had a lot in common. We thought about the world in the same way.

I glanced back at my mom and Hailana. Eight months ago, when I thought the merQueen was just a frail, benevolent old woman, this picture might have reassured me. But now that I knew the truth—that she was, in her own way, nearly as twisted as Tiamat—it scared me that my mother had been such good friends with her.

Backing away from the pictures, I dived deep and didn't stop until I'd gotten to the shelves of pearls. I reached for an iridescent pink one that was only about the size of a pea, then stopped at the last minute. I wanted to know what memory was there— wanted to know everything I could about my mother—but I had to admit I was a little scared, both emotionally and physically.

Last time had hurt more than anything I could ever remember, and I wasn't keen on reliving that pain. At the same time, though, I knew I would be forever locked in this emotional quagmire concerning my mother if I didn't try to understand her.

Closing my eyes, I gathered my courage and then, moving forward, I grabbed the pearl.

Immediately, the pain overtook me, but it was different this time. Colder. As if Cecily had taken all of her emotions, all of her misgivings, and walled them behind a sheet of thick, unwavering ice.

I shivered. It felt like I was pressed, full body, up against that ice. No big deal at first, just a little nippy, but after a few minutes it began to ache and then burn until the frigid touch of the ice worked itself inside of me. Until that innocuous skin-to-cold contact became almost unbearable.

I shrieked—I couldn't help myself—tried, just like last time, to drop the pearl. It didn't work, but then I hadn't really expected it to. The ache, the agony, grew worse and just when I was at the breaking point, I was thrust into another memory.

Though my mother looked the same, I got the impression that she was older here than in the last one, which meant this had happened sometime after she'd met my father. After she'd left our family and returned to the ocean.

Cecily was standing in front of a beautiful coral reef, her long hair flowing behind her, and though this image too was just a little out of focus, her green tattoos sparkled with an iridescence so brilliant that I had never seen its match. In front of her were three merpeople—two men and one maid. They looked tired, beaten, in no way capable of harming anyone.

In my mother's head, I saw their crimes—speaking up against Hailana, disagreeing with how she ran things, complaining about her decisions. I wish I could say it surprised me that they were being punished for this, but it didn't. Even today, Hailana was very careful about who she let disagree with her—and where she permitted it. Mostly, it was just her Council, in closed chambers.

My mother seemed to draw herself up, to gather her power, and I waited for her to carry out Hailana's orders. To banish these people who had really done nothing wrong. I prayed that was it, that she wouldn't have to imprison them—

A blinding flash of light encompassed the scene for one long second, two. When it cleared, and I'd recovered from what felt like a first-degree burn to my retinas, I saw the three people on the ground, Cecily standing over them with a face so blank it could have been carved from stone.

And that's when it hit me. Cecily, my mother, had just murdered those people in cold blood.

My stomach revolted, and I dropped the pearl seconds before I was blindingly, joltingly ill.

PART THREE

Amplification

*"Every wave, regardless of how high and forceful it crests,
must eventually collapse within itself."*

—STEFAN ZWEIG

Chapter 15

Where have you been? Kona wrapped an arm around me while I was swimming by, whirling me back to face him.

I stared at him blankly. I was so out of it, so caught up in the nightmare I had witnessed in Cecily's cave, that I hadn't even seen him.

Where have you been? he repeated. *I was worried.* His face was inches from mine, and he looked more disturbed than I had ever seen him.

It was that distress that finally got through to me, finally yanked me from my own reverie and back into the present. I reached out a soothing hand, laid it on his cheek. *I've been out. Exploring. I needed to take a break. Why?*

I thought you might be with Sabyn.

I shook my head incredulously. *After everything I've done to placate you about Sabyn, you really thought I would spend extra time with him. Seriously?*

I don't know. You disappear for hours without a word, even knowing how worried I am. I looked everywhere for you—and him—and neither of you were around. What else could I assume but that you were together?

Though it so wasn't the time or place, I wondered fleetingly where Sabyn had gone—since he obviously hadn't been with me—but then that thought drowned in the tidal wave of my indignation at being interrogated when I really needed my boyfriend to just be there for me.

What else could you assume? Oh, I don't know, Kona, maybe that you could trust me like you expect me to trust you? Or maybe you could assume that I know how worried you are about me even being near him and that I would never, ever, do anything to deliberately hurt you like that?

I sighed, tried to figure out a way to make him understand that I was being careful. I knew he was acting like this because he was worried, because just the thought of Sabyn being near me stressed him to the breaking point, but something had to give. We couldn't go on like this.

Maybe you could have assumed that after all your warnings, and knowing how freaked out you are by Sabyn even being here, that I would never go behind your back with him? Those would have all been good assumptions.

I turned away from him, started to move in the other direction.

Don't swim away from me, Tempest, he said furiously, reaching for me again. I wasn't taking it this time, though, and I lashed out, sent a mild surge of power straight at him that wouldn't hurt but did slam him back a good four feet. It worked only because he wasn't expecting it, but I didn't care. Never in my life had I put up with a guy manhandling me, and I sure as hell wasn't going to start now.

Don't touch me, Kona.

What is with you? he demanded.

I think that's my question, isn't it? You're the one being completely irrational.

We squared off across a small oyster bed, both of us confused. Both of us angrier than the situation warranted. I knew it, just as I knew I should tamp down on my temper and actually talk to him. Yet I didn't want to do that right now, not over something so trivial and yet so important. He was the one who'd grabbed me, who'd spewed ridiculous accusations all over me. And he was the one who was acting like a total ass.

Look, I told him. *I'm not doing this with you. I don't know what's going on, I don't even know what happened between Sabyn and Annalise, because you won't tell me. Which is fine—your family, your privilege, whatever. But that means I don't have to tell you everything going on in my life either. And you don't get to jump down my throat every time I turn around just because I don't report to you every second of the day.*

I was just worried.

Were you really? I looked him up and down contemptuously. *Are you sure about that? Because I'm about to shatter into a thousand pieces here and it doesn't look like you give a damn. It doesn't look like you care about anything but your hatred for Sabyn.*

That got to him. I could see it in the way Kona's shoulders slumped and in the shamed look he couldn't hide. He ran a hand over his face, across the back of his neck, and when he lifted his head again there was concern, real concern, in his eyes. *What happened, Tempest?*

You don't actually expect me to answer that, do you?

Please. I'm sorry. He reached a beseeching hand out to me.

I knocked it away before he could touch me. *You're saying*

that a lot lately, but it doesn't seem to matter, does it? Five minutes later
you're jumping to the same wrong conclusions. I'm sick of it.

Sabyn chose that moment to swim by. *Trouble in paradise, Tem-*
pest? He ran a hand down my arm and across my lower back, and
I jumped at the shock of electricity that pulsed through me at his
touch. Like always, it paralyzed me for a second, made every
brain cell I had freeze up. Before I could recover, he leaned down
and whispered, *Whenever you get sick of whiny ass over here and want*
to try for a real man, remember I'm first in line.

I shrugged him off, started to *tell* him off, since I was completely disgusted with the way he was using me to get to Kona.
But it was too late. Before I could even say a word, Kona launched
himself at Sabyn with a roar. Then the two of them were rolling
across the ocean floor, pounding on each other for all they were
worth.

A crowd was gathering, and rather than deal with everything
that entailed, I turned and just swam away. My training session
could obviously wait, and with the way I was feeling, if I didn't
see Kona for a month, it would probably be too soon.

The jerk.

I had planned on stopping by the refugee tents to visit Liam
and Mahina—she had been working there every day—but found
myself coasting up to the castle instead. It turned out the person
I most wanted to see right now was Hailana. She knew more
about this thing between Kona and Sabyn than she had told
me, and I wanted answers.

She was in her chambers with her secretary, drafting some
kind of letter to the other clans. Asking for solidarity against Tiamat was my guess, but then, I'd been wrong before. About a lot of
things.

She looked up as I entered the room. *Tempest, come in.*

I can check back later, if I'm interrupting something.

No, not at all. She nodded to her secretary, who hustled out of the room with the large chalkboard she was using to take dictation. Later, the notes would be transcribed onto a special seaweed paper that held up for years against the harsh salt water of the ocean.

I've been waiting for you. She waved her hand, beckoned me closer.

I approached warily, ready to bolt at the first sign that she was going to try that whole squeezing my heart thing again. But she seemed calm, almost happy. Although her fingers trembled a little as she reached for her bottle of passion fruit iced tea, and again I was reminded of just how old she was. And just what was expected of me when she finally died.

Sabyn tells me you've been doing very well in training. She beamed at me. *Which is saying something, as he's not prone to giving compliments.*

Yeah, well, I think he might be exaggerating. I took a seat in the chair across from her desk—it was a little lower than Hailana's, to ensure that her visitors were never taller than she was.

Oh, I don't know. I watched you out there myself yesterday. You looked very good. She paused. *Although, I admit, I was hoping for a little more.*

More? I asked, confused. *You mean, more energy?*

Perhaps. Although, to be honest, I was thinking along the lines of another talent. She eyed me closely. *I know you can call storms, bring down lightning. And that you wield energy in quite a powerful manner.*

Isn't that enough?

Of course, except . . . She sighed. *Your mother could do so much more.*

As I sat there, waiting for her to get to the point, I got the distinct feeling she was playing me, in the exact same way Sabyn liked to play Kona. But even knowing that, I fell for it, leaning forward in my chair like an eager puppy dog. She was just that good.

Thoughts of what I had seen in the cave, of what my mother had done, filled my head. My stomach pitched and rolled and for a second I thought I was going to be sick again, despite my empty stomach. I told myself to ignore it, to let the image go. I had to if I hoped to hold my own against Hailana.

You know, she continued, *usually the more time passes after a mermaid's seventeenth birthday, the more powers she gets. That you had so much power so quickly made me think that you were going to have a lot of surprises in store for us.*

She quirked one perfectly shaped eyebrow and I couldn't help it. I thought of the electricity thing I'd done with Tiamat's goons.

Of Kona explaining how rare that kind of magic was.

Of the voice deep inside myself that had warned me not to tell Hailana.

Did Hailana somehow know about it? Had I slipped up in practice, used it without realizing? I racked my brain, tried to think of every move I'd made, but nothing came to mind. I didn't remember wielding electricity against Sabyn or anyone else he'd brought in to train with us. Except . . .

Except that nearly every time Sabyn touched me, we both lit up like the Electric Light Parade my mother used to drag us to see at Disneyland every summer. I'd thought it was a training thing, something that wasn't all that unusual. But what if it was the giveaway? Was that bizarre reaction between us what had tipped off Sabyn and, in turn, Hailana?

I fought the urge to scream in frustration. I hated this. Hated not knowing all the things I should, all the bits and pieces that went into life down here. On land, it wasn't easy—especially with all the mermaid stuff that had grown almost impossible to hide—but at least up there I understood what was expected of me. What I needed to do to keep myself safe and sane. Down below, it was a whole different story, and I kept feeling like I was a couple of scenes behind the pack.

I studied Hailana, tried to gauge what she was getting at. If she were fishing and I didn't react to it, maybe she would let the subject drop. I hoped so, because everything inside me said that if she knew of my most recent talent, how easily I had killed those men, that I would find myself following even more closely in my mother's footsteps.

I didn't want to do that, *couldn't* do that. For seven years I'd sworn I wouldn't be like my mother, wouldn't make the same choices she had. And yet, here I was, in her city, with her queen, living her life—or as close to it as Hailana could get me. Again I thought of those people I'd seen my mother kill remorselessly, again I shoved the memory away.

Tried to focus instead on the problem at hand.

I didn't know what to do, didn't have a clue what to say to her. I needed Kona, who knew so much more about this life than I did. I had questions for him, needed answers, but he was so wrapped up in protecting me from the perceived threat of Sabyn that he'd forgotten the ways in which I really needed him.

Tempest? Are you listening to me? Hailana's voice, much sharper than it had been before, dragged me back to the present. From the impatient look on her face she'd been talking for quite some time, while I'd been drifting in la-la-land, trying to make some sense of the world that was slowly crumbling around me.

Sorry, Hailana. It's been a rough couple of days. Sabyn's a tough trainer.

That's why he's good for you. Jared wasn't pushing you, and that isn't going to do us any good. When Tiamat comes back for you, she's going to come with everything she's got.

I know. It was pretty hard to forget, what with everyone reminding me of that fact every time I turned around.

There was a long silence as the merQueen waited for me to say what I had come to say. But it was harder than I thought to just blurt it out now that I was in front of her. Looking down, I traced patterns on Hailana's desk as I tried to get my thoughts in order.

Are you okay, Tempest? she finally asked.

Yeah, of course. I was just . . . I looked up into her narrowed gaze and knew that it was now or never. If I didn't ask her my questions soon, I never would. *Did you choose Sabyn on purpose? Because you knew it would upset Kona?*

Mmmmm, now we get to the heart of the matter. Is the selkie prince threatened by such a strong, handsome merman spending so much time with you?

The selkie prince, I repeated, *is upset because he doesn't like Sabyn. But I think you know that.* I watched her carefully, trying to catch any flicker in her expression. She didn't so much as blink.

Is he still beating that drum? she asked. *It was an accident—Annalise fell and injured herself severely—with Tiamat's help. Sabyn tried to save her, but he couldn't. Everyone knows that but Kona.*

I was reeling a little bit at the knowledge of how Kona's sister had died, but I wouldn't give Hailana the satisfaction of seeing he'd never shared the details with me.

So you knew about Sabyn's history with Kona, how Kona felt about him, and you decided to have me train with him anyway? I asked, just to clarify things. I already knew it was true, even before she answered. Hailana did what she wanted, when she wanted to do it, and to hell with anyone else's feelings.

I don't make decisions for my clan based on keeping the selkie prince happy, she told me blandly. *I'm truly sorry if my choices have caused any stress between you.*

Yeah, and if I believed that . . . I didn't need to see the sudden cagey look in her eye to know that she was playing me. Of course, a lot of what she'd done lately seemed to have been with the express intention of causing trouble between Kona and me. The fact that we were letting her, that we were falling right into line with her schemes, was no one's fault but Kona's and mine. I would even bet that Sabyn was making all those crazy comments to me, not just to get under Kona's skin, but on direct order from her. The straightforward approach wasn't really Hailana's style.

Is that all you wanted? she asked. *To find out about Kona and Sabyn?*

That was my cue to leave, to get up from the desk and walk out before this meeting descended into the free-for-all our conferences so often became. I started to say yes, started to get up and swim to the door, but in the end, I couldn't do it. There was another question burning inside of me, one that was so important I trembled with the need to have an answer.

Tempest? she prompted. *Is there something else?*

What was my mother's real job for you?

I'm sorry?

You say she was a priestess, say that she was your right hand. You also tell me that you want me to follow in her wake, but you've never actually told me what she did for you.

That's easy. Hailana's eyes were frigid, ferocious, as they looked me over. *She did whatever I asked of her. And she kept her mouth shut about doing it. In time, you'll learn to do the same thing.*

That was exactly what I was afraid of.

Chapter 16

I was numb when I left Hailana's office, the terror inside of me so great that my mind just shut down. I couldn't help it, didn't know if I even wanted to. Any more and I was afraid I would start screaming and never, ever stop.

I didn't know where to go, so I ended up wandering down the small, quaint streets at the back of the city. They were lined with antique stores filled with goods from ships lost to the ocean hundreds of years before, galleries with beautiful underwater sculptures and other waterproof art, even saltwater tea and taffy shops.

I walked into my favorite little drink place, ordered a red algae and dulse iced tea. As I waited for them to brew it, I walked over to the window, looked out into the courtyard. And saw Kona sitting there, nursing a Kombu beer and looking quite a bit worse for wear. I guess I shouldn't have been surprised to find him here—he was the one who first showed me this place, after all.

The barista called my name, and I signed the credit slip that would be charged to Hailana—her version of a salary for me—then rounded up my tea and an ice pack or three before making my way out to where Kona was sitting. He glanced up when I slid into the seat next to him, did a double take. And then smiled the crazy, lopsided grin of his that had been making my heart flutter since the first time I saw it.

Tonight it was a little more lopsided than usual, thanks to Sabyn's fists.

Looking good, I told him, pressing one of the ice packs against his bruised jaw.

Yeah, well, you should see the other guy.

I laughed, because I knew that was what he wanted. *I can imagine.*

His hand covered mine, where I was still holding the ice against his face. Neither of us said anything for a while, probably because we didn't know where to start. Finally, figuring I might as well jump in, I said, *I was at—*

He spoke at the exact same time. *I'm sorry.*

We both paused, smiled some more. Ducked our heads. Who knew making up from a fight could be so awkward? Usually Kona just swooped me into his arms for the mother of all make-out sessions. Then again, I guess this fight was too serious to just be swept away in the current . . .

I was a jerk. I'm sorry, he told me. *I knew you were upset, but I was too furious to care. It won't happen again.*

I shouldn't have gotten so angry, I answered. *I know Sabyn is a hot button for you, and if I'd just said we weren't together you would have calmed down and we could have talked.*

He closed his eyes, breathed in a long draw of water, then sighed it back out. *I'm glad you weren't with him.*

And I'm glad you kicked his ass. He totally deserved it.

He really did. Kona pulled my hand from his cheek, brought it to his lips instead, and kissed the center of my palm in the way he knew drove me insane. *I'm sorry I grabbed on to you like that. You should have kicked my ass.*

I almost did.

He continued to press kisses up my palm to my wrist. He paused there, gave a long, lingering lick that had me shivering and clutching at his shoulders.

I love you, I murmured, pressing my own lips to the spot behind his ear, the one I knew made him crazy.

His arms came around me, lifted me onto his lap. *I love you too.*

I wrapped myself around him, grateful that I was in human form. He pulled me tight against him and I saw stars. Judging from his suddenly choppy breathing, I think Kona did as well. And then he kissed me, really kissed me, and it was everything I loved rolled into one endless moment.

A dazzling sunrise sweeping across the beach at dawn.

Cherry Garcia ice cream dribbling down my fingers on a hot summer day.

Catching that amazing, perfect wave and riding it all the way in.

I wanted to stay here forever, pressed against Kona so tightly that it was hard to tell where I left off and he began. Everything was good here, better than good. I didn't have to think about Hailana or my mother, didn't have to worry about Tiamat or my family back home.

I could bury my hands in Kona's hair, wrap my arms and legs around his body, and just sink into him and all the emotions that rocketed through me when we touched.

He pulled away too soon. *So, you want to tell me what was wrong this afternoon? I know I was a dick earlier, but I'd like to listen now.*

Did I want to tell him? Originally, I'd held the cave close to me, hadn't wanted to share this new look at my mother with anyone. But after this morning, after what I'd seen, everything felt tainted. Wrong.

It would probably be easier if I showed you. I glanced at his poor, beat-up face. *But it's about two hours from here. Do you think you're up for it?*

I'm fine. Sabyn punches like a little girl.

I snorted. *No, he doesn't.* I had the bruises to prove it.

Still. I'm fine.

Okay. Drink your beer and we'll go. I picked up my tea, drained it in three long gulps. Kona beat me anyway.

The swim out to my mom's cave took closer to three hours than two because we spent a lot of time fooling around. Racing and then spinning, making sand angels on the bottom of the ocean floor. Kissing. It was the most fun I'd had in weeks, and it reminded me of all the reasons I'd fallen for Kona to begin with.

By the time we got to the cave I was feeling, if not better, then at least more resigned about what I'd found there. Or at least that's what I told myself when we swam through the stalactite maze in the front room.

When we got to the narrow passageways—the ones I'd barely fit through—I stopped with a gasp. *I forgot,* I told Kona. *There's no way you're going to be able to fit through here.* His shoulders were twice the width of mine.

How narrow is it? he asked.

I held my arms up in a close approximation of the passageway.

You're right. What's down there, anyway?

I still didn't know how to explain. *My mom* . . . Even though I wasn't actually speaking, my voice broke. I couldn't force any other words out.

Kona nodded, like he understood, though I could see the baffled look in his eyes. He took the necklace that contained his seal skin from around his neck, found a little bit of open space in the cave, and in a dazzling display of silver light, he shifted.

I'd seen him as a seal before—of course I had—but he didn't change often. I think because he believed it underscored the differences between us. Which I guess was true, but it didn't matter to me. It's not like Mark and I were any more compatible, mermaid and human. Besides, Kona was beautiful to me, and that was when he wasn't in the middle of shifting. When he was, he dazzled me.

When I became mermaid, nothing particularly special happened, except I grew a tail. When he shifted, the whole room lit up with spectacular silver bursts of light that I wanted nothing more than to reach out and touch.

And then it was done, and Kona, in his long, black seal form, was swimming in circles around me. I laughed, reached out a hand to touch him. He was smooth and sleek, cool and slippery to the touch.

Come on, I told him. I knew he understood me, but if he answered back, I couldn't tell. In this form we couldn't communicate.

I dived deep, followed the passages, one after another, until we got to the room I was aiming for. Kona swam behind me, and every once in a while I would feel him brush against my feet, tickling me.

It was good. It kept me sane. Without him, I'm not sure I'd have had the courage to come back here. Not after last time.

Then we were there, in the room with the memories, and Kona was back in human form. And naked. Even though it embarrassed me a little, I couldn't help stealing a few glances as he shimmied back into his board shorts and looked around the room. The second he saw what was there, he pulled me into his arms and held me as tightly as he could.

Tears of the moon, he murmured softly. *I'm sorry, Tempest.*

What did you say? I asked, confused.

The pearls. He nodded at the wall. *They're called tears of the moon down here, because they can be charmed to hold regrets.*

Is that what I'm seeing when I hold them? My mother's regrets?

In one form or another, yes. He swam forward, reached out to brush a finger against a large lavender pearl.

Don't do that! I told him.

He stopped abruptly, yanked his hand back. *I'm sorry. I know they're yours. I've just never seen them before in my entire life. I've heard about the magic that goes into making them. I've just never known anyone who actually went through the process before.*

He glanced at me. *She made these for you.*

I don't know about that.

I do. It's hard to create these, takes a long time. There's no other reason Cecily would have gone through the hassle if she hadn't wanted you to see, to know. Almost involuntarily, his hand crept out to brush against one again.

Don't, I said, louder and more strenuously this time. When he looked stricken, I added, *It hurts. When you touch them. It's excruciating to hold one in the palm of your hand.*

Really? he asked. *How many have you looked at so far?*

Only three. They were . . . hard to get through.

I bet. Do you want to do another one? I could leave, if you like.

No, I told him. *Stay. That's why I brought you here. I wanted you to understand where I went, what I was doing. Why I feel the need to come even though it's probably not the smartest move.*

He looked shame-faced. *I'm sorry. I really am. You were right—I should have known.*

It's fine. I wrapped my arms more tightly around him and squeezed. *Thanks for coming with me.*

Don't be silly. He glanced back at the wall. *Have you tried any of the sea-glass pieces yet?*

I shook my head. *No. I guess I just assumed they were the same thing. Aren't they?*

I don't think so. I mean, I've never heard of them before, but . . . I have a hard time imagining Cecily just randomly changed her mind about what she wanted to use. There must be a reason she switched to sea glass.

Should I— I reached for a piece of smooth, red glass, then stopped. I didn't know if I was strong enough to go through another memory like what I had seen earlier. At least not right now.

Kona seemed to understand without my saying a word. *Whatever you want to do, Tempest.*

I nodded. Then figured it would probably be easier to do this with Kona than without him—at least this time. If I were alone and saw my mother kill someone else, I'm not sure what I would do.

Decision made, I closed my fingers around the glass and braced myself for the pain.

It never came. Instead, a soothing warmth spread out from where the glass lay in my palm—down my fingers to my arm and then through my whole body, inch by inch. It was an extraordinary feeling, especially after the agony that had come with the pearls.

Are you okay? Kona asked anxiously, when I didn't say or do anything. *Does it hurt?*

No, I told him, right before another memory unfolded in front of me.

This one was different though. It was still hazy, still out of focus, but while it was my mother's recollection, for the first time it didn't center around her. Instead, it centered around . . . me.

I was wearing a purple swimming tank and a pair of black boy-short swim bottoms, and I was in the water on my surfboard, with the number four pinned to my chest.

The second I saw that number, that outfit, I knew where I was: at a surfing competition in Hawaii. I was fourteen—I didn't have my Brewer board yet and was instead using the yellow-and-fuchsia one that had been my favorite for years.

I'd won the competition, and Roxy had wanted to sponsor me, but my dad wouldn't let them. He'd told me I was too young for sponsorship, and no matter how much I begged, he hadn't budged. Not on that.

But how had my mother known? I wondered as I watched my dad sweep me into his arms when my final score was announced and we knew I'd won. Moku and Rio were both there, jumping around and screeching like crazy people. When my dad put me down, four-year-old Moku yanked on my bathing suit top until I picked him up and twirled him around. By the time I put him down, we both looked dizzy as we stumbled onto the sand. It only made us laugh harder.

It had been a good day, was a good memory for me despite my mother's absence. She had left three and a half years earlier, and I hadn't laid eyes on her again until I'd followed Kona into the ocean.

But if this memory could be believed, she'd seen that day, knew everything about it. Had she been there, then, watching us the entire time? Too scared, too ashamed, too filled with duty to come ashore and celebrate with us? The idea made me sad, especially when I let myself think about how much I'd missed her back then. It felt strange to realize she had been there and I just hadn't known.

I let the sea glass go, let it slip from my fingers and tumble through the water to the cavern floor. As it fell, I wondered how many other times my mother had been there, watching, and I hadn't known. Was this a one-time thing, or was each of those pieces of sea glass filled with a memory of me, my brothers, my father?

If they were, if she'd been watching all along, what did that say about the way I'd always felt about her? Did it change things, when so much of my anger came from her abandonment of us?

When I thought of her there, watching, I didn't feel angry. I felt lost, like I'd missed an opportunity that would never come around again. Why hadn't she tried to talk to me? Why hadn't she said something? I'd needed her so much and by the time I'd finally found her again, it had been too late.

I'd thought that becoming mermaid would make things easier, but the more information I received the harder it became to answer anything in black and white. Suddenly, the shades of gray were more alive than they had ever been.

I was reaching for another piece of glass, wanting to see— wanting to know—when an overwhelming sense of doom, of panic, washed over me. It pressed in from every side, smothered me. Terrified me. I tried to get a handle on it, to figure out what was happening, but everything was jumbled up in the all-encompassing horror sweeping through every inch of me.

Kona reached over, pulled me against him, and something about the solid heat of his skin brought me back from the edge. Kept the hysteria at bay. And that's when I knew.

I grabbed on to Kona with hands that shook. *Something's wrong*, I told him. *Back at home. Something's happened to my family.*

Chapter 17

What do you mean? Kona asked, confused. *What's wrong?*

I don't know, I told him. *I don't know, I don't know, I don't know.*

I shot straight up, swimming for the cavern's exit with every ounce of energy I could muster.

Tempest, hold on! Kona caught up to me, wrapped his arms around my waist.

I spun in his hold, nearly decked him before I caught myself. *Let me go!* I screamed, struggling against his hold. *I have to get home. I have to get—*

I know, he told me calmly. *I'll go with you. Just calm down, breathe for a second. Tell me what's going on.*

Something's wrong. I don't know what. I don't even know how I know. But I feel it, in here. I pounded on my chest. *Something terrible has happened.*

All right, then. Kona nodded, never questioning my certainty. *Let's go.*

We both shifted, then swam through the cave like our tails were on fire. Once we hit the open ocean, Kona shifted back, got dressed, but I stayed in mermaid form. I needed to get home as quickly as I possibly could.

Panic rocketed through me with every stroke I took, burning with the certainty that someone I loved was hurt. Badly. *Not Moku*, I prayed as I swam grimly beside Kona. *Not Moku, not Moku, not Moku. Please don't let it be my sweet baby brother.*

But then I didn't want it to be Rio or my dad either. *Please,* I prayed, *please let them all be okay.* Even as I said the words, I knew it was too much to hope for. I could feel the bad news closing in, wrapping itself around me like a tourniquet that cut off my ability to think, to breathe.

You need to tell Hailana, Kona told me, *before we get too far away.*

She'll say I can't go, and I won't listen. It'll end up being a huge thing, I warned him.

She'll want you to go. I told you before, Hailana understands.

I stopped my disbelieving snort just in time to keep myself from sucking up a whole bunch of water—maybe I was finally getting the hang of this thing.

Tempest . . .

Fine, I'll do it. But when I tried to reach out to her, she wasn't close enough. And I wasn't strong enough to initiate communication from this far away.

I told Kona what was wrong and he held the bridge. It took only a few seconds for me to reach Hailana. She was in another Council meeting and pissed that I wasn't there with her.

I have to go home, I told her. *Something's wrong.*

You can't leave now, she answered. *There's no way. We need you here.*

They need me there.

You can't keep doing this, Tempest. Her voice was stern. *You chose your path. Your loyalties lie with us now.*

They should, I knew, but it wasn't as easy as she was making it out to be. I'd walked away from my life on land, but that didn't mean I could just forget it ever existed. I had spent seventeen years of my life with my family. Trying to stop caring overnight about what happened to them was impossible, even if I wanted to. Which I didn't.

I'm going, Hailana.

Queen Hailana! she shouted at me.

Fine. I'm going, Queen Hailana.

If you disobey me in this, Tempest, there will be grave consequences when you return. Consequences you will not enjoy. Trust me.

The thought that maybe I wouldn't return snaked through me, but with a quick, guilty look at Kona, I cut it off before it could even fully form.

Then I'll deal with the consequences when I return, I said.

I'm forbidding you to go!

You don't own me—you can't forbid me to do anything.

Tempest—

Drop the bridge, I told Kona, who looked disturbed but did as I asked.

I'm not heading back to Coral Straits, I told him, *so don't even bother suggesting it.*

I wasn't going to. I'm just shocked that she wouldn't let you leave. There must be something big happening.

The only big thing going on is that Hailana is a total witch. She's pissed because I won't fall in line and do exactly what she wants, twenty-four hours a day.

He laughed. *You make her sound like a fascist.*

She is.

Oh, come on, she's not that bad.

I started to tell Kona about the hints she kept dropping regarding our relationship, trying to get me to lose faith in him, but figured that, one, he wouldn't believe me, or two, he would try to figure out how I could have misinterpreted what she'd been saying.

I could also tell him that she said his sister's death was accidental, that it wasn't Sabyn's fault, but that was crossing the line and I knew it. Kona would tell me about his sister's death when he was ready. For now, I was going with his interpretation, because for me, a choice between the two of them would always come down to Kona.

For one brief, stupid second, I wondered if he would make the same choice between his kingdom and me.

Come on, he suddenly said, grabbing my hand and pulling me toward an influx of warmer, faster-moving water. *Let's shoot the current. It'll shave a good hour off our time.*

That was the last conversation we had for a long while. We were both too busy concentrating on swimming—through exhaustion and beyond—to have any energy left for something as mundane as talking. Still, I was grateful that Kona was there. I felt so lost, so confused, so frightened, that I swore the only thing keeping me sane was the feel of his strong, lean body beside me.

All I could think about was that I was just like my mother. She'd left, and maybe she'd kept track of things with us, maybe she hadn't, but she'd never been there. Not when I needed her, not when my dad and brothers needed her. And now, here I was, an ocean away when something bad happened to my family. If I hadn't been in that cave, connected to them through my mother's memories, would I even know that there was a problem? Or would I be swimming along, living my life without ever knowing that something was wrong?

You doing okay? Kona asked.

Yeah. What else could I say?

That I felt like I was going to rip apart into a thousand different pieces?

That the guilt was nearly killing me?

That if we didn't get to La Jolla soon I was really afraid that I might lose what was left of my mind?

Hey, it's going to be okay, Kona said.

I know. I wouldn't let myself think any other way.

Come here. He pulled me into his arms. *You're exhausted. Let me take over for a while.*

I'm fine, I said, but I relaxed against him anyway. I was so exhausted that I was trembling with every pull of my arms through the water.

You don't have to be Super-Mermaid, you know. Your body's been through hell these last couple of days. Just rest for a few minutes, okay?

I nodded against his chest. *Thank you,* I told him, kissing his bicep.

You're welcome. His voice was solemn when he answered, which made me think he understood just how many things I was thanking him for.

We made it to the beach near my house about ninety minutes later. It was crowded, filled to capacity with surfers, swimmers, and sun worshippers, so I shifted in the water pretty far from shore, then took my bikini bottoms from Kona, who'd shoved them in his pocket when I had shifted to mermaid.

After all the vital areas were covered, we swam to the beach. We walked out of the water together, then I slipped my hand into Kona's and we ran up the sand I hadn't set foot on for over eight months. As we ran, I prayed we weren't too late.

Chapter 18

The house was empty when we got there. I rang the doorbell again and again, waiting for one of my brothers, or the new housekeeper/nanny my father had hired when I left, to answer. But no one came, and I grew increasingly freaked out with each second that passed.

"Is there another way in?" Kona demanded, already checking around the porch for a key.

"The spare is hidden on the back patio. Or at least it used to be."

"Let's go, then."

The gates into our backyard were also locked, so we hopped the fence like my brothers and I used to do when we forgot to bring our keys to the beach. There was none of the lazy joy of those days in our movements now, though. I was as close to frantic as I'd been in a long time. It was the middle of the day in the heart of summer and my brothers weren't at home. Nor were they on the beach, which was usually their favorite place.

I tried to convince myself that it was no big deal, that they were shopping or at a movie or maybe even on vacation. But I knew better. I hadn't come all this way on a hunch. I knew, without a doubt, that something was very, very wrong.

Kona found the key underneath the rim of the outside bar, right where my dad had always kept it, and in seconds we were both inside. What I saw there wasn't encouraging.

A carton of milk was sitting on the counter, open and spoiling, while a half-eaten bowl of what was once Cheerios rested on the kitchen table. The box was on its side, with half the contents spilled on the floor in front of the key holder—like my dad had knocked it over in a rush to get his keys and then hadn't bothered to pick it up.

Which wasn't like him.

"Dad!" I yelled, taking off running through the house. "Moku? Rio? Dad!"

There was no answer, but that didn't stop me from shouting as I ran from room to room looking for someone or something that would tell me where they were. There was nothing, not even a note, although why would there be? It wasn't like my dad just expected me to drop by . . .

"It's okay, Tempest. We'll find them, but you need to calm down."

Kona slid his arms around me, pressed a soft kiss to my temple. And that's when I realized I was crying. More like sobbing, really, and I couldn't seem to stop. Fear was a wild tsunami inside of me, swamping everything else.

Kona held me until I could finally get myself under control. "First of all, do you think your dad still has some of your old clothes?" he asked when I started breathing again. "And maybe something for me to borrow? We can't exactly go running around town like this." He gestured to our damp bathing suits and sandy feet. I'd been so panicked I'd forgotten to wash off in the outside shower.

"Yeah, right. Clothes." We were standing in the middle of my dad's room anyway, so I crossed to his closet and pulled out a surfing T-shirt and a pair of shorts for Kona to wear. Thank God my dad liked his shorts baggy, because Kona was so tall that nothing else would have worked.

I left him to take a quick shower in my dad's bathroom and went in search of my room, the only place in the house I hadn't checked for my dad and brothers. What I found there nearly had me bursting into tears all over again.

Nothing had changed.

Not one thing, except my bed was made, and I remembered that I hadn't bothered with it before heading out to the beach all those months ago. Other than that, the room was exactly as I had left it—right down to the painting I'd been working on still resting, half-finished, on the easel near the window, and my pre-calc homework sitting on my desk.

Maybe I should be glad my dad hadn't messed with my stuff, but there was something intensely sad about the fact that nothing had been touched. Like it had just been waiting—*they* had just been waiting—for me to come home.

The thought had my heart breaking wide open.

Where are they? I asked myself for the millionth time. I crossed to my dresser, pulled out a purple tank top and my favorite pair of jeans. After a quick shower using my old shampoo—which was still in the adjacent bathroom—I shimmied into them. It felt strange to be wearing regular clothes again after so long. But it was a good strange.

Kona tapped on my door as I was sliding my feet into a pair of sandals. "Where do you want to start looking?" he asked. He was wearing a pair of flip-flops, but his feet were so much bigger than my dad's that his toes and heels extended over the front and back. I probably would have laughed if I wasn't so panicked.

"I need to call my dad's office, see if they know where he is." I was already reaching for the phone.

I dialed my dad's private number from memory, and his assistant answered right away. "How is he, Bobby? What did the tests show?"

My stomach plummeted. "It's Tempest, Sylvia. What tests? What's wrong? I came home and—" My voice broke.

"Oh, sweetheart, I'm so sorry. Moku had an accident on the beach yesterday. He's been in a coma for the last twenty-four hours."

I know she said more, but I couldn't hear it over the roaring in my ears. My legs gave out and I hit the ground, hard.

৵

Not my baby brother, not my baby brother, not my baby brother, I repeated to myself over and over again as Kona drove my car—which had still been sitting on my side of the garage like it was waiting for me—to the hospital. We were going about twenty miles above the speed limit, and I fought the urge to scream at him to go faster. Especially since neither one of us was exactly carrying a license—and Kona didn't even own one. The only reason he was driving was because I was too upset to think, let alone pay attention to the road.

Let him be okay, I pleaded with whatever higher power was out there. *Please, let him be okay.*

We pulled into the parking lot of Rady Children's Hospital, and Kona sped straight to the front doors. "Go on in," he told me grimly. "I'll park and meet you up there."

I didn't even pause to say thank you, just headed for the front desk at a dead run. "Moku Maguire," I told the two women sitting behind the information desk. "What room is he in?"

"How do you spell the name?" the one on the left asked. She had gray curls and wore hot-pink glasses and a teddy-bear shirt. I wanted to strangle her as she slowly pulled her keyboard closer and waited, fingers poised over the keys.

"M-O-K-U," I said through gritted teeth. "M-A-G-U-I-R-E."

She leisurely typed the name in as I imagined snatching the keyboard away and doing it for her. After what felt like forever, she glanced over the top of the screen, her expression ripe with sympathy. "He's in the Critical Care Unit, honey. But only family is allowed."

"I'm his sister. What floor is the CCU on?"

She told me and then I was running for the elevator, banging on the button over and over again, like that would somehow make it come faster. It was as if there were two of me: the calm, rational one and the one who was a step away from losing her mind. Guess which one was in control.

Kona caught up to me just as I stepped on the elevator. He tried to wrap his arm around my waist, but I shrugged him off. I felt like any wrong move, any drop of sympathy, and I was going to start screaming and never stop.

The elevator dinged on the appropriate floor, and we stepped off, only to be confronted by a bunch of signs pointing in other directions. I tried to read them, but the letters kept blurring in front of my eyes. "Where do we go?" I asked Kona as I frantically rubbed the tears away. "Which way do we go?"

"This way, baby." He reached for my hand and this time I didn't pull away. Instead, I let him guide me down the hallway to the nurse's station, each step closer to the CCU an agony of fear and horror inside of me. *Let him be okay*, I prayed again. *Please, don't take Moku from me. Not Moku.*

We finally found the nurse's station, a relatively quiet area walled behind glass. There was a line in front of me, and I waited impatiently, feeling the whole time like I was about to jump out of my skin.

Finally, finally, it was my turn. "Moku Maguire," I said at the front desk.

The nurse looked me over. "Name, please."

"Tempest Maguire."

She typed it into the computer. "I'm sorry, but you're not on the list of approved visitors."

The words hit me like a blow, and I probably would have fallen then if Kona hadn't been there to hold me up. "That's because my dad wasn't expecting me." I stumbled over the words. "Is he here?" I demanded. "Is Bobby Maguire in there right now?"

Again, she checked the screen. "He is."

"Please, can you get him? He doesn't know I made it back to town. Please, tell him I'm here. I need to see my brother. I need to know—" My throat tightened up.

The woman nodded. "Let me see what I can do, sweetheart. Why don't you go sit in the waiting room, and I'll see about getting your dad out here." She pointed to an open door about twenty feet away.

I didn't want to go to the waiting room. I wanted to see Moku. But while her eyes were sympathetic, her demeanor was implacable, and I knew I wasn't going to be able to get around her.

Kona and I walked slowly down the hall to the waiting room. I kept turning around, trying to catch a glimpse of my father coming through the brightly painted double doors that guarded the CCU.

We were hovering in the entrance to the waiting room when I saw him barreling through the doors and into the reception area near the front desk, a slightly crazed, completely disbelieving look on his face. "Tempest?" he called, looking both ways.

"I'm here, Daddy. I'm here."

And then I was running straight into his arms and the biggest bear hug I'd ever had in my life.

Chapter 19

Hours later, I sat by Moku's bedside, willing him to wake up. So far, it hadn't worked.

Beside me was Rio, my now fourteen-year-old brother. Since only two of us were allowed in at a time, my dad was outside in the waiting room.

I think he believed that sending Rio and me in together would help break the ice between us, get us talking. Not so much. Oh, my brother kept stealing glances at me out of the corner of his eye, like he couldn't believe I was really there, but he wasn't saying a word. Even worse, he didn't exactly look happy to see me.

In fact, he looked downright angry. Not just at me, but at the whole world. In the eight months that I'd been underwater, his appearance had undergone a radical change. The surfing tees and board shorts were MIA, replaced by black jeans and T-shirt, a chained belt, and spiked, black leather bracelets. His shaggy blond surfer's cut had been shaved into a Mohawk he spiked up with a copious amount of gel, his flip-flops replaced by

Doc Martens. I was also pretty sure he was wearing my favorite black eyeliner.

I had no idea what to say to him at this point, especially since my first few tries at starting a conversation had been shut down. Viciously. Still, I wanted to reach him. *Needed* to reach him. Now that my brothers were right in front of me, this inability to communicate with either of them was driving me completely insane.

"How are the waves?" I asked Rio when I caught him looking at me for about the thirtieth time.

He snorted. "Brutal. Or did you think Moku was in here because he wanted a vacation?"

"Rio . . ."

He didn't answer. Instead, he deliberately turned his back, his obvious dismissal leaving me to deal with my recriminations and fears alone. There were a lot of them.

Every time I thought about what had happened to Moku, I felt horror ripple through me. When I had first asked, my father said my brother had been out at the beach early yesterday morning, catching some of the smaller waves. Rosa, the babysitter/housekeeper, had been with him, but in the end, that hadn't mattered.

He'd gotten caught in the undertow, and judging by the bruises, the doctors thought he'd hit his head on a rock right before the drop-off. Whatever had happened, he'd ended up passing out and had been underwater for over seven minutes before Mark and Logan had finally managed to find him and fish him out.

Thank God.

Still, he should be dead. That's what all the doctors had hinted at, what every bit of medical science told them. Yet here he was, in a coma, but alive. My dad thought it was his mermaid half that kept him from dying, but whatever it was, I was grateful.

Still, it wasn't enough. Nobody knew if Moku would come out of the coma or not, and if he did, the doctors weren't sure what kind of brain damage he'd have.

My dad kept saying his mermaid half would protect him, but I wasn't so optimistic. If the last eight months had taught me anything, it was that the last thing being a mermaid protected you from was pain and suffering. In fact, it seemed to make both worse.

Still, I refused to think about all that yet. Refused to worry about it. I just wanted Moku to wake up. I closed my eyes and tried to believe that he was going to be all right, that somehow everything would be okay. It had to be. I couldn't lose Moku too. I just couldn't.

"It never would have happened if you'd been here." Rio finally spoke, his words hurling across the silence between us. They struck me, sharp and poison-tipped, just as I was sure he'd intended. Though I fought not to react, I felt their impact all the way to my soul.

"I'm sorry," I told him. "I'm so sorry." And I was. If this was what had happened to my family in my absence, then I'd never been more sorry about a decision in my life.

"Yeah, I can tell," he answered with a totally disgusted glance. "You looked really sorry when you were in the waiting room, hanging all over your boyfriend—or whatever the hell you call that weird animal thing you're dating."

"He's a selkie."

"He's a *freak*."

"Come on, Rio." I glanced at Moku with a sigh. "You really think this is what he needs right now?"

"How the hell would you know what he needs?" Rio reached over and shoved me in the shoulder, hard. Something he'd never done before.

I ignored the sudden sharp pain, made worse by the sensitivity of my skin above water. "I don't." God, it grated to admit that. "Not like you do."

"That's right, you don't. You haven't been here—not for him. Not for anyone."

"I didn't know—"

"You didn't *care*! It's not the same thing. And now *we* don't care, not about you. Why don't you leave? Why don't you get the hell out of here? No one wants you around anyway."

"Rio—"

"Go." He tried to drag me out of the chair but I was too strong for him. Frustrated, hurting, he started shoving the chair toward the door. "Just go!"

"Rio, stop it!" I was getting angry now too. "I'm not going anywhere."

"Yeah, right. The second your loser boyfriend wants you, you'll be gone. So you should leave now, before Moku wakes up. I won't let you hurt him again."

That took the fight right out of me. "I promise you, I won't leave while Moku is hurt."

"But you *will* leave, so what does it matter when?" He choked on a sob, and for a second I saw the lost little boy he was trying so hard to hide. And then he was gone, hurtling past me and out the door.

"Rio, stop!"

He didn't. I needed to follow him, to chase him down and make him talk to me—really talk to me—but I didn't want to leave Moku alone, not even for a few minutes. At the same time, Rio shouldn't be alone right now either.

Biting my lip, I lowered my head to the side of Moku's bed and just breathed for a few seconds. If I'd had my cell, I would have texted my dad in the waiting room, told him to look for Rio. But I didn't have a phone anymore. I didn't need one in my new life.

God, it felt strange—and terrible. It used to be that I believed I could fit into whichever of the two worlds I chose. These days, though, it felt like I was as ill equipped to deal with my old life as I was my new one.

So, what was I supposed to do now?

"Oh, Moku," I whispered. "Please, please don't do this. Please come back to me. I miss you so much."

I threaded my fingers through his cold, limp ones and squeezed tightly. "Come on," I cajoled. "Don't you want to see me? I'm dying to talk to you. I have so many stories about sharks and sea turtles and the coolest coral reef I've ever seen. It makes the ones in Hawaii look like nothing. I swear, there was every color in the rainbow. You would have loved it.

"And just last week, I had an up-close-and-personal encounter with a great white shark. I survived, obviously, but for a while there I was pretty sure it was going to eat me. I've never seen that many teeth so close—"

"I'm not sure if you should finish that story. I don't think my heart could take it."

I turned toward the door, where my dad was leaning against the wall, his casual stance belying the pain in his eyes.

"You saw Rio?" I asked.

"Yeah. I called my secretary. She's going to give him a ride home."

"He's really mad at me."

My dad sighed. "He's really mad at the world, Tempest. You're just a small part of it."

"I'm sorry." It was hard to look him in the eye as I said it.

"Nothing to be sorry about, darlin'." He tried to smile, but his lips trembled a little at the corners. He looked drawn, tired, and about ten years older than he'd seemed when I left. No matter what he said, I knew these last eight months had been hard on him. On all of them.

"What are we going to do, Dad?"

"We're going to keep talking to your brother until he wakes up." He slid into the chair beside me, looked me full in the face. "He *is* going to wake up, Tempest."

"I know," I told him, because anything else was unthinkable, unsayable. But fear—huge, looming, overwhelming fear—throbbed inside of me with each rise and fall of my too-human lungs.

With every beat of my too-frail human heart.

Kona was sprawled in a chair in the waiting room when my dad finally convinced me to leave Moku. He'd given me a hundred bucks and instructions to "pick up some food and then get some sleep." I almost laughed. I didn't think I'd ever be able to sleep again, at least not without nightmares playing through my head of Moku nearly drowning.

Still, he was right. I needed to go home, to talk to Rio. To show him that I still loved him even after choosing the sea. Too bad I had no idea how I was going to accomplish that.

Leaning down, I brushed a few strands of Kona's hair out from in front of his eyes. When that didn't wake him, I dropped a light kiss on his lips.

His gorgeous silver eyes blinked open and he smiled sweetly at me. "You okay?"

"I've been better."

"I know. I saw Rio."

"Yeah. Hard to recognize him, isn't it?"

"Oh, I don't know. He still looks a lot like you."

"Perpetually angry?"

"I was talking about the stubborn jaw and don't-screw-with-me expression, but whatever works." He grew serious. "How's Moku?"

"No change."

"I'm sorry."

"Yeah, me too. We're supposed to pick up some food and go back to the house. Feed Goth Boy. Dad will be home when visiting hours end."

"Okay. Let's go." He stood up, still holding my hand.

We headed for the door, but when we got there somebody was coming in just as we were trying to leave. I brushed against him in passing and my entire body went nuts. Goose bumps, shivers, electric shocks. The whole nine yards. Plus the hum of my powers suddenly kicked into top gear.

I stiffened, gasped in surprise. Turned to look back at him the same second he turned to look at me.

I knew, even before our eyes met, but it was still a shock. For him too, obviously.

"Tempest?"

Without conscious thought, I stepped forward to meet him. "Mark."

Chapter 20

Kona stiffened beside me, and I felt more than saw his hands clench into fists. It was only for a second. Then he was relaxing, pulling away from me, extending his hand for Mark to shake. I glanced up at him, a little shocked at the easy smile on his face when I could feel the tension radiating through him.

"Hey, Mark, how are you?"

Mark looked at Kona's hand for long seconds before taking it. "I've been better, Kona. How are you?"

I didn't hear Kona's answer, didn't hear much of anything but the roaring in my ears as the two of them exchanged obviously fake pleasantries. From the second my dad had told me what happened, I'd known I was going to see Mark again, if only to thank him for saving Moku's life. But I hadn't expected to see him here, hadn't expected to see him *now*.

I was completely unprepared.

Even worse, I couldn't think of anything to do that didn't involve throwing myself into his arms and showering him with kisses of gratitude. I had a feeling that wouldn't go over too well with Kona, though.

In the end, I settled for saying, "Hi, Mark," and leaning into him for a quick, casual hug.

But nothing between Mark and me had ever been casual, and the way he wrapped his arms around me this time, pulling me close, was no exception. The second he pressed his body against mine, it was like I had never left. In a flash, I remembered everything I once was. Everything we once were together.

It was like coming home.

Except my powers went crazy, my body lighting up as energy hummed through me.

Kona cleared his throat and I pulled back reluctantly, a little unsure of how many seconds—or minutes—had passed while Mark just held me.

"Thank you," I told him awkwardly. "For saving Moku. For watching out for him when I couldn't." From the time he was born, it had been my job to take care of Moku. How could I have forgotten that?

"No sweat, Tempe. You know I love Mo." Mark looked down at the ground, shuffled his feet a little. "I just wish I could have found him sooner."

"He's going to come out of this. He'll be okay." I blinked my eyes a bunch of times in a useless attempt to banish the tears.

Kona cleared his throat again. "I'm going to go wait in the hall. Give you a couple of minutes to catch up."

My knees turned to putty at the suggestion, and I glanced at Kona incredulously. It was obvious, from his tightly locked jaw to his white-knuckled fists, that he had no desire to leave me alone with Mark. And still he'd made the suggestion. That unselfishness, that determination to put my needs above his own, was just one of the reasons I'd fallen so hard for him.

Which was also why I couldn't take him up on the offer. I wanted to, would love nothing more than to stay right here talking to Mark for as long as I had a voice, but it wasn't right. It wouldn't be fair—to either of them.

"No, that's okay." I forced the words out. "We need to get going. Rio's probably starved."

Mark stepped back. "I didn't mean to keep you." His voice was stiff now, his jaw rigid, and I could tell I had hurt him by refusing Kona's offer—as much as I would have hurt Kona by taking him up on it.

Though they were being total gentlemen, I still felt like a rope in a tug-of-war contest—caught between two opposing sides. Belonging equally to both of them. It made my head throb.

"Don't be stupid," I told Mark. "We owe Moku's life to you."

"Logan helped. He's going to try to stop by later, after he gets off work."

"I'll come back then. After I spend a little time with Rio—"

"And take a nap," Kona interjected. "You're exhausted."

The proprietary way he said it irritated me to no end. Probably because I knew it had a lot more to do with Mark than with me.

Mark didn't rise to the bait, though. Just stepped farther back and said, "Don't let me keep you. I'm just going to stop in and see Moku for a few minutes. But I'll tell Logan to look for you later."

"Yeah, please. I want to thank him too."

"It's nothing you wouldn't have done for us." His phone beeped and he pulled it out, glanced down. "That's your dad now. I guess I'll catch you around, huh, Tempest?"

"Sure. And thanks again. I don't know what would have happened if you hadn't been there." Though I meant every word, they came out stilted, which drove me nuts. For years, Mark had been a lot more than my boyfriend. He'd been my best friend, the person I wanted to spend more time with than anyone else besides Moku. And now we could barely look each other in the eye. It was awful.

Mark shook his head, grinned, and for a second I caught a glimpse of the old Mark, the one I remembered. The one I could talk to for hours without either one of us running out of things to say. "It's good to see you, Tempe." He reached behind me, yanked twice on my ponytail like he used to, and then he was gone. Slipping past us and out of the waiting room door before I could think of something, anything, else to say.

∞

The house was even more gloomy than when we'd left it earlier. A summer storm had rolled in while we were at the hospital, turning the normally bright blue sky a dingy gray that made my normally sunlit house downright depressing.

"Rio!" I called as soon as we got inside. "I brought dinner!"

There was no answer. Kona and I exchanged worried looks. I headed for the stairs, but Kona stopped me with a gentle arm around my waist. "Why don't you let me try to talk to him?" he suggested softly.

I remembered the way Rio had looked when he'd spoken about Kona earlier. "Maybe that's not such a good idea."

"I had ten younger brothers and sisters," he reminded me. "There's not much he can say that's going to shock me."

"He's not exactly in a good place right now. I mean, he's never been the sunniest kid, but he wasn't like this either. Plus, I think he blames you for my leaving as much as he blames me. Maybe more."

"I know. Which is why he and I might as well get this all out in the open now." Kona cocked a brow. "I'm not planning on going anywhere, so he needs to get used to me. Right?"

"Right." I knew I didn't sound convinced about sending him in to see Rio, but that was because I wasn't. I loved my brother, but he could be a real jerk when he wanted to be. And right now, it was pretty obvious that he really, really wanted to be.

While I waited for Kona to come back down, I cleared up the mess that had been left in the kitchen before laying out the food we'd picked up. Rubio's fish tacos—Rio's favorite. I just hoped Kona managed to talk him out of his room.

I didn't hear anything from upstairs—no yelling, no slamming doors—but I didn't know if that was a good thing or not.

I got glasses, filled them with ice.

Pulled sodas out of the fridge near the bar and put them on the table.

Got napkins and placed them next to each person's glass.

Washed my hands for the second time since I walked in the front door.

Emptied the dishwasher.

Started to fold the napkin into origami dolphins—

I couldn't take it anymore. I was going up to see what was happening. For all I knew, the two of them could have killed each other . . .

I was halfway up the staircase when Rio appeared at the top

of the steps, Kona directly behind him. Rio looked pissed (big surprise), but he didn't say anything when he slid past me on the stairs. Neither did Kona, who didn't look anywhere near as haggard or worn out as I'd expected him to. God knew, Rio could try the patience of a saint.

We settled around the table, and I watched this strange, black-clad Rio eat. And at least that was familiar—he still devoured his food like a raging wildebeest was going to plow into him at any second. Strangely, that gave me hope.

At least until I got a good look at his face. His eyes were bloodshot—really bloodshot—and I wasn't sure if that meant he'd been crying or smoking pot. The fact that I didn't know illustrated better than anything else just how much things had changed around here while I was gone.

Rio had always been a pain in the butt, but he'd also been pretty much a rule follower—more so than either Moku or me. And the fact that I was now worried about him doing drugs . . . Part of me wanted to go back to that day eight months ago and change my decision—to hell with the consequences.

I tried to talk to Rio a few times, and he answered grudgingly. He didn't say anything major, but still, it was a start. One I really appreciated.

I glanced at Kona. *What did you say to him?*

Nothing major. Kona smiled. *Just guy stuff.*

Ugh, seriously? I sighed hugely to let him know I wasn't buying it. *I swear, it's times like these that remind me you really were born two hundred years ago. And that is* not *a compliment.*

He just laughed. *So temperamental. That's why they call you Tempest, right?*

Whatever.

I glanced at Rio and the smile froze on my face. The semi-relaxed look he'd worn at dinner was gone, and it was pretty easy to figure out what had caused it, even before he said, "God, you two really are freaks." And just like that, all the progress Kona had made evaporated.

"Rio." I tried to get him to meet my eyes, determined to have it out with him.

He was back to ignoring me.

"Rio," I said again, this time louder.

Still no answer. He got up and threw his trash away.

"Rio!" He was going to talk to me whether he liked it or not. I started across the kitchen after him, but Kona slipped up behind me, slid his arms around my waist. It felt like an embrace, but at the same time I knew he was doing it to hold me back, calm me down.

It might even have worked had Rio not chosen that moment to turn around and stare at me, his eyes flat and dead. I watched open-mouthed as he very calmly, very deliberately, flipped me off. Then he turned the volume all the way up on his iPod before heading for the stairs.

I lunged after him, wanting to strangle him and plead with him all at the same time. Once again, it was only Kona that held me back.

"Give him time," he murmured in my ear. "Once Moku wakes up, things will get better."

"*If* Moku wakes up." I shoved against his arms. "You can let me go now. I promise not to chase him down and pummel him."

"Well, thank God for that." Kona reluctantly dropped his arms. "Maybe it just makes me feel better to hold you."

"I think you've got that backward." I laid my head on his shoulder. "How did I screw everything up so badly?"

"You didn't. Sometimes life just happens. It takes a while before everything catches up between how things are and how we want them to be."

"Is that what this is?" I asked. "Fantasy lag? Like finding out Santa Claus isn't real?"

He grinned, rubbed my shoulders. "Something like that. Just a little more painful, maybe."

"A lot more painful," I corrected.

He sighed. "Yeah, I know. I'm sorry, baby. I'd fix this if I could."

"You got Rio downstairs. That's something." I looked at him curiously. "How *did* you do that?" I asked again.

"I told him I'd kick his ass."

"What? Kona!"

He held his hands up in mock surrender. "I'm joking, I'm joking. I apologized."

"For what? You didn't do anything."

"I stole you away, didn't I? And then I told him I understood how he felt."

"And he just believed you?"

"He did after I listed a whole bunch of those feelings. Which wasn't hard—it's not like I haven't been exactly where he is right now."

"Oh. Right." I blushed a little, ducked my head. "Is that why you're being so good to me right now? Because you remember what it's like to have your family so fragmented?"

"First of all, I'm taking care of you because I love you." He paused, ran a hand through his hair. "But yes, I remember what it was like to spend days waiting, terrified that my sister was going to die, and I know what it's like to lose a brother suddenly, when you're least expecting it. Either way sucks."

"I'm so sorry. I didn't think. I should have realized how hard all this is for you."

He shrugged. "No harder than it is for your family. I miss Oliwa and Annalise. Every day I miss them, but that doesn't mean I can blame the whole world for it."

It was my turn to soothe him. I scooted behind him, lightly rubbed his shoulders. "I know what happened to Oliwa—"

"Yeah. You killed his murderer, who had turned traitor and sold us all out to Tiamat." He said it like he was proud of me.

I ignored the way my stomach clenched at the mention of something I spent every day trying to forget. "Yes. But what happened to Annalise, Kona? I don't want to pry, but . . ."

"But Sabyn told you he wasn't responsible. Right?"

"I didn't ask Sabyn. I wouldn't do that."

He sighed. "I know you wouldn't." He glanced at the clock. "Are you sure you want to do this now? You must be exhausted."

"I'm wide awake. But if you don't want to tell me . . ."

"I'm not sure. It's really hard to talk about."

I could imagine. Just the thought of losing Moku had me so turned around that I could barely function. I couldn't imagine how I would feel if one day he was just gone. No wonder Kona wanted to kill Sabyn.

Blowing out a long, slow breath—like he was about to do something he'd regret—Kona crossed to the table. He sat down in one of the chairs, pulled me into his lap. Then buried his face in my hair and breathed deep. "How is it you can still smell like raspberries, even after months under the sea?"

I melted a little, but didn't answer him. Every day that passed, Annalise's death—and Sabyn's part in it—seemed to loom a little larger between us. I wanted it out in the open and this seemed to be the time for it, especially now that everything in my own life was so precariously balanced. Still, I'd pushed far enough. It was up to him.

Kona seemed to understand, because he passed a hand over his face, then began to talk. Slowly, haltingly. "Annalise was my favorite. To be honest, she was everybody's favorite. My mom's, my dad's, all of ours, really. She was just . . . good, you know? Just deep down sweet and innocent and good, which is sometimes hard to find in the ocean, as I'm sure you're figuring out. No hidden agendas, no nefarious plans, no ulterior motives. She was just sweet because that's who she was.

"Anyway, she fell for Sabyn when she was young—really young. She was born seventy-five years after me, so the age difference between my friends and her, back then especially, was huge. Not that any of that mattered to her. She tried to follow us everywhere—sometimes we would allow it because she was just so damn cute, but other times we'd send her back, if it was too dangerous. She didn't have much power, but then she didn't need it. We were all willing to switch off taking care of her, keeping her safe.

"I think Sabyn was flattered by her attention, at least at first. He didn't take her seriously—none of us did. She was just a baby."

He stared out the huge picture window behind us, but I

knew he wasn't seeing the ocean. He was seeing a lifetime ago, long before I was even born. The thought weirded me out a little. For the first time I think I began to understand what it meant to be with someone who was two centuries older than I was, even if he only looked about eighteen.

"But she didn't stay a baby. She grew up and she was beautiful—my dad's guards had a hard time keeping all the merboys and selkies away from her." He snarled when he said merboy. "She never noticed them, though. She only had eyes for Sabyn. Which we still laughed about, until one day, when she was looking at him, I caught Sabyn looking back.

"I told him she was off-limits—he was too old for her, too powerful, too dark. I mean, we'd been friends a long time and I knew what he was like. He went through the maids like they were candy." His laugh was bitter. "Hell, they were candy for Sabyn. Something to keep him amused for a few days before he found someone else. He'd never hurt any of them at that point, at least none that I'd heard about. Anyway, he agreed, promised me he'd stay away from her."

"But he didn't."

"No. They started dating and it got pretty serious, pretty quickly. I was pissed about it and I acted like a total ass to both of them. Maybe if I hadn't, she would have come to me. She'd always come to me before when she had a problem, always trusted me to fix it for her. But not this time. This time she confronted him on her own."

"He was cheating on her?"

"Of course. He could say he loved her, but Sabyn isn't capable of loving anyone but himself. I never blamed him for that, not with the way he was raised. But she was my sister, you know? There were a million mermaids out there who would do anything to be with him. Why couldn't he just leave her alone?"

He wasn't asking me, but I answered anyway. "Because he's a selfish prick with no impulse control?"

Kona laughed, but there was no humor in it. "Yeah. Pretty much. She followed him one night, caught him with some mermaid from an Australian clan. They had a huge fight and he hit her. She came home with a whole side of her face bruised and swollen up. She didn't tell me it was him, but I knew.

"I went after him, beat the hell out of him. It was my job to protect her, you know?"

"I know." I smoothed my hands through his hair, pressed soft kisses along his jaw. Did anything I could think of to soothe him. His eyes were wild now, dangerous, and he was shaking so badly I thought he was going to fly apart.

"Maybe if I hadn't, things would have ended differently. They would have been okay." He shook his head. "I don't know. But Sabyn, he's got a really bad temper. He keeps it under wraps most of the time, but it's there, never far from the surface. And it turned out he'd been pissed all along that I didn't think he was good enough for Annalise. Absolutely furious. And he wanted revenge, but he's such a coward that he didn't come after me like a normal person would. Like I thought he would. He went after her instead."

I thought of Sabyn's power, of how he'd slammed me into the dirt again and again, like it was nothing to him. Imagined how much worse it would have been if I didn't have as much power as I do. Suddenly, I was terrified to hear what else Kona had to say.

"She didn't stand a chance. He turned on the charm, apologized, promised her it would never happen again. She wanted to believe him, no matter what I said, so she did. That was her mistake, her stupidity. But she didn't deserve to die for it, you know? She didn't deserve—"

He stood up abruptly, like he'd forgotten I was on his lap, and nearly dumped me on my butt.

"Sorry," he said as I scrambled to put my feet on the floor, but I just shook my head. Now that he was getting the story out, I didn't want to interrupt. He needed to finish or all that poison was going to end up destroying him.

"He said she'd fallen trying to get away from Tiamat and her goon squad, had even managed to kill a few of them to make it look good. But I saw my sister's body, saw the bruises around her throat and on every inch of her.

"Sabyn and I were friends for over a century. I know how he fights, know what it looks like when he hits someone with all that power behind it. Hell, I'd fought him myself. There's no doubt in my mind that he killed my sister. I couldn't prove it, though, and no one wanted to listen."

I thought back to what Hailana had said, about how she'd made it sound like Annalise had simply had an accident. "No one wanted to believe that it was him and not Tiamat," I said.

"No one wanted to believe that one of the most powerful mermen in existence, a prince of the most powerful clan in the Pacific, could be such a monster," he answered bitterly. "So we burned my sister, scattered her ashes, and that bastard, that sick, twisted son of a bitch, acted like it was nothing. Like she was nothing. And now, now he's started on you, and I can't just sit there and wait for him to kill you too."

He whirled around, lashed out so quickly that I never even saw it happen. The huge, decorative mirror that hung on the breakfast nook wall shattered, pieces raining down everywhere, hitting the wood floor while blood streamed from a hundred different cuts on Kona's fist.

Chapter 21

"Going somewhere?" my dad asked as I tiptoed into the kitchen. He was slumped in a chair, a huge mug of untouched coffee at his elbow.

"Visiting hours start at eight. I don't want to be late."

My mother's grandfather clock chimed out the hour with five deep gongs. As the last one slowly faded, my father smirked. "Yeah, because it takes three hours to get to Linda Vista."

"It could. With traffic . . ."

"Come sit down and talk to me." He patted the chair next to him with a pointed glare. "You look like hell."

That's because it had taken me hours the night before to get Kona—and the mirror—cleaned up. To get him calmed down enough to sleep. And then I'd spent the whole rest of the night tossing and turning, long after I heard my father come in a little after midnight.

"You don't look much better, you know," I told him.

"Yeah, well, you're the one I'm concerned about." He hugged me, brushed a kiss on the top of my head. "I missed you, kid."

"I missed you guys too."

He nodded, and his throat worked a little, like he was trying hard not to cry. "Moku's going to be okay."

"I know." I reached for his coffee, took a sip. Tried to swallow despite my tight throat and nearly choked to death.

After he finished patting me on the back, my dad said, "I'm really glad you're home."

I nodded again. It was all I could manage.

"How long are you here for?"

"I don't—I can't—"

"Okay, then." He put a hand over mine, calmly waited until I stopped babbling. "We'll take it one day at a time."

"That would probably be a good idea." I paused. "Rio's still asleep. So will you tell me the truth? What do the doctors *really* say?"

Long seconds passed and, as I watched him watching me, I wasn't sure he was going to be completely honest with me. Maybe he couldn't, for his own peace of mind. The thought had the ball of fear and self-loathing twining tighter in my stomach, until it took every ounce of concentration I had just to sit still.

But in the end, he shook his head. "They don't know. They can't figure out why he wasn't brain-dead when Mark and Logan pulled him out of the water, and they still don't know why he didn't die on that beach. And it's not exactly like I can tell them it's because he's half mermaid, can I? They say his chances of waking up are only about fifty percent, but I don't believe that. Your mother went through worse and survived . . ." His voice trailed off and I knew he was lost in remembering.

I thought of my mother's cave, of the memory of how my

parents met. She *had* survived worse, but, "Dad, Mom was completely mermaid. Moku doesn't even have gills yet."

"He survived somehow, Tempest. And I won't believe that he made it through all that just to . . ." His voice trailed off. "No. He's going to be okay."

"Of course he is." I said it forcefully, surely, because I wanted to believe it as much as my father did. Getting up, I poured myself some coffee, then brought it to my nose and just breathed it in. In the ocean, I drank a lot of different types of sea vegetable tea, even told myself I enjoyed them, but as I stood here with a cup of coffee in my hands, I realized it wasn't close to being the same.

No matter how much I wanted it to be.

"So, can I make you some pancakes?" My dad walked to the fridge, opened it. "We still have over two and a half hours before they'll let us into the CCU."

"I'm not that hungry."

"It seems that every time I see you you're telling me that." He started to mix the batter up. "I can't do much to take care of you these days—let me do this, okay?" There was a lot more tension in his voice than the question warranted.

One more sign that Rio and I weren't the only ones having a hard time with this situation. "Do you have blueberries?" I asked.

He smiled at me, the first genuine one I'd seen from him since I'd gotten home. "I do indeed."

We worked together in companionable silence, almost like I'd never left. I made pineapple-mango smoothies while my dad flipped blueberry pancakes, and within fifteen minutes we were seated at the table, shuffling food around our plates and pretending to eat. At least the smoothies seemed to go down okay.

"So," he said again, after he gave up faking and pushed his plate away. "This boy upstairs."

"Kona?" I froze, a deer in headlights, with my smoothie halfway to my mouth.

"Yeah. Kona." He said the name like he was trying to find hidden nuances to it. "Is it *serious* between you two?"

"I, uh, well. We, umm . . ."

He laughed. "I guess that answers that question. Does he treat you well, darlin'?"

"Dad!" I ducked my head. "Do we really have to do this now?"

"Yes. We really do. I don't know how long you're going to be here. I sure as hell don't know when you're going to be back again once you leave. I need to make sure you're taken care of."

"I can take care of myself."

He sighed. "I didn't mean to insult your feminist sensibilities, Tempest. It's just that you're still new to life down there and I want to make sure you've got everything you deserve."

"Well, that sounds ominous," I tried to joke.

"You know what I mean. I want to make sure you have good friends and that they care about you."

"Kona loves me, Dad. He does too much for me, to be honest."

"That's good." My dad nodded. "That's exactly what I want to hear."

"I bet." I rolled my eyes, then didn't even try to pretend I wasn't changing the subject. "Is Rio coming with us to the hospital?"

"Let him sleep. He's not taking this whole thing very well."

"It doesn't seem like he's taking anything very well," I said, bringing up the subject that had been bothering me since I'd first seen my brother last night.

My dad wouldn't meet my eyes. "Give him time. He'll adjust."

"He's had eight months."

"And already he's a lot better than he was when you first left."

I turned stricken eyes to him and he cursed. "Don't look like that. I was trying to explain that he's getting back to normal."

"Yeah, right. Normal is the first thing I think of when I look at that Mohawk on the top of his head. I barely recognized him." I stacked the plates in the dishwasher. Then, without turning around, said, "I'm really sorry, Dad."

"We're not going to go through this again, Tempest. I love you and I'm so proud of you for making the decision that was right for you. That's the only thing I've ever really wanted. As long as you're staying true to who you are and what you want out of life, I'll always be behind you." He rubbed a comforting hand down my back, then glanced at the wall behind the table.

"Hey, what happened to the mirror that was hanging there?"

I froze. "The mirror?"

"Yeah, you know the one. Big. Rectangular. Ocean-type frame? It's been hanging there for ten years, Tempest."

"Oh yeah. It kind of broke last night."

"Broke?" His eyes narrowed. "That thing survived three children and four earthquakes. How the hell did it break?"

"Ummm, it kind of, fell off the wall?"

He cocked his head to the side. "Do I even want to know?"

"Probably not."

"All right, then. Give me fifteen minutes to shower and dress and we'll head out. We can beat the traffic," he told me with a wink as the clock rang out six times.

I fought the urge to run down the hall and smash it into bits. I hated that damn clock and everything it stood for. My mother had insisting on buying it about a year before she took off, and no matter how many times I'd pleaded with him to get rid of it, my dad had refused to listen. He'd kept it for years, just in case she returned.

Which was why I made no move to destroy it. It was one of the last things my father had from my mom and he took spectacular care of it—even if he now knew that she was never coming back.

I watched my dad head upstairs, then left a note for Kona and Rio telling them where we were going. When that was done, I settled down to wait for my dad. Sketching aimlessly on a piece of scrap paper, I worried about what my dad had said, poking at the words over and over again, even when I knew I should give it a rest. Like a little kid with a loose tooth, I just couldn't leave them alone.

I needed to live the life that was right for me, he'd said. Which sounded good in theory, until you realized that the more time I spent underwater, the less sure I became about which life I really wanted.

Glancing down at what I had drawn, I nearly winced.

Surfboards. Row after row of surfboards. Of course. They were a part of both worlds, spending most of their time on land but only serving their purpose when in the water.

Was that me? I wondered. Or was I looking at the first art I'd done in eight months and seeing only what I was most afraid of?

By the time my father rolled back into the kitchen, dressed in jeans and a T-shirt from his surfing company, I still hadn't found the answer.

∞

My dad and I sat by Moku's bed all morning, talking to him about anything and everything we could think of. My dad told him about the vacation he had planned for the three of them next month. They were going to Australia to visit Sergio, my dad's best friend and surfing buddy. Moku adored him, followed him around like a puppy dog whenever we saw him.

When even the mention of "Uncle" Sergio didn't rouse him, I decided to tell stories that focused on my underwater exploits. I told the best, most exciting ones I could come up with, but it didn't matter. He didn't stir, didn't squeeze my hand. Didn't so much as flutter his eyelashes.

At one point Rio texted my dad. He and Kona were coming by the hospital around two thirty to relieve us—not that I actually thought anything could do that, except Moku's full recovery. For the moment, however, I'd settle for a little of that peace of mind I'd tried to give to my father.

"I'm going to go stretch my legs for a few minutes," I told my dad before letting myself out of Moku's room.

I didn't know where I was going, only that I needed to move. It was hard to breathe in Moku's hospital room, or up here in Linda Vista at all. I was too far away from the beach, from the ocean, and I swear I could practically feel my skin drying out the longer I stayed here. Already the soft cotton of my jeans and T-shirt chafed painfully.

There was a garden area on nearly every floor, filled with flowers and trees and play equipment for the kids who got tired of sitting in their rooms all day. I found the one on this floor, spent a few minutes walking around it.

There was a little boy, no more than three, toddling back

and forth with a huge red four-square ball. His mom kept asking him to throw it to her, but he wouldn't let go. He just held on to it and ran around in circles as she laughed and tried to keep him from getting tangled up in his IV.

He charmed me with the mischievous smile he shot his mother every time she got a little exasperated with him. The way he held his hand up to her face and patted her cheeks. He was adorable, and I couldn't help wondering why he was in the hospital.

I ended up settling near the basketball hoop, a large, orange ball in my hands. I dribbled a little, made a couple baskets, but it wasn't exactly exciting to do it on my own. Still, I needed to move, to exercise. I'd spent the last eight months in an almost constant state of motion. Sitting around doing nothing for the last twenty-four hours actually physically hurt.

"I'll play you. Whoever gets to fifteen first, wins."

I turned around at the familiar voice, and there he was. Mark. My powers sparked to life inside me.

"I think I should get a handicap. You were MVP of the team two years in a row."

"Three," he said, his smile dimming a little as we both realized how much I'd missed.

"Right. Three. Congratulations."

He held out his hands for the ball. "I'll spot you three points."

"Four points. And I start." I whirled around, dribbled a couple of times, then threw the ball at the basket. It went straight in.

I whooped. "Did you see that, baby? Nothing but net."

"Should I rethink your handicap?" Mark asked, rebounding the ball and then dribbling it up the half court and back.

"Not on your life." I threw myself in his way and shoulder bumped him. It was a total foul, but he didn't call me on it. And he made the basket anyway.

I ran for the ball, tried to take it up the court, but he was right there, arms spread wide, body bumping against and tangling with mine.

I laughed. I couldn't help it. It was so much like the old days when we'd played—no rules, no called fouls, just a driving desire to win coupled with the joys of friendship and so much more.

I ducked around him, deliberately brushing my body against his the way I used to. It still worked like a charm. He stumbled, his beautiful brown eyes going dark and molten.

I ran down the court, but he was with me every step of the way, his arms caging me, his forearms brushing softly against my ribs.

My powers exploded through me, shocking me. I fumbled, dropped the ball, and he laughed, a low, wicked sound that sent chills up and down my spine. Then he picked up the ball and ran it back.

I cursed, took off after him, and this time it was I who twined myself around him, trying to reach the ball. My hands skimmed his sides, his lower back, his flat, well-muscled stomach as I attempted to pry the ball away from him. It wasn't working until I leaned forward to get that extra inch of reach, and pressed my breasts tight against his back.

It was his turn to fumble, to drop the ball, but when I reached for it, he grabbed on to my forearms, turned me until we were facing each other. I tried to duck my head, to look away, but he wouldn't let me. He followed, his eyes burning right through me.

It was one of the most intense moments of my life. Standing there in the empty garden, Mark's body inches from mine. A current of awareness rippling between us, dark, powerful, undeniable. And so overwhelming that I could feel it swamping me, pulling me under. Dragging me back to the way things had always been between us despite the distance of the last few months.

"What are you trying to do to me?" he demanded hoarsely. "Are you trying to drive me completely insane?"

"No. Of course not. I—"

"I see you *everywhere*. In the water, on the street, in the halls at school. Even when I know it isn't you, I still think, maybe . . ."

His hands tightened on my arms and he pulled me closer, until our faces were only an inch or two apart. "I see you every time I close my eyes. I dream about you, about what it was like when you were mine. That's the only time I'm happy anymore, those moments when I'm half-asleep, when you're right there, so real that I can practically touch you.

"And then I wake up and remember that you're gone, and it nearly kills me. Every goddamn morning, I get to relive losing you all over again."

"I'm so sorry, Mark. I'm so, so sorry." Tears were running down my face. I tried to stop them, but I couldn't. Not now, not with him.

"When I saw you in the water, I really thought I was going crazy. And I didn't even care if it meant I got to talk to you, to hold you. But you *were* real and you kissed me blind, then you just disappeared again, like it was nothing. Like we were nothing."

"No!"

"*Yes*. I went back every day at the same time and waited for you for hours, even after the good waves were gone. I was sure you'd come back, sure you couldn't just kiss me like that and leave again. But you did. If Moku hadn't gotten hurt, you never would have come back. I would have been out there waiting for you forever." He let me go so quickly that I stumbled. He caught me, steadied me, but then turned away, shoulders bowed, hands shoved into the pockets of his shorts.

"And then, when you finally do come back, you bring *him*. Kona." He all but snarled as he said the name. "Every time I think about the fact that I introduced you two eight months ago—"

"But you didn't."

"What?" He turned back to look at me.

"I'd met him before, a few days earlier. He came to our beach looking for me—that's when he met you."

His eyes narrowed. "The bastard."

"It's not like that. I mean, it's complicated."

"Why? Because you're a little different?"

"I'm more than a little different." I took a deep breath and then blurted, "I'm mermaid, Mark. That's a pretty big deal."

He didn't answer for a long time, and when he did speak it was in the quiet, musing tone he got when he was attempting to figure things out. "So I'm not crazy. That really was your tail."

"Yep. It really was." I studied him, tried to figure out how he felt about my not being completely human. For once he was hard to read, but it looked like he was taking it better than I'd ever imagined.

Finally, I just asked him. "Does it bother you?"

"What? Your tail?"

"Yes! No, I mean, not just the tail. The fact that I'm mermaid. That I'm not like you and I never will be."

"I don't know."

"Mark."

"I'm serious. I really don't think so. It doesn't feel like it bothers me, but then I wonder, shouldn't it? Maybe I'm not that freaked out because I always knew you were hiding something big."

"What do you mean?"

"You think I didn't notice how cold you always were, except in the water? How you never needed a wet suit? I was out there the day you nearly drowned, Tempest. I saw your legs just collapse beneath you. Shit, I even saw you turn purple. It's hard to ignore the whole glowing thing. Or the mystical tattoos that just showed up on your back, no redness, no irritation, nothing."

"You didn't—" My voice failed and I had to start again. "You didn't care?"

"The only thing I ever cared about was you. I kept trying to get you to talk to me, kept trying to show you that it was okay. I even gave you that mermaid necklace for your birthday, thinking it would say what I couldn't. But you practically threw it back in my face."

"I didn't—I thought—" Shit, I kept stumbling over myself. Why were the right words so hard to find? "It was supposed to be a secret."

"And you didn't trust me enough to keep it?" He looked incredulous. "We've been best friends forever, Tempest. Even when we weren't dating."

"I know, I know. It's just . . . I could barely handle what was happening to me, and I'd always known about mermaids. How could I expect you to handle it too?"

"You could have at least given me a chance."

"Maybe I would have if you hadn't dumped me for a cheer-leader."

"Really? I dumped you? You're the one who came to me that day at my house."

"Do you not remember Chelsea? Everyone knew there was something between you."

"I did that for you."

I laughed incredulously. "Yeah, right. Because what girl doesn't want to lose her boyfriend to the captain of the cheer squad?"

"You were already gone! You think I didn't know there was someone else? You think I didn't know that you didn't love me anymore? She was nothing. Window dressing. Saving face. Whatever you want to call it. I knew you felt too guilty to end things, so I helped you do it."

The shock of his words reverberated through me, like cymbals crashing too close to my ears. "You're not still with her?" The words fell out of my mouth before I even had a clue I was going to say them.

"I was never *with* her. We went on a couple of dates, then broke up—or whatever you want to call it—a few days after you disap-peared. I love *you*, Tempest. I've always loved you."

PART FOUR

Run-Up

"The winds and waves are always on the side of the ablest navigators."

—EDWARD GIBBON

Chapter 22

Fifteen minutes later, I was still reeling from Mark's revelation.

He *still* loved me?

After all this time?

After I'd run away with another guy?

After I'd confessed that I was mermaid?

He loved me even then?

It boggled the mind, not to mention the heart. My heart.

I didn't know what to say to him, or how to act now that he'd admitted he never cared about Chelsea. It shouldn't matter, I knew it shouldn't, but somehow it did. Which was ridiculous, because I loved Kona. But I loved Mark too, and always had.

Closing my eyes, I barely resisted the urge to bang my head against the nearest wall. Maybe a concussion would make this whole thing easier to understand.

"So, are you going to say something?" Mark asked as he handed me a Dr Pepper from the vending machine. Which was one of the coolest, and easiest, things about being with him—he knew all of my likes and dislikes, my favorites and my no-way-in-hells.

Kona was still learning, trying to figure me out, but with Mark everything just fell neatly into place. Like the way he knew I loved Dr Pepper, blue M&Ms, and reading French existentialists. That I liked putting together gigantic puzzles with really small pieces and collecting obscure red sea glass, but that I wouldn't touch anything that tasted like root beer, contained peanut butter, or in any way resembled reality TV.

Mark had held my hand through all eight Harry Potter movies and hadn't laughed when I cried at least twice in every single one.

It used to make me uncomfortable that my boyfriend knew so much about me (except, of course, for the really big thing that I hadn't been able to tell him). Now that he wasn't my boyfriend anymore—and it turned out he already knew about the really big thing and didn't think it mattered—it felt different to be understood so well.

It felt good.

Comforting.

Like I couldn't disappoint him, no matter how hard I tried.

With Kona, I always felt like I was trying to live up to who he wanted and needed me to be, but with Mark I could just be who I really was. Teenage girl, mermaid, friend, surfer, human. With him, there was no pressure to save the world, which—after the week I'd had—definitely did not feel like such a bad thing.

"I don't know what to say," I finally admitted. It was a crappy answer to his declaration, but the best I could come up with, since my brain had soared into overload.

"You could start with how you feel about me."

"It's not that easy, Mark."

"Sure it is. Either you love me or you don't."

"That's not true. I do love you—of course I do—but that doesn't mean anything is going to change, or even that it *can* change. My life is so mixed up right now—between how crazy things are at the place I've been living for the last eight months and dealing with Moku—"

"I'm sorry." For the first time since I'd seen him today, Mark looked ashamed. "I shouldn't be pressuring you. How is Moku?"

"He's the same—and I can take the pressure. I just don't want to make any decisions right now because I'm afraid I won't think them through."

"I don't want you confusing what happened with Moku with how you feel about me. Which is why I shouldn't even have brought this up right now. It's just, when your dad said you'd gone for a walk, I couldn't stop myself from looking for you. I told myself it was just to make sure you were okay, not because I wanted to push you into something you aren't ready for. Yet here I am, doing just that." He blew out a frustrated breath. "Nothing like an ex-boyfriend pledging his undying love to put a damper on the mood, huh?"

"That's not what I was saying."

"I know. I just feel like an idiot. I could have timed this better, at least waited until Moku got out of the hospital."

Right then I fell a little bit harder for him. His certainty that Moku would recover was exactly what I needed to hear.

"But then you'll be gone, right? Disappearing into the sunset with Kona all over again."

I was a little surprised he'd brought up Kona—especially without so much as a flash of the jealousy I was used to from him. I didn't want to upset Mark, but at the same time, I wasn't going to lie to him. Not ever again. "We'll stick around for a while, make sure Moku's doing okay."

"So, you're definitely planning on staying with him then." Suddenly, he was concentrating really hard on tearing into the pack of M&Ms he'd bought. When it was open, he fished around for a few seconds, then handed me five blue ones.

"Yes." Why did it suddenly make me so uncomfortable to admit that?

He nodded, then turned his head so I couldn't see his eyes. "So, is he, like, a mermaid too?"

"They're called mermen but no, he isn't. He's a selkie."

"A selkie?" Mark turned back to me, a confused look on his face. "You mean one of those seal things from Irish legends?"

"It's a little more complicated than that, but yeah. One of those seal things."

"They're real?"

"You'd be surprised what I've run into under the surface. Legends are filled with real creatures—at least the ones in the sea, anyway."

"Huh." He shook a bunch of M&Ms into his palm and then tossed them absently into his mouth.

"What?"

"Nothing. It's just weird."

"Finding out some fairy tales are real?"

"Being dumped for an actual animal. It's never happened to me before."

I laughed. I couldn't help it—he looked so disgruntled, so annoyed. "Yeah, well, I've never been dumped for a cheerleader before, so I guess that makes us even."

"We already went over that. I didn't dump you."

"Yeah, well, I didn't actually dump you either."

"Oh yeah?" The smile was back, that sweet, happy grin I'd fallen hard for before we ever left junior high. "So does that mean we're still together, then? I mean, if no one got dumped . . ."

"Mark."

"What? I'm just asking what it means." He scooted closer, brushed a stray curl out of my face.

"It means—" There were a million different things I wanted to say, a million different ways I wanted to say them. But in the end, nothing sounded just right. Not now, when Moku was in the hospital. Not when I was still mermaid. And definitely not when I'd spent most of the night lying next to Kona, watching over him while he slept.

This weird triangle thing was giving the word *complicated* a whole new meaning.

In the end I settled for generic, and a little lame. "It means I need to go. I wanted to just try and breathe for a few minutes, and I've been gone almost forty-five." It might be a crappy answer, but it was also the truth. At least partially. I did want to get back to Moku, was worried about staying away from him too long.

It wasn't the only answer, though. I was confused, really confused. I loved Mark, but I was afraid it wasn't enough. Not if that love needed to survive long separations that involved me growing a tail and helping to rule a mermaid clan. I also loved Kona—sometimes I was convinced I loved him too much. That

I was going to lose myself inside of him until one day the person I've always been just ceased to exist.

Even worse, I felt trapped. Not just between two guys, but between two worlds. And it wasn't like I could have both. That was the one thing I was certain of in this whole situation. Well, that and the fact that I couldn't—wouldn't—play one guy against another while I tried to decide where I best fit. Not this time. Both Mark and Kona deserved so much more than that.

Mark's smile dimmed as he reluctantly pulled away. "Right. Moku. That's why you're here, after all." He stood up, reached out a hand to pull me to my feet. For the first time, I realized it no longer hurt when he touched me. Not like it had before I'd become mermaid, which was strange because my skin still felt sensitive when it touched anything—or anyone—else on land. "Sorry, Tempest."

"Don't be stupid." I punched him lightly on the arm, trying to keep things on some sort of even keel. "It's my fault. But I can't think, can't breathe, when Moku's like this. After he wakes up—"

"I know. Totally my fault. Let's get you back to the CCU."

For the first time, the silence between us was a little awkward. As we walked back down the winding hallway to Moku's room, I racked my brain for something to say, but I couldn't think of anything. Instead, my brain was flashing a warning at me in blinking neon letters. D.A.N.G.E.R.

I knew it, understood it, and still couldn't bring myself to push Mark away for good. Besides, which part of my life *wasn't* dangerous these days?

When we got back to the Critical Care Unit, Kona was standing to the side of the double doors, his hands shoved deep into the pockets of his borrowed shorts. He was still, looked completely tranquil, but I could sense the storm raging deep inside of him. He was obviously still suffering from the sadness and anger of the night before. And when he caught sight of me walking with Mark, his beautiful silver eyes clouded over completely. He didn't say a word, didn't take one step toward me, but then he didn't have to. I could sense his hurt and confusion as clearly as I had sensed Mark's in the weeks before I chose the sea.

"Tempest."

I glanced up, found Mark staring at me with the intense look he usually reserved only for catching really monster waves. "I know this isn't the right time. I know he's over there waiting for you, but I can't leave until I say this."

He paused, seemed to gather up his courage. Then, when my nerves were at their breaking point, he softly whispered, "In my head, you've always been my girl. No matter what happened between us, no matter how many times we broke up, no matter what I told myself about letting you go, I've never been able to think about you any other way than as the girl I love, the girl I want to be with—even if you are with him. You're it for me, Tempest. You always have been and I'm pretty sure you always will be. I love you."

He didn't give me time to answer. He just leaned forward and brushed a sweet, tender kiss across my cheek before he turned to walk away.

I watched him go and as I did, my foolish, fickle heart—already so shaky and confused—cracked right down the center.

⚭

Kona was pissed. Really pissed. I could tell by the way he looked at me—or wouldn't look at me, to be more specific. Not that I blamed him. If he'd heard what Mark said, which I was sure he had despite Mark's whispers, he probably felt like punching his hand through another mirror. Or worse, straight into Mark's face.

"Hey, how are you doing?" I asked, softly rubbing my fingers over his battered knuckles.

"Not so great." He didn't even glance my way as we walked to the car. It was ten o'clock and visiting hours were long over. My dad had left at eight to take Rio to a friend's house, and I had stayed as long as they would let me, trying to fly under the radar. It had worked for a while, but eventually Moku's nurse told me I needed to go.

Kona had been waiting in the visitor's lounge. Silent, uncommunicative, angry, but definitely waiting. That had to count for something. Didn't it?

We finally got to the car, and after he'd slid behind the wheel, I said, "Sorry it took me so long to come out. It's just hard to leave him."

Kona muttered something under his breath.

"I can't hear you," I told him.

He didn't answer.

"Kona?" I prompted. I didn't know why I was pushing it—whatever he'd said obviously hadn't been good—but then again, I deserved it. And if we didn't talk about his suspicions, if we just slipped them under the rug, they were going to grow and grow until everything turned ugly.

"I said, it doesn't look like Moku is the only one you're having trouble leaving."

And there it was. The sore that was festering between us. "We were just talking, Kona. Nothing happened."

"If by talking, you mean he was pledging his undying love for you, then yes, you were just talking."

"It wasn't like that—" I stopped, because I didn't know what to say to make this okay, for either of us.

"He told you he loved you and called you his girl, like you were some kind of property for him to own. It was exactly like that." He slammed the car into a lower gear, took a corner much faster than the speed limit allowed.

"And you just stood there and let him talk," Kona continued. "You didn't even bother to tell him we were together!"

"He knows we're together! He knew you were waiting for me—or didn't you hear that part of the conversation?"

"Oh, I heard it. I heard everything and I didn't once hear you telling him to back off." He glanced at me as he took another turn too quickly.

"I'd already told him that I couldn't be with him—before we came inside."

"Is that what you said? That you *couldn't* be with him—not that you didn't *want* to be with him? No wonder he didn't back off. I wouldn't either, not when it seems obvious that you don't know *what* you want."

"I love you, Kona!" I reached for him, tried to hold his hand as we zipped onto the freeway.

"Maybe you do—"

"Maybe? You know I do!" Dread crawled through me, an overwhelming feeling that my entire life was spinning out of my control.

He screeched to a stop in my driveway, slammed out of the car, and headed toward the beach without a backward glance.

"Where are you going?" I demanded, scrambling after him.

"Don't follow me."

"Kona! Stop! Please. Where are you going?" I grabbed on to his arm, but he shook me off.

"I need to be alone for a while, Tempest."

"We can work this out—"

He whirled to face me, even as he whipped his shirt over his head. "How can we work it out?" he demanded furiously. "You're in love with someone else!"

"But I love you too! I do, Kona. I really do!"

He froze then, a stricken look on his face, and I realized I had confirmed all of his fears.

"I didn't mean that," I whispered.

"Yes, you did."

And then he was running for the water, moving so quickly that his form blurred, blending into the darkness of the night.

Chapter 23

Three days later, I was still sitting by Moku's bed, willing him to wake up. The minutes were creeping by slowly, and while part of me wanted them to speed up, to pass in a blur that kept me from thinking about the shambles my life was in, the other part of me was grateful. If time kept going slowly, it meant that Moku hadn't been in a coma as long as it seemed. It meant that there was still a decent chance that he would wake up. We hadn't reached the week mark yet—the doctors still talked about him opening his eyes as if it were a real possibility. But they visited less, showing up only once a day instead of two or three times like they had when I first got there.

The door opened and I didn't bother to turn around, figuring it was the nurse coming to do her hourly check on Moku's vitals. My dad had just left a few minutes before to take a walk, and I wasn't expecting anyone else. Rio was still being an ass, refusing to talk to me or come to the hospital to see Moku while I was there.

"I brought you some lunch."

I whirled at the sound of Mark's voice, my powers once again going nuts at his proximity. He was standing by the door, a vanilla milk shake from In-N-Out Burger in one hand and a small bag in the other. It was the first time I'd seen him since he'd told me he loved me.

"I, umm, I'm not hungry."

"You never are when you're stressed. But you need to eat." He pulled the rolling table over, set out a cheeseburger and fries. "I almost went for something healthy but figured this might tempt you more."

"You've been avoiding me." They weren't the words I'd been meaning to say, but once they were out, I didn't regret them.

He shook his head. "I was giving you time. You've got a lot going on right now."

"Yeah, well, I don't think that's going to change anytime soon."

"Moku will be fine, Tempest."

"I know," I said, just in case my little brother could hear me. But I wasn't feeling very optimistic. I'd done everything I could think of to bring him around and nothing was working. I didn't want to lose hope, but it was hard. I was terrified of losing him. Couldn't imagine what the world would be like if I had to live in it, forever, without his sunny smile.

"Look at me," Mark said, squatting down so I had no choice but to look into his eyes. "Repeat after me. Moku is going to wake up."

"Mark—"

"Say it!"

I sighed. "Moku is going to wake up."

"Wow, that was impressive. Could you try saying it like you mean it next time?"

"This is stupid."

"No, it's necessary. I think you need to remind yourself that someday soon this is all going to be just a bad memory. You and Moku will be back on the beach, swimming and trying to escape from imaginary sharks, and you won't even remember how discouraged you feel right now."

He took my hand, brushed his lips over the center of my palm, then curled my fingers inward. "Go ahead. Say it like you mean it."

"Moku is going to be okay."

"I can't hear you."

"Moku is going to be okay!"

He smiled. "One more time. So that it really sinks in."

I practically shouted the words and was shocked at how good it felt to say them with such assurance. There was something about the total confidence in the statement, delivered so loudly, that gave me back the hope I had started to lose.

"Thank you," I said, giving him my first real smile in days.

"You're welcome." He handed me the milk shake. "Drink up."

I took a long sip, then whispered, "I missed you. When I was gone, I missed you like crazy."

His shoulders slumped on a huge exhale and his eyes closed for one second, two. "I've waited almost nine months to hear you say that."

"It doesn't mean—"

"Shhh." He tapped two fingers against my lip. "Let me savor the admission for a few seconds, okay?"

I laughed. I couldn't help myself.

We sat there for a while, not talking. Both of us lost in our own thoughts. I drank my milk shake and ate a few of the french fries before sliding the burger over to Mark. He looked like he was going to argue, but in the end, he just shrugged and took a big bite. I guess he was enjoying the peace as much as I was.

I'm not sure how long we sat there, but I slowly became aware of someone trying to reach me. I could hear a voice, faint, echoing, in the back of my head, like it was coming from a long distance and I wasn't quite on the right frequency.

At first, I tried to ignore it. Since Kona had disappeared without a trace, I figured the only person who had enough power to reach me this far away was Hailana. And I didn't want to talk to her—or listen to all the ways I wasn't as good as my mother because I had chosen to be here for my family instead of training with my clan.

But whoever it was seemed insistent, and eventually I dropped my guard, let him or her in.

Tempest? Kona sounded far away and more than a little annoyed.

Kona? Where are you?

I'm with Zarek. I went to him to see if he could help heal Moku.

Excitement thrummed through me. Why hadn't I thought of that? *Can he?*

He doesn't know, since Moku is still completely human. But he's willing to try. We're on our way—as long as it's okay with your dad.

I'll make sure it is, I told him. *Thank you, thank you, thank you.*

Don't get too excited, Kona warned. *We don't know if he'll be able to help.*

Still. It's something more than sitting around and waiting to see what happens. I'll never be able to thank you for thinking of it.

I've never wanted your gratitude, Tempest.

There was an awkward pause as we both thought about what he did want. I glanced at Mark, who was looking at me strangely, almost as if he could sense that something was going on.

I turned my head so I wouldn't have to look at him while I communicated with Kona—the combination completely freaked me out. *When are you going to be here?* I asked. *I want to let my dad know so that he can meet Zarek.*

We're moving fast, so probably three or four hours.

I'll make sure we're ready.

Okay. He paused, like there was something else he wanted to say.

What is it, Kona?

Nothing. I guess I'll talk to you when we get there.

Be careful. Tiamat's been awfully quiet the last few days.

He didn't answer.

Kona? I said sharply. *Are you still there? What's wrong? What happened?*

Everything's fine. I have to go now.

And then he was gone, and I was left torn between excitement and dread. It would be amazing if Zarek could help Moku, could wake him up. I was frantic to see his eyes open, frantic to hear his voice tell me about all the things I'd missed. But at the back of my head were two questions that I just couldn't ignore.

What would I do if Zarek couldn't help my brother?

And what was Kona being so secretive about?

∞

Four and a half hours later, I stood on the right side of Moku's bed, holding my little brother's limp hand. My dad and Rio stood to the left of me, and opposite us were Kona and Zarek. We'd managed to get all of us into the CCU together for a few minutes—a very few minutes—by explaining that Zarek was a spiritual leader in our church. It was a stretch, especially for a man covered in forest-green tattoos who also sported three earrings and a number of other piercings, but the nurse didn't hassle us too much, as we'd been pretty good about obeying the rules the rest of the time.

Which was a very good thing, because my father had made it crystal clear that Zarek was not getting near Moku without him being there. I tried to explain that Zarek had saved my life less than two weeks before, but that had been a mistake. What I'd hoped would be reassuring had only ended up stressing my dad out more.

"What are you going to do to him?" Rio asked Zarek belligerently. "You better not turn him into a freak, like the rest of you." His contemptuous look raked over Kona, Zarek, and me.

"Rio!" my dad barked, looking angrier than I had seen him in a long time. "Keep your mouth shut or get out."

Rio folded his arms across his chest and glared at my dad, but he made no move to leave. Which was good. If this worked, Moku was going to want to see him there.

That's all that mattered, I told myself as I shoved the hurt his words caused deep inside myself. Rio wasn't trying to be a jerk—well, he was, but only because he was so hurt and angry himself. I couldn't take what he said seriously and hoped Zarek and Kona didn't either.

"What are you going to do?" my father asked. "Will it hurt him?"

"No." Zarek's voice was calm, confident, and I felt my own

nerves settling at his obvious assurance. "I'm just going to check him over, see if I can find anything inside him that needs healing."

"How are you going to do that?" my dad asked, but Zarek was already in the zone. Eyes closed, body swaying, hands hovering an inch or two above Moku's stomach, he looked like every bad-movie version of a charlatan. I could feel the suspicion emanating from my father and knew that the only reason he was giving this a try was because I had been so insistent.

Still, he was poised and ready to yank Zarek away from Moku at the first provocation. It wouldn't do any good, since Zarek, in essence, arrowed his energy straight into Moku. But I didn't tell my dad that. Some things he was better off not knowing.

The next ten minutes passed in tense silence as Zarek did just that—propelling his entire consciousness deep into my brother's body so that he could heal his injuries from the inside out. I think the only thing that kept my father standing there as Zarek grew completely unresponsive, was the fact that we could actually see small things healing on my brother.

The cuts on his right arm gradually faded and then disappeared. The same with a bruise on his jaw and a scrape along his temple.

"He's really doing it," my father whispered in awe. And Zarek was—slowly but surely healing every wound my brother had, leaving only slightly pink scars behind.

Then Zarek's breathing shifted, grew more intense, like he was expending a lot of energy though he hadn't moved at all. A light sheen of sweat coated his face and the hands he still held extended over Moku began to shake.

Is he okay? I asked Kona silently.

This is what a selkie healing looks like, especially if someone's been— He stopped abruptly.

Been what? I demanded. *Just tell me.*

If someone's been gravely injured.

So Moku really is in that bad of shape? He wouldn't have woken up without Zarek?

I don't know; I'm not a healer.

I bit my lip, struggling to keep my breathing even. *I'm scared, Kona. I'm really scared.*

I know you are, baby. He walked around the bed until he was standing behind me. Then he slid an arm around my waist and pulled me back against the comforting warmth of his body. *"It'll be okay,"* he whispered in my ear and in my head at the same time. *"If anyone can help him, Zarek can."*

I just want him to be okay. I need *him to be okay.* I buried my face against Kona's chest, breathed in the sweet, salty smell that was a combination of the water he loved and the sunlight that danced across the waves.

He stiffened a little, and I froze, hating this new awkwardness between us. Then his hand came up, rested on the back of my head as his fingers absently sorted through my curls. *Just a little longer,* he told me. *Let Zarek work a few more minutes.*

It was more like forty than a few, but eventually Zarek lowered his arms and opened his eyes. He was sweating profusely and the shaking had spread to his entire body. I reached out a hand, grabbed him seconds before he fell.

"Are you okay?" I demanded.

"Just drained," he told me. "I'll be fine after I sleep."

"And Moku?" my father asked. "How is he?"

Zarek started to answer, but at that moment one of the monitors attached to Moku's chest started to beep.

"What is that?" I asked, panicked.

Kona pulled away, turned me to face the bed where Moku lay. And that's when I saw it. His eyelashes fluttered briefy.

"Moku?" I called, clutching his hand excitedly in both of mine. "Moku, it's Tempest. Can you hear me?"

He didn't answer.

"Moku, please come back to me. To us."

"Come on, Moku. We miss you." My dad added his own hoarse entreaty to mine.

Our pleas must have gotten through, because the limp little fingers laying so passively in my hand suddenly squeezed mine. A smile stretched across his little face. And the monitors, all around him, went crazy.

"Moku?" my dad asked, leaping forward to grab his other hand just as my baby brother opened his eyes.

Chapter 24

"Tempest?"

"Yes, baby?" I leaned over and smoothed Moku's hair back from his face. It was the middle of the night and he was having trouble sleeping, drifting in and out of awareness.

After he'd woken up from the coma yesterday, the doctors had run about a billion tests. They were all shocked at Moku's incredible recovery. When all the results came back, Moku was pronounced healthy, yet they hadn't been quite ready to release him, seeing as how he'd been in a coma many of them had begun to consider unrecoverable.

So he'd been downgraded, put in a regular hospital room for forty-eight hours, and if he had no relapses, we would be able to take him home. We were about thirty-six hours into that forty-eight-hour stretch and I'm not sure which one of us was more anxious. My dad had wanted to send me home and spend the night himself, but from the moment he'd woken up, Moku had not wanted me out of his sight.

Which was okay with me, as I felt exactly the same way.

We'd played games, eaten pizza and ice cream delivered by Mark, played a new Pokémon game (also from Mark) on Moku's DS, watched enough TV to burn my retinas, and basically had as good a time together as we could manage with him in a hospital bed. The nurses had even let me take him out to play basketball a little bit this evening. I'd hoped it would tire him out enough that he could sleep, but he kept having nightmares. Whether from the MRI and all the other tests they'd run or from his near-drowning experience, I didn't know.

"Are you going to leave again?" he asked, his voice tinier than I had ever heard it.

"No, sweetie. I'm not leaving this room until you get to come home with me."

"That's not what I meant."

"Oh. Right." I sighed. "I don't know how long I'm going to stay, Moku."

"So you *are* leaving again?"

"Eventually, yes."

His lower lip poked out just a little and tears filled his eyes. He tried to blink them back, but that only made me feel worse.

"Don't go. Please. Everything's awful when you're not here."

As I reached for his hand, guilt was a suffocating weight on my chest, pressing down a little harder with each tear that rolled slowly down his cheeks.

"Oh, baby, I wish I could stay forever."

"Why don't you? No one is making you be mermaid."

I laid my head down on the bed next to him, tried to think of a way to explain things so that he would understand. Which was pretty much impossible, as half the time *I* didn't even understand the life I was living or the choices I had made.

"You're right," I finally told him. "No one made me be mermaid. But that doesn't mean that people don't need me or depend on me now that I am. If I stay here, who's going to help them?"

"If you leave, who's going to help me do my homework? I'm going to have really hard homework this year because I'm in third grade. Dad's always busy and Rio's mad all the time. He says really mean things and if you don't stay, he's going to think all those things are true."

"Baby, Rio's just upset at the world right now," I said, and while it was true, I still had an overwhelming urge to kick Rio's ass. He could be as big a jerk to me as he wanted, but he needed to lay off Moku. It made me sad to realize things between them were worse than ever.

"No, he's just mad at you. I don't want him to be mad at you anymore."

"Moku, sweetie, it's not that easy. Even if I came back for good, things would be different than they used to be."

"They don't have to!"

How sick was it that even as I was trying to convince Moku that I couldn't go back, not really, I was halfway wishing I could? My life would be a million times easier if I didn't know about Tiamat or Hailana or my mother's relationship with both of them. If I'd never heard of that stupid prophecy or learned of the power I could wield.

The idea wasn't a revelation to me, but for the first time since I became mermaid I really thought about it. If I could change everything—if I could wave a magic wand and have everything about these last eight and a half months disappear—would I?

Would I give up being mermaid?

Give up knowing what really happened to my mother?

Give up Kona?

If it meant keeping my family safe and together, would I really be willing to give up all the good things that I'd gained?

It was the million-dollar question—one I didn't have an answer to. Not now. Not anymore.

Before I could say anything else to Moku, there was a knock on the door and I grabbed on to it like the lifeline it was. "Come in!" I called brightly, rushing over in case the nurse decided to come back later. The last thing I needed right now was to be left alone with Moku and more of his questions—if things kept going at the rate they were, I'd end up a basket case before the night was done.

But it wasn't the night nurse on the other side of the door. It was Kona.

"What are you doing here?" I hissed as I urged him inside. "You'll get us in trouble—no visitors after eleven o'clock!"

"You're here," he said casually.

"Because I'm spending the night. But everyone else had to go home, even my dad. Only one person is allowed to be here after visiting hours!"

"Come on, let me stay. I promise I'll hide when the nurse comes to do his vitals." He flashed his crooked grin and I was lost—he knew it too. With a rub of my arm, he squeezed through the partially open doorway and headed straight for Moku.

"Kona!" Moku said, nearly bouncing out of bed. He'd

decided Kona was okay earlier in the day when he'd brought him the world's biggest ice cream sundae. "Did you get ice cream?"

Kona laughed, warm and deep and real. "No, no ice cream. But I did bring this." He held up a bag from the local bookstore.

Moku's enthusiasm visibly waned. He had dyslexia, so reading had always been a problem for him. "Oh. Thanks."

"Go ahead and open it—it's not what you think."

Warily, Moku opened the bag, then squealed when he saw a sketchbook, colored pens and markers, and three how-to drawing books. One was on sharks and other ocean creatures, another was on dinosaurs, and the third was favorite cartoon characters.

Moku was in heaven—my little brother loved to draw even more than I did. He opened the shark book and dived right in, drawing a pretty good rendition of a huge hammerhead shark.

"How did you know he liked to draw?" I murmured to Kona.

"I've seen your artwork, and Cecily's. So I took a shot."

He pulled the second chair in the room over to where I was sitting, then, once settled, wrapped his arm around my shoulders. I sank into him, grateful some of the tension between us had dissipated in the last couple of days.

"I missed you," he said softly, his fingers playing through the tips of my hair where it met my shoulders.

"Me too." I kissed his cheek before laying my head on his shoulder. "Thank you for getting Zarek."

"You don't need to thank me for that."

"I'm indebted to you. I always will be."

"Why?"

I stared at him incredulously. "You saved Moku. How can I ever repay that?"

"You needed help and I tried to help you. That's all. I thought that was what you were supposed to do when you loved someone."

And there it was. The six-ton killer whale in the room. "It is," I told him. "But not everyone is willing to swim two days through treacherous waters to do that, especially when they're angry. So thank you."

"Will you stop it? You make it sound like you're about to dump me."

I rolled my eyes. "Seriously? That's what you got out of that?"

"I don't know anymore."

His silver eyes were dull, and more than a little bit nervous as he looked at me. But before I could say anything else, Moku crowed, "Look at this!" and held up his finished drawing.

"It looks fantastic!" I told him. "Good job."

Kona echoed my sentiments; then we both watched, bemused, as Moku tore a piece of paper out of his sketch book and started folding it industriously.

"What are you making?" I asked after a minute of watching him fold the first top of the paper into triangles.

Both Kona and Moku looked at me like I'd grown another head. "A paper airplane!" they exclaimed at the same time, then grinned at each other.

"Obviously," Moku continued, making a few more folds that finally turned the paper into a recognizable form. But when he pulled back his arm and sent it soaring, it crashed straight into the ground.

His shoulders slumped. "They always do that," he mumbled to himself.

"That's because you're too tip heavy," Kona said. "Give me a sheet of paper and I'll show you how it's done."

"You know how to make paper airplanes?" It was my turn to stare at him incredulously.

He looked down his nose at me in what I had come to think of as his princely look. "I'm a guy, aren't I?"

"You're a two-hundred-year-old underwater prince!"

"Which is why I've had over fifty years to perfect the technique. Watch and learn, sweet Tempest. Watch and learn."

"Excuse me, but I am quite the paper airplane designer myself, you know."

"Really?" he asked, one eyebrow raised. "Well then, let's have a competition, shall we? I'll show Moku how to make my airplane and then you can show him how to make yours and we'll see which one goes farther."

It was a challenge, pure and simple, a toss of the gauntlet that Kona knew I would never be able to resist. "Fine. You're on."

"Awesome!" crowed Moku as he ripped more paper from the sketchbook. "Show me how to keep it from crashing to the floor, Kona!"

"Oh, I see how you are," I teased him, pretending to be miffed. "No loyalty at all."

"Aww, don't be mad, Tempest. It's just that Kona's a guy and guys are better at stuff like this."

My eyes widened and I stared at him, mouth open, for long seconds. Kona choked on a laugh, then became incredibly absorbed in the pattern of the wallpaper. "That is completely sexist!" I told Moku indignantly. "Not to mention ridiculous! Who's been telling you that stuff while I've been gone?" I knew it wasn't my dad, who'd spent my entire life telling me I could do anything I put my mind to.

"Rio said—"

"Oh, really? Rio said? It seems that pipsqueak has had a lot to say these days, hasn't he?" I took one of the pieces of paper determinedly. "I'll show you how to build the world's best airplane."

Kona snorted and muttered something under his breath that sounded an awful lot like "Good luck!" Which, of course, only annoyed me more.

The next few minutes were spent aligning, calibrating, folding, and refolding, until finally there were four airplanes—one made by Kona, one from me, and then the two done by Moku as we taught him how to make the planes.

I was honest enough to admit that Kona's looked more elegant than mine, not to mention flashier. But I'd been doing my design for years and was confident in its ability to kick Kona's pretty little plane's butt.

The rules were simple. Whichever two of the four planes went farthest would have a fly-off and whoever won the fly-off would have bragging rights for life.

"Are you ready?" I asked when we were all lined up against the back wall of Moku's room, planes at the ready.

"Yes!" crowed Moku, who was so excited he was practically jumping up and down. "Let's do this!"

"All right, then." Kona winked at me over my brother's head. "Count us down, man."

"Three, two, one, go!" We let the planes rip.

Kona's flew the fastest, but it crashed and burned before

reaching the halfway point of the room. Mine went the far-thest, followed by Moku's version of Kona's plane.

Moku retrieved the airplanes, then counted us down for the fly-off. And then bragged hugely as his plane soared all the way to the opposite wall.

"Design will tell," Kona said with a smug grin.

"Give me a break," I answered. "Your design failed miserably."

"Excuse me? I believe my design just kicked your plane's butt, thank you very much."

"That was execution from the aerospace engineer over there," I said, nodding to Moku, who was yawning sleepily as he climbed into bed.

"That's not true, Tempe. Kona helped a lot." Moku was noth-ing if not loyal.

"Thanks, man." Kona ruffled his hair and I bent to give my brother a kiss on the cheek.

"Go to bed," I told him. "If you're in good shape tomorrow, the doctor is going to let us take you home."

"He better let me go home. I'm sick of this stupid old hospital."

"I know, baby." I turned off the lamp near his bed so that only the dim light from the bathroom remained. Then started to unfold my chair into a bed.

"I should probably get going," Kona said, sounding as awk-ward and unhappy at the prospect as I was. That he'd taken the time, and energy, to do all this for my brother, reminded me of why I'd fallen in love with him to begin with.

He was brave and strong, and yet so considerate that it made everything inside of me melt, turn gooey. He was a prince, heir to the throne, and could have let that privilege turn him into a totally different person, one who would never consider flying planes with a sick little boy well after midnight.

"You can stay for a while," I told him. "I mean, if you want. This bed isn't the most comfortable, but if we squeeze you could lie down on it with me." I pulled a sheet out of the closet, draped it over the cushions.

"I could probably do that." Kona smiled and my heart squeezed just a little, like it always did when he looked at me like that.

In the end, he stretched out on the makeshift bed and I cuddled up against him, my head pillowed on his bicep and my hand resting on his stomach. I loved being near him like this, soaking up the delicious warmth that emanated from his every pore. Especially here on land, when I was always freezing, no matter how much clothing I had on or how hot it was outside.

We lay there like that for a while, long after Moku had fallen asleep, and I didn't want the night to end. I knew that everything was changing, that soon nothing would be as it once was. I didn't know exactly where the feeling was coming from, but it was there, deep inside me. A strange vibration that warned me something big was coming, something different and life altering and previously unknown.

"I have to leave soon," Kona said, and I rolled to my side, pressed my mouth to his. I didn't want to go there yet. Not now, when I was trying so desperately to find a way to fit the two halves of my life together.

He kissed me back, but it was a different kiss than I was used to. Softer, sweeter. The heat was still there, of course, but as Kona's lips moved over mine, no fireworks burst behind my eyes. No dynamite was ignited. Instead, it was a slow, steady burn that had my heart beating heavily but not racing, my body melting instead of exploding.

I wrapped my arms around him, buried my face in his neck, and held on tight, praying that this wasn't it. That he wasn't saying good-bye to me, not now when I couldn't imagine a life he wasn't a part of.

Moku snuffle-snored a little in his sleep and Kona reluctantly pulled away. As his lips relinquished mine, I remembered where we were and flushed in embarrassment. Nothing like losing myself in a kiss when my hurt brother lay just a few feet away.

"Why do you have to go? Can't you stay a little longer?"

He pulled me closer and I buried my face in his neck, breathed in Kona's unique scent. I barely resisted the urge to beg.

"Things are getting worse. Tiamat's raised an army and they attacked another clan."

"Not Coral Straits!" I said, panic fluttering in my throat. Was this what he'd been hiding from me, what he hadn't wanted to tell me?

"No. A selkie clan this time, which was why it was so hard for me to find Zarek and get him back here. The clan has called on my family for help, and we need to be there for them. We've been allies for hundreds of years."

Guilt assailed me. Kona had dragged Zarek away from people who really needed him when it was his job to help them. If times were normal, I'm sure he would have come willingly. But something told me that to get Zarek here Kona had been forced to play the role of future selkie king to the hilt.

I felt sick at the thought of selkies who might have—probably did—die while Zarek was swimming here. Felt even more sick at the thought of staying on land when so much was happening under the ocean. At the same time, though, just the thought of leaving Moku right now had fear racing through me. Basically, I felt damned if I did and damned if I didn't.

"I need to come with you," I said. It wasn't a question, but I wanted it to be.

"You need to be here for your brother." He rolled over, tilted my chin up so that we were looking directly into each other's eyes. "Do you think I don't understand? I have siblings, too. If I'd had just one more day to spend with Annalise, do you think I wouldn't have taken it?"

"But Tiamat—"

"Has been around for thousands of years, as has this fight. It isn't going to change overnight." He brushed soft kisses across my forehead, then down my temple to my jawline. "Take the time you need."

He kissed me again and this time it was just like it always was—colors exploding behind my eyes, fire racing through my veins. Love bursting through me.

"And then come back to me, Tempest," he whispered so softly that I almost didn't hear him. "Please, come back to me."

Chapter 25

The first night Moku was back at home, I had terrible nightmares. It was the only time my whole family had spent the night under the same roof in nearly nine months, so I should have been thrilled we were all together. Not to mention that Moku had been given a clean bill of health—something the doctors still didn't understand.

And I *was* thrilled about both those things, I told myself as I climbed out of bed in the middle of the night. It was just that I was also worried—about what Kona had said *and* what he hadn't.

Deep in the heart of the Pacific, things were going very badly, very quickly. They had to be, or else there was no way Tiamat would be brazen enough to attack both a selkie and mermaid clan within a week of each other. And while she hadn't destroyed any major underwater cities—or any major underwater clans— she *had* picked those with powerful allies. Allies whose people and resources would be stretched while helping the others.

All of which meant she thought she was strong enough to stand against the combined strength of not just the two clans she'd attacked, but also against both Hailaina's and Kona's clans—whatever trouble we chose to bring to her doorstep. So something was going on. I just needed to figure out what.

I padded down the hall on silent feet, trying my best not to wake anyone. My dad was exhausted from all the time he'd spent in Moku's hospital room, and Rio, well, I just didn't want to deal with his brand of snark in the middle of the night.

Outside the house, the wind howled and I jumped a little, then shook my head at my own idiocy. Stupid dream. I didn't remember the specifics of it, just the overwhelming sense that something was very wrong. My whole body felt strange, like I was moving through mud. Like the weight of it was slowly pressing down, smothering me. Crushing me.

I took a deep breath, tried to force air into my starving lungs. Told myself it was okay, that I was being stupid, that maybe I was having a panic attack. It wasn't like I could actually be smothered standing in the middle of my hallway.

It had been days since I'd so much as felt the water on my toes, let alone been surrounded by it, and I was feeling the loss. My lungs hurt—like breathing air for this long was just too harsh for them. My skin itched and burned with dryness no matter how much lotion I used, and there was a restlessness deep inside of me, a pressure that screamed to be relieved.

Without making a conscious decision to do it, I was out the front door, padding down the block and across the street to the beach that had always been such a big part of my life. The second my feet touched the sand the fear from the nightmare was gone, the dull ache that had been inside of me for days dissipated, the tension I'd carried melting away.

Just get your feet wet, I told myself as I walked to the waterline. God only knew what was lurking offshore waiting to grab me. This was one of Tiamat's favorite stomping grounds, after all.

Something about that thought caught my attention, niggled at the back of my brain. I tried to figure out what it was, what I was missing, but the harder I tried to understand it, the more elusive the thought became. It was right there, not quite fully formed, waiting for me to extract it. But I couldn't reach it, no matter how hard I tried.

Besides, everything Kona told me put Tiamat thousands of miles away tearing up the Pacific's power structure. Which was awful, but should mean my late-night dip went unnoticed.

More at ease now, and unable to resist the siren call of the ocean, I waded a little deeper—enough to get my knees wet and send relief coursing through me. As the water lapped around me, all my fears and worries dissipated, replaced by pure, unadulterated pleasure. Joy. Excitement.

I moved out farther without making the decision to do so. In seconds, I was up to my waist, then ducking down until my shoulders were covered. As long as I was careful, I told myself, everything would be okay.

A part of me hated how good this felt, how necessary. It was the part that longed to be normal, to be human. The same part that wanted to stay here, with my family, forever.

But another part, one that I feared was growing larger by the day, relished the feel of the water against my skin. That part wanted to go under, to dive deep, to submerge itself and never come back. Just the thought had me stumbling backward a few steps. Toward the shore and my house and the family I refused to give up.

Suddenly, something wrapped itself around my upper arm. Alarm and anger raced through me as I whirled to face the threat, my other arm raised to deliver a shot of pure energy to whoever dared come to this beach, to the beach where my family and friends swam. This time, I would send a message to Tiamat that warned her to stay away from here forever.

Except it wasn't Tiamat or one of her minions behind me. It was Mark, a wild look on his face as he took in the soaked tank-top and boyshorts I had been sleeping in. My heart stopped and my blood ran cold as I used every ounce of strength I had to pull back the energy and stop the fatal blow that I had aimed right at him.

"Tempest, wait," he said, almost as frantic as I was but for completely different reasons. "I've been watching for you. Don't go. Not yet. I'm not ready to lose you again. Not now, before we even have a chance to—" He stopped, tried again. "Please."

My heart started again, in a frantic staccato rhythm that was impossible to control—or ignore. There was a roaring in my ears and a blurriness to the world around me.

I'd almost killed Mark.

I'd almost killed Mark.

I had almost killed Mark.

The words chased themselves back and forth in my head, a macabre mantra that turned my knees weak and made my blood boil. If I had hit Tiamat or one of her minions with that energy blast it would have hurt them badly. But Mark . . . Mark was human. He couldn't have withstood the strength of that blast.

I really had almost killed him.

Panic-stricken, terrified, operating under a driving need to assure myself that he was okay, I threw myself at Mark, hitting him square in the chest and knocking both of us back a few feet and down into the shallow water. It swirled around our legs and hips as I straddled him, tangling my fingers in his shaggy blond hair.

"Whoa! What's wro—"

I didn't give him the chance to finish. Instead, I tugged his head back so I could look into his beautiful eyes, see the life still shining in their dark chocolate depths. And then I kissed him with all of the fear and relief and longing that were rocketing through me.

The world exploded.

A crazed kaleidoscope of spinning colors whirled around us, between us, and heat spilled through me, enveloping me in a frenzy of emotion with no room for thought. Only action. Only sensation.

Leaning in to Mark, I pulled him even closer, until there was no space between our bodies, nothing between us at all but the thin, wet fabric of our clothes. And even that was too much for me right now, when the horror of what I had almost done was a nightmare burning inside of me.

I tugged at his shirt, shoved it up so that I could run my hands over the warmth of his stomach and chest. So that I could feel the hard, fast rhythm of his still-beating heart.

Mark yanked his mouth away from mine and I tried to protest, but then he was skimming his lips over my jaw, down my throat to the ragged rise and fall of my chest. He kissed the hollow of my throat, licked drops of salt water from my collarbone before trailing kisses along the deep V of my camisole.

"I love you," I told him, the words bursting out of me as I slid my own mouth down his temple and across the rough stubble of his jawline. "I love you so much."

I kissed him again and it was as powerful, as amazing, as it had been the very first time. I never wanted it to end. Fumbling with the hem of my own shirt, I tried to pull it over my head so we could be closer, but Mark put a hand over mine, stilling my frenetic motions.

Pulling his lips away, he wrapped his arms around me, pressed me back to his chest. And just held me, his breathing harsh and disjointed in my ear as he tried to calm down a little. Mine sounded the same—I knew it did—but I didn't care.

"Mark, please," I begged as I kissed his shoulder, his chest.

"Tempe, what's going on?"

"Don't you want me?"

His laugh was harsh, painful. "Tempest, I want you so badly I can barely see straight. But not like this, in the shallows where anyone can look out their window and see us. And not when you're obviously freaked about something." He grabbed my hands, held them tight in his own. "Please, tell me what's going on."

I shook my head. Closed my eyes. Laid my head on his chest and tried to relax. To breathe. Just breathe.

I didn't know what to say to him, how to explain what had almost happened. I didn't want him to know. He'd taken the mermaid thing pretty well—better than I had ever expected. But that didn't mean he could deal with everything that came with it, particularly the dark, powerful stuff.

In the end, I didn't answer his question and he didn't push me to. Instead, we lay there, tangled together—half in the water, half out of it—until the multihued dawn broke slowly over our small part of the Pacific.

◈

"I want to go to the beach," Moku whined as I placed a plateful of pancakes in front of him.

"The doctor said you needed to take it easy for a few days," I reminded him.

"I don't want to take it easy. Besides, in a few days you're going to be gone again. I want to go to the beach with you, Tempest! I wanna watch you surf!"

I sighed. "Look, how about we make a deal? You eat your pancakes and then we'll go sit on the beach for a while."

"But I want to go swimming! It's boring being sick."

"Boring or not—Dad will kill me if anything happens to you. He'll be back in an hour. If he says you can go in the water, then you can. Until then, it's the sand or nothing."

He sighed, obviously annoyed. "Fine. It's better than sitting in this stupid house, anyway."

"See? Things are looking up already." I brushed a kiss over the top of his head. "I'm going to go change into my swimsuit. Eat your pancakes and we'll go."

A few minutes later, Moku and I had cleaned up the kitchen and were on our way down to the beach. He was practically dancing with excitement and I wasn't much better. It had been a long time since I'd hung out with my brother at the beach, and if I was lucky, maybe some of my friends would be there too. Scooter and Bach, Tony and Logan. Brianne. Mark. My stomach did a little flip at the thought.

We had barely crossed the street before I saw them. All five guys were in the water, paddling their boards out to catch a wave while my girlfriends Brianne and Mickey watched from shore. It had been so long since I'd seen my friends, and watching them now made me realize just how much I'd missed them.

"Look, Tempest, Mark's the first one up!" Moku said, pointing at the water. Sure enough, in his bright orange and white Hawaiian board shorts, Mark was hard to miss as he caught pretty decent air.

"He looks good," I told Moku.

"Not as good as Logan! Look!"

I smiled as my best bud took the next wave, and ended up shooting the barrel. He rode it all the way in, while Bach and Scooter snaked Tony.

Logan was getting ready to paddle back out when he saw me. A huge grin split his face and then he was sloshing the last few yards to the shallows. Moku and I ran down to meet him.

"Tempest! I heard you were back!" he yelled as we got closer, his Australian accent as heavy as ever. "It's about time you made it down here."

"She was at the hospital with me," Moku told him seriously.

"I know, man." He reached out, ruffled my brother's hair, then pulled him into his side for a one-armed hug. "I'm glad you're all right."

"Thank you for saving him," I said, throwing my arms around Logan's neck in a huge hug.

He laughed and picked me up, swung me around. "Mark did most of it. I just held his hand when he got scared."

"Moku?" I asked, confused, because I thought he'd been unconscious the whole time.

"No. Mark." Logan winked at me before his blue eyes turned serious. "It's good to have you back, Tempest Maguire."

"It's good to be back, Logan Callaway. Except, I probably won't be staying all that long—"

"I know. Mark told me."

My eyes bugged out of my head. "He told you?"

"About you going to school in Hawaii for the year? Yeah. A kind of homage to your mom. I think it's cool. Still wish you were here, though."

"I kind of do too, Logan." I rested my head on his shoulder.

A couple minutes later, Mark dropped down next to Moku on the towel we'd set out. "How you feeling?" he asked.

"Good," Moku answered. "I'm not sick anymore."

"Glad to hear that." He held his fist out for a bump, which my brother was only too happy to give him. "So, what are you doing up here then? Don't you want to go in the water?"

Moku sighed. "Tempest won't let me. She says we have to wait to clear it with Dad." His tone said that I was obviously the worst sister ever.

Mark glanced at me apologetically. "She's probably right. Dads tend to get bent on stuff like that."

"Still, she doesn't have to sit here and watch me like a baby. She can surf. Right, Logan?"

"Absolutely," my friend answered.

"Maybe I don't want to surf. Did you ever think of that, smart guy?"

The only response I got to that was three of the most

incredulous looks I had ever seen. Which just went to show how well these guys knew me.

"I'll hang with Moku for a while. Take my board. It's not a custom-made Brewer, but the shape isn't that different from yours." Mark pushed my shoulder lightly. "Go," he told me. "Have fun."

Logan was already on his feet, reaching for my hand to pull me up. "Come on, just one. It's been forever since you surfed with us."

It had been forever since I'd surfed, period. And to do it on an unfamiliar board? I'd probably make a total ass of myself. At the same time, though, the waves *were* calling . . .

"Okay, just once."

Mark snorted, muttering something under his breath that sounded a lot like, "Yeah, right."

"Just once," I reiterated to Moku. "You'll be okay?"

He rolled his eyes. "Really, Tempest? Mark saved my life once already. I think he can handle watching me sit on the beach."

"Whoa! You got owned," Logan said with a grin. "Come on, let's go shock the hell out of Scooter, Tony, and Bach. It'll be fun."

"Okay, fine. Let's do it." I grabbed Mark's board, which was a little longer and more unwieldy than mine—he was taller and weighed more—and ran for the water. Once I was on it, though, I realized he was right—the shape was pretty much the same as the Brewer I had used for months before becoming mermaid.

"You ready?" Logan asked as we started paddling out.

"I was born ready, thank you very much."

"Yeah, yeah, big words. Let's see if you can actually pony up."

"Let's see if you can *keep* up."

We kept paddling until we got close to where the other guys were. "Hey, Tempest!" Scooter hooted. "Good to see you out here, girl!"

"Good to be out here!"

The other guys added their greetings, but before we could do anything else, a huge wave started surging. "Party wave!" Bach yelled, and we all started hauling ass straight toward it.

It was going to be a monster, I could tell, so I braced myself, duck dived down, and came up exactly where I needed to be. A quick glance at Logan told me if I didn't move it, he was going to be up before I was, so I rushed it a little. Got my feet, found my balance, and then promptly got knocked ass over tea-kettle into the wave.

I hit hard, rolled, morphed just enough to let my gills do the work for me, then made my way back up to the surface in time to watch Logan and Bach find the sweet spot.

"Dude!" Scooter said as I climbed back on Mark's board and made my way over to him. "The waves in Hawaii not up to snuff or something? You almost never get worked like that."

"It doesn't look like you did any better," I said, punching his arm. But he was right. I had been totally worked over—I just didn't know if it was because of the board or because I was that out of practice. I was really hoping it was the board.

He pretended to be wounded from my punch. "Yeah, well, I'm not some crazy good surfing goddess. I'm allowed to get worked."

"This is true," I teased, then nodded behind him. "Another one's coming. Wanna try again?"

"No doubt."

We started paddling.

"This one's a monster!" Scooter yelled. "You sure you want to do this?"

"Who are you talking to?"

He just laughed. I shifted my weight, watched as the wave got closer and closer. Then I duck dived down for extra momentum, came up right where I was supposed to again, and tried this whole surfing thing one more time.

And it was magic. Beautiful. Like I'd never, ever left. Within a second of finding my legs, I'd also found the sweet spot, and then I just rode. Up and over, I got great air and finished with a nice run down the center of the barrel.

I glanced toward shore, where Moku was cheering for me. I waved at him and Mark and then started the trek back in.

"You done so soon?" Scooter asked.

"I've got to get back to my brother. Maybe I'll come out again tomorrow morning, stay for a while."

"We're going for pizza later. You should come."

I smiled, grateful and a little amazed at his easy acceptance. I'd disappeared on them twice, without a word, yet my friends were willing to just take me back. "I'd like that," I told him. "I missed you guys."

"We missed you too. Besides, you look much better in a bikini than Tony does."

"Since when does Tony wear a bikini?"

"Come to Frazoni's with us and I'll tell you the story."

"Bribery?"

"Hey, I'm not proud. We need to hang out before you head back to paradise. Plus, I want to hear about those waves off

Waimea—my parents said they'd spring for a trip next month. Maybe you could show me around."

"Yeah, maybe," I told him, but the lie made my stomach hurt. I hadn't surfed Hawaii in more than two years, and I wasn't going to be anywhere near there when Scooter made it over.

By the time I got back to Mark and Moku, my brother had convinced Mark to take him into the water on his surfboard. "Like a raft ride," Moku told me. "I swear, no swimming."

He looked so hopeful and I'd come so close to losing him, that I couldn't resist the puppy dog eyes for long. So I traipsed down the beach with them, and when we got to the water, we put Moku on the surfboard between us. As we floated him around the shallows, I was careful to stay on one side while Mark stayed on the other. Moku giggled and kept trying to talk us into making it wilder, but aside from a few bumps here and there, we kept it calm.

At least until I looked onto the shore and saw my father running at us, waving his arms like a crazy man. "What's wrong with Dad?" Moku asked.

"I have no idea." I turned to Mark. "Watch him, will you?"

"Sure." He looked as concerned as I felt.

As I hit the shore, I heard my father yelling, "Get him out, Tempest! Get Moku out of the water!"

I didn't know what was wrong, and I didn't stick around to find out. I just dived for Moku, whipped him off the surfboard and waded to shore with him in my arms. When we got there, my dad all but ripped Moku away and started checking him over.

"Dad? What's wrong? I was careful. He's fine."

For long seconds my dad didn't answer, just continued to

check Moku's arms and legs. When he was convinced my brother was okay, he handed Moku to Mark, who had come to see what all the commotion was about. Then he pulled me a few steps down the beach for privacy.

"It wasn't a surfing accident," my dad told me fiercely.

"What do you mean?" I asked, confused.

"Moku's near drowning. It wasn't a surfing accident. That thing, that witch that went after you when you were ten. She was here. It wasn't a bump on the head that nearly killed him. It was her."

Chapter 26

It was like my father had started speaking another language. "What?" I asked, unable to truly understand what he was saying. "Tiamat was *here*?" My blood ran cold, even as a freight train roared through my head. "How do you know?" I whispered. "I thought you were at work when Moku was hurt?"

"Rosa. It scared the hell out of her. It's why she hasn't been here for the last week—she quit after I asked her not to call the police and report what happened."

"What did she see?"

"Moku going into the water like he was in a trance. When she called him back, he didn't respond or act like he heard her at all, which is totally not like him. And then, when she started to pull him out, it was like something was holding on to him, refusing to let go. I tried to convince her it was seaweed, but she knew better."

God, it really was the same as when Tiamat had come after me all those years ago. It was a horrifying thought.

"Tiamat was here," I said again, just so there was no misunderstanding. "At *this* beach. And she attacked Moku."

"Yes. That's why I don't want him near the water. What if she comes back and we can't fight her off? I almost lost you that night in Hawaii, almost lost him the other day. I won't risk it. Not again. I'm not losing any more of my family to that damn ocean." He looked so tormented that it nearly ripped me apart.

"She won't get her hands on him, Dad." Lightning suddenly crisscrossed the sky, slamming into the sand so hard that the very ground around us trembled.

My father jumped and screams echoed down the beach before being drowned out in the loud boom of thunder rumbling through the air. Pitch-black clouds rolled in from nowhere, letting loose a heavy curtain of frigid rain that had people screeching and running for their cars.

"We need to go in," my dad said, glancing at the sky even as he reached for my arm. "This storm looks dangerous."

He had no idea just *how* dangerous it could be.

I yanked my arm from his grasp, but even as I did, I reached for the control Jared had so painstakingly taught me. For the discipline I'd spent the last eight months working on. But it was gone. Had evaporated like so much mist in the face of Tiamat's newest attack on my family.

I could feel the energy building, feel the power gathering inside of me. I tried to deflect it, threw my arms out wide and sent wind skittering across the surface of the water in a last-ditch attempt to keep from unleashing all the pent-up fury and horror inside of me.

It didn't work.

"Go!" I told my father and Moku. "Get to the house."

"You need to come with us!" my father shouted, wrapping an arm around my shoulder. "This storm can kill you."

"It's my storm," I shouted, backing down the now-abandoned beach. "It won't touch me!"

"Tempest!" my dad called as he made a last grab for me and failed, his fingers sliding harmlessly off my elbow.

"Get Moku inside!" I shouted to him, trusting he would do as I asked.

I didn't know where I was running to, exactly, knew only that I was trying to get away from all the prying eyes and lingering tourists who obviously didn't know enough to get in out of the rain.

I stopped running about a mile and a half down the beach, at the edge of a sheltered alcove that had been completely cleared out. This was it. I needed to get a grip on the terrible power and rage that would consume me if I let it. Already I felt it churning inside, racing through my blood, lighting me up like a gaudy Christmas display.

Had I learned nothing, then? Had all those months, trying to learn control, just been marking time?

The wind started picking up, blowing hard enough to get the water churning and to send sand flying in all directions. It was okay, I told myself, trying to get back some semblance of control. Moku was fine. Tiamat hadn't been able to hurt him as she'd wanted to, hadn't been able to get him to come to her.

But she had tried. She had tried to hurt him, tried to control him, tried to take him. Everything I had done, everything I had given up, had been for nothing. Tiamat was still a threat to my family and I hadn't been there to protect them.

Hailana had promised me months ago that Tiamat would have no use for my brothers. That, supposedly, neither Rio nor

Moku possessed the kind of power I had and therefore wouldn't be of any interest to Tiamat. Obviously that wasn't the case. Of course, that was probably why Hailana had lied. Because she'd known there was no way I could possibly build a life under the ocean if my family wasn't safe.

Just the thought had the power sizzling through my every cell. The wind circled me, whipped around, until I was almost consumed by the energy of it. And by the electricity that flowed into me like it had that time in the ocean, turning me into some kind of semi-conductor.

Feeling like I would be ripped apart at any second, not knowing what else to do, I threw my arms up and sent the current crashing outward. It scorched my fingertips as it exploded from me, rending the sky in half as lightning bolt after lightning bolt slammed into the earth. And still it wasn't enough. Still I could feel the power swelling, building, until I was all but consumed by it. I didn't know how to channel this much energy, this much electricity. It made those moments when I'd fought Tiamat's henchmen seem like nothing, made the storm where I'd nearly killed Kona seem like child's play.

Standing here on the beach, wind ripping past me, water roiling and churning around me, lightning blistering the earth as thunder boomed overhead, I thought this must be what it felt like to stand in the eye of a category-five hurricane. Grasping desperately for sanity in a world gone crazy around you.

Closing my eyes, I tried to focus, tried to find a way to harness the energy, to bring it all back inside me, but by then it was too huge, too powerful. So instead, I fought to channel it, to send it blasting into the sand, into the earth.

My first attempt knocked me off my feet, threw me five yards back into the rocky walls of the cave. I hit hard enough to knock the breath right out of me, and for long, helpless seconds I just sat there with aching lungs, trying to figure out why the world was going fuzzy around me.

If I passed out, would everything stop? Or would my body just take over? Because at the rate I was going, I would spawn a tsunami—or at least a cyclone. Not willing to take the chance, I forced myself to my feet. Stumbled closer to the water.

"Tempest! Tempest, no!" The words reached me as if from a long distance, and I almost ignored them. Would have ignored them if I hadn't seen Mark running across the sand toward me.

"Stop!" I screamed, throwing a hand out. The power behind the movement stopped him in his tracks and then slammed him to the ground, as the lightning continued to strike around him. It was like the nightmare with Kona all over again, when he had come to help me and I had accidentally struck him with lightning. That time, the ocean had healed him, but Mark wasn't selkie. If he came too close, I could kill him.

I started backing away, trying to get as far down the beach as possible. Anything to give Mark a chance to get away. Only he wasn't trying to move back—he was scrambling toward me. And even though the wind was so strong that he'd lose his footing every few steps, he was gaining ground, refusing to give up.

"Mark, no!" I screamed again, but I don't know if he heard me or if my warning was lost in the wind that whirled and roared around us.

Terrified, desperate, I turned away, flung my hands toward

the ocean, and unleashed everything I had. Energy exploded out of me, shot straight into the water in an outpouring of power that went on and on and on. I could feel Mark struggling through the wind behind me, trying to reach me, but I couldn't turn around. If I lost focus now, even for a moment, we'd be finished.

Because while the lightning and thunder were dying down a little more with each second that I continued to blast my power into the water, another problem was developing—the waves. They were growing larger and choppier, hitting the beach faster and higher than they ever had before. I tried to pull back, to temper the energy I was leveling into the water, but it was too little, too late.

A few hundred feet out, a huge wall of water was starting to build, each of the waves flowing into it, adding to it, even as it moved closer to shore. *I'm doing this*, I thought in horror, as I watched the swell seethe and grow.

"Holy shit!" Mark said, staring up at what had to be a forty-foot wall of water. "Tempest, we need to get out of here. Now!"

"This is my fault," I told him.

"It's just a freak storm." He tried to grab on, to pull me to his version of safety, but the second he touched me he was knocked straight off his feet. He didn't fly all the way to the cave, like I had, but he hit the ground several feet away. I wanted to run to him, to check and make sure I hadn't just electrocuted him.

But the wave was growing even higher, and I had the feeling if I so much as moved, it was going to come crashing down, not just on Mark and me but on our whole neighborhood.

I kept my hands raised, the power funneling straight into the ocean—into the giant tsunami that loomed above us—but I closed my eyes, breathed deep. Tried to clear my mind and center myself the way Kona and Jared and even Sabyn had taught me. It was harder than it had ever been, with not only one of the guys I loved in the line of fire, but also my entire family.

I would not do this to them. I would not hurt one more person that I loved. Not like this, not with the powers that my mother gave me. Cecily had controlled the rampaging energy inside of herself. I could—I would—do the same.

Doing anything else would make me just like Tiamat.

As I calmed myself down—narrowed my attention, controlled my emotions—I became aware of more than my sense of betrayal. More than the rage and the terror, more even than the seductive frenzy of the magic that burned inside of me.

The wind was hot against my face, the sand cool on my toes. I glanced down as I tried to gather enough strength to end this, and saw, at my feet, a piece of sea glass. The same color as the seething heart of the Pacific but no bigger than the average oyster shell, it looked like so many of the pieces on the top shelf of my mother's cave that it gave me pause. Splintered, for one second, the concentration I had worked so hard not to let falter.

The ocean rumbled, roiled, heavy splashes of water dropping down on Mark and me from the wave I was barely holding back. It brought me around. Then I was reaching down, scooping up the piece of glass and holding it tightly in the palm of my hand. Years of being tossed and tumbled through the ocean had dulled the edges so that I didn't slice my hand open, but it was still sharp enough to hurt. I barely noticed.

Instead, I was remembering those times in the cave when I had seen my mother's memories and had wondered how she'd managed to trap them inside the glass and pearls. Something told me this was it. This outburst of power that was almost uncontrollable.

I glanced over at Mark, who was watching me with a combination of awe and fear, and told myself there was no way I was going to mess this up. He'd stuck with me through everything and I would not let him pay for that with his life.

Throwing the glass up in the air as high as I could, I aimed every ounce of magic, of power, I had straight at it. Electricity blasted into the glass, suspending it in mid-air and lighting it up from the inside until the entire world around us was a bright, glowing blue. The sea glass hovered there, a large crack appearing down the center of it, but it didn't shatter. Instead, it absorbed every ounce of energy I poured in.

Around me, the wind died down, the thunder and lightning stopped altogether, and slowly, so slowly that at first I thought I was imagining it, the wave began to break down. Drop by drop, inch by inch, it began to melt back into the simmering sea.

And still I kept the power flowing straight into the glass, draining myself of magic and emotion and power. Burning myself out in an effort to stop the destruction that still hovered at the tips of my fingers.

I'm not sure how long I stood there, pouring everything I had into that tiny piece of glass. Long enough for exhaustion to replace energy and frustration to replace fear. But in the end, it was worth it. The wave dissipated. The storm died into nothingness. Soon the only reminder of my loss of control was the destruction left in the wake of the storm and the cracked piece of sea glass that dropped harmlessly at my feet.

I bent down to pick it up, but it was burning hot. I wanted to leave the sea glass there, to bury it deep in the sand and pretend the last hour had never happened, but doing so was impossible. I'd sent every drop of power I had into that thing—who knew what kind of memories it would show the next person to handle it?

Ignoring the blister that was rising on my hand from the heat, I held the glass for one second, two, then used whatever strength I had left to launch it as far into the ocean as I possibly could. It soared for long moments before sinking below the still surging waves.

"What was that?" Mark staggered up to me, looking like he'd just run the longest marathon in history—and come in last.

"You knew I was different," I answered.

"Different, yes. Able to light up a major metropolitan area under your own power, no." He smiled to show he was joking, but I could see the truth.

I let him pull me into his arms, spent a few minutes drawing comfort from him in a way I never had been able to when I was completely human. But he felt so good. So strong and safe with his heavily muscled arms wrapped around me that I never wanted to leave.

I couldn't stay here forever, though, much as I wanted to. Not when Tiamat was a threat to everyone and everything I cared about—here on land and in the ocean. There was something deep inside me again, pushing me to hurry. Telling me that something awful was about to happen.

At the same time, though, I couldn't stand the idea of leaving here. Not now, when I had just found Mark and my family again. Not now, when I had so much to say to my friends and to Rio, who could barely stand the sight of me.

Still, the sense of urgency grew with each second I was on land, until my skin was once again so sensitive that I could barely stand the feel of Mark's calloused hands resting on my shoulders. Tiamat was up to something. But what was it? What use did she have for my brother?

Unless . . . unless Hailana had been right all along, and she hadn't needed Moku. Not really. What she'd needed was Kona and me out of the way for a few days so that she could run unchecked through the ocean, doing whatever she wanted. She would still have to fight Sabyn and Hailana, would still have to fight Kona's family, but without the two of us she would have a much better shot at wreaking havoc on our clans.

In those moments, everything clicked into place and I knew.

"I have to go," I told him.

"What? Now?" He reached for me.

I pulled away from Mark. For one long moment he looked devastated. And then his face closed up and he stepped back, letting me know he was as hurt by my leaving as Kona had been a few days earlier by my choosing to stay.

"Will I see you again?" Mark asked stiltedly. "Or is this it?"

"I want to say yes, of course you'll see me again."

"But?"

"But this thing I have to do . . . I don't know. I promise you, though, if there's any way for me to come back, I'll do it."

Fear for me replaced the hurt on his face. "What are you doing, Tempest? Where are you going?"

I shook my head, then kissed him with all the aching wishes

and could-bes that stretched between us. "Tell my dad—" I cleared my throat, tried again. "Tell my dad and my brothers that I'll miss them."

The idea of leaving my family here, vulnerable to anything that Tiamat wanted to do to them, killed me. But leaving her out there, knowing she could strike at any time, made it so much worse.

This, what she'd done to Moku, was her calling card, her call to action, and I would not disappoint her. Not now. She'd already killed my mother. She'd nearly killed my brother. There was no way I was letting this go, no way I was leaving her free to attack everyone else I cared about.

I gave Mark one last hug, then ran for the water. When I got there, I turned to find him staring at me, anguish and anger at war on his face. "I love you," I told him. "I swear, if I can find a way out of this, I'll be back."

"I'm going to hold you to that." He jogged the short distance between us, yanked me hard against him, and gave me the kind of kiss that made my head spin and my body melt. "I love you, Tempest Maguire, and you had damn well better come back to me. Or I will find a way to come after you."

He stepped away, and I took one last look at his beloved face. Turned and had one last glimpse of my house, where my family waited for me. Then I was gone, plunging into the surf and diving deep.

As the ocean closed over my head, I told myself I was doing the right thing. The only thing. Going after Tiamat once and for all was the only way to keep everyone I cared about safe.

Chapter 27

It was a long, hard swim, and I was exhausted by the time I got close to Coral Straits. I'd tried to reach Hailana, tried to reach Kona, but despite the crazy power that seemed to have taken up residence inside of me, I still wasn't able to communicate over long distances, not unless someone else was holding the bridge for me.

Still, I wanted them to know I was going after Tiamat. That this time she had gone way too far. If she hoped to take me on, that was fine. I was used to it and could take care of myself. But to go after my baby brother . . . I was done playing around. One way or the other, this thing had to end.

I knew it was dangerous, knew there was a chance I'd end up dying right along with her, but I couldn't let that matter. If no one else was going to try to end her, I would take on that job. And relish it.

Was this what my mother had felt like when she'd left us to fight for her clan? This burning need for retribution and to keep her family safe? Yesterday I would have said it wasn't enough to justify leaving us the way she had—nothing was—but as I contemplated the fact that I had just dived into the ocean without so much as a good-bye to anyone but Mark, I finally understood that sometimes, there was no other way. If I'd stopped, if I'd gone back to the house and hugged Moku, I'm not sure I ever would have found the strength to leave.

I would have to talk to Hailana, figure out the best way to go after Tiamat. While normally I wouldn't trust any advice from the merQueen, on this I had no doubt she would help. She wanted Tiamat gone at least as badly as I did—it was why she put up with my attitude, after all.

I swam into the city, determined to head straight to Hailana and make her see me, no matter how angry she was about my leaving. But the second I zipped out of the trench and into Coral Straits, horror overwhelmed everything else I was feeling.

The city had been destroyed. Most of the buildings were nothing more than rubble, the refugee tents reduced to scraps of material. I slowed down, dived deeper to see if I could figure out what had happened, but it was getting harder to see. And that's when I realized—the weird, slightly rosy cast to the water wasn't my imagination. It was blood. Gallons and gallons of blood.

I started to gag, swam higher to get away from the slick feel of it in the water, and as I got closer to the heart of the city I realized where the blood was coming from. There were bodies everywhere. Some intact, some torn into so many bloody pieces that it was nearly impossible to imagine that they had once been mer. Small groups of survivors were slowly carting away the dead, one by one, but their efforts seemed futile. There were so many.

Unsure of what else to do, I swam straight toward the square at the center of the city, where, if the body count was anything to go by, most of the fighting had taken place.

I gasped at the sight of the girl who always brewed my red algae tea. She was lying flat on her back, a gaping hole where her heart used to be.

I whimpered at the sight of Mahina's uncle, sword still in his hand, facedown in the street. There was an arrow through his neck.

Sobbed at the sight of little Liam curled into a protective ball, a spear protruding from his narrow back.

I swam over to him and lifted his body in my arms. Tried to see if there was some way he had survived, some way he could have—but no. He was dead.

Rage—huge, overwhelming, suffocating—rose up within me as I surveyed the death and destruction. With it came an amazing clarity, one that too late allowed me to understand Hailana's warnings. She'd told me if I went home it would be the end, but I hadn't believed her. Hadn't been able to understand what she was trying to tell me.

I'd thought she'd simply meant she'd punish me, would kick me out, but that hadn't been it at all. I'd been so arrogant, so blind, so filled with dislike for her that I hadn't listened. And now all these people had died. I was as responsible for their deaths as Tiamat.

But surely Hailana could have slowed her down? And Sabyn, who had more power than any merman I had ever met? Where had they been when this had happened?

Or had Tiamat somehow managed to kill them as well?

Gently placing Liam back on the ground, I shot forward, winding through the buildings and debris as quickly as I could. It seemed like it took forever, and I encountered more and more dead along the way. Most of my clan had been executed in the streets.

Finally, *finally*, the palace loomed in front of me. It was partially destroyed, the area where I lived reduced to nothing more than rocks, but the merQueen's quarters looked like they might be intact. I dived through the closest opening and made my way to her rooms.

She wasn't there.

I searched the whole castle, found it abandoned.

Panic set in then, a wild, rampaging thing that filled me with urgency and horror.

I barreled back outside, into the ocean, looking for someone who might be able to tell me what happened to her. And ran full-on into Mahina, sent us both tumbling head over heels until we managed to right ourselves.

Oh my God, you're alive! I wrapped my arms around her and hugged her tightly.

She returned my hug, burying her face in my neck. I could tell by the way her shoulders shook that she was sobbing. I didn't know what to do, what to say, so I just held her and let her cry for long minutes.

When she finally raised her head, her eyes were swollen and painful looking, but she was composed.

What happened? I demanded.

Tiamat . . . and Sabyn.

Sabyn? I asked incredulously.

They're together. MerQueen Hailana thought that he was her secret weapon, that together you two could do anything, but it turns out he's been with Tiamat all along. They waited until you were gone and then yesterday, they attacked.

All of Kona's warnings and accusations came crashing in on me. He'd been right and I hadn't trusted him, not completely. I'd believed that Sabyn was a jerk, but I hadn't known how untrustworthy he was. Hadn't known that he was a traitor.

I'm sorry. I didn't know. It was a poor excuse, but all I had to offer. I couldn't even look at her while I spoke.

How could you have? They played everyone. She shuddered. *My uncle . . .*

I felt tears burning my own eyes. *The rest of your family?*

They're okay. Mom and Dad took us out to the plate shelf, to the market there. When we came back, this is what was left. We haven't found my uncle yet, but he isn't among the survivors, so—

I saw him. His body, I mean. I can take you to him, if you'd like.

She shuddered. *Yes. Let me get my dad and brothers so they can . . .* She couldn't finish.

Within half an hour, we had collected her uncle's body and brought him to the surface, near Hailana's castle. Mahina's mother and sisters organized a small funeral pyre for him, and we had a funeral right then, with none of the pomp and circumstance we'd had for my mother nine months before. But it was better than the mass funeral pyres that were being lit at other places on the island. At least his was personal and his family was there.

When it was over, I left Mahina with her grieving family and walked over to Hailana's castle. It, like everything else on the surface, was completely intact. Tiamat was a fearsome enemy, but unlike the rest of us, she could never leave the water. She couldn't shift beyond the mermaid-type shell she usually employed, couldn't grow legs or lungs. She was tied to the ocean, unable to breathe on land.

Which meant that anyone who had been up here—and who had not rushed into the water at the first distress cries—was alive. This was where the injured had been brought to be tended and this was where Hailana was, according to the rescue personnel I had asked.

I found her in her bedroom, propped up in bed and looking more frail than I had ever seen her. Both of her eyes were swollen almost shut, her left arm was broken, and I didn't think there was a spot on her body that wasn't bruised or cut. She had fought hard to save her city and her people. "So, you've come back." Her voice was weak and strained, but unaccusing.

"I have."

"You saw what happened?"

I wanted to apologize to her as I had to Mahina, to acknowledge my culpability in the situation, but the words stuck in my throat. After everything that had happened between us I had trouble bowing to her, even though she looked like she was one step away from death. At the same time, I didn't know what else I could have done. If I hadn't gone home, if Kona hadn't come with me and brought the healer, Moku might very well be dead now. I knew Hailana expected my loyalty to be completely to her, but it wasn't and it never would be. My mother had put the clan above her family. I wasn't sure I'd ever be able to.

"Yes," I finally said.

"You must be thrilled to find me so humbled." A tear leaked out of the corner of her eye.

"No," I repeated. "You couldn't have known—"

"I should have. I made some huge miscalculations, Tempest, and they have cost my clan its last chance at survival. We are doomed now."

"There are survivors. We can rebuild—"

She snorted, the first time I had ever heard such an unelegant sound come from her. "Most of the clan is dead or injured. Who is left to rebuild? After everything I've done to keep them safe, I ended up destroying them. I am finished as their queen."

I didn't know what to say. She *had* made mistakes and when the deaths were dealt with, when the shock had worn off, people would be furious that she had brought such a powerful enemy right into the heart of the city. She hadn't meant to, had thought Sabyn was on our side, but it was her job to seek out the truth. Underestimating Tiamat and misreading Sabyn so completely were terrible, terrible mistakes.

Still, I couldn't leave her like this, miserable and guilty and closer to death than I had ever thought possible. "The clan can survive," I told her. "We can prepare—"

"Oh, *we* can, can *we*? And where were you today, Tempest? The clan needs a strong leader, one who sticks around when things get tough. If that leader isn't going to be me, who will it be? You keep running off to play at being human even though you clearly aren't. How are you going to lead these people?"

"I have no desire to lead your clan, Hailana. I've told you that before."

"*Your* clan, Tempest. Or it would be if you ever chose to accept us. But you run between us and the selkies and the humans like you're ashamed of what you really are."

"If being a mermaid means I have to—" I forced myself to stop before I said something that I would regret. She was weak and badly injured, after all.

But Hailana only laughed. "Have to be like me, you mean? Or like your mother?"

Now that she'd said it, I wouldn't back away from the truth. "Yes," I answered, agreeing with both parts of her statement.

"Oh, my sweet, naive little Tempest. I didn't start out this way, you know. No one does. But centuries of fighting Tiamat and a world that can't accept our existence, centuries of fighting for my clan's very survival, have changed the way I view things. I once had high principles and a rosy vision of how the world should work. But that vision isn't practical. Sometimes, when you're in charge, when people live and die on the decisions you make, you can't afford to keep your hands clean. Sometimes you do things you know you'll regret."

I thought of Cecily, of the way she'd killed those people without a flicker of remorse. "And if you do that often enough, you stop feeling bad about anything. That's the flipside of moral compromise, isn't it, Hailana? Pretty soon you can't tell right from wrong."

"Look at you, so sure you'd never compromise those pretty principles of yours. But how do you know? You've never been tested." She swallowed with difficulty, tried to push herself up a little more on the pillows, but was too weak.

I moved to help her, but she waved me away. "I think that's all about to change. Come talk to me in a week or two about your fine, upstanding morality. If you're still alive, that is."

Dread filled me at her words. I wanted to turn, to walk away, so badly. Because if I stayed, I would be giving her the satisfaction I had denied her for so long. But at the same time, I couldn't not know. I couldn't leave here in ignorance if it meant that people suffered because I wouldn't play Hailana's game.

"What do you know?" I asked.

"A lot more than you, Tempest."

"Really? Is that how this is going to work? You drop cryptic hints, I ask you to explain, you laugh in my face? You really want to play it that way, when *our* people are in danger?"

"Our people are fine for right now—no one is in imminent danger."

I lifted a brow. "Then why are we having this conversation?"

"Because we aren't the only things under the sea, are we?"

"What's that supposed to mean? I don't have time for your riddles, Hailana. People are—" I broke off in terror as her meaning finally sank in. "The selkies?" I whispered. "Tiamat is going after Kona and his family?"

Hailana made a point of glancing at the clock by her bed. "My guess is she's already been and gone. Who even knows if your selkie is still alive?"

"You didn't warn them?" I asked, trying desperately to reach Kona. As always, I couldn't reach far enough.

"Warn them? How was I supposed to warn them? My clan is in disarray, my powers burned out—"

"You could have tried!"

"Or I could have kept my mouth shut and hoped Tiamat decided to have mercy on my clan. Attracting her attention now is a very stupid move." She reached for me with her good arm, her hand closing around my wrist with shocking strength considering her condition. "Let it go, Tempest."

Kona! I called out, using everything I had to try to send the message across the ocean at him. *Please, Kona, answer me.* There was no response.

I pulled away from her, headed across the room at a dead run.

"Tempest!" Hailana called after me. "You have to think of what's best for the clan. You have to think like a mermaid . . . and a queen."

"I can't sit around and watch while people die needlessly."

"You won't be able to stop it."

"No, what I won't be able to do is live with myself if I don't try."

"And that—that weak little heart of yours—is why you'll never be half the woman your mother was."

"Thank God for that." I slammed the door on my way out.

Chapter 28

I was still shaking by the time I hit the main road that led to the castle. "Hey!" Mahina grabbed my arm as I raced by her. "You're running around like your tail is on fire."

I didn't answer her. I was too busy screaming for Kona in my head. *Where was he?* I wondered frantically. He couldn't be dead. He just couldn't be!

"I'm sorry. I have to go," I told her.

"Go where?" she asked incredulously. "Look around, Tempest. We need you here."

"Tiamat's taking aim at the selkies. Hailana didn't warn them."

Mahina got it right away. "Kona?"

"Yes. He's not answering me. I have to get closer, have to—"

"Come on. I'll go with you."

"What about your family?"

"They'll understand." She grabbed my hand and we ran down the beach to the water.

"What's the fastest way to get to Kona's territory from here?"

I asked her. Besides being a genius, she had a better sense of direction than a GPS. If anyone could help me find a way to do what I needed to, it was Malina.

"Through the Wailana trench."

"Let's do it then."

"I want to pack a few things first. So should you."

"We don't have time."

"Then we'll make time." She started running toward her family's land house. "I'll meet you here in ten minutes."

Even as I cursed her, I ran back into Hailana's castle. Went to the room I kept there and put together a backpack filled with extra clothes and the only weapon I could find—a knife Kona had given me months earlier for protection.

Then I ran outside. Mahina was already there, a black water-proof bag slung over her own back. Together, we plunged into the water, diving deep. Neither of us bothered to shift—the trench was so narrow that it was hard to use our tails effectively. Better to traverse it in human form before shifting.

Thank you, I told her as we swam.

Give me a break. Nobody else needs to die today. She paused. *Except Tiamat.*

I've got no argument with that.

As we swam, I kept trying to reach Kona. But when we were within a half hour of his territory and still nothing, I thought I was going to lose my mind. Even if I couldn't hold a bridge at this distance, there was no way I could be this close to him without Kona knowing and contacting me. Something terrible must have happened.

Images of Coral Straits after the attack zoomed through my

head. I closed my eyes, tried to block them out, but all I could see was Kona lying somewhere, dead or dying. Just the thought had my stomach pitching violently and for a minute I was sure I would throw up.

He's dead, I told Mahina desperately. *That's the only explanation. He has to be dead.*

Don't go there yet, she answered, but I could tell by the grim tone of her voice that she thought the same thing.

I let him go.

What?

When we were in La Jolla. I knew something was wrong, and I let him leave without me anyway.

That's understandable. Your brother—

It wasn't just about my brother. It was about Mark. And Kona knew it.

Mark? she asked, turning to me with wide eyes. *I thought that was long over.*

So did I. But being back there, seeing him . . . Everything got so confused. I love him, Mahina. I really do.

What about Kona?

That's the thing. I love him too. I don't think I knew how much until— I swallowed more water, coughed. *Until this happened.*

The long, deep trench that led directly to Kona's city loomed in front of us, and I barreled down it, leaving Mahina to follow in my wake. I was swimming as fast as I could, as fast as I ever had, so that when it emptied out into the city, I ended up skidding across the ground much as I had the first time I'd ever come here. I'd been rushing to make sure Kona was okay that time, too.

I ended up stopping inches from one of the selkies in seal

form. It was lying on its side on the ocean floor and at first I thought it was just resting. But then I understood—it was dead.

I scrambled up, backed away, and realized I was in the middle of my worst nightmare. Kona's city looked even worse than Coral Straits had. Thousands of bodies littered the ground—in seal and human form—each one a little more horrific looking than the last.

Oh my God! Oh my God! Ohmygod, ohmygod, ohmygod! I screamed, turning around and around, trying to find Kona. Trying to see if he was down here. If Tiamat had—

I don't know if he's here, I told Mahina, bordering on hysteria. *I can't tell the difference between them in their seal forms. I didn't see him like that enough. I don't know. I don't—*

Hey! She grabbed me by the shoulders, gave me a firm shake. *You have to get it together!* She pointed at a few live selkies in human form. They were going from body to body, checking to see if anyone was still able to be saved. So far, it didn't look like they'd found anyone. *Let's go ask them if they know where the royal family is.*

It was a massacre, I told her dully. *They didn't stand a chance. They weren't prepared at all. Hailana could have warned them. She could have—*

Don't think about that. Not now. She looked around grimly. *We'll deal with Hailana's crimes later. Let's go see about Kona first.*

We swam over to the selkie healers. As we got closer, I realized one of them was Zarek. I threw myself at him, grabbed on to his arm. *Kona?* I asked, unable to formulate the words to ask what I really needed to know.

We haven't found him yet. He shook his head grimly. *The king—* He choked up, cleared his throat. *The king and queen are over there.* He pointed behind him to two selkies in human form, both of whom were being wrapped in long pieces of fabric. Tiamat had gotten her revenge on Malakai, after all.

I gasped, stumbled, would have fallen if Mahina hadn't been there to hold me up. *Have you checked above?* she demanded of Zarek.

We did a cursory sweep through the house—no one was there that we could see.

Let's go, Mahina told me. When I didn't budge, she started dragging me along behind her.

He's not up there, Mahina, I told her desperately. *He's down here somewhere. He's—* My voice caught on a sob as I tried to accept the impossible. Tried to make myself understand the inexplicable. Kona couldn't be dead. He just couldn't be.

Sitting down here isn't going to help anyone. Let's go check the surface, just to be sure.

Her indomitable will firmly in place, she tugged me toward the narrow, vertical passage that would take me to the island where Kona's family made their home. I didn't fight her because, honestly, I didn't have the energy. Trying to make a decision was impossible, especially as an abyss of agony yawned wide inside of me.

When we got to the passage, Mahina pushed me forward. *You go first.*

I didn't question her. I couldn't. I just stretched my arms over my head and pushed up. There was barely enough room in the narrow, rocky chute for me to move my arms and legs, so it was slow going, just like always. I finally made it to the top, bursting into the warm water of the inlet that brought me to the beach right in front of Kona's castle.

Mahina was right behind me, and together we slowly made

our way to shore. The beach was lined with injured people, while others attended to them. They were all positioned close to the water, and I remembered, suddenly, how salt water healed them. Which made me wonder—just how badly, and quickly, had those down below been injured that being immersed in the stuff had provided almost no protection?

No one spoke to us as we made our way over the sand to the giant castle. When we got to the front door, I knocked as loudly as I could, praying for Kona's butler, Vernon, to open it. If he was there, I told myself, then everything would be okay. He would know where Kona was. Vernon would never let anything happen to any of the royal family.

But then I remembered Kona's parents, lying dead beneath the surface, and knew that nothing was going to be okay again. Even Vernon, with his incredible organization skills and implacable manners, couldn't make it so.

When no one came to answer the knock, Mahina reached forward and pushed the door open. I walked in, glanced around. The foyer looked exactly the same as it always did, nothing out of place, nothing broken, just like at Hailana's. Zarek had said they'd done a cursory search of the place, but that didn't mean anything. Kona and his brothers and sisters could be upstairs, injured. Unable to call for help.

I ran for the stairs, took them three at a time. Even as the logical side of my brain told me it was impossible, that Tiamat couldn't make it up here, I didn't stop. I had to check, had to know. I hit the fourth floor in thirty seconds flat and took off down the hall toward Kona's room.

The door was closed and locked, but a quick shot of energy

had it buckling in front of me. I burst into Kona's sitting room, screaming for him, but he wasn't there. I went through to the bedroom, the bathroom, even his huge walk-in closet. But there was no answer. He really wasn't here. He really wasn't—

I turned to tell Mahina, and as I did I caught sight of graffiti scrawled across Kona's bedroom wall. Written in a red liquid so dark it was almost black were the three-feet-high words:

THE NEW SELKIE KING REQUESTS YOUR PRESENCE AT THE SAHUL SHELF.

Eyes wide, heart hammering in my chest, I forced myself to cross the room. To get up close and personal with the message I was sure I would see in my nightmares for the rest of my life. Reaching out, I touched the letters, which were still a little wet, and came away with the viscous liquid on my fingertips. It was thick and a little clotted and smelled faintly of iron.

At the first whiff of it, the room started to spin around me and my knees gave. I hit the ground hard, but it barely registered. I was still wrapped up in the knowledge, in the horrified realization, that I was staring at a very large message written entirely in Kona's blood.

PART FIVE

Overtopping

"There's no secret to balance. You just have to feel the waves."
—Frank Herbert

Chapter 29

"Where's the Sahul Shelf?" I asked Mahina when I could reason again. It had taken a few minutes—for a while all I could think of was how much blood Kona had to have lost for them to be able to write those gigantic letters on the wall.

Who had done it? I wondered absently. Tiamat couldn't leave the water, so had it been Sabyn? Or some other traitor to the mer and selkies that we didn't yet know about?

I was lost in thought, devastated by the idea of Kona as Tiamat's prisoner and desperately trying to figure out how to get him back, so it took me a while to realize Mahina hadn't answered me. I turned to look at her, only to realize she was on the floor too, looking much paler than her Polynesian skin tone should allow.

"Is that blood?" she finally asked hoarsely.

"Yes."

"Kona's blood?"

"Yes." After everything we had seen today, it surprised me a little that this was what had sent her over the edge. Then again, it *had* done a hell of a number on me as well.

"He really is dead, isn't he, Tempest?"

"I don't know." I looked back at the message, read it for the hundredth time. "I hope not."

There must have been something in my voice, because Mahina snapped her head around to look at me. "You aren't actually planning on going there, are you? It's a trap, Tempest."

"I know it's a trap, Mahina. I'm not stupid. But if he is alive, I can't just leave him there. At her mercy."

"She'll kill you. That's what this is all about—you know that. Take away every source of advice and knowledge you can turn to and then lure you in. She figures you're going to be easy pickings, especially since Sabyn was your trainer and knows everything you can do."

"Not everything," I said grimly as I pushed myself to my feet. Never had I been so glad that I'd played my training sessions so close to the vest, not revealing to Sabyn what my newest powers were.

"What does that mean?" Mahina asked.

"Where is the Sahul Shelf?" I repeated.

"I won't tell you. You can't do this."

"Then I'll find it on my own." I headed for the door.

"Tempest, wait!" Mahina trailed after me. "This is suicide!"

"It's suicide *not* to do it," I told her. "This is Tiamat's big stand. She thinks she's broken us, thinks she'll be able to take me out the second I show up and then there will be nothing left of the prophecy to stand in her way."

"Well, then, she'd be right. That's exactly what's going to happen if you do this."

"Kona is king now. You realize that, right?"

"So?"

"So without him, what do you think is going to happen to his clan? We can't just stand by and watch it go down. They're our most powerful allies. Besides, Hailana as good as told me that she's done as merQueen. Which means there will be a power vacuum with our clan."

"Especially if you run off and let Tiamat kill you! We all know you're supposed to be the next merQueen."

Just hearing the words come out of her mouth made me nervous. Not about dying, because at this point, not going after Tiamat was as much of a death sentence as trying to stop her. She wasn't going to be content with Kona, wasn't going to be content with shattering our clans. She'd be back and, weak as we were, we wouldn't be able to fight her.

Still, the idea that I would take over, that I was *supposed* to be queen . . . It certainly wasn't the first time I'd heard it—Hailana had implied as much when I'd spoken to her earlier, and people had bandied the idea around almost as long as I'd been underwater. But the thought of it, the idea of becoming so completely mermaid, didn't sit nearly as well with me now as it had all those months ago.

"At the moment, being queen is the last thing on my mind. It's much more important for Kona to be king than it is for me to be merQueen. I *will* save him."

"And die doing it."

A shiver worked its way down my spine. "If that's what it takes."

"You're insane," Mahina protested even as she followed me out of the house and back toward the water.

"I don't expect you to come with me," I told her. "Believe me, I know exactly how dangerous this is."

"Which is why you can't do it alone. But I'm warning you, if you get me killed, I'm going to haunt you forever." She looked across the inlet to the huge expanse of ocean. Then said with a sigh, "Australia's that way." She pointed to the right.

"Australia?" I asked.

"You wanted to know where the Sahul Shelf is. It stretches from the coast of Australia up to New Guinea."

"All right, then." I dived into the water, then waited for Mahina to do the same.

You don't have to come, I told her one more time. *You should stay here—*

Shut up and let's go before I change my mind. She started swimming. *And where the hell else would your best friend be besides right here, risking her neck with you? Haven't you ever read Harry Potter?*

I smiled despite the gravity of the situation. *Just call you Hermione, oh brilliant one?*

Exactly.

We went back through the passage, swam over the death and destruction in the city, and out to the open ocean through the trench.

Mahina headed right, but I stopped her. *We need to go this way.*

You're turned around, Tempest. Australia is in the opposite direction.

Yes, but there's something we need to do first. You said Tiamat had taken away my every source of advice.

Well, yeah. She pretty much did, didn't she?

There's one left. I dived deeper. It was easier to travel fast the closer to the ocean floor I was.

Who? Mahina demanded.

My mother.

I sped toward Cecily's cave, blind and deaf to anything but getting to those pearls. They were her regrets and memories, yes, but I didn't believe they existed only to torture me, physically and emotionally. Maybe it was wishful thinking on my part, but maybe, just maybe, there was advice in that cavern that would help me do what my mother had. That would help me defeat Tiamat—if not forever, then at least until the clans could grow strong again.

Three hours later, we hit the cavern fast, so fast that I nearly slammed right into the rock formations that decorated the first room.

Where are we? Mahina asked her first question in hours.

This cave was my mother's, I told her. *She left memories for me here.*

Mahina caught on quickly. *So, if we're lucky, there will be some kind of how-to-take-down-Tiamat instruction manual?*

If we're very, very lucky.

We coasted through the passages, avoiding the fire coral, and within minutes ended up in the pearl-lined chamber.

Holy crap, breathed Mahina as soon as she saw them. *That's a lot of memories.*

Tell me about it.

Now that I was here again, staring at all those pearls, what I had planned seemed like a daunting task. Or, to be honest, more like an impossible one. How was I supposed to find the right memory among all of these? If each of them hurt as much as the other two had, I wouldn't survive long enough to die at Tiamat's hands. My mother would take care of me for her.

Tracy Deebs

Still, I'd come all this way in a last-ditch attempt to find something. I had to try.

Swimming forward, I zipped around the circle, coasting by the pearls, waiting for something, anything. A sign, maybe, or an electric current like the one that had pulled me here to begin with. But there was nothing. Finally I gave up and just grabbed a pearl.

I braced myself for the pain, and it didn't disappoint—fire licked through me. But I didn't fight it this time. Instead, I let it take me over in one incendiary rush. It was intense, but before the pain had even begun to dissipate, the memory started playing before my eyes.

This time my mother was with Hailana above water, and it only took a minute for me to realize that she was making a deal with the devil. Or pretty close to it. They were arguing over something, someone, with my mother asserting that it wasn't time, that *she* wasn't old enough yet while Hailana insisted that *she* was. It didn't take a brain surgeon to figure out they were talking about me, any more than it took one to realize my mother had completely sold me out by the end of the conversation.

I couldn't say how it still managed to surprise me, but it did.

I dropped that pearl, reached for another. This one was Cecily as a young mother, completely overwhelmed. I was sitting in my high chair screaming while she tried everything to comfort me. I didn't stop until my father came home and swept me into his arms. We went down to the beach and he held my hands while I toddled along the water, my face still stained with tears.

I threw the pearl down in disgust. On another day, at another time, this would all be completely illuminating. For now, however, none of these memories were getting me any closer to finding Kona than I currently was. I stepped back, looked around the chamber, hoping for some kind of inspiration.

My eyes fell on the sea glass and I remembered that first one I'd looked at, of my surfing competition. I felt like an idiot—wouldn't the information about what I needed to do to defeat Tiamat be in the sea glass, not the pearls? Good things, not regrets?

I reached for the closest piece, a red one, but something stopped me. Instead, I picked up a shard of purple sea glass—rare and beautiful, it called to me in a way the others didn't.

The second my hand closed around it, memories bombarded me from all sides. My mother locked in bloody battle with Tiamat. They fought viciously, horribly, using whatever weapons they had at their disposal. My mother blasted Tiamat with all the power she had, but the witch only laughed—until that power reached through her defenses to slam against her tender underbelly.

Then she retreated.

I dropped the sea glass, picked up another purple one. Saw Tiamat wound my mother this time. She fooled her, feinted, got her from behind. And once her scaly tentacles were wrapped around Cecily, there was no getting out. My mother would have died if Hailana hadn't managed to cause some damage of her own.

On and on I went, pulling one piece of purple sea glass off the shelf after another. I was focused, in a frenzy, determined to learn everything I could about this monster who had taken so much from me. I could sense Mahina behind me, and though she couldn't do anything, her presence comforted me. Even though I would never let her get close enough to fight Tiamat, the fact that I wasn't alone now—that I wouldn't be alone during that long swim to Australia—meant more than I could ever tell her.

Memory after memory poured through me and out into the chamber, showing Mahina and me Tiamat's strengths and weaknesses. Showing us how she fought and the best way to counter her. Some of the battles my mother and Hailana lost, some they won. Sometimes Malakai was there and in some of the most recent, so was Kona's mother. I absorbed as much knowledge from the battles as I could, but in none of them was Tiamat actually vanquished. Much like my own battle with her, there were setbacks—on both sides—even a desertion of the field. But in the end, she always rose stronger than ever.

I watched the last memory—of Malakai, Hailani, Cecily, and a couple of other people trying unsuccessfully to end Tiamat—and felt my hopes dissipate. It wasn't here.

I looked around the chamber. Maybe I was wrong. Maybe the answer wasn't necessarily in the purple pieces. But there were so many others. There was no time to look at all of them.

Still, it wasn't like I had a better idea. I reached for a green piece of glass and found one last purple one hiding behind it. My heart jumped and I reached for it, then hesitated at the last minute. This was it. My last chance at figuring out how to defeat Tiamat. If the secret wasn't here, then it didn't exist and I would have made this trip in vain. While the other battles had been interesting to watch and had given me glimpses of Tiamat's fighting style, none had been the advice—the road map to taking her on—that I'd been hoping for. If this one was just more of the same, then I didn't know what I would do. How I would beat her and get Kona back.

With a deep breath and a silent prayer that this was somehow everything that I was looking for, I closed my fingers tightly around the glass. It bit into my hand, even drew blood despite the worn-down edges, and I knew it was because I was squeezing it so hard.

Behind me, Mahina gasped in alarm, and when I didn't respond, she tried to pry my fingers from around it. I held on even more tightly, refusing to budge, and was rewarded with a memory unlike any other I had experienced.

It started with me seeing a long, dark tunnel in my mind's eye. Then I was tumbling down it, flipping head over heels again and again and again.

When I came to a stop, I was disoriented, confused, my head spinning. At the same time, there was an overwhelming sense of danger. A powerful need for me to get my senses back and be on the lookout.

I shook my head, tried to stumble to my feet—I was still in human form—but before I could do much more than push to my knees, I was hit by a powerful blast of energy that sent me reeling all over again. This time, when I came to a stop, I was ready for the next attack and managed to roll out of the way of the energy surge.

As I lay there, panting, I glanced down at my hands and saw a scar in the center of my palm. A scar I didn't have, but that my mother had had for as long as I could remember. It was as I stared at that odd, diamond-shaped scar, that I realized this wasn't my fight. It was Cecily's. In this moment, in this memory, I was not just watching my mother battle Tiamat. I was living the battle—as her.

The realization galvanized me, had me paying more attention as giant blasts of power slammed into the wall right above my head. I ducked and swerved, twisted and turned in an effort to get away from the sea witch—who definitely had the upper hand here. It was in all of this dodging that I got my first good look at the wall I had been plastered against more than once.

It wasn't a rock wall at all. It was the side of a ship. On closer inspection—which I got when one of Tiamat's blasts sent me careening face-first into it—I realized it was wooden. An old Spanish Galleon from back in the days when Christopher Columbus had landed on North America. But what it was doing in the Pacific was anyone's guess, unless the Spaniards—or someone else—had attempted to navigate both oceans.

Something about the ship gave Cecily an idea. I didn't know what it was, which was the oddest thing I'd ever experienced—it was like I was in her body, performing her actions, but using my brain. Even with all the magic I'd experienced since being under the ocean, I'd never dreamed such a thing was possible.

Before I'd recovered from that shock, Cecily was racing toward Tiamat, throwing another blast of energy at her with every foot of territory she covered. Soon, it was Tiamat who was on the run, Tiamat who was tripping and tumbling through the water.

It was no different than any of the other fights I had seen between my mother and the sea witch, at least until Cecily slammed Tiamat with enough power to light up a small city for a week. As Tiamat reeled, my mom took advantage of her distraction to dive straight toward the ocean floor. Once there, she burrowed her way under the sand and rocks until she'd created a deep tunnel of sorts that ran beneath the ocean floor and came up next to the old Spanish ship.

As I got my first good look at the ship—and the color of its wood—I realized that the desk Hailana was so proud of had come from this ship. This battle.

Tiamat, crazed with rage and pain, shot through the tunnel after Cecily. And that's when I finally understood what my mother was doing.

Quick as a flash, she blasted through the outer wall of the galleon. Out came thousands upon thousands of gold coins. Manipulating every ounce of magic she had, Cecily used her energy to lift the gold up and funnel hundreds of pounds of it into the opening she had just created in the ocean floor. Then, before Tiamat could even realize what had happened, she whipped the remainder of the gold to the other side of the tunnel, blocked in that end too.

Tiamat was trapped—at least until she could tunnel through another portion of the ocean floor.

I kept wondering how this had managed to trap Tiamat for five hundred years when it had taken my mother only about ten minutes to dig the entire tunnel. But then Cecily seemed to get an infusion of power, an influx of energy that made her phosphorescence near blinding.

Malakai lending her his power? I wondered, remembering the way Hailana's Council had said my mother hadn't done this alone. At that moment, Cecily stepped back and did exactly what I had done once before with her magic—pulled electricity from the water around her. She was able to channel so much that she didn't just cause a big explosion like I had. She actually melted the coins.

Rivers of molten gold flowed from both ends of the tunnel, filling the entire thing and catching Tiamat in the burning metal. The monster screeched as she burned, but Cecily didn't even pause. Creating a minicyclone much like the one I had spawned earlier on the beach, she created a tunnel right through the center of the melted gold, letting the frigid sea water flash freeze the stuff from the inside out. Tiamat, who had to be surrounded by water—who couldn't function in any other conditions—ended up being almost totally encased in hardened gold. Barely able to move or breathe or function. The only thing keeping her alive at all was the small amount of sea water she had access to from the tunnel that had flash-frozen the gold.

It had been a miscalculation on Cecily's part—she'd been trying to kill Tiamat not trap her. But that didn't stop her from completing the job by fashioning a nearly unbreachable cage.

The miracle, I realized as I watched Cecily layer on more and more molten metal—silver as well as gold—wasn't that my mother had managed to contain Tiamat for hundreds of years. It was that Tiamat had ever gotten out.

That alone warned me just how powerful she had become in those years trapped below the ocean floor. Which did not bode well for me. At all.

Chapter 30

Let's go, I told Mahina as I scooped up two of the pearls whose memories had already been expunged, just in case we needed something to trade with along the way.

Sure, she agreed, though she was watching me with a frightened look on her face.

Did that last memory help you figure out what you need to do to stop her? my friend asked as we made our way back out to the ocean.

You couldn't see it?

No. I saw the others, but that one was weird. You just checked out, and except for a little bit of thrashing around, you didn't move again until you opened your eyes. It scared the crap out of me.

I'm sorry. It was weird for me too. And no, I really didn't get any great ideas from it. Unless there's a bunch of gold lying around the Sahul Shelf.

Gold?

Yeah. I told her what I'd seen. *Any ideas?*

We need to run in the opposite direction. Melting gold using just energy? Good luck with that.

It wasn't just her regular energy. It was this electric thing—

What's the difference?

I don't know how to describe it. I guess you have to see it to understand.

I'd rather not, to be honest. She shuddered. *Well, at least we know to go for the underbelly, right? That's where she's most vulnerable.*

Yeah, because I can so see her giving us a shot at that.

Mahina stiffened. *I was only trying to help.*

I know. I'm sorry. I wasn't trying to be obnoxious. I'm just messed up.

Me too. She smiled. *It's okay.*

I paused as we left the cave. *Now, which way is Australia from here again?*

Still right. She rolled her eyes, grinned.

Mahina talked as we swam, once again explaining the whole direction thing, and I let her drone on—mostly because I knew it gave her something to concentrate on besides where we were going and what we would do once we got there. Plus, the sound of her voice was kind of soothing. It kept me calm, which was important, since I pretty much felt like I could wig out at any second.

Australia was about a forty-hour swim from where we currently were—and that's if we traveled full speed the entire time. Unfortunately, neither of us had slept in close to twenty-four hours and the last thing I'd had to eat were the pancakes I'd made Moku for breakfast back on land.

We needed food, needed to rest, but it wasn't like the ocean had an all-you-can-eat buffet on every corner. Which meant I was either going to have to get over my squeamishness about killing a fish for food (sushi, anyone?) or we needed to find a sea-vegetable patch pretty quickly.

I was totally pulling for the latter.

Mahina, who was going through a vegetarian phase, was also on board with that plan, so as we swam we kept our eyes peeled for anything that might look like food. Closer to Coral Straits, we had huge fields of crops, but out this far it was pretty much every creature for itself.

I reminded myself I had more important things to worry about than the rumbling in my stomach. In less than forty-eight hours I would be going up against Tiamat, and this time, there would be no element of surprise on my part. She was expecting me and sure to be armed with Sabyn and a bunch of her other loyal subjects— including a sea monster or two.

Does it surprise you? I asked Mahina abruptly. *That Sabyn turned traitor?* I was thinking of all of Kona's warnings, of the way we'd fought over his concern for me. Knowing what I did now, I felt like such a fool. Why had I given Kona such a hard time?

I don't know. I always got a creepy vibe from him, even when I was admiring his fine form, but I figured that was just because of the stories. Did I think he would sell us out to Tiamat? Not a chance.

I'm an idiot. I let him train me, even when it drove Kona around the bend. But, except for the first day when it seemed like he was trying to kill me—

Which he probably was.

Yeah, I know that now. Except for that, he wasn't a bad trainer. He didn't teach me any offensive stuff, but he taught me stuff about defense I'd had no idea about.

Yeah, probably so he'd know how to get around you later.

I sighed. *Yeah. Probably.*

I ran a hand over my face, tried to ignore the bone-deep weariness that was invading my every cell. How was I going to save Kona? If it was just a matter of trading myself for him, I would do it in a heartbeat. He was so much more important to life down here than I was and besides, the idea of saving myself at *his* expense made me literally sick to my stomach.

But it wouldn't be that easy. My brain flashed back to the last time Tiamat and I had squared off in a major battle. I had tried to outthink her then, had attempted to figure out what she had planned—for me and my mother. I'd failed, and my mother had been killed. I couldn't handle the idea of failing again, of losing Kona the same way I'd lost Cecily.

Was I strong enough for this? I knew I didn't have a choice—I was doing it. But was I really strong enough to take Tiamat on or was I just fooling myself? Was I leading Mahina into a slaughter?

Thank God I knew not to rely on anything Sabyn had taught me, but I still felt like those sessions with him left me vulnerable. He knew how I moved, how I thought, my favorite means of attack. Nothing quite like parading your weaknesses out in front of the enemy for him to scrutinize . . .

And thank God for Kona, who had warned me over and over again not to trust Sabyn. Not to mention the warning deep inside that had kept me from showing him the strongest of my powers. The fact that he didn't know about the electricity thing might be the only advantage I had in this whole mess. Because while Sabyn might have learned my attack patterns, I'd also learned his.

Tempest, look! Mahina pointed toward the ocean floor and then suddenly dived deep. Not sure what she'd spotted, but knowing her eyesight was better than mine due to all the years I'd spent on land, I followed her without question.

And nearly wept with joy when I realized she had found an undersea garden. After paying the admittance price—which ended up being one of the pearls I'd pulled out of my mother's cave hours earlier—we raided the garden mercilessly.

As we ate, and rested our exhausted tails, I thought about all the things I didn't know about Tiamat, all the things I didn't know about life in the ocean overall. Part of me couldn't believe I was doing this, risking everything in a fight that didn't have to be mine. But at the same time, I couldn't ignore what had happened to my mother. Couldn't ignore what had happened to all those selkies and merpeople. Or what was happening to Kona right now.

Taking on Tiamat might not be the smart thing to do, but it was the right thing. As long as she was around, no one would be safe.

So, I said to Mahina as casually as I could, *what am I going to be dealing with here?*

She paused, a bunch of sea lettuce halfway to her mouth. *With Tiamat?*

No, with the climate in Australia. It was my turn to roll my eyes. *Of course with Tiamat. I've already met the Lusca,* I said, referring to the huge sea-monster thing that had ripped my mother apart almost a year ago. *But what other creatures does she have lying in wait?*

I'm not really sure. Mahina thought for a minute. *There are* stories, of course, but nothing that I know for certain to be fact. A lot of them are just mythology, after all.

I refrained from mentioning that both Tiamat and the Lusca were considered mythological creatures—and therefore fake—by most of the world. The fact that we knew the truth didn't make their existence any more believable to most of the population.

I still want to know, even if they are fake. Better to be prepared.

Well, it's not like I have a lot of up-close-and-personal knowledge of Tiamat, but I can tell you what I've heard, Mahina began reluctantly. *The Lusca is usually never far from her—you saw that. But she has other creatures that work for her as well. The shark-men, the bunyip, Ceto and Scylla, and, of course, the Leviathan.*

She looked at me expectantly, but I couldn't respond. It was like everything she said after shark-men was in Greek. *What's the Leviathan?* I asked. They called whales leviathans, so maybe she had a huge whale that did her bidding? But how menacing could a whale be? Most of them ate plankton, for God's sake.

The Leviathan is a sea monster, kind of like the Lusca. But it's more of a dragon. He's the most powerful creature in the ocean, or so everyone says.

Terrific. I blew out a long breath. *And the rest of those things you mentioned?*

She sighed, ran a hand through her hair. *They're also sea monsters. Ceto is pretty much chaos personified—her favorite pastime is sinking ships and bringing down planes that come too close to her lair.*

Where's her lair? I asked warily.

It's in the Atlantic—between Bermuda and Puerto Rico.

I choked on a piece of dulse. *You mean, the Bermuda Triangle?*

I don't think it's actually a triangle, Mahina answered. *More like a rectangle. Why?*

I started to explain about the myths and lore associated with that part of the ocean, but decided it could wait for another day. I had more important things to do right now.

As we ate, I continued to question her about Tiamat's allies. Scylla, it turned out, was another kind of sea creature—the only one left of her kind. When in her natural form, she had two snakelike heads and the power to create whirlpools and sinkholes wherever she was. Like Tiamat, she could transform into mer form with magic and the blood of mermaids.

And bunyip, while not as frightening as the three sea monsters Tiamat had at her beck and call, didn't seem like anything to fool around with either. Water demons who lived near Australia and who ate human and mermaid flesh, they were fanged and vicious and frightening as hell. At least according to Mahina.

Terrific. Why had I wanted to know what I was swimming into again?

Before long, we were on our way. We swam and swam and swam, until my tail and arms were exhausted and it was all I could do to keep my body moving in a forward motion. I knew it was wrong to push myself like this, knew Mahina and I should find some place to rest for a few hours, but just the thought of stopping again was impossible. Not when Kona was in danger, his life hanging in the balance. Not when so many people had already died. This thing needed to end and it needed to end soon.

We're almost there, Mahina told me as we swam by a huge coral formation. *The Sahul Shelf is only about an hour away.*

Okay, thanks. Part of me was grateful we were so close—I wasn't sure how much longer my nerves could hold out—but another part of me was absolutely terrified. We had swum all this way and I still didn't have any more of a plan to rescue

Kona than I had when we'd started. I had hoped something would come to me on the swim, but plotting and scheming had never really been my thing. I'm more of a straightforward, in-your-face kind of girl—something I was afraid was going to get all of us killed before this day was over.

Kona? I tried my hardest to build a mental bridge long enough to reach him. Not that I was holding out much hope. He could be drugged, unconscious, hurt . . . anything could have happened to him in the last four days. But still I had to try. Just the idea that Kona was gone—

Tempest? His voice was faint, faraway, and for long seconds I was terrified I had imagined it.

Kona! Are you all right? I demanded.

Go back, he told me. *You shouldn't be here.*

Typical male. He'd been protecting me for almost a year, and it was obvious he had no intention of changing that behavior, even though he was the one in need of rescuing now.

Where else should I be? I asked him. *I can't leave you with Tiamat.*

Yes, you can. This is what she's been waiting for. She wants you dead, out of the way, so she doesn't have to worry about being challenged again.

I thought of all the death I had seen at Coral Straits and in Kona's territory. *It doesn't seem like she's particularly worried about that anyway. I'm so sorry about your parents, Kona.*

Yeah, me too. I could hear the defeat in his voice and couldn't stand it. Kona had always been so strong, so sure of himself. The idea that he was now the one who needed reassurance felt strange. But he had just lost most, if not all, of his family. How else would he be feeling?

Where are you? I asked him. *We're coming up on the Sahul Shelf, but I don't know which part of it you're on.*

Silence was my only answer.

Kona? I screamed, suddenly panicked. Had Tiamat found out he was speaking to me and killed him?

I'm here, Tempest. He sounded infinitely weary. *You need to go back, before it's too late.*

And you need to stop whining and tell me where you are. Because the only place I'm going is to find Tiamat—with or without your help. I paused. *Though I would really prefer your help.*

You can't win. She's ready for you. She's been waiting for days, prepared to kill you on sight.

Like that's a surprise? Tell me something I don't know.

Please, I'm begging you. Don't come.

Kona. I said his name softly, wishing I could reach through the bond and reassure him as he so desperately needed. *I'm going to find a way to get you out of there. So you might as well give me all the information I need. The more I know, the better prepared Mahina and I will be.*

Mahina? You brought Mahina with you?

Well, the volunteers weren't exactly lined up around the block. Besides, I trust Mahina as much as I trust you. There are only a couple people in the world I would say that about.

For a second, my brain went to Mark, and a bone-deep sorrow swamped me. I might die down here tonight, and Mark would never know what had happened. Neither would Moku or Rio or my dad. The idea of them waiting for years for me to come back—as we had for my mother—made me more than a little bit crazy. If only I could see Mark and my family one more time . . .

Tempest? Are you still there?

I'm here, Kona. And I'm not going anywhere until this thing is done. So, please, please, if you know, tell me where you are.

This time, he was the one who didn't answer. Long seconds ticked by and then finally he whispered, *We're on the north part of the shelf. Tell Mahina we're close to the Sahul Reef. She'll know what I'm talking about.*

I closed my eyes as relief swamped me. *Thank you. Now, who's there with you?*

He hesitated.

Kona, do you want me to get my ass kicked? Who's there with Tiamat? Sabyn? The Lusca?

Sabyn and a bunch of shark-men. Ask Mahina about Scylla and bunyip.

I already have.

And you're still coming? Are you suicidal?

I didn't answer that. Instead I told him, *You'd come for me.*

Damn right I would. But this is different.

Because I'm a girl?

Because I love you and I don't want anything to happen to you.

It's going to be fine, Kona.

Another long pause. *I can't change your mind, can I?*

No. Through the bridge, I tried to show him my certainty, my resolve.

I could feel him making a decision, his own resolve suddenly as strong as mine. *Then there's something else you should know,* he told me.

What?

She was hiding him for the big reveal, hoping it would throw you off balance when you need your concentration most.

The knots in my stomach multiplied. *Tell me,* I demanded. *What is she hiding?*

He took a deep breath, braced himself. *She kidnapped him, brought him down here. He's got a tank of oxygen strapped on, but I'm not sure how long it's going to last.*

Moku? I asked as terror seized my entire body.

No. Mark. Mark's here too, Tempest.

Chapter 31

His words sent me reeling, both literally and figuratively. I stopped dead in the middle of the ocean and Mahina slammed into me, hard. We both went flying.

What the hell? she demanded when she'd righted herself.

I couldn't answer her, couldn't formulate words in my head. Instead, my thoughts, my consciousness, my very soul were filled with one long scream.

Tempest? Kona again, sounding panicked. *Are you all right?*

I didn't answer.

Tempest, damn it, don't shut me out. Answer me. Are you okay?

He's alive? I finally managed to choke out the words.

He's fine for now, just a little banged up. Kona paused, like he was debating whether or not he wanted to continue. But finally he said, *We're pretty deep. I'm not sure how long humans can stay at this depth without having problems.*

I took off then, swimming faster than I ever had before, faster even than I'd seen Kona go. Mahina struggled to stay with me, but it wasn't long before she fell behind.

Where am I going? I shot the words at her. *I'm looking for the Sahul Reef?*

She didn't ask how I knew, but then I figured she didn't have to. It was pretty obvious that something had lit a fire under me. *If it's the one I'm thinking of, it's about ten miles north of here.*

Are you going to be all right? I asked her. Not that I was stopping. The idea of Mark throwing a pulmonary embolism or slowly being crushed beneath the weight of the ocean was killing me, pushing me to faster and faster speeds.

Go, she answered. *I'll catch up.*

Within minutes, I reached a huge coral garden that I figured must be the Sahul Reef. Instead of passing over it, I dived deep and hid among the animals' branches. I got stung by a coral again, but it was better than last time—either because it wasn't fire coral or because I was slowly becoming immune, as so many of the other mermaids were.

Either way, I wasn't moving—this was a good place to wait for Mahina and to try to figure out what tricks the sea witch had up her sleeve.

Where's Tiamat? Mahina asked when she found me.

I'm not sure. I know she's close—I can feel her. It's like this darkness is pressing in on me, making it hard to think or move.

Sounds like a spell—she's not taking any chances with you.

At that moment, two of the ugliest creatures I had ever seen swam by. Glowing yellow, they had strange misshapen heads; large, pointy ears, and small, humanlike bodies covered in big, mismatched scales. *Bunyip?* I asked Mahina.

Yes. She shuddered.

In the back of my head, I was aware of Kona trying to talk to me, but I ignored him. I couldn't afford any distractions right now and one more bombshell like the last one he dropped would mean game over.

We barely dared to breathe as they passed by us, armed with spears and obviously on patrol. But once their backs were to us, I started weaving my way through the coral in an effort to stay undercover while I followed them.

What are you doing? Mahina hissed.

I didn't answer, figuring it was pretty obvious.

They'll catch us.

Or they'll show us where we need to go. I don't know about you, but I don't want to just swim up on Tiamat accidentally.

How do you know they're not leading us into a trap?

Do you have a better idea? I demanded.

No, she huffed. *But I really don't want to die today—can I just throw that out to the universe?*

I think the universe is aware.

The bunyip continued on their path, giving every indication that they were oblivious to us following them. I could only hope they weren't leading us into an ambush. In a perfect world, I would be able to scope out the situation before going in blind. I was more than aware that probably wouldn't be the case—here, but hope springs eternal.

Kona. I called him again.

What? he roared. *Where are you?*

Sorry. We were hiding from the bunyip.

I felt him recoil. *Where are they?* he demanded.

Where are you? I countered. *Are you out in the open ocean or are you in a cave?*

About a mile past the reef, there's a sunken ship. She has us in the hold, at the bottom. And, Tempest, she has hundreds of soldiers in and around us just waiting for you. Bunyip and the sharks, plus the others.

I figured. I paused, then spoke to both him and Mahina, wanting my friend to be in on the conversation as well. *You say you're a mile north of the reef?*

Yes. But there's no way for you to sneak up on us. I told you that already. You have to go, try to get out of here before she realizes you're close.

Don't worry about us, Kona. I glanced at Mahina. *We've got this.*

Mahina shot me a thumbs-up sign even as she looked ready to puke.

I have to go now, I told him. *I'll talk to you again when I'm safe.*

Tempest! Kona shouted suddenly. *Tempest, no! She's moving troops. I think she knows you're here. The bunyip must have seen—*

More likely, you're tipping her off, I told him. *Somehow I don't think Tiamat could fail to notice the fact that you're suddenly freaking out.*

She doesn't know I can talk to you. She gave me something that was supposed to inhibit my powers. Instead, it knocked me out completely. I haven't been awake that long.

Does she know you're conscious?

No.

Good. Try and keep it that way. Are you and Mark alone?

No. That's what I keep trying to tell you. You can't win—

I'll see you in a little while, Kona. I promise.

I broke the connection, then slowly, stealthily, made my way out of the reef. No one attacked, so I was hoping we'd have a few minutes before the next patrol came by. Of course, if things went according to the hastily manufactured plan in my head, we would need only a fraction of that time.

What are you doing? Mahina hissed. *They'll see us.*

Not if I have anything to say about it.

I shifted back to human form—for some strange reason my magic always worked better when I had legs—shimmied into my bikini bottoms and called the power up inside of me. I could feel it growing, getting stronger, seething just below the surface as it sought an outlet.

I refused to let it loose, at least not yet. Instead, I gathered more and more energy from the waves until my entire body was vibrating with the strength of what I was trying to hold deep inside myself. When I couldn't contain it any longer, when it felt like I would break apart if I amassed even one more drop of energy, I focused on the ground and let it all go at the same time.

In seconds, I'd created a twenty-foot-long passageway straight down into the ground. *Come on*, I told Mahina, diving in. We hit the end of the passage in less than a minute, so I used small blasts of energy to continue building the tunnel, much like my mother had done in that last memory.

I need to know when we've gone exactly one mile, I told Mahina. *Do you think you and your weird geography talent can calculate that precise of a distance?*

Seeing as how the alternative is death, I'll give it my best shot.

You do that.

I turned my head to grin at her, but she just glared. *I don't know how you can laugh at a time like this.*

Because the alternative was to start screaming again, and that wouldn't help anyone.

Going back to work, I pulsed out another section of the tunnel, then another and another. It was slow work, and I couldn't help wondering how my mother had done it. She'd created one of these so fast that I barely had a chance to blink before she was out the other end.

My inability to do the same was not exactly inspiring confidence.

How much farther? I asked Mahina after nearly an hour of blasting out piece after piece of the tunnel.

At least half a mile, she told me.

You have got to be kidding me. I stopped for a second, pulled back. Really looked at what I was doing. I was blasting away, pushing outward and compacting the dirt against the walls of the tunnel as I went.

It was working, but it certainly wasn't very time or energy efficient. I was already exhausted and I hadn't even started battling Tiamat yet. There had to be a better way of doing things—I just needed to figure out how.

I thought about surfing, about how I duck dived under the water to get better momentum and control. Thought about the way I always twisted my hands when I went to break the surface because it made things cleaner, easier. And wondered if there was a way to use that same barrier-breaking twist down here.

An idea came to me—strange and outlandish, but it could work. It wasn't how my mother had done it, wasn't how anyone else I knew would do it, but maybe it would work for me.

Back up, I told Mahina, scooting after her a few feet back up the tunnel. Feeling stupid, but willing to try anything at this point, I stretched out on my stomach, hands above my head. And then I started pulling the energy back in again. Not gathering a little bit at a time to do the small blasts I'd been working with, but enough to do that first blast again.

Enough to set every nerve in my body to vibrate.

Taking a deep breath, I tried to do what I had when I'd created that long, silver spear against Sabyn. I visualized what I needed from my magic, and then I let the power loose.

I spun like a top at high speed, my flexed fingers tunneling into the earth so fast that I covered yards in mere seconds. Like a drill bit going into wood, I twisted my way through the tunnel at an amazing speed, going and going and going until Mahina yelled, *Stop!*

I fell to the ground, exhausted and more than a little dizzy.

How did you do that? Mahina asked incredulously. *I've never seen anyone spin that fast in my whole life.*

I have no idea. I just know I don't ever want to do it again. I clenched and unclenched my fists, trying to stretch out the cramps in my fingers.

Now what? she asked.

I looked straight up, visualizing what might be above us. *Now we find out how close we actually are.*

She looked pale. *What happens if we come up right in front of them?*

We duck?

You are really on a roll today. An absolute riot.

I do what I can.

Before I started digging my way out, I decided to try one more thing, just to see if I could get a bead on where exactly we were. *Kona?* I called again.

Tempest? Where are you? It's been forever!

Yeah, well, I'm a little busy. Say something else, will you?

What do you want me to say?

You sound closer.

So do you. Where are you? He also sounded terrified, but I didn't tell him that—especially since I knew his concern was all for me.

I'm not exactly sure. Is Tiamat still with you?

Yes, along with a few of her henchmen. Please, don't do anything stupid.

A little late for that, isn't it? I was crawling along the tunnel while he spoke, trying to find the spot where he sounded the loudest. *Keep talking,* I told him.

What are you doing, Tempest?

Trust me. How's Mark?

He's still out. Or, like me, he's pretending to be. I'm not sure.

Are you both tied up? Or locked in somewhere? How is she holding you?

We're chained to iron posts.

Of course they were. It wasn't like Tiamat wanted to make this easy for me or anything.

Okay, I told him, *I think that's the best I'm going to get.* I'd crawled about forty feet back down the tunnel to the spot where he was at his absolute loudest.

What does that mean?

It means close your eyes and relax. I'll be there soon. I injected a lot more confidence into my voice than I was feeling.

Tempest, please. He sounded broken, defeated, completely un-Kona-like. *I don't want you to do this. Do you hear me? Don't make me watch you die, please. I love you and I can't—* His voice broke.

Tears filled my own eyes, but I batted them away. *It's going to be fine*, I told him huskily, knowing I was lying but not caring. Because I hadn't come this far to turn back without even trying to save him and Mark. *I love you too. Be ready.*

Tempest! Tempest, no!

I cut the connection completely, slamming a wall up in my mind so I wouldn't hear his desperate pleas.

This is it. I turned to Mahina. *Are you ready?*

Oh yeah. Can't wait.

We tunneled straight toward the surface, using the small energy blasts again as I didn't want to take the chance of going too fast and blowing right onto the surface. I could feel the consistency of the dirt changing, getting wetter, and I knew we were close.

Taking a deep breath, I reached for the backpack I'd given to Mahina for safekeeping. Pulled out the knife I'd stuck there a few days ago. *This is for you*, I told her, sending as much energy into it as I could. Within seconds, the blade burned hot enough to raise blisters. *It's not much, I know, but—*

She knocked me with her shoulder to shut me up. *Hey. It's fine. I figure I'm going to spend most of my time ducking behind you, anyway. Besides, I have a few tricks up my sleeve.* She gestured to her own backpack. *Now, get out of my way.*

She shouldered past me.

I grabbed on to her arm, horrified. *I'm going up first.*

Really? Have you never watched any of those human cop shows? You're the one who can blast people at a thousand yards, so you need to go up second. To cover me.

Mahina, there's no way I'm letting you do that.

You don't have a choice. She reached her arms above her head and, using every ounce of strength she possessed, plunged straight through the thin layer of dirt at the top of the tunnel and onto the ocean floor.

Chapter 32

I piled out of the tunnel about two seconds after Mahina, arms extended and energy blasting in all directions. I dropped two of the shark-men before I even had a chance to look around and figure out where we were.

But the second I turned, I realized we couldn't have picked a worse spot to come up if we tried. Kona and Mark were nowhere in sight, although the ship Kona had spoken of was only about five yards away. That was actually the good news. The bad news was that we had somehow managed to emerge in what looked like the middle of a strategy session.

Sabyn, the traitorous bastard, was at the front of a group made up of bunyip and shark-men, while a half-human, half-snakelike sea serpent stood a little bit to the side, speaking to another group of bunyip. Her top half was human and as beautiful as Tiamat's, except this creature's hair was long and black, while her skin was honey colored. *A Polynesian version of the sea witch?* I wondered as Mahina hissed, *Scylla.*

Our eyes met across the expanse of ocean, and I watched as

hers widened in surprised comprehension. She went for a spear that was stuck into the ocean floor right next to her, but I had already created a spear of my own and now hurled it straight at her chest. With a cry of rage, she jumped out of the way, but not before it took a huge chunk of skin, muscle, and scales off of her hip.

I turned to face a smirking Sabyn and his crew, but Mahina was already lobbing a series of what looked like homemade grenades straight into the middle of the group. As they scattered, she grabbed my arm and yanked me toward the ship. We made it behind the bow just as the first one exploded, followed by detonations of the other two.

Shock waves ripped through the water, and when I peered around the corner it was to see numerous bunyip and sharkmen lying on the ground. Some of them were in pieces, and those that weren't still didn't look like they were going to be getting up anytime soon.

What the hell were those? I demanded.

Something I've been working on for a while. I've only ever detonated one before, so it's nice to see that it worked. Although I am curious about the range—the blast wasn't quite as powerful as I was anticipating.

Can we be curious later? You know, when our lives aren't depending on how fast we move? Scooting back from the ship, I took aim at the hull and let loose a massive energy blast that ripped right through the thin sheets of metal that made up the bow of the twentieth-century warship. *Let's go,* I told Mahina, heading through the hole I'd created.

I glanced behind me in time to see Sabyn break free from

the chaos outside and head straight for us. A few feet behind him was Scylla, a murderous look on her beautiful face.

It was definitely time to get moving.

Once inside the ship, Mahina wanted to pause and get her bearings, but she hadn't seen what was coming. *Move it,* I shouted at her, locking my hand around her wrist and dragging her forward. We were in a room filled with machines—pumps and gauges and strange-looking metal contraptions that looked like they had once been important.

We're in the engine room, Mahina breathed in awe, trying to take in everything at once.

Look later, I told her as I swam low, trying to get lost beneath the machinery. I had made it halfway across the room, Mahina at my heels, when Sabyn and Scylla burst through the hole. Though we had crammed ourselves into a crevice so small it was impossible to turn my head to watch them, I knew they were there. Partly because of the glow of their phosphorescence as they made their way down the narrow aisles and partly because the temperature of the water had dropped about twenty degrees.

I'd felt the drop in temperature outside as well, but had chalked it up to the difference between the tunnel and the open sea. Now, however, I wondered if it was Scylla who had that effect on the water, as I'd never felt a difference like that around Sabyn before. Was she doing it on purpose? Trying to freeze us into compliance? Or was she just so evil that the cold was a natural by-product of her existence?

Either way, Mahina squirmed in terror as Scylla got closer, and to keep her from moving I ended up clamping a hand down on her shoulder. *Don't move,* I told her fiercely.

They're going to find us. She sounded as close to hysteria as I had ever heard her.

Not if you don't give us away. Just be still for a minute—

I can't. Her voice rose until it was a high-pitched whine deep inside my head. *We have to go. We have to move. She's going to kill us if we stay here.*

As Mahina pushed against me, crying a little, trying to get out, I knew that there would be no reasoning with her. Any second now, she would give away our hiding spot and whether I liked it or not, we were going to have to take on two of Tiamat's most powerful allies.

Do you have any more of those grenade things in your bag? I asked her.

Only two. The distraction worked, had her focusing on what she could do to help instead of her utter certainty that we were about to die.

Shit. Two wasn't going to do us much good, especially not if we still had to face Tiamat, a hoard of bunyip, and God only knew what else. Still, it would be stupid to save them for later if it meant dying now . . .

Get one of them out, I finally told Mahina, and Scylla must have felt the vibrations from her movements because the sea witch stopped in her tracks. Then turned and faced our hiding spot dead on before beginning to swim toward us.

Are you ready? I asked Mahina, who whimpered even as she pulled out the grenade, as well as the knife I had given her.

Scylla must have alerted Sabyn to our presence, because the next thing I knew, he too stopped his mad dash to the other side of the room and began making his way back toward us.

Mahina stiffened, tried to scoot out of our hiding place with the knife extended in front of her. *Not yet,* I cautioned.

But they're getting closer.

Not close enough to use that, I told her. *Trust me, give it just a few more seconds.*

I kept my voice low and soothing, trying not to spook Mahina—or myself. Because if I was honest, I was one small step from wigging out as well. Still, that was exactly what they wanted, and I wasn't going to give them the satisfaction. Wasn't going to just roll over and let them kill us.

I waited, breath held, for one of them to make a move. But even as I postponed our attack, I was working, thinking, channeling energy and using it the same way I had seen Sabyn do during our "training" sessions.

Layer after layer, I quickly built a spear that was as sharp as a scalpel and probably three times as deadly, based on the power I was resolved to putting behind it.

It's almost time, Mahina. Scylla was close, very close, because I could see the pink tinge to the water splashing over to us. She was obviously still bleeding, which, disgusting as it was to be this close to so much blood, could be an advantage for us. We just had to find a way to exploit her injury.

Scylla stopped a few feet away and just waited. Beside me, Mahina grew more agitated, but I still refused to let her strike out with the knife.

She who moves first loses. It was one of the first things Jared had taught me and I had lived by it for months now. Striking first meant lowering your guard, exposing your weaknesses. Waiting was a way to show your strength.

Almost, almost, I said to Mahina. Let her get a little closer. *Let her—*

My plan went completely awry when Mahina thrust her arm out prematurely, then pulled back through the water for all she was worth. The knife plunged into Scylla's upper tail and the witch howled in agony.

Since it was too late for the attack I had hoped to launch, I sprang into action. Leaping up, I shoved Mahina behind me. She refused to let go of the knife as she went, so it ripped out of Scylla almost as quickly as it had gone in. Scylla screamed in rage and pain, and though I knew I was going to regret it later, I went for her instead of Sabyn. I figured it was better to finish her off early than to leave her injured and constantly have to watch my back.

Except it wasn't that easy, because injured or not, Scylla still had a few tricks up her sleeve. As I moved closer, hoping to finish her off, I came into contact with the bloody water. The skin on my stomach started to burn, to blister, and I reared back in pain and shock.

Her blood is poisonous! Mahina shrieked. *Don't let it touch you!*

It would have been nice if you'd warned me of that earlier!

Diving deep just as Sabyn sent a blast of energy crashing my way, I rinsed off the tainted blood, then wound my way around the machinery to come up behind Scylla. As the current was flowing toward her and Mahina, I hoped standing in the opposite direction would keep me away from the blood.

She half turned, shot a blast of energy straight at my head. I ducked and it missed me, thank God, but it was a little too close for comfort, especially in these cramped, crowded quarters. Besides, Sabyn was gearing up for another attack—after training with him for all those hours, I could sense it in the way he held his body and the air of expectation that surrounded him.

I braced myself for whatever he had planned, even as I turned, plunging my energy spear straight through Scylla's heart. She screamed, clawed at it . . . and was dead before she hit the floor. I backed up quickly to avoid her blood.

Go, Mahina! I screamed as I squared off against Sabyn. *Get out of here!*

My best friend didn't have to be asked twice. She scrambled for the hatch, was almost halfway through it when Sabyn casually reached out a hand. He made a fist like he was grabbing something and yanked hard. Mahina reeled backward, slamming brutally into one of the machines.

She didn't get back up, and when I screamed her name, there was no response at all.

Give it up, Tempest, Sabyn said in a bored voice. *She's dead.*

The words hit me hard, sent me reeling, but I refused to acknowledge them, let alone believe them. He couldn't know what kind of shape Mahina was in any better than I did, couldn't know—

I shoved thoughts of my friend to the back of my mind when Sabyn started to circle me, which was no mean feat in quarters this cramped. Yet somehow, he managed it.

I stepped back, turned with him, unwilling to let him out of my sight for a second. Our eyes met and he smiled, but it was so filled with malice and evil that it made me shudder. How had I ever thought, even for a second, that he might be a decent guy?

We don't have to do this, you know. His voice was soft, sibilant, seductive. *Tiamat doesn't want to see you die.*

I snorted. *You could have fooled me.*

No. Wasting powers like yours is stupid. If you joined us, we could rule all the waters in the world.

Yeah, because turning my powers over to some ugly-ass sea witch with delusions of grandeur makes so much more sense than fighting you. Besides, she should give up the whole recruitment thing. It didn't happen when she killed my mom, and it's not going to happen now.

Tempest, we could help you.

I don't want your help. I was also circling now, so that the two of us were mirroring each other's movements as we faced off—each shifting in an effort to keep the other in our sights.

Everything inside of me demanded that I attack now, lashing out while he was still trying to talk me into joining his side of the fight. But, again, Jared's training raised its head and I knew I had to stay alert, wary, be ready to deflect his move, which meant I couldn't strike first. It had ended up working out all right with Scylla, but only because her attention had been fractured. Sabyn was focused entirely on me and I knew one wrong motion would mean my death. The smile on his face told me that he would enjoy every second of ripping me apart.

So we continued to circle. For long, endless, exhausting minutes, we spun, each waiting for the other to make a move. I was growing antsy, freaking out a little. Mahina still hadn't moved, hadn't said a word.

Every instinct I had, every ounce of friendship inside of me, screamed to look at her, to check on her even if it was only visually. But I knew that as soon as I did, as soon as I glanced away, that one moment of inattention would be the end of me. I resisted the pull, stayed focused on Sabyn.

That intense focus was the only thing that saved my life.

When Sabyn struck, it wasn't the in-your-face assault I was used to. Wasn't silver arrows or massive blasts of power. Instead, it was subtle, insidious. At least at first.

The water around me began to churn, to spin. I thought it was a rogue wave coming through, spurred by the amount of power concentrated in such a small area. But then I realized the movement wasn't just natural current. The water was actually spinning around me, creating a whirlpool effect that began turning faster and faster, locking me in place.

I tried to back away, to stumble through it, but it moved with me in ever constricting circles, spinning so fast that the centrifugal force made it almost impossible for me to get enough water into my gills to breathe. The world was going gray, and I knew I had to do something fast if I was to have any chance at all, but the lack of oxygen—combined with the clawing panic rising inside of me—made it almost impossible to strategize.

Not so tough now, little Tempest, are you? Sabyn taunted me. *And this is just the beginning. It only gets worse from here—unless you want to put a stop to it. All you have to do is join us and this can go away.*

As he spoke, the whirlpool got tighter and tighter until I swear I could feel, not just the water, but also Sabyn's fingers around my neck, strangling me. *Come on, Tempest.* The whisper sounded in my ear even though he was several feet away. *Swear your allegiance to Tiamat, to me, and all will be forgiven. If you ask nicely, I might even let your little pet human go home.*

What about Kona? I could barely get out the words.

Sabyn's hands felt like they were wrapped around my head

now, crushing my gills, truly preventing me from breathing. I clawed at them, tried to pry them away, but it was impossible because in reality, there was nothing tangible there. Only the sensation of being strangled, plus the knowledge that time was running out.

You see, Kona and me, we go way back, Sabyn said. *And I must admit, I have some scores to settle with him. I won't lie—it's going to be a lot of fun watching him die. But that doesn't mean poor little Mark has to die too. I have nothing against him. Of course, it's kind of hard to hate him when all he does is lie there like a vegetable.* Sabyn laughed. *Which he'll be, very soon. I think he's only got about an hour of oxygen left in the tank Tiamat found him. Even if you tried to get him out of here . . .* Sabyn shook his head. *It's a long way to the surface.*

I shuddered in horror and fear, which only made Sabyn laugh louder. He was so sure of himself, so proud of the way he and Tiamat planned on exterminating two of the people I cared about most in the world. Not to mention Mahina, who was lying at my feet and who might very well be dead right now.

Rage burned in my gut, a blind, red-hot fury that Sabyn was doing all of this. Sabyn, whom the merQueen had trusted. Sabyn, whom *I* had trusted—for a little while anyway.

The anger gave me strength I wouldn't have otherwise had, strength to stop fighting the whirlpool, to stop struggling for air, to just relax into it. It was obvious that Sabyn felt my sudden surrender and was instantly suspicious—I could feel it in the way his body tensed, see it in the wary look in his eyes as he watched me.

But it was too late. All his bragging, his pride, had given me the one-second opening I needed. My hands dropped away from my gills, and in a couple seconds I managed to yank enough electricity from the ocean to power a small city. Then I reached for him, all trembly and submissive, and he was stupid enough to lower his guard a second time.

That's when I struck, pumping thousands of volts of electricity—via lightning—straight into his chest, directly at his heart.

He didn't have a clue what hit him.

Chapter 33

The whirlpool didn't so much die down as explode outward when Sabyn stumbled back, clutching his chest. As the water seethed and roiled around us, I watched, completely dispassionate, as he fell to the floor of the ship. And then I hit him with another blast, one that ripped right through him, charring flesh even as it split the skin of his abdomen wide open.

It was a truly gruesome sight, but I didn't flinch. I don't know if that said something about who he was . . . or who I was becoming.

Quickly backing away, I hauled Mahina up and threw her over my shoulder as I moved toward the door, not willing to turn my back on Sabyn for a second. He might be down but he wasn't necessarily out—I'd been around sea creatures long enough to know how that went.

And sure enough, just as we reached the hatch, the door slammed shut. The waves caused by the abrupt motion bounced and pinged off everything, including me. They were strong enough, and I was just off-balance enough carrying Mahina, that they slammed me into a wall. My concentration wavered for only a second, but like what had happened with Sabyn, the lapse was just long enough for him to strike.

He chose a high-pitched vibration that filled the entire engine room, oscillating off all of the metal and filling the water with a noise so piercing and shrill that it was impossible to bear. I screamed, slammed my hands to my ears, but it didn't seem to matter. The vibration wasn't just outside anymore. It was inside of my head, violently shaking me apart.

I dropped to my knees in an effort to escape the sound. I wanted it to stop, *needed* it to stop, but since I had no idea how Sabyn was doing it, I couldn't even begin to think of how to counter. Of course, that was assuming I would ever be able to think again. Because right now, the only idea running through my head was the fear that my brain was literally going to explode. Already, I could feel blood, thick and viscous, leaking out of my ears. As I wiped at it, I wondered vaguely if this meant that my eardrums had burst or if something more serious was going on. I knew I should be concerned, but the noise made it impossible to do more than formulate that emotion in theory.

Even worse, Sabyn actually started healing the wounds I'd inflicted on him, slowly closing them up until nothing was left but a couple livid red scars across his chest. I didn't even know how it was possible—he was a merman, not a selkie, and mer-people normally didn't heal anywhere near that fast. I should know.

Frightened, confused, and more desperate than I wanted to admit—even to myself—I sent a blast of energy straight at him, but my brain was so scrambled that I couldn't find much power to put behind it. Sabyn deflected it easily and lobbed back one of his own that had me ducking and moving for cover.

I wasn't very fast, as I was still carrying Mahina. Turning my body so that any blast from Sabyn would hit me and not her, I tried to dive behind one of the huge storage containers that stood at the end of each of the machinery aisles. But even as I tried to get to safety, I knew there wasn't much shot of me making it.

Still, I had to try. I shifted to the left one second before a blast of energy whooshed past me and slammed into the wall just to my right. I knew I had only seconds before he came at me with another shot, and not knowing what else to do, I dived for cover. It was a gamble—for long seconds I was completely exposed—but running around waiting to get hit was easily as dangerous.

I braced myself for impact, either from the ground or from a fireball from Sabyn, but it never happened—instead, Mahina leaped back into action. Pushing herself off my shoulder, she twisted around and lobbed a grenade straight at Sabyn.

We didn't bother sticking around to see how he was going to handle this latest attack.

Instead, I course-corrected and we careened off the front wall before I dived for the door—determined to get out of the engine room before the grenade exploded. I was thrilled Mahina was okay and didn't want anything to change that—especially not a grenade of her own making.

We made it, with about three seconds to spare. And then I was barreling down the hallway, my brain functioning a million times better now that the horrific noise had stopped.

Put me down, Mahina hissed, but I ignored her. Out here, where I wasn't trying to avoid a million different pipes and gauges, it was a lot easier to carry her—plus I wasn't sure she'd even be able to swim or shift.

I was more powerful in my human form, but I definitely wasn't faster, so we hit the narrow, circular stairs at the end of the hall only seconds before a volley of spears flew down the hallway. They slammed into the wall directly above where we'd been floating. Since I was sure there were more where those had come from, I didn't bother for a look at our newest attackers. Instead, I took the remainder of the stairs three at a time and then ducked into the first available doorway.

I was expecting the worst, and from the way Mahina had tensed against me I knew she was too. But there was no one in the room, thank God. After double bolting the door—hooray for military ships—I slowly set Mahina on the ground.

It's about time, she said grumpily. *I was beginning to feel like a two-year-old.*

Would you rather I'd left you back there?

No. She paused, then grudgingly added, *Thanks for the rescue.*

I think that should be my line. I eyed her cautiously. *How are you feeling?*

I'm fine. She pushed herself up, swam a little. *I've just got a hell of a headache, thanks to psycho-merman.*

You probably have a concussion. I looked around the room for the first time. It was completely empty except for a few chairs knocked over on their sides. But there was another staircase built into the wall opposite us. It was leading down. I stared at it for a minute, calculating, then turned to Mahina.

How far from the bottom of the ship do you think we are? I asked.

Judging from the lack of windows in any of these rooms, not far. Plus the engine room is usually pretty low down. Why?

I nodded at the staircase, saw understanding dawn. *What room do you think this is?*

She shook her head. *It's hard to tell without any of the original contents, but I wouldn't be surprised if it had been some kind of storage room.*

Which would what? Make the cargo hold below this?

I don't know. Maybe. She sighed heavily. *You're going to make me go down those steps, aren't you?*

No. But I'm going. You can come or stay here alone . . .

She beat me to the first stair. *You go first this time. I've had enough violence to last me a lifetime.*

So had I, but I was smart enough to know there was much more to come—and it didn't matter what order we took down the stairs. Still, after everything she'd done to help me, I was plenty willing to take the first hit here. It was what I had always planned on anyway, before Mahina had suddenly decided to play hero.

I moved down the stairs cautiously. My balance was a little off—a result, I think, of whatever damage had been done to my ears. But sounds were so distorted in the water normally that it was hard to tell if my hearing was okay or not.

I braced myself, almost expecting to find Tiamat at the bottom, waiting to blast me into next week. And if not her, at least some of her bunyip and shark-men. But there was no one, nothing—except for another staircase.

I was shaking now—a combination of adrenaline and fear

rocketing through me so fast that it was difficult to stand, let alone swim. Still, I crossed the room and headed down this staircase as well.

Kona, I called as I hit the first step. *Can you hear me?*

Oh my God, Tempest, you're alive. What the hell were all those explosions? He sounded as shaky as I felt. He also sounded close. Really close.

I started slowly down the staircase. *Do you know where Tiamat is?*

She's here, with me.

Sabyn? I took another step.

I haven't seen him in a while. Where are you?

On the stairs. Four more steps and I was about a third of the way down the staircase. As I made the first turn, I realized it wasn't pitch black down there like it had been in the other two rooms—instead I could see a few glowing lights in different colors.

Silver, red, a muddy green.

I froze, trying to figure out what to do next. *I think I've found you.*

Tempest, go back. There's no way you'll survive—she knows you're here and she's got a perfect shot at the staircase from where she's standing.

I can't leave you.

Yes, you can. You have to.

Stop whining, Mahina cut in, *and think of some way to distract the sea witch from hell, will you please? We just need a second.*

Which was why she was the genius in this equation—or at least I thought so until I saw the last grenade was clutched in her hand.

Don't throw that! I squealed.

Yeah, because I'm going to risk killing the loves of your life, she told me privately. *What the hell did we do all this for if I was going to just fry them in the end?*

Exactly what I'd been thinking.

I braced myself for Tiamat's attack, but before I could take another step, I heard Kona. Not on our private channel but on one that anyone—even Tiamat—could hear.

Give it up, Tiamat. If you're still here by the time Tempest finds me, she'll kill you.

So, you're awake, dear boy. I was wondering when you were going to join us. A ripple of waves flowed past us as she moved. *And I think you're giving your girlfriend a little too much credit.*

Really? If you're not afraid to fight Tempest, why did you bring so many reinforcements? You must know you can't beat her.

For long moments, there was no response at all. Then, *Feeling awfully brave today, aren't we, Prince Kona?* She gave a low, angry laugh. *Or should I say King? I have to admit, killing your father gave me more pleasure than I've had since I watched that bitch Cecily die.*

Her voice dropped to a sibilant hiss. *And you're still alive because I thought this would be amusing. But don't push me too far. She's already here—I don't need you as bait anymore. Or that useless human toy of hers . . .*

Kona made a choking sound, like he was in pain. That, combined with her obvious threats about him and Mark, had me jumping the last section of staircase. The water cushioned my landing, and I crouched as close as I could get to the ground considering I was floating. Mahina landed right behind me.

Mark and Kona were sitting on the floor in the middle of the room, backs against an iron pole and heavy chains wrapped around them—just as Kona had warned me. Tiamat was next to them, her back to the staircase as she towered over Kona. Her spiky black tail was curled close to her body, as she leaned over and raked her poison-tipped claws down Kona's face.

Behind her, facing outward through a variety of holes blown in the bottom of the ship, were bunyip and shark-men galore. Others were focused on a staircase about halfway across the room. Within seconds, I realized that Tiamat was also watching that staircase. Mahina and I had come down a small, back stairwell that led into a sheltered alcove off the main cargo hold. No one was paying any attention to it at all.

Thank God.

We had finally caught a break.

But even then, Tiamat was turning, her green eyes glowing with a maniacal light.

I let loose a bolt of electricity aimed straight at her before ever making the conscious decision to do so. She deflected it easily.

Tempest. Her smile was razor sharp and ugly as hell, despite her beautiful face. I shuddered as I realized she was even better looking than the last time I'd seen her, more proof that she had gorged herself on the blood of the mermaids she had so recently killed.

Let Kona and Mark go, I told her in a voice that revealed none of my fear. *And maybe I'll let you live.*

She laughed, and this time there was nothing fake about it. *Let me live? Look around, Tempest. Coral Straits and all of its allies are in shambles. Hailana is one small step from death's door. The selkie empire has been destroyed. Let me live? I think you have that backward. Maybe, if you are very, very smart in the next few minutes, I'll let you live.*

She glanced behind her, to where the shark-men and bun-yip eyed me eagerly. *But to be honest, that's not very likely.*

My stomach tightened and terror slid, ice cold, into my veins. *What do you want?*

Want? She shrugged. *Nothing. Look around. I have everything I want right now. And if something else comes up in the future, well then, I have more than enough power to take it. Whatever it is.*

Then why am I here? If you have everything you want, why do you need me? Or Mark? I deliberately avoided looking at Kona. *He can't help you with anything.*

Ah, but he is amusing to keep around. She floated over to Mark, who was watching everything with eyes so wide I could see the whites all the way around his irises. I knew he couldn't hear anything that we were saying, which must have made this whole thing even more terrifying for him. Tiamat trailed one razor-sharp nail down his cheek.

I wanted to reassure him, to find a way to tell him that everything was going to be okay, but I didn't know if that was the truth. Every second that counted down was another second wasted of Mark's precious air supply.

We have to do something, I told Mahina. *Mark's not going to last.*

Uh, not to be pessimistic, but I don't think we're *going to last.*

Not helping.

Sorry. She blew out a long breath. *Okay, we need to even the odds.*

There's forty of them and two of us. I'm not exactly sure how you plan to make things more even . . .

We need to get Kona out of those chains.

Yeah.

How are we going to do that? Mahina asked.

I have no idea.

Not sure what else to do, I moved forward. Tried to draw Tiamat's attention away from Mark and back to me. It worked a little too well, as not only did she focus on me, but so did her huge band of henchmen.

Now that I think about it, Tiamat said as she glided toward me, *I do want something from you, after all.*

Of course she did. She hadn't set up this whole nightmare for the amusement factor alone. *And what is that, exactly?* I shifted so I was between her and Mark and Kona. It left my back vulnerable, but that seemed a small price to pay.

Your blood.

Her hand snaked out and grabbed on to my wrist. She was stronger than I thought, and when she yanked me toward her I didn't have enough strength to resist. I tried to pull away, but Tiamat was having none of it.

Hold them! she shouted, and a dozen or so bunyip converged on Mahina and me, some restraining Mahina in the corner, the others grabbing my arms and legs, my shoulders and hips. Offering me up to Tiamat like some kind of ancient sacrifice.

Your mother promised you to me seventeen years ago, Tiamat said as she leaned over, her red painted mouth gaping macabrely. *And then denied me every time I came for you. That ends tonight. With your blood and Kona's energy, I will be invincible.*

Her grip tightened on my arm as she dragged me—and the bunyip holding me—even closer to her. And then, with one powerful slice of her nail, she ripped my wrist wide open. And began to drink.

Chapter 34

I screamed. I couldn't help it. Everything inside of me shut down, every thought, every breath, until the only thing left was pure, animalistic fear. My heart raced, my nerve endings burned, my senses blurred into nothingness as endless seconds passed, the most drawn out and frightening of my life. And still I screamed. I screamed and screamed and screamed.

Even as I did, I kept waiting for her to finish, to say she'd had enough or that it was a mistake, that she didn't really want my blood. Though one of the first things I'd learned down here was that mermaid blood really did give Tiamat power. It gave her beauty and strength and magic, and she drank until the mermaid in question was dry—I had seen enough to know she wouldn't stop until I was dead. And yet, despite all my knowledge, it had never before occurred to me that one day she would actually come after *my* blood.

Which made me a total and complete idiot. Kona had said that certain people had more powerful blood than others. Why wouldn't Cecily's daughter have blood of incredible strength and magic? Combined with the power of Malakai's son? Tiamat really might end up invincible.

I screamed louder as the knowledge of my imminent death began to sink in. I'd been prepared to die helping the others escape—but I hadn't been prepared to go out in the opening battle, as the dumb blonde in the horror movie who everyone knew deserved to die because she was TSTL—too stupid to live.

Well, maybe not everyone.

Behind me, Kona and Mark were going crazy trying to get to us. I could hear them even over the shrieks of protest in my head, yelling and cursing and yanking against the chains that bound them. I knew, in those moments, that if they could have gotten free, they would have torn Tiamat apart with their bare hands. Or died trying.

That knowledge calmed me down somehow, let me think even through the scalding pain radiating from my wrist and up my arm. I was bleeding out pretty heavily now, the world around me beginning to grow fuzzy. A large part of my brain was paralyzed, unable to do anything but screech as she drank from me. But another, smaller part kept telling me to do something besides scream, to somehow find a way to escape.

That was the part I needed to listen to.

Ignoring the soft, slurping noises Tiamat was making, ignoring the excruciating pain of being drunk alive, I focused instead on the burning I could feel in my stomach—not pain so much as the touch of gathering electricity. Closing my eyes, I focused on the water, on the electric charge, and began to amass more and more power.

I pulled the energy from the water around me, from the ocean beyond the boat, from the sea floor that beckoned to me. It filled me up, scalded my insides, made my skin boiling hot. I could feel it radiating up from me, but more, I knew the bunyip were getting uncomfortable. Shifting their hands, their stance, moving around restlessly in a way they hadn't even a few moments before. It was only a matter of time before their skin broke and blistered like the skin of my stomach had—except this time it wasn't from Scylla's poison, but from the heat I was making no attempt to hide.

It still wasn't enough though. I felt like there was more energy to gather, more power to consume, to build.

There were nearly fifty people in the room with me, fifty living beings with life energy of their own. With my eyes closed and my senses seeking, it wasn't like I could miss it. Before I really understood what I was doing, I started to pull that force inside me as well.

My body trembled under the impact of it all, and I remembered those frightening moments on the beach when I had feared I was going to literally ignite. That I was going to turn supernova and suck everyone and everything around me into the black hole I created.

That fear was back, sharper and more real than it had ever been.

But unlike the instance on the beach, there was nothing I could do to stop it this time, nothing I could do to temper it into something softer, less catastrophic. Terrified, desperate, I had put my body in the driver's seat and this was the result.

I only hoped I didn't end up hurting Kona or Mark or Mahina. I reached out, tried to warn them, asked Kona to shield the three of them, but I wasn't sure if Kona or Mahina could even hear me. I was pretty far gone, my powers stretched to the breaking point. And still the electricity grew.

As if from far away, I heard the bunyip start to whisper among themselves.

Heard Mahina's muttered *What the hell!* and Kona's murmured *Tempest, baby, what's going on?* But I didn't respond to them. I couldn't, not now. Everything I was, everything I ever could be was focused on this wild, free, electric being I was becoming. This force that was about to be unleashed.

And still my power grew, until my back arched under the strength of it, until my hair took on a roiling energy of its own, until my whole body finely vibrated with the energy it was filling up with, the energy that it could no longer contain.

A shudder worked through me, a convulsion that started in my feet and shook my entire body in a close approximation of an epileptic seizure—my brain's response to the overload I was forcing it to carry. Again and again I seized and trembled, until the bunyip backed away in fear, and even Tiamat, who had continued to glut herself on the power cocktail that was my blood, looked up from what she was doing.

That's when it happened. The second her mouth lifted from my vein, I exploded outward in a burst of energy so great that I blew out the walls of the room, the walls of the ship, had us spinning and turning and lighting up on the ocean floor in a way no one had ever seen before.

The energy blasted out of my body much like a nuclear explosion without the mushroom cloud, encompassing everyone and everything in my path. The bunyip holding me turned to dust from one second to the next, and Tiamat literally went up in flames.

She shrieked then, trying to put the fire out by rolling on the ocean floor that had replaced the boundaries of the ship. And still I didn't stop the outpouring, couldn't stop it. It reached toward the other bunyip, toward the shark-men that were attempting to flee in fear. But they had hurt me, hurt Mark and Kona and all those other mermaids and selkies. It incinerated them on contact.

Tempest, stop. Look! Mahina screamed from behind me. Kona must have heard my request for his protection, and had shielded her, because while her nose was bloody, the skin of her arms and face blistered from my heat, she was still in pretty good shape.

But her burns weren't what she was concerned about. It was the chain wrapped so tightly around Mark and Kona. It was boiling, almost melting, and as it did, it was searing a powerful brand into their chests and upper arms wherever it touched.

The sight of them in pain reached the small part of me that was still there, that had not ceased to exist in the rage of power and heat that was consuming so much of what was in its path. Forcing myself upright, I tried to rein it in, tried to pull the power back inside myself now that it had done its job.

It was agonizing. Miserable. Impossible. Yet I managed to do it, one small current at a time. Not letting the power go, as I still had more battles to fight, but leashing it, holding it down, wrapping it tightly inside of me.

The second she sensed that the danger had passed, Mahina was across the room, prying the chain from around Kona and Mark. *Come on, we need to get out of here.* I couldn't tell if she was talking only to them or if I was included in the conversation. All I knew was that every single being still alive in the room—and there weren't many—was looking at me like I was a cross between the Leviathan and the devil himself.

It barely registered as all hell broke loose.

Sabyn, a huge army of bunyip and shark-men at his heels, hit the ocean floor in a blinding flash. He leveled an energy arrow straight at Kona's chest, let it fly. Kona intercepted it with a wave of his hand, and it fell, harmlessly, to the ground.

It was the opening salvo in a battle that should have been over in seconds—we were that outnumbered. But somehow, we managed to hang on.

Grouping together in the middle of what had once been the cargo hold, backs to each other, Kona, Mahina, and I faced out in every direction—with Mark in the middle to protect him—and prepared to fight.

Now that I had contained the monstrous energy suck inside of me, I couldn't release it again. It had burned itself out in that one fiery blast that had gone on and on and on, had burned me out until my control was nothing but a shaky shell.

I could still fight, still shoot energy blasts, but that super-nova effect had consumed itself—maybe a little too soon.

Positioning myself next to Mark, who was lugging around an oxygen tank—and two of the guns Mahina had apparently found among the cartons of weapons still in the hold while I'd gone nuclear—we worked together to fight off this newest prong of the attack.

Sabyn and a burned and blistered Tiamat had fallen back, were watching as the bunyip and shark-men charged. Mark and Mahina shot anything that got within a few feet of them—as bullets travel only a short distance underwater—while Kona and I used our own powers to blast the creatures back.

We need to get out of here, Mahina hissed. *Unless you're going to go all nuclear again, we don't stand a chance against this many people. Tiamat's hurt, but Sabyn is still in great shape.*

I know, I know. Any ideas? I asked her and Kona. A quick glance at Mark showed that he was more than holding his own—and that his oxygen tank had only about fifteen more minutes left in it. Whatever we were going to do, we had to do it now.

As it became obvious that we were surviving, Tiamat and Sabyn entered the fray one more time. Sabyn with that sneaky, terrible whirlpool of his that surrounded us, robbing us of the ability to breathe, and Tiamat with her spells and magic that hit each one of us differently.

Though she wasn't touching me, I could feel the poison in her razor-sharp claws as she punched straight through the raw, angry skin of my stomach and started to squeeze my heart, much as Hailana had done all those months ago. Except Tiamat wasn't trying to make a point. She was intent on killing me, and with so much of my blood running through her veins, it was child's play. She was scarily in tune to what I could do and what I couldn't.

I shot a blast of energy at her, but she dodged it easily even as she squeezed her fist tight. It was too much. I stumbled, dropped to my knees.

Kona came to my rescue. Blasting through the walls of the whirlpool Sabyn had created, he sent his own energy straight at Tiamat. She was so busy concentrating on me, relishing the pain that she was inflicting, that she didn't notice until Kona's fireball connected straight with her vulnerable midsection.

She went down with a scream of rage, hitting the ground hard enough to loosen her grip on me. It was all I needed. I climbed to my feet, prepared to blast her with everything I had left. But Mark was already there, emptying the clip of his gun straight into her like some kind of commando in a war movie.

She didn't die. Mere human bullets couldn't kill a sea witch of Tiamat's magnitude, especially not slowed down as they were by the water. She was injured though, badly enough that Sabyn dropped his attack and swam to her. He picked her up in his arms, and after sending a powerful volley of arrows our way—hundreds of the things came soaring at us, forcing us to focus on them instead of him and Tiamat—Sabyn retreated.

We were left with a battalion worth of bunyip and shark-men, all of whom looked nervous, confused. Like they didn't know if they should keep fighting or surrender the field. A few of them started backing away while others rushed forward. Reaching deep inside of myself, I laid them flat with a couple more energy blasts.

Then I swam over to the bunyip who had been acting as leaders. Stood over their fallen forms and thought about killing them all, just to ensure this never happened again. I could do it. I had the power—not to mention the little voice urging me to end them for everything they'd put my friends through.

But I flashed back to that moment in my mother's cave, where she'd stood over three unarmed merpeople and killed them in cold blood. I remembered my horror, my shock. My disgust. And knew that I could never hurt these bunyip, no matter what they had done. They were unarmed now, practically defenseless against us, and I. Was. Not. My. Mother. Nothing, not even this brutal of an attack, could make me cross that line.

Leave us alone, I told them, *and I'll let you live. But if even one of you attacks us, it's open season. We will kill you all.* I shot a bolt of electricity into the floor of the boat, inches from one of the most powerful bunyip's heads.

He must have gotten the message because no one followed as Mahina, Kona, Mark, and I slowly made our way through the carnage and out of the ship.

Do you think they're out here, waiting for us? Mahina asked anxiously.

I think they're long gone, I answered. *Tiamat was in bad shape. It will take a while for her to recover from the beating she received today.*

What about Sabyn? Mahina continued.

I glanced at Kona, knew that Sabyn's days were numbered. There was no way the new selkie king was going to let him live, not after everything he'd done to Kona's family . . . and to me.

We'll deal with Sabyn later, Kona said, straightening up. *Right now we need to get—*

I gasped, cutting him off. Because as he stood, I realized something none of us had noticed before. One of Sabyn's final arrows had hit the mark, ripping through Kona's side and embedding itself deep within him.

Chapter 35

Kona seemed to notice at the same time I did, or maybe the adrenaline coursing through him finally wore off, because he suddenly collapsed in a heap right at my feet.

Oh my God! What do we do? I dropped to the sea floor next to him, pressed my hands against the wound, and tried to stop the blood flow.

We get him to a healer, Mahina told me grimly. *It has to be bad if his body can't heal itself. I don't know if there are any around here or even if they'd help him if there were. The Australian clans are really tight-knit. They don't like outsiders.*

I'm fine, Kona said, but already his breathing was labored, his beautiful silver glow dimmed.

No one was talking to you, I told him archly. *We need to stop the bleeding or we won't be able to take him anywhere.*

I know. Mahina was already scouting around the ocean floor, looking for God only knew what.

What are you doing? I asked. I didn't move to help her—I was too busy putting pressure on Kona's side—but Mark had stumbled over to a different spot and was trying to help her search for whatever it was she needed.

Red algae, she told me. *It'll clot the blood if we apply it directly to the wound.*

I turned to tell Mark what red algae looked like, and remembered I had no way to communicate with him. I couldn't get inside his head the way I was in Mahina's or Kona's. I ended up waving to him, gesturing him over.

Once I got him situated, with his hands over Kona's wound, I sprang into action, fanning out to look for anything red algae might grow on. I finally found some on the outer pieces of the destroyed ship and I scraped it off before swimming back to Mahina as fast as I could.

She breathed a huge sigh of relief and pressed it straight onto Kona's side. Within a minute or so, the bleeding had slowed to almost a drip and he wasn't gritting his teeth quite as hard as he had been.

Red algae is also a painkiller when applied directly, Mahina informed me.

Thank God. My knees went weak with relief. *What do we do now?*

We try to find that healer. She glanced to both sides of us, as if she could tell our location just by a quick look around the ocean floor. *I think there's a selkie clan north of here*, she said doubtfully, as if something about the whole situation had made her lose faith in herself.

There is, Kona said. *I think they're about seventy miles north.*

Seventy miles isn't bad, I told myself as I helped support Kona's weight. About a half-hour swim from where we were if everything went as planned.

Mark got on Kona's other side, helped support him by drap-
ing Kona's arm over his shoulder.

Are you ready? I asked Kona, pressing my cheek to his.

As I'll ever be. His smile was a little strained, but it was there.
And his silver phosphorescence wasn't quite as dim as it had
been.

We started out, a little slower than I'd anticipated courtesy of
Kona's wounds and Mark's human limitations. But we hadn't
gone more than a few yards when a strange, high-pitched beep-
ing noise started. My already abused eardrums ached in protest.

What is that? Mahina demanded.

Mark turned stricken eyes to us as he pointed to himself . . .
and his oxygen tank.

Shock raced through me as I studied his gauge. With everything going on, I had completely forgotten the air situation. Now,
according to the gauge, Mark had only five minutes of oxygen
left. And that wasn't enough time to get him to the surface.

I looked between Mark and Kona frantically. What was I
going to do? Kona was nowhere close to being out of the woods
yet. We hadn't found a healer, his wound could burst open at
any minute with all the swimming he still had to do, not to
mention the fact that he'd lost a lot of blood.

And Mark? Mark didn't have enough air to get to the surface.
And even if he did, it wouldn't exactly matter. We were in the
middle of the Pacific Ocean, somewhere off the coast of Australia. What was he supposed to do if he even made it to the top?
Bob around until some passing boater picked him up? And what
was he supposed to say? He was far from home with no money,
no passport, nothing.

I bit my lip and tried not to freak out as precious seconds leaked away. I'd known all along that I was going to have to make a choice like this one day, a choice between the two of them, but I'd never dreamed that it could be a life or death situation—for either of them, let alone both.

In the end, though, it wasn't much of a choice. I looked at Kona, waited until his beautiful silver eyes met mine. *I'm sorry*, I told him. *I can't let Mark die.*

I know.

I turned to Mahina. *Get him to a healer. Keep him safe. Please.*

I will. But you better get moving. She nodded at Mark.

I know. I crossed to Mark, smiled at him. He was amazingly calm considering he was on the brink of death. I didn't know if that was because he didn't realize how far down we were or if he was just more stoic than I could ever imagine being. Either way, I wasn't going to waste a second more.

I pointed up and he nodded. Then wrapped an arm around him and pulled him close, so that our bodies meshed from shoulder to hip. He waved at Kona and Mahina, mouthed the words *thank you*. And then we were ascending, moving slowly toward the surface. We couldn't go too fast because we were a long way down and rising too quickly could end up killing him. Decompression sickness was nothing to fool around with.

At the same time, it wasn't like he had enough oxygen left to do everything we needed to. Which meant, soon enough, we were going to have to make a choice between leveling up and rushing to get him air.

But not yet. For now, we were going to do everything we could by the book. And pray, by some miracle, that it was enough.

I hated that we didn't have a gauge to tell us how deep we were or how many feet we had ascended. I tried to remember how many feet we were allowed to ascend per second—I think it was somewhere in the thirties. Thirty-one? Thirty-seven? I decided to compromise at thirty-five to be on the safe side. Of course, that was all estimation too.

I counted to sixty, moving up as slowly as I could, trying not to surpass thirty-five feet a minute. After about four minutes, I made him stop. Level out and hang for a while as his body rid itself of excess bubbles from being down so long. Mark was trying not to breathe much, using only enough oxygen to keep himself alive, but after a few minutes of hanging out at this level, his tank gave one long beep right before it shut down.

For the first time there was real panic in Mark's eyes, panic that mirrored the fear deep inside of me. How was I going to get him up in time? How would I keep him alive? The surface of the ocean was a long way off . . .

I shoved the worry down, closed my eyes, and tried to think. There had to be a way out of this, had to be a way to keep Mark safe. We hadn't fought through everything with Tiamat and Sabyn just to give up now. I took a deep breath, blew it out slowly . . . and that's when it came to me.

I ripped the breathing apparatus from Mark's mouth, ditching the oxygen tank altogether. Then took another deep breath in through my gills and placed my mouth over his, creating a seal between our lips, and breathed the oxygen into him.

His hands tightened convulsively on my hips as he took in the first breath, and held it for a few seconds before breathing it out. I shook my head, mimed holding his breath, and he nodded. He already knew what I was trying to tell him. He'd just needed that life-affirming breath to make sure everything was still in working order. I didn't blame him.

Breathing deeply again, I did the same thing. Leaned over and brushed Mark's cold lips with my own until he opened them a second time; then I breathed more air into his mouth.

He held the breath inside this time, his brown eyes staring straight into mine with so much love, so much concern, so much *awe*, that it filled up every empty space I had inside of me. I stroked a hand down his cheek, then wrapped my arms around him and memorized the feel of him for all time.

We started to climb again, slowly and carefully. When he finally blew the air out in tiny bubbles, I breathed for him again. And again. And again.

It took a long time, but eventually we reached the surface. The second his head broke through the water, Mark took a series of long, ragged breaths. Then he cupped my face in his hands and kissed me like it was the end of the world. Like this was the last kiss he was ever going to have. I wrapped my arms around him and kissed him back.

When Mark finally lifted his head to grin at me, he said, "I love you, Tempest. I really, really love you." And then he kissed me again.

This time when we broke apart, I said, "We've got to figure out which way Australia is."

He grinned and pointed behind me.

"How do you know?" I asked, turning.

"How do you not know? How much time have you spent in this ocean now?"

"More than you."

"Exactly my point." He kissed me a third time, and it was so full of joy and happiness and excitement at being alive that I couldn't help the tears that sprang to my eyes. "I've got to tell you, Tempest, you sure know how to show a guy a kick-ass time."

Kick-ass was right. "I nearly got you killed."

"You saved my life—and everybody else's. I can't believe how amazing you are."

"Yeah, real amazing. It takes an awesome girl to get her guy kidnapped and nearly murdered."

"Yeah, well, it takes a more awesome girl to save that guy. And the kidnapping was so not your fault. It was the evil sea-bitch all the way. I can promise that I definitely won't be fooled by her damsel in distress routine a second time."

"Is that how she got you? Pretending to need help?"

"Yeah. Said she'd hit her head when her board got away from her. I tried to get her back to shore—"

"Of course you did." Because that was just the kind of guy Mark was. Decent, caring, always willing to risk his neck for someone who needed it. Especially me. How many times, now, had he nearly died because of me?

The thought made my stomach cramp, so I shoved it aside. "We need to get you to land."

"Yeah, well, I'm not sure what I'm going to do when I get there."

"I actually have an idea about that," I told him. "But it depends on where in Australia we end up."

"I'm betting on Sydney."

I smiled. "I can only hope we'll get that lucky."

Mark laughed, started to swim toward where he believed land would be, but I stopped him. "Seriously? Like you haven't been through enough today?"

"What do you mean?"

"I mean, you're not exactly adapted for this. Settle back and let me do most of the work."

"Oh yeah?" The gleam in his eye was speculative—and more than a little interested. "And how is that supposed to go, exactly?"

"Like this." I shifted quickly, tucking my bikini bottoms into the pocket of Mark's wet suit, then wrapped my arms around him like Kona always did me. The thought gave me pause, but I pushed it aside. I had to take care of Mark before I could get to Kona. Until then, Mahina would have to make sure he was all right.

And then we were off, traveling toward land at over a hundred miles an hour.

Mark laughed, whooped. "*This* is a kick-ass ride," he called to me.

His response made me smile, and despite everything, I relaxed and enjoyed the sun beating down on our backs as we raced through the water to safety.

We hit Sydney Harbour about an hour and a half later. I laughed when I saw the Opera House. "You were right," I told Mark.

"I usually am. But, Tempest, what are we going to do here? I don't even have a passport."

"I know. One of my dad's friends from his surfing days docks in Sydney most of the time during the winter. Dad and the boys are planning on visiting him next month, but if we're lucky, he'll be here already."

It took a while for us to find Sergio's boat, simply because there were thousands docked around the harbor. But my family had visited Sergio here two or three times in the last few years, so I had a pretty good idea of where to start looking. Eventually we found it—a small, pretty yacht named *Surf's Up*.

It was early morning in Sydney, so I was hoping I'd find Sergio around. Last time we visited, he'd slept on the boat, but a lot could change in a year. I was proof of that.

Still, when I called to him from the dock, his shaggy black hair appeared within a couple of minutes. "Who's there?" he asked, his Italian accent sounding completely out of place down here.

"It's Tempest, Sergio. Bobby's daughter."

"Tempest?" His whole head came out this time and he eyed me in surprise. "You're looking good! But what are you doing here?"

"It's kind of a long story. Can we come aboard and tell you?"

"Of course, of course." He ushered us in with a wave of his hand. "Just let me put some pants on and get the coffee started. I'll be up in a minute."

It was more like seven minutes (I knew because I was fidgeting the whole time, trying to figure out how long it would be before I could get back down to Kona), but when Sergio finally made it topside, he had a tray of coffee and croissants with him. Mark and I tried not to fall on them like starving wildebeests, but we failed miserably.

Sergio eyed us with amused indulgence. "Been swimming?"

he asked, taking in our wet clothes. Mark had shed his wet suit a while back and was now in just a pair of board shorts.

"Something like that. Look, I know this is awful, but I can't really explain how we got here. Can you just trust me when I tell you we weren't doing anything illegal and help us out?"

He laughed. "You sound more and more like your mother every day." But he was quick to offer his help. "Can Mark's parents send a passport to him? If so, he can stay here until it arrives and then we'll get him on a plane home."

"In a few days. He can't fly yet. He's been . . . diving."

"He can stay as long as he needs to," Sergio replied.

It was exactly what I hoped to hear. "Thank you, Sergio. I don't know what I would have done if you hadn't been here."

He just smiled his easy surfer's grin. "Hey, no worries. I'm looking forward to surfing with the two of you this afternoon—seeing if you can still hold your own Down Under."

I laughed, then made my excuses. Much as I wanted to stay with Mark, I needed to get back to Kona as well. To make sure he was okay, and that Mahina had gotten him to a healer. I also had to check on Hailana and the state of her clan. *My* clan now.

Mark walked me as far down the harbor as we could go, then wrapped his arms around me and held me tight. I breathed him in, the salty, sweet scent of him melting me inside a little, like it always did.

"I'm sorry," I told him. "I'm so sorry."

"For what?" At my very unamused look, he said, "Oh, right. That whole kidnapped by the evil sea-bitch, nearly blown apart by some crazed merman, running out of oxygen under the water thing. You're sorry for that?"

I laughed, as I knew he wanted me to. "Yeah, pretty much."

"No problem. It was a hell of a date."

"Is that what you're calling it? A date?"

"I don't know. What should I call it? A one-night stand?"

"It's not like that."

"Tell it to me straight." He stepped back. "Am I ever going to see you again?"

"Yes! Of course. But Tiamat and Sabyn ruined almost everything. I have to go help fix it."

"Of course you do." He looked out over the harbor. "What about Kona?"

I didn't know what to say, didn't know how to fix this whole ridiculous love triangle thing we were embroiled in. "I don't know. I have to talk to him. He's got a lot going on right now."

Mark's jaw worked back and forth. "Does he?"

"His parents just died. He's got to become king—"

"He's a king? Seriously?" Mark turned his back on me and walked a few steps away. As he did, I thought I heard him mutter, "No wonder I've never stood a chance."

"It's not like that, Mark." I chased after him, got in his face.

"Then how is it, Tempest? How the hell is it? I love you. You say you love me. And yet every time I turn around, you're running back to him."

"I have to make sure he's okay. And I'm not running to *him*. I'm running back to my clan. It's devastated, the merQueen is injured. I have to do what I can to help."

"And then what?"

"What do you mean?"

"After you've done all your mermaid stuff, and you've

checked on Kona and he's told you he loves you. What. Happens. Then."

"I don't know," I told him. "Okay? I don't know."

"Well, then, you better figure it out. I can deal with all the mermaid stuff, even deal with crazed sea creatures that are the things nightmares are made of. But I will *not* be your sometime boyfriend, hanging around waiting for you to come back to land after you've had your fun with Kona."

And then he turned and walked away, the too-small flip-flops Sergio had loaned him slapping angrily against the dock.

I didn't try to stop him. But then, how could I, when everything he'd said was true?

Chapter 36

By the time I found Kona and Mahina, they were halfway home. Mahina had gotten Kona to a healer, and he'd done enough good that Kona was swimming on his own. There was still a scar on his side, red and bumpy and angry looking, but all of the important things were healed.

Is Mark okay? Mahina asked when I caught up to them.

He's fine. I didn't look at her or Kona as I spoke. I couldn't, not while Mark's ultimatum was echoing in my head.

Good. Kona smiled at me, but it was strained. Tired.

It's going to be okay. I brushed a hand over his shoulder.

I don't think I can do this, Tempest. I'm not ready to be king. This time he was the one who couldn't look at me.

I know. But you're going to do a great job. Everyone knows that you'll be amazing.

I miss them. I know my mom was a pain, but the idea that she's never going to nag me again, never try to get me to settle down and be more respectable, is awful. And my dad—I still had so many questions for him about what it means to rule wisely.

I thought of my mother then, about how the memories she had shown me saved my life—and kept me from making some of the mistakes she had. The idea that Kona would never have that chance devastated me.

It's going to be okay, I repeated.

He just shook his head. *And what about you? Hailana's in bad shape and you're the only one she's—*

Don't. Please, don't go there. I can barely keep it together as things stand now. If you say the Q word I'll lose it.

Hiding isn't going to change anything.

Yeah, well, it's worked for me so far.

That's debatable. Mahina couldn't resist adding her two cents.

We swam quietly for a while, all of us completely exhausted from what we'd been through. We stopped to eat when we were hungry, to sleep when we couldn't swim anymore. But in general, we just kept moving, determined to get home as soon as we possibly could. At the same time, I know we were all anxious about what we would find.

As we swam, I couldn't help wondering where Tiamat was, what she and Sabyn were planning. But I figured we would know soon enough—it wasn't like she ever really played her cards close to her chest. Except for that blood thing. I really hadn't seen that coming.

I glanced down at my arm, at the long, deep scab there. I probably should have gotten stitches, but it was too late now. I tried to tell myself a scar there was no big deal, but for me it kind of was. The last thing I wanted to do was think of Tiamat every time I saw my arm. Then again, it wasn't like I was ever going to forget what she'd done, or how close she'd actually come to killing me.

Mark was right. It was the stuff nightmares were made of, and I had a feeling I was going to be seeing Tiamat in mine more often than usual.

Do you think they'll be back soon? I asked suddenly.

I expected to have to explain myself, but Mahina and Kona must have been worrying about the same thing—they knew immediately who I was talking about.

I hope not, Mahina said. *I need a little recovery time. I think we all do.*

So do they, Kona told us. *Tiamat was in bad shape when Sabyn pulled her out of there. And without her, I'm not sure how much power he really has.*

What about his tattoos? I asked. *They're signs of his power, and he has more of them than anyone I've ever seen.*

I wouldn't be so sure about that. Kona exchanged a glance with Mahina.

What does that mean?

I take it you didn't look in a mirror when you brought Mark to the surface. Kona reached over and traced a finger over my shoulder, then down my rib cage and across my stomach. I followed the path, saw that my entire torso was now covered in purple tattoos in the same shape and pattern of those on my back.

Where did these come from? I demanded.

They were there after you did your little exploding sun trick. Once the light died away, these were hard to miss, Mahina answered. *Not that I'm surprised. I've never seen anything like what you did.*

Me, neither. Kona shook his head, looking more than a little awed.

I don't know how I did it. These weird powers keep showing up—it was just part of the whole electric thing.

Kona nodded. *I know. And I guarantee you, Tiamat and Sabyn are scared to death after seeing what you could do.*

Give me a break. I'm still pretty damn scared after seeing what they *could do. Sabyn healed himself after I practically split him in two. How is that even possible?*

My guess is they've been sharing blood for a while now—combining species' powers like that has a tendency to make both more powerful. For a while anyway, Mahina said.

Is that why she wanted my blood?

Yep.

But what did she mean about Kona's energy? I asked. *She wanted my blood and his energy.*

Selkies' actual powers aren't blood based, like mermaids' are, Kona said. *Any power we have comes from the way we channel energy from the ocean. The better we are at doing that, the more power we have.*

So, you're really good at that whole water-channeling thing, then? To be as powerful as you are?

His smile faded. *I'm good but nowhere near as good as my father was.*

I didn't know how to respond to that, so I didn't say anything. Neither did Mahina.

We made it to Kona's territory a couple of hours later. The cleanup had continued during the days we were gone and the city was almost back to normal—just with a lot less people out and about than it usually had. Some were barricaded in their houses, hiding, while many others had died in the attack. Either way, I felt miserable swimming through to Kona's castle and figured he must be feeling about a million times worse.

I went on land with him, to the castle, took him inside

while Mahina waited in the ocean. She said she needed a nap, but I knew it was because she didn't want to intrude.

The house felt so empty without his parents and siblings there—I hadn't realized how used to their presence I'd grown in the last eight months. They were a loud, big, boisterous family and it seemed strange to be here without them. Again, I knew it was a million times worse for Kona. Only two of his brothers and two sisters had survived Tiamat's attack, and they were sitting in the media room watching TV. They jumped up and greeted him, but their jubilation only lasted a few seconds before they were once again looking as blank and devastated and lost as Kona did.

I didn't know what to do for him, didn't know how to help. After my mother had died, I'd been too frozen inside to let him help me. I wondered if that was how he was feeling now.

"Do you want me to stay?" I asked after hugging his brothers and sister and offering them my condolences. "I can—"

"You need to get back to Coral Straits. I know you must be anxious to see what's going on."

"It doesn't matter. If you need me, I'll be here."

He smiled sadly, and the expression on his face was so much like the one on Mark's when we said good-bye that I did a double take. "It's fine, Tempest. We both know this isn't where you want to be anyway."

"That's not true." My heart fluttered a little in panic. I wasn't ready to do this—dealing with Mark had already thrown me for a loop. Having to also deal with Kona . . . it was too much for me to handle right now on top of everything else.

But I couldn't tell him that, not when he was an even bigger emotional basketcase than I was. So I just waited to hear what he had to tell me.

In the end, he didn't say anything at all. Just kissed my forehead and whispered, "I'm tired. Can we talk about this later?"

"Sure. Of course." I felt like I'd just been spared a trip to the guillotine. "Get some sleep—you were close to death a couple days ago."

"So were you."

"Yeah, well, I'm resilient like that."

"Thank God." He pulled me to his chest and hugged me. I hugged him back, dropped a soft kiss on his shoulder. As I did, I realized that I would always love Kona, always be grateful to him and have mixed-up feelings for him. But the way I loved him was different from how I loved Mark. With Kona, it was sweet and comfortable and lovely. Which was nice—I wasn't denying it.

But it wasn't the same wild, crazy excitement I felt whenever I saw Mark. My heart didn't skip a beat, my palms didn't sweat, my powers didn't jump. Some might think that was a good thing—I certainly had for a while—but now I wasn't so sure. I liked the way I felt when I was with Mark, loved the tingle he still gave me even after all these years.

Not that I was going to tell Kona that. Kicking someone when he was down was much more a Tiamat thing to do than a Tempest one. But when I pulled away, I realized Kona already knew. It was in the sad smile he gave me.

In the friendly way he squeezed my shoulder.

In the kiss he brushed across my cheek instead of my lips.

"Kona . . ."

"Don't worry about it, Tempest. We both have a lot on our minds right now."

"But—"

He put a finger on my lips. "You need to get going. Hailana is probably having a stroke wondering where you are. And I have a kingdom to run. It's not like I have time to do the whole love-triangle thing right now, anyway."

Ouch. His words hurt, even as I understood the truth in them. Still, I knew I could fight him. Right now, I could fight this thing that he was doing. I could throw my arms around Kona and tell him I loved him and I would never give him up. If I was ever going to do that, this was the time for it.

But in the end, all I said was, "Are you kidding me? Hailana probably knows more about that fight than you and I do. Her informants are everywhere."

He agreed, a sad look in his eyes, and I left after giving him another hug. As I got into the water where Mahina was waiting, I vowed to be there for Kona whenever he needed me. He had a terrible, awful time in front of him and he was going to need all the friends he could get. No matter what happened with Mark or Hailana or this whole mermaid thing, I was not going to let him down.

&

The scene at Coral Straits was just as miserable as the one at Kona's house. Maybe even more so, as Hailana lingered close to death's door. I went to see her as soon as I got back and she barely recognized me. She was shaky, weak, almost impossible to follow. In the space of a week, she'd gone from a formidable, if old, opponent to a weak object of pity. It made me feel awful.

The next couple of weeks passed in a blur as I worked tirelessly to help get Coral Straits back in shape. We upped our patrols, trained more soldiers, cleaned up the destruction Tiamat and Sabyn had left behind. And tried to slowly put the pieces of our lives back together.

I was having a hard time with it—partly because I was trying to do the job of a merQueen without ever taking on the actual title. As long as Hailana was alive, it would be hers. When she died, *if* she died, I would think more about what my responsibilities were and what I wanted to do with them.

I'd been back under the ocean about four weeks when my first chance for a break came. I told myself I was going to hang out with Mahina, go shopping, have fun, but in the end I did what I knew I would do all along. I swam home to San Diego.

I didn't know what Mark was going to say, didn't know if he would want anything to do with me, since I'd been gone a month without so much as a word to him, but we needed to talk. Needed to see if the spark was still there. If he still felt for me what I was beginning to think I would always feel for him.

It was night when I came ashore, and I was better prepared this time. I pulled a sarong and tank top out of my waterproof backpack, slipped them on over my swimsuit, then made my way slowly up the road to Mark's house. He lived only a few houses down from me, and I smiled as I passed the house I'd grown up in. I was dying to see my dad and brothers again, but I had to do this first. I'd traveled the whole world, yet after everything was said and done, I'd ended up falling for the boy next door after all.

I knocked and his mother answered. Her eyes grew wide when she saw me, but she welcomed me in and ushered me to the backyard. I knew exactly where Mark would be—next to the beach, his favorite place to think was a large, double hammock his mother had hung up years before.

Sure enough, he was there, kicked back, arms folded behind his head as he studied the myriad stars in the late-night sky. "I'm fond of Pisces, myself," I said, pointing at one of the constellations.

Mark jumped at the sound of my voice, then nearly fell out of the hammock. "Tempest?" he asked, climbing to his feet.

"Yep."

He glanced back up at the sky, where I'd pointed. "That's Aquarius."

"Oh. Sorry. You've always been better at this than I am."

He didn't answer, so we just stood there, staring at each other. "You didn't come all this way to talk about the stars."

"I came because I missed you."

"Did you?"

"Yes. I'm sorry it took so long. Things were . . . difficult. The merQueen is sick and I needed to be there, to help."

"I'm sure you did."

I was getting a little annoyed. I didn't expect him to greet me with open arms, had figured I'd have to do a little groveling, but . . . actually, I had hoped he would greet me with open arms, now that I thought about it.

"Is that all you have to say? I came this far to see you." I got in his face and his eyes narrowed, his hands coming up to circle my biceps.

"What do you want me to say?" Mark asked.

"Tell me what you're thinking. Tell me what you want from me."

"I'm thinking that this whole mermaid thing of yours is turning out to be more complicated than I expected."

I stiffened, backed away. Subconsciously, I'd been expecting this all along. I thought I'd prepared myself for it, but I'd been wrong. I'd really hoped . . . I cut the thought off before it ever really formed. "I know. I understand."

He put a finger under my chin, lifted my face to his. "What is it you think you understand?"

"If I didn't have to live this life, I wouldn't want any part of it either."

"That's not what I said, Tempest."

"No, but it's what you meant, right? It has to be, because no one in their right mind would actually sign up for this shit." My breath hitched on a sob.

He closed his eyes, pulled me against him. "I can't do this," he murmured against my hair.

"Can't do what?"

"I can't pretend I didn't miss you every second you were gone. Your life is crazy, I know that, but I don't care. I never said I wanted you to change, only that I wanted to be a part of your life." He leaned down and swept his lips gently over mine. "*Want* to be a part of your life. I love you, Tempest. Even after everything that's happened. Maybe even more, after what I saw you do down there."

"It didn't freak you out?"

"I didn't say that, especially when you went all, I don't know, nuclear? But I figure that just means I've got a lot to learn about loving a mermaid." He rested his hand on my cheek and I turned my head, kissed the center of his palm.

"I'm going to have to go back again. I'm not here to stay."

"I know that. But you won't be gone so long next time, right?"

I thought of the mess down below, of Hailana and Tiamat and everything I still had to do to help make things right. "I'll be back as soon as I can."

He nodded. "Good enough." Then he paused, stepped back. Cleared his throat and looked out at the fruit trees that lined the edge of his backyard, his hands shoved deep into the pockets of his board shorts. "Kona—"

"I know."

"If you want him—" He cleared his throat again. "If you still want him . . ."

"Yeah?" I asked, eyeing him curiously.

"Then that's too damn bad." Mark's eyes were dark and brooding and more intense than I had ever seen them as he pulled me close. "You're *my* girl, Tempest. And this time I'm not stepping aside. This time, I'm keeping you."

And then he kissed me, really kissed me, and I forgot the long list of reasons we weren't supposed to be together. Because Mark was mine too.

And *I* was keeping *him*.

ACKNOWLEDGMENTS

Usually, when I write my acknowledgments, I save my editor and publishing house for last, but this time I really have to thank them first. Especially my incredible, amazing, wonderful, and patient editor, Stacy Cantor Abrams, who put up with more from me on this book than any editor should ever have to. Thank you, Stacy, for everything you've done for Tempest and me. I appreciate it more than I can say. Thank you, thank you, thank you.

For everyone at Walker Books, who took my dream for Tempest and turned it into not one but two beautiful books that awe me every time I look at them. Thank you so much for all the hard work you put into my books. I love everything about them.

For my fantastic agent and very dear friend, Emily Sylvan Kim, who started me on this journey nearly three years ago now. Thank you for always listening, no matter how outlandish the idea. I can't imagine trying to do this without you.

For my mother, who is always there when I need her, and who kept my house running and my children fed while I wrote like a madwoman.

For my boys, who put up with the most miserable summer on record so I could finish this book. Next summer, Disneyland. I promise.

And for the three most amazing writers and friends I have ever had the privilege of knowing: Shellee Roberts, Emily McKay, and Sherry Thomas, who make this writing gig so very much fun. Thanks for always being there.